EVERNIGHT PUBLISHING ®

www.evernightpublishing.com

ELLIS KAYE

Copyright© 2019

Ellis Kaye

Editor: Karyn White

Cover Art: Jay Aheer

ISBN: 978-0-3695-0071-7

HOW A HEART BEATS

DEDICATION

For my family and everyone who believes in a happily
ever after…

With special thanks to my tribe at the DFW Writers'
Workshop, Amy Brewer, Liz Larson, and to those of you
whose names I used. In all fairness, I never thought
anyone would read it.

xoxo,

ek

HOW A HEART BEATS

Ellis Kaye

⌢•••◆•••⌢

Chapter One

It's not superstition. It's a known fact. Shit happens in threes.

A sterile brightness glared overhead. Controlled chaos buzzed below. The trauma room pulsed with tonal beeps, wailing alarms and hushed, hurried voices. Olivia Aberdeen surveyed the team and the calm hanging over the half dozen bodies bustling around the stretcher.

She counted the minutes. A precious three. One-hundred-and-twenty seconds. A virtual lifetime of, "C'mon. Lord. Please let this be it."

Except it wasn't. It rarely ever was, and all too soon, slow, accepting motions replaced swift determination. One by one, her work family stepped back. Huddles of royal blue, green, and grey stood, shoulders slumped, emotions hidden by a hand or a dejected gaze at the bleached white floor. The chief ER resident hung his stethoscope around his neck and backed away. Everyone seemed ready to accept fate. And the rule of threes.

Fuck that.

"No. No. *No!* One more. One more round," Liv pleaded, pounding away at the toddler's chest. Mackenzie Collins, County Med Emergency Department's third code of the night. The team knew what the outcome would be when they got the ambulance call, but this one had to turn around. It *had* to.

She pinched back angry tears and fought to keep her voice even. Detached. As professional as an ER nurse could be when facing her third death of the night.

"She's a baby! C'mon, y'all, one more."

Sweat dotted her forehead. They'd done everything. Lines, drips, meds. And more rounds of CPR than she could count. There were no more "Hail Mary's" left to pass. She forced her eyes open and searched the room, trying to connect with one person who still held onto hope this would be the life they'd save today.

Pale and conflicted, a medic wiped the sweat from his face with his green scrubs, then took over compressions. Liv backed away, bent at the knees, exhausted, and hungry for air. First time or five-hundred, it was the longest three minutes of her existence to stand over a person and beat life into a heart.

The resident elbowed for more room at the head of the stretcher. Grim faced, arms folded, it was up to him to say they'd done enough, to say with finality a mother would never speak to her baby girl again.

He took a sobering breath then blew it through his nose. "All right, Liv. One more. Push a high dose epinephrine, and someone grab me the ultrasound machine. Let's see if we can get something back to defibrillate. How much longer until the parents arrive?"

People rushed around, falling into roles without direction. The mark of a good trauma team. And even though Liv was new and a transplant southerner in the great blue north, she melted right in.

Liv checked the Braslow's tape and grabbed the corresponding medication to the baby's size. She'd thank the Lord later for the invention that made medical math almost foolproof, and used the time now to ask God for one of his miracles.

"Epi's in," she answered, hoping the little heart would flutter back to life.

A head popped around the curtain. "Family's here. I had the chaplain escort them to the private waiting room."

A hushed discussion bounced from person to person. Parents and family were encouraged to come back and witness the last efforts. People in the business of saving lives were taught it's important for closure, but that's bullshit. Regular people didn't need to see the torture doctors and nurses put their loved ones through, or the mess. But it was the right thing to do.

Liv pulled in a breath, hoping to find composure mixed in with the tainted oxygen. "I'll go," she said, shouldering the responsibility, but the idea of doing this for the third time in less than twelve hours tore a hole in her gut no amount of Mylanta would fix. She caught the eye of the resident. He dropped a dollop of lube onto the sono machine and pressed it against the little one's chest. Liv held her breath. *Everyone* held their breath.

"Stop compressions, please." Habit drew her eyes to the monitor hanging at the foot of the bed. Expecting the worst, she prepped for the flat line that meant death, but there was movement. A quiver. Liv's heart jumped into her throat.

Professional decorum be damned, Liv bounced on the balls of her feet and pointed at the monitor. "That's fine v-fib!"

She dove to her knees and fumbled through the

defibrillator settings. The black cloud hanging over the room cracked with a ray of light. Hope. And Liv latched on.

The resident closed in on the screen as if he couldn't trust his eyes. "Well I'll be goddamned. Let's get her going! Start with two jules per kilo," he ordered, but Liv was three steps ahead.

"Done. Charging to fifty." The pack at the end of the stretcher did the rest. The room went silent. The defib signaled ready. "Everyone clear."

The gaggle of nurses, medics, and respiratory therapists jumped away with Liv's command. The little body jolted off the mattress. She seemed to hover in midair. The moment she settled back down the baby girl was back.

"Good God! She's in a normal sinus." Another nurse rushed to the baby's side and squeezed a breath into her lungs. The doctor pressed his fingers into the hollow of her neck. His face split into a wide smile.

Olivia mirrored it, but not before glancing at the ceiling and through to Heaven on the other side. The conversations quickly went back to the unit hot gossip and what time the Starbucks should open. Everyone knew this was a tiny blip in the girl's outcome, but the ER had done their part. They'd saved the life. The rest would be up to God and the Pediatric ICU. Liv massaged at the CPR muscle strain running down her neck and turned to get the family. A hard sigh heaved from her chest, relieved she wouldn't be starting the conversation with "I'm Nurse Olivia. I'm sorry, but we did everything we could."

"Hey, Liv."

She stopped. The resident broke away from the fashionably late attending rubbing sleep from his eyes.

"That was a good call."

****

The rhythmic rock and sway of the 'L train was going to be her downfall. There wasn't a Monster big enough to keep Liv's eyelids from rolling shut. It didn't matter that she was squished by strangers, or saturated with the noxious stench of BO and bleach—because it probably came from her, she was one hard minute away from falling asleep and finding herself at the airport.

Again.

She crinkled her nose, and discreetly tried to sniff her pits. The hipster wedged into her side shifted. Something clung to the wrinkled, faded blue scrubs she'd worn the last fourteen hours—she just hoped it wasn't the residual funk of the crash GI bleed she'd pawned off at shift change.

The prospect of sweet sleep taunted her with a soothing chorus of hisses and hums, and home was an eternal six stops away. Liv's eyes fluttered shut, and her head bobbed to the side. A smack against the Plexiglas shook her into consciousness. She grimaced, pulling out her cellphone. Manners be damned, and she set up to break a cardinal rule of the 'L, ignoring the judgmental leers from the other commuters. They hadn't been up for twenty-four hours on four hours sleep.

"C'mon, Lottie. Answer. Answer. Answer..." she chanted to the ring, imagining the voice on the other end. Breaking the second rule of common courtesy, Liv took to calling her best friend before an acceptable hour for a well-bred southern lady.

"Livy, I swear someone had better be dead," Charlotte drawled into the phone, her usual warm voice clogged with sleep. Even if it was after eight Georgia time, Charlotte Van Sutton didn't rise before nine without fresh coffee and a homemade peach muffin on her dressing table.

The 'L's disembodied conductor announced Clark and Lake.

"Talk to me, Lottie. I've got to make it five more stops."

"And I've got fifty-eight more minutes before Nanny brings me the twins."

Liv's brow furrowed. Of all the people she'd grown up with in the world of Savannah affluence, she never thought Lottie would fall into that hotbed of hypocrisy and pretentious laziness. Still, Lottie was her family. Livy and Lottie, cradle to the grave.

Liv forced a smile into the phone. "How are Ashton and Louise? Walking yet?"

Charlotte groaned a muffled sentence, which meant she was shifting to sit up in her one-thousand-thread-count sheets and down comforter. "Walking, yes. Sleeping, no."

And that affected her how? Nanny Kemp had been the twins' nanny since before they were born, catering to a pregnant Lottie's pampered whims. An awkward pause filled the line. The best time to talk to Lottie these days was after four PM and her late afternoon julep; the juicy gossip didn't get discussed until brunch anyway.

Liv got an elbow in the ribs, hardly accidental. "Sorry, Lottie. I just needed to…"

"Stay awake. I know." Finally, Liv heard the compassion she expected from lifelong friendship. "If you must work, why don't you work during the day like a normal person?"

"Everything good happens after three in the morning. Or don't you remember senior year and all our TriDelt debauchery?"

Liv almost heard the reminiscent grin erupt on Lottie's face. "For some reason I don't remember much of that at all. I have no earthly idea why that would be of course."

"They say it gets easier. You should have seen what I got to do last night..." Liv said, feeling her excitement crescendo into storytelling mode.

"Why don't you just come home, Livy? It's got to be gettin' cold up there. C'mon. 'They who must not be named' won't bother you... You can stay with us in the guest house."

"It's been almost two years, Lottie, you don't need to lump Logan into the same category as Lord Voldemort."

"Oh, I wasn't talkin' about that asshat cheater ex-fiancé of yours. I was talkin' about your Momma. You know she's..." The voice dropped. The inside of the train went dark.

"Lottie, you there?" Liv yanked her iPhone from her ear and scowled. No signal.

The grumpy hipster sitting to her right threw herself into a standing position. She leered into space and clicked her tongue.

"Ya see? That's why you don't talk on the 'L. Rude."

Liv ignored the brashness and shut her eyes, praying for the polite patience bestowed upon southern born ladies. Why did the Lord test her so frequently? The 'L stopped, and her eyes opened. The twerp vanished, and she had just two stops left. She could almost smell her sheets and the prospect of not suffering through a day's worth of night shifter's insomnia should've made her giddy, but the mention of Logan's name ached in her gut. The pain and embarrassment suffered at the hand of Dr. Logan St. James of Chatham County Hospital and his scandalous preference for little blonde playthings had long healed over, but left her scarred and forever tied to the city she'd never call home.

Liv rubbed at her flat stomach and the pain that never went away. Little girl flights of fantasy combined with a delicious and sexy workplace romance. Never again.

To her right, another nurse rose to her feet. Blessed with the label of statuesque since toddlerhood pageants, Liv made the best of County Med's boxy, blue scrubs. And yet silly girl envy curled her lips. Petite, sensuous. A lovely pixie with curves for days. Even the leggiest beauties would be green for such a killer little body working her hourglass beneath nurses' famously unflattering uniform. Liv's polar opposite except for the exhaustion etched beneath their eyes.

Despite the minor itch of feminine jealousy, Liv tingled with camaraderie. Kinship. Solidarity for all who save lives while the rest of the world sleeps.

The feeling must have been contagious. "Whoever told you it gets easier is a lying douchebag. All of this," she said, gesturing to her oval face strained with lack of sleep, "is why we get paid extra. Early Botox slush fund. I'm sure you don't remember, but I'm Torey. I sat through hospital orientation with you a few months back. You work in the ER? Olivia, right?"

"It's just Liv." She laughed and cautiously evaluated her surroundings. It was never hard to spot a nurse, but that doesn't mean they want everyone to know they work in the armpit of the hospital. The train car jerked along the track. Torey took it in stride. "I'm part of the county ER burnout program. I take care of tiny humans now."

Liv scrunched her face working to make the connection. In the nursing world those specialties were like going from Nancy Pelosi to Ann Coulter.

"ER to NI? That's a pretty big leap."

Torey shrugged. "Take a big leap, or take a big leap into the lake."

Liv sighed. The bedside nursing struggle was real. "Burnout's a bitch."

"And now my patients are two pounds and change," Torey added. Liv stretched her aching back. That sure as hell seemed like a tick in the better job category.

"So what do you do to flip? Meds? Booze? Combo of both?"

Liv grinned. Secretive. Sultry. "Glass of red wine, bubble bath, and a date with my battery-operated boyfriend."

Torey's stoic exhaustion cracked. "I name you my new best friend. That's what's missing with those baby nurses. The crass funny." The train slid to a stop. "This is me. You back tonight?" Liv gave her a sleepy nod. "Ugh, yeah. Me, too. Hope you get some rest. I'll see you around." With a friendly smile and wave, Torey scurried off the train.

One more stop. She could make it one more stop. The train groaned forward. The best thing to do would be to stand, stand and resist the sway. Sleep crept in, weighing her down like warm honey oozing over her limbs. With strength she never knew she possessed, Liv lumbered upright. The doors split open, and the usual onslaught of oncoming passengers was non-existent. The Franklin Park platform was a ghost town.

A shout rang out.

"Someone, call an ambulance!"

Liv rolled her eyes then glared at the sky. "Oh, for cryin' out loud…"

****

It wasn't fair. Didn't doing the right thing count for something? She didn't want a reward for helping a stranger after falling down a flight of escalator stairs. She didn't want payment for using her favorite white lab jacket as a pressure dressing. Sleep. That's all she wanted, but no amount of Benadryl and red wine would bring down the high of saving a life.

Liv ambled along the platform and glanced at her watch. Escalator guy sucked up an hour of sleep. The autumn morning sun blazed its way to brunch. She frowned, full of stupid self-pity. Every joint ached and cried in stiffness. But her brain buzzed, wired with adrenaline and the juicy images of a pulsing arterial scalp laceration. Rather than turn down her block, she went straight and crossed the intersection, risking death by cab and drunk bike messenger to her local library.

She waved at the sweet old ladies who worked the checkout line, her eyes instantly connecting with her favorite librarian and next-door neighbor, Rose Loveitz. Rose had a sneaky habit of letting Liv check out stale reference books she'd use in lieu of her old cocktail of Ambien and alcohol.

Mrs. Loveitz looked her over with a sympathetic glance. If twelve hours in the pit hadn't left her covered in dead skin flakes and filth, Liv'd run over and give the first friend she made in Chicago a hug. Instead she winkled her nose, miming disgust and pressed through to the back. Hidden behind the outdated *World Book,* atlases, and the bathroom were the remnants of the library's card catalogue.

Liv opened a drawer at random and ran her fingers along the aged and brittle stack of four by six cards. "All right Flynne-comma-Augustus, whaddaya got for me?" Exhausted, she needed to squint to read the faded typeset.

"*The Migration Habits of the Philomachus Pugnax*… Yup, I think you'll do." She yanked the card from its drawer and slammed it shut. A loud crack echoed through the stacks. It was a life lesson Liv learned in high school. Nothing put her to sleep faster than reading something she give zero fucks about, and today that was going to be birds.

She grumbled her favorite list of curse words as an evil sunbeam seared through the old metal blinds. The building was ancient. Hot as balls in the winter, freeze your nips off in the summer with graffiti commemorating the Bulls' first three 'peat from 1993 tagged the work tables. Rows of little box Macintosh computers had green screens that still played *Oregon Trail*. The moment she walked through the doors a year and a half ago, she fell in love. Although, she secretly wished she'd found a fancy dry cleaner, or laundromat. In her world away from Savannah affluence, it meant she did her own laundry, and a yearly pap smear was a more enjoyable alternative.

Liv navigated the maze of shelves with ease, but the book acted like a beacon pulsing with light as she traveled down the aisle. Relief cloaked her weary body as her fingers connected with the spine. Elusive sleep lurked. A satisfied smile pulled on her lips.

"Ah, Augustus, where have you been all my life?" She inhaled the stale pages, and the weight of her chronic sleep deprivation pressed on her shoulders. The devil in the form of a two-minute power nap called, and Liv surrendered.

****

Stiff backed and irritated, Anderson Cole paced through the library stacks. Why in God's name was a bathroom impossible to find?

"She's got to be flipping senile…" he muttered, looking back at the octogenarian working the checkout desk.

The labyrinth of outdated reference books seemed

to multiply like a bad Disney movie where the hero would have to choose between pissing himself or death by pride. He caught the eye of an attendant shelving books, but it'd be snowy day in Aggie August before he asked where to find the toilet two times in one visit.

Way to perpetuate the male stereotype, idiot.

His hands trembled from too much caffeine while his groin tried tear open from three too many overpriced, big-city, blood-of-virgin lattes. He'd have done just about anything to keep his mind off the call. The offer. The means to move on from the broken life he left behind in Texas. But death due to a ruptured bladder would have been real low on the list.

His cellphone vibrated in his pocket. Andy ripped the phone from his jeans, ignoring the judgmental leers and shushes he'd get after breaking the library vow of silence, but a sound caught his ear. A snore. Muffled. Feminine. Except it grew into a cough. The heavy snore of an insomniac.

The phone persisted, and he looked down. The snore interrupted what would have been a horrible mistake. It wasn't *the* call. Talking to the train wreck on the other end would ruin the day. Week. Hell, why stop there? The rest of his damned existence.

If there was one thing he'd learned in the last fifteen months and twenty-three days, there was no timeline long enough for the grieving. He didn't have the patience to be the gentleman his mother raised, and no amount of time above the Mason/Dixon would retrain the years of southern etiquette. He hit "end" and shelved the crazy on the other end for another day.

Andy searched the next aisle over. Sure enough, he found the source. Her. Peaceful, serene and completely upright, a nurse by the looks of it. Not a sexist assumption. Just connecting the dots. Shift workers' insomnia, blue scrubs, and white shoes. Didn't require a fancy degree to suss out.

He checked his watch. No one intended to be asleep in the library at nine AM. Blame the fairy-tale hero complex, but he felt compelled to rescue the woman from an inevitable ground level fall. The fact he had a preference for peaches and cream redheads had absolutely nothing to do with it. At least that's what he'd tell himself after waking her up.

****

A hand grabbed at Liv's elbow, pulling her from a delicious sleep. "Eh … hello? Hello? Miss?" She fell over, startled, and swung in the direction of a deep, twangy voice. "Whoa, easy there, Tyson."

She blinked herself awake.

"Geeze, sorry!"

Mortified, she forced her eyes on the floor and rubbed out the numbness at her shoulder and left hip. Liv took a risky peek at her life-sized alarm clock. Huge mistake. She sucked in a breath. Being a supreme specimen of good-looking, he checked off no less than four of her favorite male attributes in the one-second glance. Tall, blue eyes, wavy black hair, and the perfect five o'clock shadow. Only she would take a swing at the real life McDreamy. He caught her glance and smiled. Lazy and adorable.

Unbalanced and unprepared, Liv ignited. The concrete floor turned to mush, and she all but fell over. For a second time.

In a gallant flash he placed a steadying hand on her back as she flung her hands out for help. His grip reached the width of her waist and his fingers connected at the skin of her hips. Her heart sputtered in her chest. Electric and lightning quick, the spark sprung them apart. Sexy on a stick jumped back.

"You good?" he asked.

"Yeah … you just…"

"Surprised you. I noticed. Do you make it a habit of falling asleep in the library at nine in the morning … while standing in the avian reference section?"

Liv smoothed her hair, wishing her blush would fade. "No. I'm pretty flexible, sometimes it's auto repair, or baking… But that doesn't beat falling asleep in line at the Jewel, or on the elevator at Water Tower."

"Who hasn't fallen asleep on that elevator?"

Liv laughed and allowed another look at his face. Their eyes connected. *Shit. Bad idea.* Something inside fluttered, and it wasn't just sexy time tingles. He was reading her like an open book. The unfortunate irony was not appreciated.

"You're, uhh, so you're a nurse," he said.

Liv shook her head. She might be proud of the letters behind her name, even if they only meant "refreshments and narcotics", but it was almost a given that when strangers learned she was a nurse it was usually followed by a request to check out a mole, rash, or if it was supposed to hurt to pee.

"No. Not a nurse. Dog groomer." She grimaced. Dog groomer? Phlebotomist would have worked just fine.

McDreamy smirked.

"I never knew that would be so draining."

She was caught, but she didn't care. Their moment was over. "Thanks for the wake-up call." McDreamy's delicious charm aside, Liv hoped he'd take the hint. A gentleman would follow her lead.

"You sure you're safe to get where you're going? I don't want to worry about you falling asleep at an intersection or anything." A familiar, soft drawl slurred his words. There was no way she imagined the subtle southern twang as he pulled away.

Her heart raced as he turned to leave, and her gaze traveled to his ass. His perfect, sculpted ass, cradled by designer denim. That checked seven, and eight. Flushed, turned on, and now insufferably awake, she doubted even Augustus Flynne's bird magic would do the trick.

Liv pulled out her phone and meandered through the maze of bookshelves, her nose glued to the screen. She calculated how many hours of sleep she'd get before her shift started again. A whopping four. Liv had to fight her Momma's voice with the reminder.

"Good genes only go so far,"—polite, southern code for, "you look like hell, Olivia." She hated to agree with her mother. In fact, it was a life's passion to *never* agree with her, but this time she'd be right.

Liv swallowed her frustration, and conceded that today was just going to suck. She spotted a white card on the floor and recognized the colorful insignia. She picked up the lost library card and deciphered the name scribbled in clinical chicken scratch.

"Cole? Anderson? Cole Anderson?" she called. No response. "Two damned last names," Liv muttered under her breath. "Anderson Cole?" She tried again, and out popped Sexy on a stick, this time his lazy grin pressed into an irritated grimace, but a smile was instant after he connected her face to the voice.

"Cole Anderson? Anderson Cole?" she asked.

He nodded. A slow, swoony smirk curled from his little boy smile as he looked her up and down from the short distance. The attention was sweet and so fucking flattering, she really wished he'd cut it out and give her a reason to rein in the crazy—like insult his Momma or kick a kitten.

She cleared her throat and tried to ignore the

twinge in her belly. "Your card. I guess you dropped it back there."

"Thanks. I got it this morning, no tellin' how mad those librarians would get if I had to get two in one day."

"So which is it?" Liv asked, veering toward the check out. His eyes darted back the way he came, then swallowed what looked like a serious case of "I'm going to piss myself," a look she knew all too well.

"Anderson. Andy," he clarified in a friendly tone. The millisecond of internal conflict was wiped from his features, and he motioned for her to enter the line before him. He left a gentlemanly distance. But hormones be damned, she couldn't help herself. Liv leaned into his space and inhaled his air. A smile tugged on her lips. "I'm going to have to ask you to tell me your name, aren't I?" he pressed.

Olivia laughed, girlish and unintentionally flirty. She clenched her fingers into a fist hoping to dial down her attraction. "Liv. Liv Aberdeen."

"Well, Liv Aberdeen, can I take you for coffee? Or a drink? I don't know what time of day it's supposed to be for you," he said with the perfect blend of flirty teasing.

No stranger to offers, she sucked in her bottom lip, this time truly disappointed. She wasn't ready. But golly, it's cruel to turn down a fella so fun to look at, and without a doubt, more fun naked.

"I shouldn't. As you know I'm pretty tired, and I've got to work again tonight…"

"At the dog groomer?" Andy held Liv's gaze as if to dare her to hold onto the lie.

"Ah. Yeah, the dog groomer."

He pursed his lips and cocked an assessing eyebrow. His blue eyes deliberately traveled the length of her body, inventorying her scrubs and incriminating, undeniable white clogs scuffed and smudged with twelve hours' worth of piss, vomit and escalator guy's blood.

"Isn't that blood on your shoe?" he asked.

"I didn't say I was a *good* dog groomer."

Sexy on a stick laughed, shrugging his shoulders as if to admit defeat. "Well, all right then. Maybe I'll see you around, Liv."

A shiver shimmied down her spine and singed her panties as she heard his twang make love to her name.

Chapter Two

Andy tried to go about his day. Normal. Collected. He was a grown, dignified adult. A doctor, for cryin' out loud. And grown, dignified men, trauma physicians didn't whoop and holler after a phone call, but that's exactly what he did. Surrounded by moody strangers on the train platform, Andy searched for an open palm to high-five in celebration. Homesickness bit him in the gut. If he'd been walking around the square back in his hometown, there'd have been a handful of kind folks ready to smack his open palm.

The city seemed bigger than it had eight years ago. It had only been a week, but he already missed his King Edition, Dodge Dually. Like a novice Chicagoan, he took the wrong train and got off a stop too soon, but he still got to the hospital with minutes to spare and made a beeline for the "Doctor Only" bathrooms.

Simply put, it was the piss of a lifetime. The pleasure mixed with pain rivaled the satisfying agony of holding in an orgasm to be sure the lady got off first. He groaned. Relieved, then annoyed. It was time to get laid if he seriously compared a piss to the pleasure of a woman. Somewhere in the depths of his brain, Liv appeared. He remembered the lush flush of her cheeks and imagined the rosy color build while he worked between her thighs.

The moment burst with the flush of another toilet. Andy rolled his eyes, grumbling the kind of profanity that his Momma would have slapped him for. In the hurry to prevent from pissing himself he didn't bother checking the occupancy and now broke the cardinal rule of the john, *and* moaned like a damned pervert with his hand on his dick.

The occupied stall opened. Andy turned toward the wall of sinks to avoid any passing leer, but that didn't stop him from tossing a cautious glance in the mirror to his left. Behind him, the man removed a long white coat from a hook and dramatically shook out the creases. Heat flushed up Andy's face hoping for a stranger. Better yet, a deaf stranger. Instead, recognition was instant. *Shit.*

"Dr. Smithson," he said, relying on a formal, subdued nod rather than his cordial Texan smile.

"Dr. Cole," replied the older man with standard salt-and-pepper hair and frameless eyeglasses. He hadn't looked like the clichéd pretentious physician during yesterday's interview. Today was a different story, but it might have something to do with the fact Andy had the stones to use the swank doctors' bathroom, and the ink wasn't even dry on his contract. "Looking forward to your first shift I take it?"

Andy flicked his gaze to the wall in front of his face and shook himself clean before adjusting himself back into his pants.

"Yes, sir. Very much. I loved this department a decade ago. I'm sure this time will be no different."

Dr. Smithson ran the faucet, and tossed a critical glance at Andy's reflection before washing his hands.

"You were a great prospect, back then. It was our loss when you decided to complete your residency in Texas."

Andy grimaced. He regretted making that decision, but back then he'd carried the responsibility of keeping his new bride happy. After only four years in the best trauma residency in the country, he packed up to finish his specialty training down in Waco and Mrs. Greta Cole got to go home and live in the privileged splendor of a doctor's wife.

"It's kind of you to say that, sir, really. I am very

happy to be back."

"Although I doubt you'll have as many rodeo or roll over tractor accidents up here."

Andy stiffened and clenched his jaw tight to keep from running his mouth. The not so subtle dig at his southern roots rubbed him raw.

Dr. Smithson chuckled, fully aware he'd tweaked the Texan's pride. "I'm only joking with you, Dr. Cole. I'm sure you'll be seeing some pretty exciting stuff. The crime rate doesn't look good for our mayor, but it sure makes us look good."

Adrenaline beat through Andy's veins. He stifled the excitement with a hard swallow. Trauma junkies didn't love when people got hurt; they just wanted to be there when it happened.

The rest of the afternoon was filled with a run of the mill meet 'n greets and "Howdy there's" with the upper level staff of his department. Much of the staff remained the same from the years before, but the idea that he'd have his own crop of residents and a few select med students to inspire or destroy irritated him. Andy knew teaching would be part of job, but he'd spent the last few years in a small, rural ER, and the quip about redneck farm injuries wasn't too far off.

Doubt needled into his brain. After what happened in Guatemala. His son. All the shit he left behind—was he ready? Was he good enough? Valid questions. Valid concerns.

He followed around a trio of ED directors, including the Chief Nursing Officer. Andy remembered her from his intern years. Boisterous and unknowingly out of touch, her scrubs were the same ones his mother wore when he was a boy. "This is our new triage area. It is just steps from the trauma and major medical wing. You might remember it being a bit of a trek," she mused.

Andy flashed back to his first year of residency. Having to carry a bloody teen dumped at the front door down a maze of halls was not something to smile at. Rust and salt were still imbedded in his nose from his first gunshot wound, but being polite was ingrained just as deep.

"Yes, ma'am. Looks like a real nice update for the patients and your nurses. I'm sure they're happy to save the extra steps." Old habit tugged at Andy's cheek. His half grin. The woman stuttered at his cordial banter and led him to the main nurse's station. His stomach lurched. His pulse raced. *Excitement. Noise. Holy shit.* He had forgotten about the noise.

Bodies rushed in and around the trauma rooms. Drawers and doors slammed open and shut. Loud patients. Louder nurses and wailing harmonic dings from the bedside monitors and IV infusion pumps competed for attention. The ER secretaries magically controlled the nonstop chorus of telephones and overhead pages for doctors and STAT x-rays. It was chaos. Perfect chaos.

The long rectangular wing was the length of three of his old unit, rivaling the size of his local Wal-Mart where he grew up—and light years away from the crammed mess that was the ER he remembered from his early residency. Two dozen patient treatment rooms separated by curtains and the occasional solid surface lined the four walls that made up the critical care side. Computers on wheels, affectionately referred to as "COWs" and equipment with no official home were strewn about the large, circular nurses' station. A long white jacket hung over the unit's intubation glidescope. Andy forced a pleasant expression. Such thankless behavior. Back home the glidescope was a waste-not, want-not item he had to beg for. Here it was being used as a resident's coat rack.

A few empty stretchers were tucked away in dark corners and lined some of the blank wall space for the overflow patients that appeared to be a very regular occurrence. Thrust into the heart of the unit, Andy felt the bite from every curious gaze. Even the patients in the hall beds smelled the fresh meat. A handful of the stares belonged to a group wearing grey scrubs and short white jackets, standard issue County Med first years. He stood a little straighter, and let his gaze travel around the bustling bodies in blue. Royal blue.

On high alert, Andy looked around. What were the chances? An animated group of nurses and medics hovered over the primary board. Curiosity lured him in their direction. He'd guess the puffed-up male with a bold tattoo inked down his forearm and the longer-than-needed-to-be-taken-seriously beard would be the charge nurse. Flaunting his position with a borderline douchebag arrogance, he had more than one of his female counterparts hanging on his every word. And, this guy ate it up like fresh pie.

"Heya, fellas." Andy introduced himself with a firm, yet friendly handshake then turned his attention to the women that flocked to his side like bees to bluebonnets. His face split into a smile. "Ladies. I'm Anderson Cole. One of y'all's new physicians. Whatdya say about goin' easy on me for a few days while I get acquainted?"

He might have been out of practice, but he knew interest when he saw it. Most women lapped up the accent and dose of Texan charm. It's a shame they didn't expect it from the men in their lives.

"Oh, of course, Dr. Cole," flushed a little blonde. He glanced at her nametag. "Please, call me Andy. Nora," he corrected with his half grin. She all but fell over while a hefty swig of "fuck off" radiated from the charge nurse. Andy straightened, and the blonde flittered away with a lingering glance.

"Full house tonight?" he asked, trying to sound cordial and noncompetitive, but it came out forced. Being an ass was more natural than he'd like to admit, and having a pissing contest on his first fucking day was probably a bad idea. It didn't matter that he had a bunch of letters behind his name. Respect was earned in the Pit. He wasn't twenty-five competing for the attention of his colleagues anymore.

A medic chimed in while the charge nurse debated how to reply to the overflow of testosterone.

"Yeah. Friday nights are always a party, Doc."

"I did some time here a few years back. I remember."

The medic slugged the charge nurse's elbow, and gave him the universal, sly grin of camaraderie.

"C'mon, Javi, put Olivia with me in triage. She's going to crack soon. I can feel it."

The name grabbed Andy's attention.

"Don't let Liv hear you say that," the charge nurse said.

Andy's cock twitched before his brain heard her name. An irritating flutter buzzed in his stomach. He pushed down the flare of lust and hid the infatuated fool's grin by glancing at the floor. Holding out hope about a woman he'd just met was harmless, but a stupid waste of time. Even if the divorce papers were signed and in the mail, divorced didn't mean done. Neither did distance. Tragedy and loss would be a noose forever tying him and Greta together.

Andy lifted his chin with a non-verbal, "see ya later," but was brought right back.

"Oh, I know, but I just love getting those lace little panties of hers in a twist," the medic said. An asinine smirk curled on Javier's face.

"She does get herself wound tight when anyone calls her that, doesn't she? I'd sure like to—"

"Y'all wouldn't be talking' about a woman you work with? 'Cause that'd be mighty rude, don't you think?" He took a step back toward the pair. If it came across as threatening—good. The medic balked, then backpedaled sputtering a nonsense apology. Javier on the other hand, held Anderson's cool gaze. The charge nurse seemed intent to answer Andy's challenge.

Dr. Smithson emerged from the central station. "Dr. Cole?"

Andy blinked out of Javier's hard-assed gaze. Like a Neanderthal, he was ready to club the guy for insulting the honor of a woman. He'd pretend it's his nature to do so, not the fact he was drawn to nurse Olivia Aberdeen and wanted it to be him helping her unwind.

His new boss waved him over. "Dual trauma in ten. Let's see how much you remember."

****

Despite leaving the library hot, horny, and hangry, Liv got home and proceeded to crash. No meds, no half liter of wine, no Augustus Flynne and his *Philomachus Pugnax*. Primed for sleep, she stripped in the hall of her Lake Front Brownstone, skipped her mandatory post-shift shower and found the first horizontal surface that wasn't the floor. The chaise in her parlor would need to be burned, fumigated, or Lysol'ed to high Heaven, because not even the fear of ER cooties could stop the scorching REM rebound the second she shut her eyes.

Front and center Anderson Cole floated through Liv's dreams. Charming and sexy-as-sin, Mr. Tall, Dark, and Fuckable melted her LaPerla panties right off. Literally. Liv awoke wet, and woefully unsatisfied by an alarm clock of city noise. A jackhammer clobbering away at the sidewalk cut short Andy's deft possession of her clit, but the dream would certainly be kept in her naughty bank for a good long while.

Pressed for time, Liv hurried around her house, retrieved B.O.B. from his place in the nightstand and threw herself in the shower. A sorry case of blue "bean" was no way to start the day. She closed her eyes and focused on the warmth rippling down her back. Moist heat enveloped her senses. Anderson Cole appeared in her mind, right where she left him, towering over her, pressed into a shadowy corner of the library stacks. Carnal. Coy, he licked his lips, then kissed along her jaw, humming into her neck. Andy drilled his cock into her pelvis, reciting a list of filthy things he wanted to do to her.

"I'm going to make you come, Olivia. Right here. Right now."

Voyeuristic anticipation blossomed in Liv's belly. She worked the shower loofah into a lather and inhaled the lavender scent. Andy returned in her mind. He caressed the length of her ribs, then up to cup her breasts. Olivia mirrored the act, teasing the loofah over her nipples and down to her navel. She slid her palms through the silky, floral scented soap as Andy grazed the hard peaks with his teeth.

Liv whimpered and arched into Andy's touch. She reached for her vibrator, and flicked the switch. The familiar, low hum flooded her sex with want. She tempted it across her thighs and along her lower belly.

In a manic, devious moment, Liv reached for his cock through his jeans and squeezed. "Don't expect me to be quiet."

Andy groaned and palmed her clit. "Never."

Liv pressed the vibrator into the ache between her

thighs and gasped. Needing more, she spread her legs and leaned against the glass shower wall for support. Hot water rained from above, while Andy kept working in her mind.

"How do you want it?" he asked, rubbing his calloused palm into her sex. "Slow?"

Liv rolled her hips, pulling the vibrations into her body.

"Hmm. No. My sexy girl wants it fast."

Liv slid the vibrator through her arousal as if it were Andy's cock.

"Mmm. I want your pussy so bad, but not yet. I'll fuck you another time." Andy dropped to his knees and kissed down her stomach. He blew hot air over her clit and scratched his nails through her small patch of auburn curls before grabbing her hips. Hard. Commanding.

He locked his blue eyes to her, then dove between her legs. Liv directed the pressure right on the swollen bundle of nerves and mimicked the work of Andy's tongue. The build was instant. Direct. No rolling hills of pleasure, but an intense swell of sensations reaching to her toes and prickling her scalp. She groaned and bit her lip. So close, so fast, Liv drowned in the image of Andy lapping at her clit until her pleasure crested and she came up for air.

Liv rested her head against the glass and gulped for breath. Coming down was always the best part. She turned her face into falling water and smiled. "Well done, Andy Cole."

Now *really* short on time, Liv hurried through her daily routine, thankful to save a few primping minutes by laying off her under eye concealer. A dewy, orgasmic glow and four hours of hard sleep not only removed the purple rings etched under her eyes, but left her as cheery as a daisy and ready to save some lives.

****

Aside from the sultry start to her day, the rest of Liv's night was pretty standard. By the time midnight rolled around, she'd forgotten her lustified fantasy, fending off a contact intoxication after the third drunk Northwestern co-ed puked down her scrub top.

"Really? Ya'll need to stop soaking your tampons in moonshine," Liv huffed, wiping the girl's face. She finished her quick assessment and helped her flirty tech, Leo, prop the girl into the wheelchair. A surge of empathy flowed through her veins. Liv pulled off the incriminating Delta Delta Delta sweatshirt before sending her back. "You're making the rest of us look bad, here, hon."

The girl heaved. "Are you going to call my Mom?"

"I think a chat with your Momma would do you some good, but no, sweetheart, you're eighteen. You're an adult. A stupid one. But an adult nonetheless. Shoving straight liquor into your whoo-haa won't remove the calories, *and* it'll give you the yeast infection of your life," she preached with a compassionate smile and Savannah, Georgia, twang lingering on her lips. Liv tried not to scrunch her nose at the tang of urine and vomit, then covered the girl with a warm blanket as Leo took her out of triage and into the main department.

Liv sat back in her little cubbie and debated changing her scrubs for the second time. Another set of headlights flashed through the glass.

"Lost cause," she muttered, and stretched away some of the mid-shift lull.

"Any bets about Miss TriDelt's blood alcohol level?" asked Leo, strutting back to join Liv in the triage booth. He leaned against the door frame crossing his arms over his chest. The move drew her attention to his biceps, and the grin on Leo's face said that was the intended reaction.

A frantic man burst through the doorway.

"*Help*! *Help*! My wife's outside having a baby!" he bellowed gasping for breath. Liv jumped from her chair and ran, with Leo racing after her. She yanked her walkie from her back pocket.

"I need a stretcher and an open room, STAT! Get Labor and Delivery down here now!" She didn't wait for a reply before throwing the door open.

She found a young woman braced in the front seat, howling in pain. "My baby. It's coming! Aaggh…"

Olivia skipped her usual introduction and dove under the dash contorting herself between the woman's legs. "All right, try not to push. I need to take a look."

The instructions were met with another wail and the panicked father calling for Jesus to help. Dark and unable to see, Liv took a gloved hand and felt between the woman's legs. Her fingers met a warm squishy resistance. Liv peeked over the woman's nightgown stained with blood. The size of her belly and the bulging bag of waters only meant one thing.

"How many weeks are you, Hon?" The question didn't register with the screaming woman or her husband. "Sir!" she tried again, directing her focus at him. "When—is—your—wife—due?"

He sputtered a few incomprehensible syllables before he could answer. "January. The baby isn't due 'til January."

The mental math drew a pause. *Shit.*

Liv pressed her hand gently against the membrane containing the extreme micro preemie. More bodies arrived. Leo and the other staff reached to gather the woman from the front seat. "Forget L and D, we need the NICU team. Pull out the 2.0 intubation tube and double O blade for the doctor in case this baby decides to come. Someone get me a puke bag!" she called from between the woman's legs. She heard the click of the walkie and another nurse call for neonatology to hurry down.

The tech handed her the vomit baggie.

"Feeling queasy down there?" he teased. In the heat of excitement, a joke every now and again helped to ease the tension, but right then, it sure pissed her off. Liv hissed a curse word and flung her hair out of her eyes.

"No, if I need to catch this baby, I need it to stay warm. I've seen them put these little critters in Ziploc bags right after birth." Liv prayed, short, sweet. "Dear Lord, please don't let this woman deliver her baby in my hands." The woman groaned. Liv sensed her urgency to push.

"No! Ma'am! C'mon, short breaths. *Don't push!*" A rush of warm, salty water drenched down her arm, and a tiny body flopped into her open palm. "*Shit*! Baby's out!" Liv placed the one-pound infant in the plastic, examining it for all parts and gripped the mother's arm.

"We've got sixty-seconds until the umbilical cord stops pulsing and the placenta comes. Move her!"

Everything that happened next was a blur. Nothing she'd really remember, but the rush she'd never forget. The tiny infant was locked and loaded into a traveling isolette and Liv took her first real breath in over an hour. She leaned against the nurses' station counter and watched the one-pound baby leave encased in plastic and covered with tubes and wires.

"Impressive," said her new gal pal from the train. Torey had arrived with the NICU team for the crash delivery. Liv glanced down and smiled. Cold, congealed liquid saturated her scrub top and splattered her cheek.

"I *am,* aren't I?"

The pair looked over the perpetual mess in the ER. Dirty linens, stretchers stowed haphazardly along the walls; across the unit a pair of trauma medics donned white plastic gowns over their teal scrubs.

"A revolving door of fun," Torey quipped, a reminiscent smirk on her face. "Oh, all right. I suppose I miss this a little."

"Stay and play?" Liv tempted from her height. On cue, the homeless guy in an overflow hall bed rolled over and revealed his lilywhite hiney, then kicked off his shoes. The stench of rotting feet and sock sweat wafted over.

"Oh, yeah. Never mind. See you later, Liv." Torey waved and disappeared to the elevators.

Liv turned for the penalty box known as the triage booth when one of the lady trauma technicians came over and handed her a fresh scrub top.

"So, Liv, did you get a chance to see the new MD?" the tech asked. Great with faces, bad with names, Liv wished she could address her properly, but at least it was just friendly chatter.

"Nah, I missed him. Let me guess. He's an ass."

The ER technician laughed and elbowed another nurse in the ribs.

"His ass *is* something." She swooned, fanning herself. Liv shrugged. She didn't want to appear uninterested in the conversation and risk being rude or not fitting in. But doctors, hot or otherwise, were not on her radar. She was a woman, she'd look, stare, maybe even feel tempted to flirt and bat her lashes, but she was so very over any male in the medical profession. And above all else any male with the letters "MD" behind their name. Everyone discussed the handsome, new trauma doctor, and Liv let her mind wander back to Anderson Cole's marvelous behind.

Chapter Three

Sliding her badge through the time clock was the best part of the day. It meant she survived. As far as excitement went, delivering a micro-preemie was impossible to top, but she ended her night with a sicker-than-shit septic, diabetic patient with blood sugar of eighteen-hundred and a serum lactate off the charts. It was the nursing battle of a lifetime. Hyperkalemia. Ventricular Tachycardia. Two central lines. Prepping for emergent dialysis and timing when to fill the gut with kayexelate so the patient didn't poop all over the stretcher sapped every ounce of energy.

Liv found her new work BFF on the platform. Rooted with exhaustion, they stood side by side waiting for the seven-twenty-two. It was probably her imagination, but her body felt like it was still rushing through her twelve-hour shift.

"Off for four." Torey smirked up at her like she won the night shift lottery.

Liv's perfect posture wilted. "Oh must be nice. Off one night, then on with a call shift."

Torey cackled. "You mean mandatory overtime."

She sighed. "Yep … and it's flipping Friday the thirteenth." A pout, full of self-pity tried to emerge.

She loved her job. Loved the commitment and heart it took, but every shift—good, bad, ugly—was a giant kick in the ass. Unable to remember a time she wasn't exhausted, she wished for the kind of mother that would call and shower her with pride and praise. She wished for the kind of Momma that would make a huge fuss of their hardworking daughter. Of course she'd deny it, but she wished *someone* in her life would fuss over her. It had been twenty years since she watched the only perfect man she'd ever known lowered into the Georgian soil. And with her Daddy a lifetime gone, all forms of affection and smiles of encouragement came from her mother, and it would be a cold day in hell before her Momma would risk wrinkling her porcelain skin. Liv straightened her shoulders and threw her hair back.

Screw Momma and that pretentious stick up her ass.

"What do ya say to a night out?" she asked. The 'L train barreled down the track, then screeched, slowing to a stop.

Torey's nose scrunched tight. "Aren't you exhausted?"

"Pretty much all the time."

She laughed. "Okay, just don't expect any witty commentary."

"I don't. I'm the funny one." Liv got a shove in the arm as the two boarded the train and looked for a seat. The car, like the day before, was congested with moody city folk, their noses glued to their smart phones or e-readers refusing to acknowledge the bleary-eyed nurses that hadn't sat in fourteen hours. Too tired to grumble about the injustice, they grabbed a rail and held on as the train jarred forward.

****

It wasn't stalking. He was at the library to read. He held a book in his hand to prove it. Of course, he never bothered with the cover and when he sat down to "not stalk" Andy spent the better part of the afternoon familiarizing himself with *A Woman's Guide to Self-Love and Exploration.* Time floated away and so did his purpose when the pages opened to a rather detailed manual of how a woman should get herself off.

"Learning anything new?"

The warm, velvet purr thrust Andy from his chair.

He tossed the damning book into the vacant seat. Late afternoon sun smudged into a gloomy evening, but Liv glowed, lovely and radiant. It probably made him look like the ultimate pervert, but he couldn't keep the boyish, eager grin off his face.

"Oh, no. I'm an expert. Wrote the book in fact."

Liv pursed her lips. *Shit.* A silent, but very clear "what a douchebag," reaction. With a swift kick in the ego nut sack, Andy deflated. Except she held his gaze and grinned. Her green eyes widened. *Intrigued? Nope.*

Turned on.

Andy straightened and sucked in a breath, hoping to find a shred of manliness. It was useless. She had him the kind of stupid-giddy reserved for first crushes. "Already finished with the bird book?"

Her cheeks colored, and the blood rushed from his head to his groin. He shuffled his feet, hoping to stop his dick from becoming an embarrassment.

"Ya know, turns out, I didn't need Augustus Flynne after all."

Liv's fingers played with the spine of the book, and because he must be punished for something, she clutched the book to her chest. The move, conscious or otherwise, pushed her tits up and together. For the last twenty-four hours he'd thought of nothing else but Liv's body beneath her scrubs, but this was cruel. A clingy black sweater, a tight denim skirt that hit mid-thigh, and those annoying ankle boots he hated but all the girls here wore. Except, on her it fucking worked. Everything about Liv was too much, but not enough. Andy forced his eyes off her breasts and glared at the ceiling. A call for mercy.

On cue, one of the crones working the depository called out to Liv. Attuned to the sound of distress, Anderson couldn't ignore the winded and strained voice, or the old woman as she gripped the counter.

Liv held up a finger. "Hang on a second," she said darting off. Her spidey-sense must have kicked into hyperdrive before Anderson could take his eyes off her ass.

Liv reached the counter and, with surprising grace, hopped over and spun around to address the pale woman. Andy followed, assessing from a distance with his hand on his cellphone. No doctor in the world could stop a heart attack without resources.

"What's goin' on, Mrs. Loveitz?" she asked, reaching for the old woman's wrist. A clammy flush dotted the librarian's forehead. Liv grabbed a dainty handkerchief from inside her purse and wiped along Mrs. Loveitz's face then neck. "Andy, can you drag that chair over here, please?"

Like a lumbering buffoon he hadn't even thought to grab the woman a chair. He could crack a chest and cross clamp the aorta in three minutes, but having her sit down never sprang to mind.

"Did you remember your Digoxin today?" Liv continued. Breathless, the woman nodded. The crowd in a library on a Friday fall evening was sparse, but the ones that were there all convened around the pair.

"Your heart's running and skipping away from you. You know what that means?"

Andy helped Mrs. Loveitz into the seat and felt her cool, moist skin. She slumped her shoulders, braced her hands on her knees and gulped down air. Her distress prickled his skin.

"She's going need an ambulance. You know, I'm a doc—"

"I know. Can you call? This isn't our first rodeo, is it, Mrs. L?"

Andy grinned and did as he was ordered. Liv had it well under control. She went behind the counter and retrieved an oxygen canister and mask, then tightened it around Mrs. Loveitz's face. "Try for some slow breaths there, Rose." Liv turned her attention to Andy mid-911 call. She motioned for the phone, a polite smirk on her lips. Maybe she was a bit of a control freak. He offered her his cellphone and crouched before Mrs. Loveitz. He took her hands in his. Her breathing had slowed, and she seemed to be more comfortable.

"Howdy, ma'am. I'm Andy Cole. It seems Liv has you well taken care of, but is there anything else you need? Something I can get you?"

Rose Loveitz shook her head, a smile erupting across her face. She tugged the oxygen mask down. "Well, now I know why Olivia looked like a smitten kitten when she left here the other morning. You are certainly a nice slice of pecan pie."

Andy dropped his gaze to the carpet, reveling in her flattery.

"No thank you, young man," she continued. "I'm fine. Olivia will have the ambulance here in a few, and she always calls me in a favor. She's a nurse in the emergency room at County Med."

He threw a glance over his shoulder and laughed. "I knew it. She tried to tell me she was a dog groomer."

"Then she must really like you."

His cheeks warmed. One day in town and he was already crushing on the prom queen. "Is that so? Howdoya figure?"

"I've never seen her stare at a man the way she's ogling you this very second. You'd think she's starving."

The flush in his cheeks rushed to his groin. He cleared his throat.

"But I know she's more than hungry," she added with the sort of affection he expected from family, but Mrs. Loveitz didn't seem tied to Liv by blood.

"So you think I'd stand a chance askin' her to dinner?"

Mrs. Loveitz grinned, then gasped for air. Andy moved her oxygen mask back on her face. "Are you a murderer or a politician?" she asked between sucks of air.

"No, ma'am."

"Live in your parents' basement with a credit score below six-hundred?"

He shook his head and put a hand over his heart. "Texan's honor."

"Well good. You pass *my* test. But for a lady who doesn't date, Olivia has very low standards: never insults his mother—"

Andy chuckled. "I got that nailed. My mother was a saint."

"Can't be anyone she works with. *Especially* a doctor."

Andy stiffened, a big ball of "what-the-fuck" wadding up in his stomach.

"Sure a workplace romance is a bad idea, but what's she got against doctors?"

Mrs. Loveitz looked over his shoulder as Liv called in what sounded like a "VIP nurse perk hook-up". She smiled, but it wasn't a *real* smile. It was a pity smile. The same smile he had to endure for months on end. The look he went thousands of miles out of his way to avoid.

"Well, it's not for me to say," she said, having to pause and catch her breath.

Andy turned his attention to Liv. Animated. Adorable. Beautiful. She found his gaze and grabbed hold. A grin that rivaled Christmas curled along her lips and everything went belly up, and bass-akwards.

He'd run off and be a garbage man if she kept looking at him like that.

"But sure as God made green apples, the Cubs will have won a world series before she'll let herself fall for another doctor. No matter the accent."

****

Liv danced off the chill in evening air waiting on the ambulance. She tossed a sideways glance at Mrs. Loveitz. Her dear friend appeared to be recovered and was busy batting her lashes at Anderson Cole. She shimmed for warmth, suddenly envious of an eighty-four-year-old woman with saggy skin and a long list of complex medical problems.

When the ambulance arrived, Liv stepped back, relinquishing a sliver of control. "This has got to be torture for you," observed the cute, baby-faced, barely legal paramedic swimming in his Chicago Fire jacket. He'd dropped a few patients in the Pit the night before. So sweet he would give a girl a toothache. But Liv always preferred steak.

She smirked at the brazen kid years out of his league as he strode by carrying his box of tools. Mr. Steak-on-a-stick finally broke himself from Mrs. L's spell and came to join her outside as the paramedic and EMT did their thing.

She pretended not to notice the questioning look on his face. And the warmth that spread through her cheeks and into her scalp. "You might have noticed. Rose is a special friend of mine. I'm a little overprotective."

"Well, it was a good thing you decided to swing back here this evening." His tenor twang all but made her panties vaporize.

It didn't take a valedictorian to put together he'd been waiting for her. And that thought alone made her all sorts of turned on.

"You know she let it slip that you're an ER

nurse."

Liv glared at her friend as she rode by on the stretcher. "Traitor. I'll call to check on you in an hour."

Mrs. Loveitz blew her a kiss, then locked her dissecting blue eyes onto Andy. Liv expected him to cower under her stare, but he absorbed it, standing taller with each second that passed between them.

"Why don't you want people to know you're a nurse?" he continued.

"Oh, the usual. Too many randos try to take off their pants."

"Man, if I had a dollar for every time I was told to keep my pants on."

Blasphemy. Andy Cole should never have pants on. Liv breathed a sobering sigh. She enjoyed him way too much. Her eyes lingered over his square chest and stubbled chin. Her imagination ran away with images from the sexified REM rebound session. Andy Cole making her come in every way possible flickered before her.

The autumn air bit into the exposed skin along her chest. She shivered, yet seared with something else. Her nipples hardened, and friction from her French lace LaPerla's shot straight to the sweet spot between her legs. A little swivel of her hips teased the silky material over her now swollen clit. Andy hadn't done much, said even less, and all she could think about was how his fingers would feel if they slid up her skirt.

"I'm usually not a fibber," she admitted, laying on her pageant princess persona. It got her out of more trouble than she'd like to admit. "But to be fair, I didn't expect to see you again."

Andy shrugged off his coat and wrapped it over her shoulders. "You mean you've never had a man wait you out at the library before?"

She tried to hide her deep inhale as he enveloped her in his warmth and woodsy sent. "Nope. You're the first."

Something in the way he looked at her set off a cascade of panic. But for the first time since she left Savannah, she wasn't afraid of the palpitations in her chest or the ache in her belly. All it did was make her want more.

The waa-mbulance slammed shut, and Liv broke herself from Andy's gaze. Mrs. Loveitz disappeared under revolving red lights and wailing sirens. Liv attempted to step away from Andy's pull, but her rebellious feet knew where the rest of her body wanted to go.

Andy placed his hand on the small of her back and guided her toward the double doors. He took a shaky breath. Arrogance when done right was sexier than tailor-made suits and dirty talk, but Andy's schoolboy nerves were about the most adorable thing she'd ever seen.

"So … ah, if you hadn't figured it out by now, I'm here because I would love to take you to dinner, Liv."

She nibbled on her lips. A charming and handsome stranger might be just what the RN ordered to keep girlie parts from expiring. But as much as *Cosmo* tries to sell it, sex weighed against her still fragile, broken heart that always gave up love too easily.

Andy must have read her silence and the conflict pinched along her brow. He straightened, like he was preparing to take a rejection like a man.

"Well, Mr. Cole, I'd love to, but I'm plum booked up tonight…" Without warning, she leaned into his space, breathed his air and knew instantly saying no would be a mistake.

"But it's just drinks with a girlfriend from work.

If you can handle a little ER shop talk, why don't you come along?"

He laughed. "ER shop talk is something I can definitely handle."

Chapter Four

Andy swirled the single malt around the base of the glass, brought it to his mouth and inhaled. Warm, buttery. He examined Liv's soft features dance in the glow of candlelight over the rim of the glass. Pulling out the chair next to him was a mistake, as there was no way to hide the fact he was staring.

Ten years in Texas came and went with little change, but Chicago's Northside had reinvented itself three times over. During his early residency, nightlife consisted of techno music dance clubs or pre-hipster bars hosting alternative garage bands and poetry slams. These days, the Gen-Xer's had moved to the suburbs and taken with it all the earliest parts of the twenty-first century. Since then the Millennials and gastro pubs had invaded. While he would never admit it, Andy rather enjoyed the sleek iron and glass, ultra-modern décor while savoring his whiskey.

The conversation could have been about unicorns, Democrats, and the Kardashians, but none of it stuck. He spent all of his energy trying not to stare into the curve of her breasts while she chatted with her original plans for the evening. He masked his disappointment when her friend arrived just after they sat down. It left no time to charm her up and casually mention he was a doctor. A doctor that—because God's got an awful sense of humor—now worked in the same damn ER she did. Soon, he'd be writing orders for her to carry out, and there was nothing sexy about telling the woman you want to see naked to do an enema. *Shit.* This was a bad idea. It was rule number one in residency. Don't date the nurses. Why was it only hitting him now, now when he was more than half crazy for her?

"Torey, this is my friend Andy Cole. Thanks for letting him tag along to our girls' night out." Liv nudged her friend with her elbow and flashed Andy the smile that went straight to his groin. That sure as fuck didn't help things.

He stood, pulled out the opposite chair and helped Torey out of her jacket. He saw the silent girl conversation in their shared glance. *Yup.* Chivalry wasn't dead, and it was easy to be a gentleman in a sea of douchebags.

"She took pity on me, really. A grown man sitting alone in a library on a Friday night. Even my mother would've been embarrassed to claim me." He winked, devilishly flirting with both women, but saved the cocky smirk for Liv. And the fact she slid her chair a little closer meant one thing—it had done its job. "So, Liv told me you're an ER nurse dropout."

To his left, Liv jumped in her seat. He couldn't be sure, but he'd bet money she just got a swift kick in the shin.

"Ask her how many times she got puked on last night," Torey countered. "Call me what you want, but my back doesn't ache, and my patients don't threaten to sue because I offered them a ham sandwich instead of turkey."

Andy laughed knowing the exact kind of patient she was referring to, the gems whining about the hospital not having premium cable, or flat screen TVs.

"You know, Liv, that baby you delivered yesterday is doing really well."

Andy's jaw fell open.

"Y'all had a delivery in the ER?"

"Oh, no. Not in the ER. Liv delivered a twenty-four-week fetus in the front seat of a Honda Civic."

****

Liv wasn't one for boasting, but she loved the rapt attention Andy showered her with while retelling the events from her shift the night before. It was the same kind of attention that had screwed her over and broken her heart two years ago. She blamed being a girl. A silly, narcissistic, pageant girl that secretly wanted everyone to think she was pretty and smart.

She broke the lock of his blue eyes and fiddled with her empty wine glass.

"It sounds more exciting than it actually was. I'm glad the little guy is putting up a strong fight."

"Don't diminish what you did," Andy said. "That's truly amazing."

"Well right after that I got cussed out by a drag queen that I'm pretty sure was high on 'bath salts' … so it's not all glamor, glitz, and glory."

"Fellacia Handcock stopped by? Haven't seen her in ages," Torey reminisced. "So, Andy. What's your story?"

Liv grinned at her new friend, thankful she turned the topic away from their less than ladylike job. She always feared blabbing too much about herself, an even more disgusting habit, but since Torey arrived there hadn't been any time to ask the down-and-dirty get to know you questions. Torey was being a heck of a wing-woman. She'd get a latte and maybe Leo's phone number out of this.

Andy took a long draw from his tumbler, draining the amber liquid in one swallow and ran his tongue over his lips as if to ensure no drop was left behind. Liv's heart sputtered, her chest flushed, and blood surged to the achy spot between her legs. God, she was wet and turned on just watching the man finish his whiskey.

"Y'all might have guessed, but I'm not from 'round these here parts," Andy said with a chuckle. His accent deepened, and like an addict staring at her next fix, Liv's mouth watered. A home-grown southern man so sexy she could cry. "I just moved up here from a small town in West Texas."

"Occupation?" Torey pressed.

Andy shot a glance at Liv.

"Dog groomer? I hear there's quite the need for them in the neighborhood."

A giggle, drunk and lively, bubbled from Liv's chest. Flirting instinct was in full force, and she rested her hand on his, then turned to explain the hilarity to her bemused friend. After the giggling subsided, Liv leaned back, unconsciously trailing her fingers over his knuckles. He pulled his hand away to bring the empty glass to his lips. The ice rattled against the rim. She brought him back with an enigmatic smile. Short of saying he was an axe wielding sociopath, there's very little he could say that would make her not want to go home with him, or break the spell of instant infatuation. "Charity work. Mission trips. Over the last few years I've made several trips to small, isolated countries in Central and South America. Brought food, water, medical attention, and other services."

Liv's jaw popped open. His blue eyes wavered, but she held his gaze, astonished, entranced. A charming, chivalrous gentleman that tended to the poor and needy who happened to be a supreme specimen of sex on a stick? He was like finding a leprechaun-riding a unicorn.

Another kick found her shin. Still in wing-woman mode, Torey tried to reel in the potentially looney woman behavior, but it went ignored, swallowed up by the tingles of a blooming crush. "Anderson Cole, you are going to make it very hard not to fall in love with you."

Chapter Five

Fucking idiot. That's what he was. Lying by omission is as bad as the sin itself. Charity? Mission work? Yes, all true. Three separate seasons working in remote villages in Central and South America providing free medical aid to poor and epidemic ravaged communities was good for the soul, but hardly altruistic. A PR stunt orchestrated by his ex-wife during Junior Women's League elections and something he kept up to escape her wrath and condescending cracks for a few weeks a year. Andy winced stumbling over the memories. He loved the work, but he also loved A/C and WiFi.

He didn't know what was worse. Purposely lying about what he did just to keep her interested in seeing him, or that Liv deemed him almost a saint for doing it.

What was the worst thing that could happen? He would have told her that he was a doctor, she'd have back pedaled and politely declined another date; they'd have a good, somewhat awkward laugh about working together and that'd be it. And truthfully, that would have been the best possible outcome.

Liv kept her hand tucked into the crook of his arm as he walked her home. They meandered in step down the sidewalk. Maybe it was all in his head, but they were already in perfect sync.

"There it is again!" he laughed. "I knew I heard a twang! Get a little liquor in you and look what comes out."

"Aw, hell. You caught me," Liv said. She looked up, slightly mortified. "I'm a Savannahian born and bred."

He stared at her, mouth open and brows pulled

tight. A confused gape easily hid the fact he was imagining her naked. "How'd you find yourself all the way up here?"

Liv took a sharp breath and cleared her throat, her gravity pulling away.

"Doesn't everyone move to Chicago for the weather? Ah. This is me." She did a little twirl and stopped in front of a towering brick brownstone. Three stories, vintage stained glass, and only one pair of double oak doors. Snap judgments aside, the intimidating, city-folk mansion appeared to be all hers.

Liv turned into him, then curled her fingers into the hem of his shirt. Their eyes connected, and while his heart stopped, his cock turned on. She leaned in and, for the love of God, purred. "I'd love to ask you up, but think I've done enough damage for one night. That moonshine hit me in all the wrong places, but you, Mr. Cole. Just the opposite."

He pressed her hard against the solid oak door. There'd be no denying the erection he drilled into her pelvis.

"Is that an invitation to kiss you, Ms. Aberdeen?"

She sucked in a quick breath, then grinned. Hungry. Wanting.

"You're damn right it is."

Andy sealed his mouth to hers and wove his fingers into her copper hair, pulling her into the kiss. His tongue parted her mouth, and she wrapped her arms around his neck. Hot and electric, he commanded more, but something slowed. His heart. His brain. Something tugged him back as if to ensure they'd never forget the moment. She came up for air, and peeped through her lashes. God, every look was a direct line to his crotch. She reached into her purse and dug around then pulled out a Sharpie. Of course a nurse would have a permanent marker in her handbag. She rolled up his sleeve, taking deliberate care to caress the tense muscles of his forearm and wrote her phone number. Beneath it in messy script she wrote.

Olivia

"Does this mean I can call you—Olivia?"

"Yes."

The hold she had on him came out of nowhere. She was smart, funny, and sexy as hell, but there was no way around it. This was going to blow up and end bad. He needed to put a stop to it, but couldn't. Not when she looked at him like that.

"Good luck washing that off." Olivia pecked his cheek, and opened the door. "G'night, Andy."

She flashed him a smile. The one that made his stomach do back flips.

"Goodnight, Olivia."

He was fucking hosed.

****

Hot and turned on, Liv needed a shower. A cold shower. She needed to nip her needs in the bud before she did something stupid, like hang outside her window and tell the sweet and fine piece of man to come back and perform a long list of delicious and naughty things to her.

Andy must have been able to read her dirty, dirty mind. Thirty minutes later he sent her a polite but slyly, filthy text message where had he whispered the words in her ear, she'd come on the spot.

Her heartrate climbed. Want flushed her skin and pulsed between her thighs just imagining the tall, Texan gentleman murmur how he had a lovely evening, but hoped to taste more of her next time. Her sex swelled. Every inch of her craved release. God, she needed to get off, but first things first. Propriety and good manners would always win out.

Liv called Torey and thanked her for a nice evening, apologizing once again for turning her into a third wheel when she was the one who invited her out in the first place. A ready compromise was met after Liv promised spa pedicures and mimosas the following week *and* Leo's phone number. He might have been a playboy, but he wasn't the type to fuck, dump, and tell.

"I'm not looking for marriage, Liv. I just need my pipes cleaned."

She sighed. "Okay… But you know they sell very good playthings for that. Far less hassle and batteries cost nothing compared to a broken heart and a shot of penicillin."

"Thanks for your concern, friend. Get some sleep."

Liv grunted. "That's the funniest thing you've said all night." She hung up the phone and stared around her home. Tonight would be an insomniac's worst nightmare.

"I should've never returned that stupid bird book."

****

Her kitchen was spotless. Her closet organized by color, season, and designer. Even with her revulsion of laundry, every item of clothing was washed, folded, and put away. Liv was stuck, smack dab in the middle of a night shifters' classic dilemma. Forcing sleep, and run the risk of waking up with the sun, like a normal person, or hoping to trick the body to sleep during the day with the very plausible chance you get none. She went with the latter and sat down at her tidy little writing desk. Late night was the best time to indulge in a few guilty pleasures. Buttercream frosting by the spoonful, Amazon Prime, and Facebook stalking.

It was evil. There had to be a special place in hell for the humble-bragger friends that littered her wall with "messy" perfectionist Instagram photos and the staged videos of their supposedly genius, Mensa-level toddlers. Liv tried to remember when any of these women could have been her friend. Of course, when you attend college at the Southern version of Ivy League, graduating magna cum laude didn't mean anything unless it came with an MRS degree. Most nights she could convince herself she made the right choice, but this was one where she felt the needling pinch of doubt.

She heaped dollop of frosting into her mouth, letting the sugar take away some of the pain that never seemed to go away as her fingers hovered over the keys that would connect her with her past. Taking a look at Logan St. James and his flavor of the month couldn't sting. Not after having such a fantastic time with saintly, tall, dark, and lovely Mr. Anderson Cole. Except it did. It would seem her ex-fiancé flew right past flavor of the month and dove straight into the quest for another missus. The new side piece was a quintessential southern beauty. Liv couldn't be sure if it was petty jealousy, or pity that bubbled in the pit of her stomach.

She would never have been happy playing the role expected of her in Savannah's elite society, but that didn't mean she didn't have the same wants out of life. She had been hell-bent on not falling into the same trap, avoiding any romantic prospect like a bad case of infectious diarrhea, but something was different about Anderson. She wanted to blame the moonshine, but she was stone cold sober when she made the decision to Stalkerbook Andy. Of course, being a grown man that wasn't a complete narcissist, there was nothing but a gorgeous profile photo of him with his arms around a little dark-skinned child taken in front of a backdrop of pure squalor.

Her heart swelled, and she had to rein in the crazy, closing the window before making a fool of herself, and—God forbid—send a friend request. That would be the equivalent of a drunk-dialed booty call, and if there was one lesson her Momma ingrained so deep it was etched on her bones, it was to make sure a man worked to woo you.

Like an answer to her naughty prayers, her cellphone rang. A 3 AM call was one of two things, and God wouldn't be so cruel and to have work call on one her night off. The delightful chime made everything below her navel tingle. But the FaceTime image that came through was a familiar as her own. Her beloved Lottie.

She fluffed her hair and pinched her cheeks before swiping to answer. For some reason she felt the need to appear put together in the middle of the night. "Lottie. Sweetie, what's goin' on? Everything okay?" Concern deepened her usual muddied twang.

"Oh, you know. Same shit different day." Her friend on the other end must not have felt the same pressure to keep up appearances. Blotched and bleary-eyed with smeared mascara, Lottie looked like her most recent companion was a bottle of JD. Liv let out a sigh when her friend took a deep swig from bottle of good ol' Jack Daniels, just as she suspected.

"C'mon, lay it on me."

"I hate men. If it weren't for the whole not liking fish thing … I think I could be a lesbian."

"You'd make any woman very happy."

Lottie nodded and pumped her chest with her half-drunk bottle.

"I really would. Wouldn't I?"

Liv's brow knitted together. She carried the

weight of worry for her friend. This wasn't her usual middle of the night call where she's stark raving mad at her husband, Dr. Theodore VanSutton. Teddy had a sneaky habit of curtailing Lottie's spending by canceling her charge cards without telling her. "I told him, Livy. I told him that I better never find out…"

"What are you talking about?"

Lottie hiccupped. The whiskey-fueled defiance and anger cracked, and she crumbled. Liv's heart broke for her friend. She knew what Lottie would say before she finished the sentence.

"There are pictures this time. It's always been idle gossip. And gossip could work in my favor. But now … Jesus, Livy. How could I let myself become my Momma?"

"Teddy's having an affair with Nanny Kemp?"

Lottie snorted. "Ha. That's a scandal I could spin, but no. Some beautiful blonde that works for the Baptist Ministry."

Liv couldn't hold in her snark and sang the song of her pre-teen generation. "Isn't it ironic?"

"Dontcha think?" her friend answered without missing a beat. "Seriously, Olivia, I don't know how I'm going to show my face. I don't want to hide in shame, but I don't want to hear the damned talk. And my poor babies." Lottie's tears fell without restraint. Liv wanted to jump through the phone to her friend on the other side, and comb her fingers through her hair the same way Lottie did the day Logan broke her heart for all of Savannah to see.

"Go wake Nanny, and the twins. Book the first, first-class tickets you find, and come on up here. You know I've got plenty of room."

Lottie's mouth fell open, then quivered into hope. "You sure?"

"Of course I am. And sweetie, if I don't hear from you by five, I'm coming to find you."

Lottie's crushed soul burst from her chest. She thrust her shoulders back, wiped her cheeks, and cleared her throat of sadness. In a breath she morphed into her strong, debutante persona.

"All right then, Livy. What should I pack?"

Chapter Six

Andy was pretty sure he broke every rule of modern courtship by texting Olivia the moment she shut her door. Like a lovestruck twit, he obsessively checked his phone for a missed message or reply and his ego had officially deflated by the time he got to his hotel. Frustrated in more ways than he could count, he threw himself into the shower and jerked off. It was a waste of ten minutes. He was just as wound as when he started, depleted of nothing but sperm and time.

He stood at the sink, towel slung low on his hips and wiped away the steam to examine his reflection. He ran a hand along two days' worth of stubble as if the coarse black hair somehow retained any piece of her. Habit had him reach for his straight razor, but Liv seemed to love the lazy-man's five o'clock shadow. Falling into a new category of pussy-whipped, he left it on the counter.

The whiskey buzz and tingle of infatuation began to wear off as he glared at the queen bed in his suite at the Peninsula on Michigan Ave. This wasn't him. A small town, country boy had no place in this kind of luxury, but still he thanked the Lord for the means to have it fall into his lap.

Andy circled the room and vowed not to look at his phone. Or his computer. Never in his life had he been a slave to that kind of technology, and it wasn't going to change solely because he'd fallen head over dick for a woman he'd just met, but that didn't stop him from jumping out of bed the instant he heard the phone vibrate against the nightstand.

Blindly, he swiped thumb across the screen to answer expecting to be greeted by Liv's warm, honeyed voice. But it wasn't Liv. It was the crazy he shelved for another day.

"Andy. So glad you decided to pick up," Greta crooned in her favorite passive-aggressive tone.

Anger simmered in his veins. He clenched his molars together to keep from falling into her trap.

"I've been busy." It was a glib lie. One shift in the Pit and an afternoon lounging in his Boxer-briefs watching ESPN college game day concocting a plan to get Liv out on a date was hardly busy.

"Of course you have," she dismissed. "I just thought you should know MeMaw's back in the hospital. They're sayin' it's pneumonia this time."

Andy frowned, the petty flare of irritation fizzling. He might have divorced Greta, but he never meant to abandon her family. "That's too bad. Be sure to give her my love."

"I went ahead and got her a room in the Lutheran Home."

He flipped. Was she trying to rub salt in the wound of their broken relationship? "Just because I'm not there, you throw your grandmother into a nursing home? That woman *raised* you. Christ, Greta, you know how I feel about that sort of thing."

"That's right, Andy, you're not here. What was I supposed to do?"

"Take care of her. Use my fucking money for something *other* than trips to the spa and Neiman Marcus. Get her in-home nursing care."

"Screw you and your self-righteous bullshit, *Dr. Cole*," Greta barked.

Andy prepped for a battle, but the line went dead. He clenched his phone in his fist ready to throw it across the room, but he took a cleansing breath and ran a hand through his hair. What did he expect? To be able to move away from his grief and her crazy, then have it be over? Never. He smirked. Greta would spit nails if she knew he spent the evening pursuing another woman. The kind of woman she'd loathe. Smart, kind, and the type of unintentionally sexy that made men pant. The mere thought of her went straight to his crotch. That was going to get old real fast. He debated rubbing out the instant hard-on while he climbed into bed and caved to one final glace at his text inbox.

Olivia: **Pretty sure that can be arranged... ;-)**

Short. Sweet. Left him wanting more. And no stupid emoji. His heart and his cock aligned. Hosed wasn't the word. He was falling in fucking love.

****

Liv's insomnia raged, and it was fair to guess she got less than four hours of sleep. There was no saying what she bought off same day delivery when she hit zombie mode as the sun started to rise a little after seven. Like always she finally fell asleep around noon and was woken up by the downstairs buzzer.

Her heart bounded within her ribs, and she flopped out of bed. Disoriented and flustered, she raced around her bedroom for her robe. The front door buzzed again.

"I'm comin'!" she hollered, knowing full well it wasn't going to be heard. There was another long draw on the buzzer, followed this time by a frantic voice over the intercom.

"C'mon, Livy, open up. It's freezing!" In the background she heard the telling babbles of early toddlerhood and the calm shush of Nanny Kemp. Lottie had arrived earlier than she expected. Liv grabbed her phone on the way down and checked the time. All right, not early. God, it sucked sleeping away the day and still being tired.

Liv reached the door and fumbled around the locks. Bleary-eyed, she threw the door open and into the open arms of her oldest friend.

"Oh, Lottie, so glad you're here! C'mon in!" she squealed. Lottie ambled through the doorway with a procession of little people and noise. Clad in her classic Burberry trench, strappy Jimmy Choo's, and oversized Marc Jacobs sunglasses, Charlotte VanSutton was the picture of southern perfection. Nanny Kemp, plump and comfortable, ushered the wayward blonde-headed babies, Ashton and Louise, right behind. Liv let go of her friend and fell to her knees to embrace her honorary niece and nephew. Like mirrored opposites, the weary little boy clung to his momma, and the little girl beamed. "Look at y'all, getting so big. Your momma didn't tell auntie how big you both have gotten."

Lottie removed her sunglasses. Red, puffy lids encased her brown eyes, and the remnants of her Dior mascara smudged down her cheeks. Just like last night, Liv's heart broke for her friend. Lottie had always been the strong one, and here she was, a mortal woman, sad not because her husband had had an affair, but because he was stupid enough to get caught with his pants down. What kind of fucked up society teaches its men it's okay to be unfaithful to your wife as long as you don't get caught and what kind of mothers teach their daughters to accept that kind of disrespect? Never in her twenty-eight years did she hate her Savannahian roots more than she did right then.

Another night shift loomed over her head. She wished for the work ethic that wouldn't plague her for taking a personal day, but surely Lottie wouldn't make her feel like a bad host for not calling in and entertaining her the minute she walked in the door.

"Nanny, I've got the guest rooms on the second

floor ready for all y'all, and the basement's full of little surprises from auntie." Liv swore she heard some grumbling about the safety of stairs as Nanny marched the twins down the hall.

Lottie pulled her brunette tresses into a high ponytail. "Are you still buying up baby toys and outfits?"

She held in a wince. "You know I can't resist a sale."

Lottie squinted Liv into focus, as if to count the bags under her eyes and assessed for the deep, terminal sadness only she could see.

The pitter-patter of little feet passed, and Liv swallowed against pain clogging her throat and painted on her FOS smile.

She waved her off. "Not now, Lot. I need to get ready for work, and you need a drink."

They rounded Liv's French country kitchen and made a pass at her wine cabinet.

"C'mon, Livy. This is not a chardonnay problem. Gimme the good stuff," Charlotte slurred in an irritated tone. She kicked off her stilettos, tossed her thirteen-hundred-dollar designer coat onto the floor, and shed her chic outer layer and fell face first into the girl Liv grew up with, but apparently that meant she'd skip the pretentious bullshit and dive straight into her stash of hillbilly moonshine.

Up in Olivia's sanctuary, Lottie changed from of her stylish travel clothes and pulled on a pair of Liv's threadbare college sweats. Faded beyond recognition, the Vanderbilt's School of Nursing insignia showed its years of marathon study sessions and trips through the sorority house washing machines. No longer a center stage member of Savannah's elite, Lottie lounged in Liv's clawfoot tub, sans makeup and drinking straight from the bottle. But she was radiant. Over-indulgent chandeliers always had a place in a lady's en-suite. The warm, filtered glow minimized all flaws, except exhaustion.

Liv sighed at the injustice, but knew sleep deprivation, no matter how bad it aged a woman, was better than being on the receiving end of heartbreak and scandal. She'd already been there. Done that. Sold the t-shirt on Craigslist.

"This feels reminiscent of senior year," Liv said, swiping on a layer of mascara. She watched her friend's response in the mirror.

Lottie choked on a swig of whiskey.

"You mean, me sitting here drunk, rambling about some stupid, southern prick while you get ready to do something responsible … like … study or go play with old people…"

"Not all of us could major in contemporary cultures." Liv winked at her friend and hopped off her vanity stool to strut into her cavernous walk-in and get dressed.

Nanny Kemp called from the bedroom to discuss dinner for the twins. Liv heard Lottie stumble out of the tub and meander down the hall, giggling at something her little ones must have done. She peered around the door. Lottie plopped herself and the babies on Liv's four-poster bed, covering the twins with blankets and kisses.

Her cellphone chimed. Liv's heart thumped in her ribs. Anderson Cole flashed before her eyes. She crossed her fingers and looked down. Andy's name illuminated the screen. A nervous flutter bubbled in Liv's stomach, but the tingles of infatuation made her bounce on the balls of her feet.

Andy: **Hope you slept well. I tossed and turned until about two. No idea why… Have a nice night at the dog groomers.**

Liv paced in a tiny circle hoping to calm down.

She wanted to bound through the door and gab with Lottie about the new fella she was crushing on, but she'd never be that insensitive.

She emerged from the closet, tucking her phone into the pocket of her scrubs and kept her gaze on the floor. There'd be no way to hide her silly girl excitement from her face, so it'd be best to avoid it altogether.

Too bad rushing out of the room looked highly suspicious.

"Livy?" Lottie called. Liv flew past her bed filled with laughing children and her way too intuitive best friend. Lottie jumped from a makeshift porthole in the blanket fort they had made.

"Oh, no you don't," she slurred, weighed down by the liquor flowing through her system.

Liv got to the door, and threw a glance over her shoulder. "I had Nanny lock up the rest of my alcohol. Order in some deep dish. The Lou Malnati's menu is on the counter. Love you!"

"Olivia-Grace MacArthur Aberdeen, get your skinny ass back over here."

Liv halted. It was a stupid thing to hide, but she was only thinking of Charlotte's feelings. She tried to imagine fishing through a four-hundred-pound man's flesh to find his dick and place a Foley catheter. Anything to muddy the telltale signs of blossoming love from Lottie.

"Fat guy with a little weiner," she hummed in her head then turned around. Yep, that was all she needed. Every trace of girlish excitement vanished with the vision of digging through an obese man's junk. They locked eyes.

"Charlotte, I'm sorry. I just didn't want to be late."

Lottie gasped. "You met a guy!"

****

It was the fib of all fibs, but somehow Liv convinced her best friend Anderson Cole wasn't a big deal. And by big deal she meant falling for a man she hardly knew. So what if she let herself get swept away with the sweet and foolish ideology of love at first sight, or quick passionate connections that defied logic? For a second time. It was all harmless. Innocent. A silly girl crush that would fade just like a tan in October. Besides, she refused to let the scars on her heart turn her into a cynical spinster. Even if the last time she fell in love it came back to bite her in the ass. Full of drunk wisdom, Lottie offered up a hefty dose of harsh reality.

"Men lie. Good ones. Bad ones. It's in their fucking DNA."

"Hm. That's weird, I don't remember learning that in BIO350."

"Seriously, Olivia. So what if he's gorgeous?"

"Sexy on a stick."

"Or smart."

"Rice and Baylor."

"Or kind."

"Did I mention he does mission work?"

"And proves chivalry isn't dead."

"Pulled out my chair, and gave me his coat."

"I will be a monkey's uncle if that man isn't hiding something from you," Lottie finished. Liv knew Charlotte wasn't just projecting her own hurt feelings. It was a reminder.

"I won't let you forget what Logan did."

Olivia frowned. She didn't need a reminder of Logan's betrayal. She had the bank stubs and two stubborn belly scars to prove it.

"I know, Lot. But let's remember who the real villain was … *is*. You know it wasn't the little blonde jezebel with a G-string hanging out of her scrubs. I can forgive a fella for thinking with his dick. But I..." Liv paused, a lump of regret balled in her throat so tight it choked her.

"I will never forgive Momma for the way she..." Liv couldn't bring herself to say the crime.

Lottie wrapped a Pilates toned arm around her neck and pulled her in for the kind of hug that answered the unsaid. Liv soaked in the love of her lifelong friend, then wiped her cheek and plastered a pageant-winning smile on her face. "Besides, I don't let myself fall in love with doctors anymore. I've pretty much sworn off anyone in the medical field for that matter."

Lottie squeezed tight, then let her go turning toward the processional of toddlers singing "Twinkle, Twinkle".

"Pretty much?"

"Eh. There's a hot guy in housekeeping. And you know how I hate to mop the fucking floors..."

"Language, please! You mind your mouth around the babies, Miss Livy," chided Nanny Kemp.

Liv flamed, mouthed an embarrassed apology, and bent down to kiss her honorary niece and nephew, pulling them into hug. Ashton cringed then let out a wail. Lottie responded in kind, swooping in to rescue him from being smothered by auntie smooches. She couldn't help but chuckle at the little boy's persistent and clingy behavior. Lottie had sworn up and down she'd never have a Momma's boy. Well, the Lord went ahead and ignored that.

"Sleep tight. See ya'll in the morning."

****

Doctors didn't punch a clock, but for all intents and purposes, Andy punched his. Charts signed, patients turfed to all the right places, and for good measure, made sure his residents were tucked in for the night. Everything was done. And done well. All that was left, was to get the fuck out before Liv and rest of the night shift meandered onto the floor.

Andy stared down the long back hall of the ER and adjusted his messenger bag across his chest. The weight and being pressed for time strangled him. The new, bass-akwards department layout got him turned around and lost. All he wanted to do was steer clear of the nurses' lounge. And escape.

A door popped open. Expecting the worst, he braced for Olivia's discovery. It was about time for that shoe to drop.

"Ah, Dr. Cole, if you don't mind. Could you hang on a second?" His medical director, Dr. Smithson, emerged from a dimly lit office and removed his glasses.

Andy raked a hand through his hair, then checked his watch. Three minutes. "Yes, sir. What can I help you with?"

"Our department will be in need of some of your expertise here in the near future."

If there was a point to his statement, he wished Smithson would get there faster.

"I'm happy to help anyway I can, sir, but … um, can we discuss this tomorrow? I've got to get going."

The Senior Physician slumped and rubbed the bridge of his nose. "Yes, of course. But, eh real quick, if you don't mind. With your recent mission travels to Central America, did you have any experience with Guatemalan Hemorrhagic Fever?"

Andy froze. His breath trapped in his lungs. He couldn't move. Couldn't blink. Couldn't process. There's no way he said "Hemorrhagic Fever". The simple virus that morphed into a virtual death sentence.

"Anderson?"

Nothing registered. Not in a way that could elicit a reply. His heart raced, and his joints burned like fire. Sweat trickled down his back. It had to have been his imagination, but his throat tried to close. A wailing ambulance siren pulled him from his thoughts.

He found his voice, but it came out dry. "I have some experience with the Blood Flu, yes. Why?"

Smithson pressed his lips together. "The mayor just accepted three hundred refugees from Guatemala, and I don't want us to be another Dallas."

Chapter Seven

After the revelation of potential pandemic disaster, Andy couldn't leave. Instead, he followed Smithson to his office and talked at length about the "what ifs" and resources needed should a patient present with symptoms. The disease was a relative unknown unless you'd spent time in the region. The Guatemalan Hemorrhagic Fever was a sinister, devastating, and lightning quick virus that leveled entire villages in a week. No vaccine. No cure. No hope. Except, for some reason, Andy had survived it.

He and Smithson spent the whole night after his shift reliving his medical experiences, and it did nothing but drain him. Andy stepped outside and huddled into his jacket, missing the mild Texas weather. The city skyline was a blended wash of grey, purple, and orange. He took a deep, cleansing breath and closed his eyes. The cool air was a power wash to the senses. The moment Smithson said "Hemorrhagic Fever," every inhale had smelled like blood and decay.

He took another breath, but this time inhaled vanilla and cinnamon. Olivia appeared in his mind, and his eyes popped open.

"Hiya, cowboy," she said, greeting him with such sweetness he damn near fell to his knees. "Fancy finding you."

"Olivia? Hey… eh, 'Morning." Like a smitten twit, he beamed and stepped into her orbit. Divine intervention stopped him from drawing her into his arms. He needed to stop staring or risk venturing into stalker territory, but Jesus, she was beautiful. No one should be that beautiful after working all night.

Her lips curled, curious, but not suspicious. *Shit.* Mental exhaustion and the stupid excitement you get from catching a glimpse of the girl you're clinically obsessed with made him forget he wasn't supposed to be a doctor—and by extension, had no reason to be hanging around an ER at seven in the morning. He'd thank the gods of stank for forcing a change out of his black scrubs the night before—and for the ability to think on the fly. "I hope you don't mind, but I was up and wondering if you'd allow me to walk you home."

All right, maybe lie on the fly.

Olivia's cheeks flushed, and she glanced at the ground as if to hide her reaction. He wished she wouldn't. The rosy shade shot right to his cock. Andy held his breath. Lying to her was going to be the death of him. Scratch that. If she suddenly wanted nothing to do with him, that'd be the death of him.

Liv looked up.

"How about you take me to breakfast first?"

****

"How'd ya find this place?" Andy asked, swirling his biscuit through his heaping helping of gravy. Liv knew this would hit the right spot. He was downright drooling the moment they stepped through the door. Ethel's Place was a hole in the wall diner city folk went to for a dose of southern comfort and hospitality.

She dotted her napkin along her lips, then laid it in her lap.

"Mrs. Loveitz. My sweet old neighbor learned pretty fast I wasn't much of a cook, so she helped me find a few places that she thought might make me feel at home."

"Well, this place fits the bill," he said and flashed his half grin. Liv's mouth went dry. He sure hit all the right notes. "How did Rose come to find you weren't much of a cook?"

She bit her lip. Most men would expect any long-term prospect to know their way around a kitchen. The only direction Liv knew was straight to the wine cabinet and left at the takeout drawer. But no point in pretending … not when the nursing cat was already out of the bag. "Let's just say Mrs. Loveitz had to explain why you keep a fire extinguisher under the sink."

Andy laughed. Fine lines hugged his eyes. Dignified. Sexy as hell. God. She was too attracted to this man. What she wouldn't give for him to open his mouth and have spinach in his teeth, something to bring him back into the realm of normal hot. Normal hot she could handle.

They had a breezy discussion about the beautiful fall neither of them was used to, how there was a supreme shortage of good Mexican food, and which deep dish joint was their prospective favorite.

"Maybe you aren't the man for me. I don't know if I can let myself fall for someone that thinks Gino's is better than Lou's."

"Well, now. Don't be hasty. Maybe I just need the right woman to show me the error of my ways."

Liv let out a nervous giggle. Her heart fluttered in her chest, and she couldn't even blame her coffee. She was used to jerks hitting on her, not swoon-worthy gentlemen who made her laugh and shamelessly turned on at the same time.

"Did you have a good night? Save any lives or have any babies to deliver?"

Hoping to calm her girlish nerves, Liv sipped an ice water and shook her head. She could go on for days about some of her better stories, but no normal person wanted to hear about a severed finger or the fella with maggots in his foot. Of course, lost butt plugs and the guy who put lug nuts on his junk were fun topics, but nothing a well-bred lady from Savannah society would discuss over breakfast.

"Just an average night, I'm afraid." Golly, that was a stupid line, but exhaustion had sucked all the funny dry.

Andy pursed his lips and nodded. Adding to the ambiance of home, a twangy country song played overhead. He took a beat to hum a few words. His amused and contented expression hardened. His eyebrows knitted together, and he broke her gaze by glancing out the window. It was the first time she'd ever seen him appear conflicted. Liv let the silence fill between them until it became too much. Her heart couldn't take it, filled to the brim with unsure worry.

"You okay over there, cowboy?" she asked and held her breath, suddenly afraid she was being a lousy date after he went through the effort to get up early and see her home from work.

"Yeah, sorry. Just a bit tired is all." His eyes found hers, light but subdued. Her stomach flipped. Heat flushed up her neck and into her cheeks. Andy smiled at the blush, which of course compounded the problem.

"Anderson Cole, I wish you would stop smiling at me like that. You're giving me a serious case of the vapors." She giggled, playing up her inner O'Hara and pressed her hand into her flaming cheeks. He reached across the table and pulled it away from her face. He locked his fingers into hers, natural, like they were meant to hold hands for a lifetime. "Why *were* you up so early?" His mouth popped open for the easy answer. "And don't you try to get away with charming the scrub pants off me. No man gets up before the sun to meet a girl they've just met."

"Heh. You got me."

Liv pressed her lips together and perked a curious eyebrow.

"I actually never went to sleep."

She let out an inadvertent chuckle and pulled her hand from his.

"Of course. Another lucky lady I suspect?" It was an attempt to tease, but it came out looney and insecure.

Andy laughed. "If by lady you mean an older man with grey hair and glasses, then yes. I was with a colleague discussing some of my time in Central America."

Liv pondered the admission with an audible sigh. Her hand relaxed in his, wishing she could scoot into his seat and feel his warmth run up and down her side.

"That completely takes away from the grand, romantic gesture, doesn't it?" he asked.

Liv shrugged and met his gaze. Andy rose from his seat and slid into the open spot next to her. Her eyes widened, trying to remember if she had accidentally said her thoughts aloud. It wouldn't have been the first time her filter failed to do her job.

Andy leaned into Liv's space. His broad chest engulfed her frame. She never felt dainty, but next to him she sure did. She inhaled and was instantly drunk on his musky, masculinity. Sandalwood and sweat charged her senses. Her head fell to the side, a subconscious invitation to allow his lips to graze the skin just below her ear.

"What if I were to tell you that seeing you this morning was like a breath of fresh air? What if I told you I've done nothing but think about you since the moment we met? Or that I think you're the most beautiful woman I've laid eyes on."

A shudder prickled down her spine as the words escaped his mouth and blew over her neck. Liv turned into him, and looked up into his hooded stare. Her heart thudded. How could this man have such an effect on her?

She learned the lesson about infatuation and love the hard way. She wasn't the naive twenty-three-year-old that fell for lines and banter. Drunk Lottie's wisdom rang through her brain, and the wound that Logan left started to pull apart. But, God, he smelled good. The kind of good that made you forget your own name.

The warmth of Andy's lips caressed the skin at her earlobe. Liv arched into it, desperate for a connection. "I'd tell you to start using those lips for something other than talking."

A low groan erupted from his chest. He brought his eyes to hers. Hungry. Wanting. Andy never broke the gaze as he brought his hands up her neck as if to hold her in place. Slow and deliberate, the build was too much, and in a moment of clarity, Liv froze then leaped back.

Andy drew away, wounded, and muttered a quick apology, something about being too forward, but Liv laughed.

"No. God, no. It just hit me that I am absolutely filthy. I can't in good conscience let you touch me."

The lines of disappointment relaxed. He flashed her "the smile", the one that made her panties combust, then returned his lips to the spot below her ear. "I promise you that doesn't bother me in the least."

The sweet bristling of his beard danced along her skin, and she couldn't help it. A soft moan escaped her lips. He wove his fingers into her hair, brought her face to his, and silenced the sound with a kiss.

Liv leaned into him, and he pressed back. Instinct parted his lips with her tongue as she molded into his embrace.

"Ahem." The intentional noise sprang them apart. The diner's owner glared down at them, full of annoyed judgment. Guilty and a little embarrassed, Liv forced her eyes into her lap, but nothing could suppress the grin on her face.

Andy sat up to take the blame for their adolescent misconduct. A perfect gentleman. "Sorry, ma'am. Truly. Miss Olivia and I got a little carried away."

"I admire fresh love as much as the next old woman, but too much of that stuff will drive away the lonely people that live off my coffee and charm."

Andy must have replied with "the smile" because without another word, she scurried away. The kiss might have been over, but it didn't stop him from sliding his hand up the back of her scrub shirt. But something in this touch was different. It wasn't just electric and demanding; it fulfilled the simple need for a connection.

Liv soaked up the sensation when her cellphone buzzed then chimed in her breast pocket. Good manners prevented her from grabbing at her cell, but something inside told her to answer. Few people called her, even fewer called in the morning because they knew she worked at night—what they failed to realize was insomnia didn't care what time of day it was.

Her phone persisted, and she glanced down feeling the dual pressure to be a good date and a considerate friend. Andy took it as an opportunity to reach into her pocket and cop a quick feel. His thumb grazed the outline of her breast. Hot. Sinful. He offered her the phone with a conniving, sexy as hell smirk.

"Unless it's another man, I don't mind."

With a hope of appearing demure, she hid her enjoyment by glancing down and took the phone. Lottie's name and picture came through the cracked screen. Equal parts concerned and annoyed at the interruption, she muttered her favorite cuss word, sliding her finger to answer. Loyalty would always win out. "Heya, Lottie. I stopped to get some—"

"Livy!" Charlotte sputtered so loud Liv flinched.

"LouLou fell down the stairs! She's bleeding! You need to come real quick!" There was a wail from her honorary niece in the background, followed by a gurgled rant from a furious Nanny Kemp.

Lottie sobbed. "S'okay, baby, auntie will be here soon."

Liv jumped from her seat and grabbed for her bag and jacket.

"I'm on my way. Ten minutes, Lottie." She hit "end", and tucked the phone into her pocket. "Sorry, Andy, but I gotta run. I'm needed back home."

Andy rose, mirroring her urgency and reached for his wallet. He tossed a handful of bills onto the table.

"Everything all right?"

"No, it's my niece—my best friend's little girl—they're staying with me, and she fell down the stairs. Apparently, she's bleeding… I'm pretty sure she's okay, she was screaming like a banshee, but I've got to go."

"Mind if I come I along?" he asked. There was no hiding the surprise from her face. "Call me selfish, but I'm not ready to say g'night just yet. Bleeding babies or not."

Liv's face flamed hot for the hundredth time this morning, and she nodded. Sure, he was probably trying to cash in on the heat of the moment, maybe take advantage of her sleep deprivation and a person's tendency to make bad decisions and swoon his way into her panties. But then again, who's to say it'd be a bad decision to let Andy break her unspoken vow to be single and therefore a bit rusty between the sheets?

She grinned. "That'd be great. I hope you're not squeamish or anything. That's why Lottie called like her britches were on fire. She hates the sight of blood."

Andy took her jacket and draped it over her shoulders. "I think I can handle it."

HOW A HEART BEATS

****

Anderson stood huddled next to Liv on the 'L platform. The mid-morning sun melted away the northern chill, but Andy was intent to savor the closeness. Every minute he put off telling her the truth was another severed stitch that held them together.

It almost happened this morning. The moment her cheeks flushed with pleasure at the sight of him after her shift. He held onto the hope that he could charm his way into revealing the truth about being a doctor—especially one she worked with—but selfish cowardice speared him through the belly. As a doctor he was trained to rationalize and calculate the dreaded "What ifs", but around her, he was just a man who couldn't get his brain, heart, and dick to get along.

Before he parted ways with Smithson, he was given a month-long print-out of his shifts and residents. Like a grunt noob, he'd been blessed with more than eight late evening or overnight shifts. He didn't need a medical degree or a fancy double major in microbiology and applied mathematics to know the odds for steering clear of Olivia while at work were not in his favor.

Liv tapped away on her phone to her frantic childhood friend. Her lips ran a mile a minute giving him the down and dirty history of their lifelong friendship. Perhaps it was a need to prepare him for what she believed would be a likely inquisition, but he could tell much of her rambling was in response to her worry for someone she deeply cared for.

Entranced, he stared into her green eyes. The heat of his stare set her cheeks a blaze.

"I'm sorry. I know I'm rambling. Are you one of those fellas that can't handle a bunch of chatter before—"

Andy silenced her with a kiss. He gripped her

waist, then slid his arms around her sides, committing the curve of her hips to memory. She sighed, molding against him. She brought her hand to his cheek and pulled him in deeper. Liv might have smelled like vanilla, but she tasted like wine. And he was sure to be drunk for days.

A robotic voice announced the arrival of the 'L, and within seconds the platform shook as it barreled closer then screeched to a stop. Liv stiffened, then pulled away. The kiss couldn't be over.

When she stepped back it was like she took a part of him with her. A spleen. A kidney. Only a fool would say a piece of his heart, but Lord help him, she'd made him that fool.

She glanced at the ground, waiting for the train doors to open. Her expression lacked the euphoria he'd expect from a kiss—that to him—could have set ice on fire. He had to touch her. To try to make sense of what she was keeping inside. Andy held his breath and laced their fingers together. Like a lovesick girl, his heart burst in his chest when she returned the pressure and squeezed tight.

"What are you trying to do to me..." she muttered. Her playful and exasperated smirk went straight to his cock.

He chuckled. "I think that's supposed to be my line."

The doors opened, and they stepped inside the crammed 'L train. It gave Andy the excuse to stand tight against her back. There'd be no hiding the effect she had on him. His erection should have been a painful embarrassment, but he didn't care. And by the seductive, sexier-than-hell grin on her lips, neither did she. He lusted after her, and she knew it.

She leaned into him, shifting her tight little

behind over his dick, teasing away his restraint. He lowered his lips to her ear and inhaled. Her warm, heady blend was quickly becoming an addiction.

"You keep doin' that," he hummed, blowing air down her neck, "you'll be seeing a very different side of me." Discreet and deliberate, he slid an arm around her sides and under her shirt, claiming her waist. He flattened his palm over the base of her stomach. His grip spread from the swell of her navel down to the crest of her thighs. He closed his eyes and clenched his jaw in want, imagining through the thin layers the slick heat of her clit.

Sultry and sweet, she rolled her hips. "That had better be a promise."

Chapter Eight

Liv didn't know who was in a worse state, little Louise or Lottie. Hungover and cranky, Lottie needed a double espresso and half a Valium. Yes, those counteracted each other, but that was how Charlotte VanSutton ran. Always on opposite ends of the spectrum. LouLou, on the other hand, only needed a dip into Liv's frozen fudge pops and a Band-Aid.

"Lottie, you need to relax. I've got this." Olivia cradled Louise in her arms and wiped the stream of blood from her face. She hummed a little ditty and tickled her toddler belly to her squeals and delight. Lottie rumbled something about needing a drink and shot daggers at Andy, who still by all guesses needed to survey the level of crazy before entering the lioness's den.

"It's awful early for a date, doncha think?" Lottie hissed in his general direction.

"In our defense, Mrs. VanSutton, I think you could make the argument it was a little late. She had just gotten off work." Andy kicked off his shoes, leaving them in the hall. He took a strong step toward her, and offered Charlotte the smirk that made Liv wet. Lottie arched an eyebrow. Liv knew the look. The silent, southern cast of judgment, but after a beat she softened and threw herself into the chaise, bathing in the morning sunshine.

"You must excuse me, Mr. Cole. I'm not myself these days."

"That's for damn sure," Liv muttered, dabbing at Louise's forehead getting a better feel for her injuries.

"I heard that," she grunted back, but showed no offense. "Give me a few hours, Anderson. Then we can have a proper chat."

"Please, call me Andy. And by proper chat, do

you mean one hundred questions to assess the strength of my character and intent for your friend over here?"

Liv laughed, pressing the sides of the puncture wound that skirted along LouLou's hairline.

"You sure got a level warning before coming here," she said, rubbing her temples. "How's my baby girl, Livy?"

Liv's heart raced a bit faster, and not because Andy had come around to place his hands on her shoulders. "I'm sorry, Lottie, but I think it's gonna need a stitch or two. I'd hate for it to scar."

Lottie drew a hand over her mouth. It was hard to tell if it was to hold back vomit or a sob for her baby. Nanny Kemp shuffled through the hall with little Ashton on a hip. He wiggled desperately to evade her clutches when Lottie was in his sight. She smiled at her boy.

"C'mere, Bubba. Momma needs your sugar."

Andy knelt before the baby girl. Bashful and beautiful, Louise beamed her Momma's trademark sassy grin. "Mind if I take a look, princess?"

The toddler replied with a quick incompressible syllable that must have meant yes because she tilted her sweet, round face up to his. If Liv wasn't already in love with this man, this tipped the scales. Andy cupped her cheeks and with a critical eye pressed the cut together.

"Does is it hurt, baby?" he asked like he expected a full-on reply.

Her ovaries all but ruptured watching Andy's attentive, tender behavior, but she wasn't shocked. She knew that with his mission work he focused much of his time with children, but something was very astute and nimble about how he examined Little LouLou's face.

Liv was ready to succumb to a crazy lovestruck girl impulse when Lottie reached over and smacked her arm. Best friend telepathy had its perks. Andy kissed the girl's nose then stood and began rummaging through drawers in her immaculate kitchen.

"Do y'all have a junk drawer in this fancy girl's kitchen?"

Charlotte huffed. "They don't have marble counters in West Texas?"

"Has someone been chattin' 'bout me?" he twanged.

Liv turned and glared at her best friend, hoping to hide the embarrassed flush in her cheeks.

"I have a rather tidy catch-all drawer next to the stove."

"So, you *do* know which one is the stove, then?"

She wanted to reply, "Right behind that sexy ass of yours", but snooty pride prevented the quip. He held her gaze. Hot and tempting. Her mouth filled with cotton.

A cacophony of silliness broke their moment. Behind her Ashton and Charlotte hummed a chorus of "Row Your Boat," with Louise bouncing in her chair clapping her hands. Nanny Kemp stood like a centurion statue over the room. The proverbial adult presiding over her drunk Mistress, a pair of adolescent, hormonal flirts, and two toddlers.

"Whatcha lookin' for, Mister?" Nanny Kemp asked.

Andy dug through the mound of expired coupons, tape, birthday candles, and batteries. Out of the blue he coughed. Another dose of mortified panic pulsed through Liv's veins. The drawer became a spur of the moment hiding place for her brand new, very expensive, and elaborate vibrator. In the name of sleep and sexual satisfaction, no expense was spared, but not something the grocery delivery service needed to see.

"Find what you need there, Andy?" Lottie chimed.

He cleared his throat.

"Ah, yes. Yes. Superglue," he said, flustered and as red as the sweater he wore. He motioned to Louise, who was now covered in chocolate fudgesicle from her chin to her toes. "This ain't much of a cut. Just a bit of super glue will keep it together and prevent a scar. No use gettin' needles involved."

"That'd mean no trip to the stupid doctor," Nanny Kemp hissed.

"Nanny!" Liv chided with a shake of her chin.

"That's not fair. Not all doctors are stupid. But that's a conversation for a different day," she mumbled under her breath. Andy shot her a curious glance, which she pretended not to see. No man wants to know a woman's dirty laundry.

"You think that's all it needs?"

Liv squatted once more to inspect her niece. Wiping away the last trace of injury, she shrugged.

"Yeah, I think you're right. No more ouchies for this little princess!"

Andy squeezed the weathered metal tube.

"You know, I could really use—"

"A Q-tip," Liv answered without thought.

"Yep. Exactly that," he said with a nervous chuckle. "Is that some special mind reading voodoo they teach y'all in nursing school?"

She paused, struck by the rare seamless moment. The kind you experience after working with or knowing someone for a long time. She dashed to the bathroom and returned in just under a minute. Engrained nursing habit had her open the package like a sterile instrument. Andy grabbed the Q-tip with a quick and steady hand.

"Thank you, Nurse Olivia. Can you approximate those edges for me?"

Liv did as she was told, smirking at what must be

an appreciation for medical television. If he only knew how full of shit those were. "Watching old episodes of *Scrubs* and *ER* doesn't give you an MD."

He chuckled. "Damn. I really hoped to impress you with my vast array of TV medicine. This may sting, baby," he warned, his Texas twang pulling heavy on his words. Liv's heart sputtered then damn-near burst. How could someone be so sexy on every damned level? His voice. His manners. The way his chin stubble was always the perfect length. Love and lust swelled in her stomach so tight her eyes watered.

He dabbed the cotton along her hairline careful to avoid as much of her blonde curls as possible, then blew it dry. Louise whimpered something about an owie, and Charlotte shot from her seat. She swooped in, full momma-bear-mode, but the cry came as a demand for the Barbie Band-Aid Liv procured from her pocket. She applied the bandage with a kiss to her booboo and plopped the little one off the stool. Louise ran into her mother's open arm.

"My babies... Mmm, Momma loves you," Charlotte said, squeezing both kids so hard you'd think their heads would pop off. Nanny Kemp stepped in, and ushered the little pair back down the hall for their morning nap.

Liv turned to Andy, ignoring the peering eyes of her best friend. He closed the distance between them. It was a double-edged blade. She needed a fix, but she knew where it would lead. She inhaled his scent, and her blood sizzled in her veins. "A nap would be nice..."

She expected more simple banter, but Andy drew her into his arms and brought her lips to his.

"Oh, hell, you two are gonna make me throw up," Lottie grumbled, staggering to her feet.

Liv grudgingly broke the kiss.

"No, Charlotte dear. That was the half bottle of whiskey you drank yesterday."

Lottie didn't argue, but waved her middle finger as she ambled down the hall. Liv turned her attention back to Andy. Her palms raised to meet his chest, and her coy smile morphed into a smirk of devilish intent.

"You made a mighty fine doctor, Andy Cole. I'm pretty sure your patient fell in love with you."

Nerves fluttered in her chest, as Andy's grip on her hips burned hot. He ran his nose along her hairline and inhaled. Her breath caught, and her brain flipped off. The ache between her legs started to grow. Inviting a man to bed wasn't her style, and she thought she'd learned her lesson about falling for one so fast.

"Would this classify as a third date?" she asked to his feet, clad in mismatched argyle. Even that was fucking sexy.

Andy's chest rumbled with laughter. The friction and heat rippled through her scrubs, teasing her nipples. She took a deep breath and looked up. Calm. Composed. Confident. All things she hoped he'd see, not the insecure worry of a spoiled, pageant princess with a crazy drunk best friend, who was falling for a man because of his looks, charm, and swoon-worthy kindness that could all be just as fake as the last man who swept her off her feet.

"Is there something special about the third date I should know about?"

Liv tugged his arm down the hall and up the narrow flight of stairs. The dark stained original hardwood floor creaked and echoed with their synchronized steps. "When a lady brings a gentleman to her boudoir, the third date is usually considered acceptable."

"This is a fancy girl house. I've never seen a

boudoir before."

She laughed. Her nerves eased with the non-heated banter, but there was nothing to distract her from the aches in her joints and stiffness in her back. Sixteen hours of strenuous lifesaving and chronic lack of sleep made her feel much older than twenty-eight.

Liv pulled Andy down the hall, into her bedroom, then shut the door. He put his hands on his hips, surveying the eclectic, feminine space. Timeless furniture, modern finishes, and a dash of personal history decked the walls. The sun poured in through the floor-to-ceiling bump-out windows with a view clear out to the lake. She crossed the room to let out the elegant, black-out silk drapes.

She loved the feeling of his eyes on her as she sauntered back. She almost forgot she was wearing a disgusting layer of dead skin flakes and unflattering scrubs. She took down her hair and shook out the waves, letting them cascade around her face. It was a bold and sensuous attempt. Andy cleared his throat and scratched at his chin.

The hard line of his lips softened as she placed her hands on the taut muscles of his upper arms. She kissed his jaw with the slimmest skim of her lips.

"Excuse me for a girl minute."

Liv walked away, headed for her en-suite. The grand mirror that hung on the wall reflected Andy's aroused face. Daring herself to be brave she slinked out of her shirt, exposing him to a tempting glimpse of her back and sliver of lace from her lilac lingerie. She locked eyes with his through their reflection and kicked the door shut.

"All right, Olivia-Grace. Battle stations."

She ran through the routine of a woman with too much dignity and pride to be seen with stubbled shins and stale coffee breath.

She heard a few telling sounds of Andy rummaging around her room. She had a naughty thrill, imagining him remove his sweater, perhaps leaving his undershirt for her to slide her hands up and under. She wasn't a gambling woman, but she'd bet a cool twenty he wore boxer briefs beneath his designer jeans. "If you're bored the remote is in the nightstand," she called, scrubbing the all the important places down with scented creams and oils.

There was a muffled laugh and the sound of Andy crashing onto her plush mattress.

"The last thing I am is bored."

She opted for a sexy and sweet satin camisole with matching cheeky lace trimmed panties and swiped a final layer of red lip stain over her bottom lip. She popped her morning birth control and tucked a condom from the bottom drawer of her vanity into the waistband of her undies. The whole refreshed package took less than ten minutes. Amazing what a little soap and fresh britches can do for a girl.

The time did nothing to dampen her desire. Her heart pounded. She had to talk herself down from bouncing out of the room like a little kid ready to play with a shiny new toy. Putting her hand on the handle she said one final prayer that he wasn't an axe-wielding psychopath and opened the door.

Chapter Nine

The moment Olivia agreed to let him follow her home he vowed not to sleep with her until he told her the truth. But she kept making it fucking impossible. He could withstand sweet smiles, sexy smirks, and avoid staring at the curve of her breasts through her boxy scrub top, but watching her dote on her little niece and care for her friend, his heart and cock had completely obliterated his brain's ability to think by the time she invited him to her bedroom.

He was thankful for the slam of her bathroom door. With his eyes on her ass he needed the loud noise to shock some sense into him. Manic, he paced the room and tore his sweater over his head. It choked him. He needed room to breathe. Think. Assess. And plan. In a calming move he ran his fingers through his hair then down to scratch his chin. Clarity came from the habit, and he remembered the goal of any ER physician. Stabilize and hope to make it 'til tomorrow.

Though he was usually turned off by frills and countless throw pillows, something about Liv's setup worked. As did everything else that could be even remotely irritating about her. Finding a flaw with the woman was about as useless as looking for a Bible in a whorehouse.

He couldn't help but laugh knowing the teenage version of himself would be kicking him in the 'nads for turning down the chance to get laid. But that's not what he wanted. He didn't just want her. He wanted to worship her. He wanted to make love to a woman who knew without a doubt where his feelings stood. And he couldn't do that and lie at the same goddamn time.

Andy threw himself on Liv's bed. A plethora of Olivia-scented pillows swallowed him whole. If he wasn't going to let himself get any, this would have to do. She hummed to herself from behind the closed door. His mind wandered and steered down a dangerous path. His cock twitched. He slammed his eyes shut as if it would erase the image of her slender back and perfect breasts defying all sorts of physics in the kind of bra that was used to make men fall to their knees.

The singing stopped. Andy was met with silence. He endured the nerve-wracking shrill of silence and waited for the shoe to drop. Liv opened the door, her intoxicating blend of vanilla and cinnamon hanging in the air. Thankful for the wood floor creaking beneath her petite frame, he followed her approach and was ready for an assault. Her warmth. Her touch. The allure of her honeyed voice.

"Sorry to have kept you waiting…" she purred as the mattress gave way. One by one she peeled away his resolve by climbing into her massive bed. Everything started to ache, bound in want and restraint. He clenched his fists feeling his body give way to Liv and her gravity.

He couldn't do it. He had to look at her. Caving to the weakness of man, he opened his eyes. His smile was instant, but his words took their time. "You're more than worth the wait."

Olivia bit her lip and flushed under the compliment. Sure, she probably thought it was a line, but he meant every word. Beneath hooded eyes he examined her, the slight upturn of her nose, the fullness of her lips. She wore a sea green lace something that barely contained her. Following the delicate line of her collarbone, he caught a glimpse of her rosy pink nipple.

Liv seemed to hover in midair and kissed his cheek.

"Are you tired there, cowboy?"

Andy let out a chuckle and selfishly pulled her to

him. She fit and formed against his chest, turned snugly into his side. Warm body on warm body. He thought he'd explode and not in a way any man wanted to. At last, his brain flipped on. He muttered his fall-back boner killer.

"*Olfactory. Optic. Occularmotor*"

"Trochler. Trigeminal. Abducens... I know those, too."

He froze. Reciting the cranial nerves would have been an ultimate fuck-up. Any nurse with half a brain knew it. While most guys likely used baseball stats and childhood memories of their grandmothers to talk their dick down, Andy recited neuro-anatomy. He stayed stock-still and hoped for divine intervention. It was a stupid waste of the Lord's time, but he didn't care. He wasn't ready for it to be over, not while she rested her body against his. Andy exhaled his silent plea, and in a breath Liv's body became sedate. Then heavy. And began to snore.

He intended to savor every minute Liv slept molded to his chest. He kept waiting for the usual, compulsive need for space. Being still wasn't in his nature, and he wasn't the kind of man to sleep spooned next to a woman. Greta had given him years of hell for it. So he tried. And while she could sleep, curled into his long frame, he lay there sleepless. Restless. And resentful.

To his astonishment, the ache in his groin began to fade, background noise to the need to figure a solution. A timeline. Just what the fuck was he going to do?

Andy caved to the invasion of Olivia-infused sleep. She danced through his dreams as a naughty nurse, slutty seductress, and as a lovely and sweet girl that made him bend to her will. No man should dream about a Sunday afternoon that didn't involve beer and football, but dreaming about taking Liv to Target to buy bedsheets and groceries filled him with as much joy and want as watching her prepare a sponge bath wearing nothing but latex gloves and her stethoscope.

He woke cold and free from the binds of Liv's slender arms. Disappointment hit him square in the chest, but a muffled snore warmed the air. Fulfilling her own subconscious need for space, she had turned away, taking every blanket with her. His eyes adjusted to the half-darkness and frowned at his morning—or afternoon—wood. The old four poster creaked as he rolled out of bed, which did nothing to wake his sleeping beauty. The last few hours more than delayed the inevitable. It made the inevitable impossible to imagine. Still, he smiled and kissed her lips, hoping it wouldn't be the last.

He tiptoed into the bathroom, took a piss and tried unsuccessfully not to peer into her closet or any other place that would fall into stalker territory. She had a shit-ton of shoes. Neat. Meticulous. Dozens arranged by height and color. Andy grinned. The nursing OCD he learned to live with as a boy was strong in that one. Growing up with a Lead Scrub nurse for a mother, he knew by age five the difference between clean and organized.

Andy pulled on his jeans, ran his fingers through what he wished was just-been-fucked hair, and backed out of her bedroom to go down to the kitchen for a sandwich. He hoped she'd have the fixin's for grilled cheese and was ready to get down on one knee when he found brick cheddar, bacon, and real butter in Liv's refrigerator.

Mid-sizzle, Andy's phone chimed. He had already thumbed through the irritating texts from Greta, listened to a voicemail from Smithson about a meeting with the Chicago branch of the CDC and another from his real estate agent saying he found a nice 3000-sq. ft. loft in Lincoln Park with two covered parking spaces. Nothing else needed to be addressed. But the number that came through was a stock hospital number. Two shifts under his belt and he was already being called on his off days to fix the messes of his residents.

"Hi, this is Andy Cole," he answered.

"Dr. Cole, sorry to bother you at home," squeaked a nervous voice on the other side. He knew instantly it was CiCi, or Dr. Cecila Martin. Bookish, bright, but so unsure of herself that it was almost debilitating. A healthy dose of fear helped to keep a doctor sharp and at the top of their game—and for a new physician, that usually went hand in hand with their first death. Dr. Martin had had three. She loomed around with the title of "Double-O-Seven" and a license to kill, but the truth was, shit happened in threes. She just didn't believe it.

The smell of golden butter ripened, and Andy flipped the sandwich to a perfect toasty brown.

"That's all right, Cecila. What's up?"

"The hospitalists won't admit the forty-eight-year-old diabetic with cellulitis from yesterday. I've been sitting on him for ten hours trying to get a bed, but they're refusing."

He frowned. "I'm sure no one wants to touch a noncompliant, drug seeker. But shit, he still needs the admission. He's had his Vanc and Zosyn IV, right?"

"Yes," she answered immediately. She must have felt like she had something to prove and had reviewed the case through and through before calling.

"How are his vitals? Blood sugars?"

Dr. Martin took a few shaky breaths as she clicked through her chart and rattled off the patient's status. A nurse distracted her with a request for pain medicine.

"Yes, that's fine. Whatever she needs," CiCi replied.

"Finally trusting some of the nurses?"

"I think it's the other way around."

Andy reached into a cabinet looking for a plate. "Stop putting pressure on yourself that doesn't need to be there. It is a teaching hospital."

She snorted. "Well I've learned a lot about prepping people for the morgue."

"You'll get there. I trust you. Everyone else trusts you. Time to trust yourself. Tell them to get off their asses. Be blunt and call people out. They don't want his shot-to-hell medical history and oxy habit tarnishing their shiny record. Who's on today?"

"Gibbons."

"He can be bought. Promise him a pair of tickets to Soldier Field on the fifty-yard line."

"Isn't he from Green Bay?" she asked.

"Exactly."

"All right. Will do. Thanks. Sorry about calling you again," she muttered. Probably a bit embarrassed, but Andy was more than willing to give the occasional ego boost when it was needed.

"You're a great doctor, but your own worst enemy. Get him turfed to medicine and get the hell out of there. I'll have plenty of I and D's waiting for you tomorrow."

Andy took a satisfying bite of his sandwich and ended the call. The butter and bacon melted in his mouth. Too many pieces of Heaven to be thankful for. He turned to sit down at the kitchen island stool and instantly locked eyes with a sharp-faced Lottie.

"I don't know what 'charity and mission work' means in Texan, but I'm pretty sure it doesn't require an

MD at the end of their name."

Words evaded Andy's brain. Panic overruled every thought. He was trained to control massive hemorrhage, to cut a hole into the throat of a person dying to breathe, but he had no idea what to say to Liv's fiery and suspicious best friend. The grilled cheese's rich deliciousness turned to sour vomit in his mouth. He choked it down, knowing his dishonesty was his own bitter pill to swallow. No more lies.

"Yes, Lottie—"

"Don't call me Lottie. Only my friends have that privilege," she hissed in a subdued quiet. He would have preferred her yelling over the ice in her voice.

He cleared his throat and tried again, breaking her disapproving glare to peer down the hall, but she would have none of that. "Olivia is still asleep. You may continue."

He took a breath. "I am a physician. As a physician, I provide free medical care to poor—"

Charlotte rolled her eyes and threw up a hand to interrupt. "That sounds very nice. Where and what kind?"

"Excuse me?"

She narrowed her eyes. "Where? And. What kind?"

Tired of swallowing his goddamn pride, Andy's temper simmered. He was guilty of plenty, but he didn't deserve a stranger's indignant judgment. He scratched his chin, rising off the stool. Lottie crossed her arms. Olivia's childhood best friend was ready to go to battle, but if he wanted to win the war over loving Liv, this was one he'd have to let Lottie win

"Well if it isn't the two people I adore most in the world," Liv chimed, warm and bubbly from halfway down the hall. The "Oh Shit" knot of surprise jumped into his throat. He looked over, ready for his world to come crashing down. He hoped Liv was wearing more than when he left, but when she bounced into the kitchen in a pair of sweats and his baggy red sweater, his stomach did a back flip.

Like an old habit he opened his arms to her, and she slid right in, placing the sweetest of kisses on his cheek. "My ears were burning. I figured y'all were talkin' about me."

Andy shot a hard glance at Charlotte over Liv's shoulder. She pursed her lips, debating how she intended to play. "You had promised Anderson twenty questions. I only made it to two," Lottie crooned in a warm, smart-assed tone. Relief rolled off his shoulders, and Liv pulled away to grab for his sandwich. She took a healthy chomp and purred.

"Mmmm. Cooks, too," she said with a mouth full of butter and cheese. She took a sniff of the coffee left over from the morning and stuck out her tongue in adorable disgust.

Andy smiled. "I can make you a new pot."

"God, no. That ain't necessary," she said pouring herself a cup. "You should see what they make me drink in the Pit. It'll put hair on your chest."

His smile faded. His neck burned under Lottie's glare. Liv rose on her tiptoes and kissed his lips. "Don't keep me waiting, Mr. Cole." She turned to head out of the kitchen and swatted at her friend. "You be nice and let him come back in one piece."

Charlotte's cheek twitched. He held her furious gaze until Liv was safely up the stairs.

"Shit. I should have known," she drawled. "Enough arrogance and charm to compete with even the most prolific of serial killers. You're a damned ED Doc."

He crossed his arms and took a cleansing breath.

"You don't know me, Charlotte."

She scoffed. "*I* don't know you? You're all the fucking same."

He understood why she was mad, but her reaction was absurd. "I'm a physician. I save lives. I help people. Good people. Bad people. People that can't help themselves. I don't know where narcissistic psychopath falls into that spectrum."

Lottie shook her head as if she expected him to miss her point. "I'm not questioning your intentions as a physician *Dr.* Cole. But there's a reason Olivia is up here in the first place. No one moves to Chicago for the pizza or weather."

Andy shifted his weight. His knees threatened to give way from the worry pumping through his body. He focused his eyes on the mirror above Liv's fireplace. It was a mistake. He hated seeing himself for what he was. A lying, selfish ass.

"I don't know what lead up to her moving here. She keeps herself locked up tight."

"Not tight enough, apparently," she muttered, shuffling her bare feet to Liv's wine cabinet. Andy raised his hand in protest. "I'll take no judgment from you, sir. So tell me. Would you work together?"

He swallowed. "Yes."

"Oh, bless your heart. You're an idiot, Anderson Cole."

"I prefer struggling romantic."

Lottie ran a hand through her hair and handed him a bottle of red with a look that said she expected him to open it. "Scratch that. You're a huge idiot. Why didn't you tell her right away?"

He peeled away the foil and found the cork. She offered up the screw.

"Long or short version?"

"Whatever is filled with more truth and less lies."

Andy twisted the screw into the cork. He drove it in harder than was needed, but something had to shoulder the brunt of his irritation, his anger, his disgust with himself. He yanked back. The bottle opened with a satisfying pop. He relaxed and looked her square in the eyes. The answer that followed was natural and sincere.

"I fell in love with her the moment I saw her. And when her sweet ol' neighbor told me Olivia would never date a doctor, I was too much of a coward to tell her the truth."

Charlotte held his gaze. No question she was waiting for a tell he was full of shit. "You have forty-eight hours, Anderson Cole. Tell my best friend the truth and accept whatever comes from it by this time Saturday or you will answer to me. And if you think I'm scary now, you just wait."

He exhaled. "All southern women worth their salt are terrifying."

"You're in no position to be cute."

He cleared his throat and looked away. "Yes, ma'am."

"She thinks she loves ya, too, you know. That's the problem. And the last man that swept her off her feet had a bunch of fancy letters behind his name, swooned the little white scrub dress right off her alabaster skin. He told her she was smart, beautiful, and that when they got married they'd fill their house with little ones for her to dote and love on. But he broke her, you see? And it took fifteen hundred miles to fix. I won't let that happen again."

Andy nodded, fearing what came out would dig him deeper into the hell he made for himself. Lottie took a sip right from the bottle.

"Call me Lottie 'round Liv. Don't want to make

her suspicious…" Her voice trailed off, and she found his eyes once more.

"Thank you for how you handled my baby girl. I think she just might fight her auntie for you to be her hero."

Chapter Ten

Of all the flipping times to not suffer through hours of insomnia. It was a crime against womanhood to have a gloriously undressed man in your bed with the intent to seduce and satisfy, only to fall asleep the moment your bodies connected. The bags under her eyes were thankful for the usually elusive sleep, but the throb between her legs hadn't been taken care of, and she woke a few hours later wired and turned on. She had a wave of guilt, expecting Andy's balls to be an awful shade of blue and vowed to make it right.

She might have been wide awake, but it didn't mean she wanted to get out of bed. Andy's scent clung to her skin. She stretched, lapping up the remaining warmth left from where his body had entangled with hers as they slept. She hoped the small fix would mollify her wants, but filling her senses with what remained only amplified her needs. The kind of needs remedied by an evening with a bottle of wine, and sultry date with B.O.B.

Desire ached in her belly. Overtaking every cell of caution, Olivia craved him. God wouldn't put a man like Anderson on the Earth if he couldn't make a woman come for days, but sex wasn't some magic cure. Her heart desired the white-picket fence. The minivan. The slew of carbon copy redheads competing for her affection. The husband who worshiped the ground she walked on. Everything she convinced herself couldn't exist, the most epic of fantasies. True love. Romance. A happily ever after.

Ready to succumb to the rest of the day, Liv pulled on a pair of sweats and slipped into Andy's sweater. The neck hung low over her shoulder, and because no one was there to judge, she shamelessly buried her nose into the rust-colored cashmere and inhaled. Her insides sizzled. She piled her hair into a messy dancer's bun, then washed her face. She took her meticulous time applying the snake oils and creams that promised to keep her porcelain skin line-free and beautiful. She hated agreeing with her Momma, but the amount of effort it took to look effortless was always worth it.

Her luxurious lakefront brownstone had its perks, but the thin turn-of-the-century walls were not one. Down the hall she heard Nanny trying to corral little Ashton and Louise, promising them a date with the Mickey Mouse Clubhouse. Liv took it as an opportunity to check on LouLou's booboo and give Nanny a much-deserved break.

"Hiya, babies!" she called, entering the large room she had on permanent reserve for guests and family, which except for Lot and the twins, was hardly ever used.

Louise came running up, brandishing her favorite pacifier. "NiNi. NiNi!" the baby squealed.

"Well, I'm just going to assume that means pick me up, Auntie!" Liv swept her in her arms and ran her fingers over the small wound held together with super glue. No bruising. No redness or inflammation. "Looks like Mr. Andy fixed you up good, baby girl." She kissed her cheek, and the little one squirmed to get free. Nanny Kemp sat swamped in a pile of books. Olivia knew she had too much pride to ask for a moment of peace, but the desperation could be read loud and clear.

"Why don't you go on and have a rest, Nanny? I've got these two lil' hellions for a few."

Nanny smiled, but shook her head. "That'd be mighty kind, Miss Livy, but I think the Missus is down talkin' to your Mr. Andy. I expect he's going to need you."

"Ain't that the truth. Let me at least help out tonight—so you can sleep?"

"Won't be necessary. I just need to find these babies a park to play at. They're used to havin' the run of the yard."

Liv approached the perpetually wary Ashton then dived to plant a big wet raspberry kiss on pudgy neck. "We'll do that tomorrow."

Heading down her back service stairs toward her kitchen, Liv heard Andy's deep, Texan twang. His voice rolled down the hall and hit her right in the feels. She wanted to hear him croon from sun up to sun down. A giddy smile split her face, until Charlotte's stern, zero fucks given voice barreled into her happy place.

****

Something was off. Unbalanced. Finding her lifelong friend and the man she was pretty sure she wanted to make babies with chatting together set her nerves on fire, and not in the fun, tingly way. She couldn't put her finger on it, but something in her gut put her on alert. It's the same feeling a nurse gets when they know their walking talking chest pain was fixin' to code on their table.

She knew Lottie was doing her part to interrogate and intimidate, but what if it all backfired? What if the strong, alpha best friend she loved and would help move a body for was hell bent on making sure she didn't fall into the same ludicrous kind of love that broke her not long ago? Andy appeared to hold his own, but the charming confidence that made her panties wet was the kind of cocky arrogance that Charlotte loathed. She'd have to explain. Clean out her skeletons. Have the conversation no girl wanted to have with their new fella.

Liv waited in her room, hugging her stale coffee for comfort. She itched with nervous energy and began to pace. When that didn't work, she obsessively organized and cleaned her already spotless writing desk. What she wanted to do was bite her nails, but courtesy of her Momma and the years of pageant training, the urge put the taste of glue in her mouth.

Finally given a reason to appreciate her thin walls, she heard Andy stride down the hall. Conversation and a childish squeal rumbled through the thin layers of plaster and wood. It gave her a second to stop whatever anxious, OCD behavior she relied on to calm down, and present herself in a way that wouldn't appear looney and insecure.

In a heartbeat Andy opened the door. He smiled. Big. Gorgeous, and one-hundred-percent fake. She deflated. "I'm sorry 'bout Lottie. She can be a little…"

"Fierce? No. Don't be sorry," he said, pushing his fists into his pockets. "The beating was worth it."

Liv grinned at his appeasing tone, but it didn't soothe her worry. She rose from her desk, her gaze on the floor. She kept waiting for a dose of courage to look him in the eye. She crossed her arms over her middle, and his sweater fell, revealing more shoulder and a flash of cleavage. He cleared his throat.

Drawing an instant conclusion, she began fumbling with the hem.

"Shit. Sorry. I'm sure you want to go… Um. Here."

Andy put a calm hand on her arm. She stilled.

"I don't wanna go anywhere, and Lord knows, Olivia, every cell in my body, wants you to take that damn thing off, but I need to say something first."

Nerves pounded color into her face as he trailed his warm calloused finger along her collarbone and up her neck. Her breath caught. He tilted her chin, and forced her eyes to lock with his. The imposter smile had pressed into a flat line. Serious. Intense. A tight V puckered between his brows. Worry washed over her. What had Lottie done?

"No, Andy. Please, let me explain. Lottie means well. But she's just overprotective." Liv stepped out of reach and sat on her bed, drawing her knees to her chest, protecting her heart.

"D'ya know why I live here?"

His lips curled. "Doesn't everyone move here for the weather?"

"She really laid into you, didn't she? I came up here to get away and not from my crazy mother, even if that is a tick in the plus category."

Andy came to sit beside her. She needed it. Him. But she'd never get it out if he kept trying to be close to her.

"Listen. None of that is import—"

She jumped up. "I ran away, Andy. I ran away because I was stupid. A stupid girl who let fine things and flattery go to her head. And she's afraid I've gone on and done it again."

"Done what again?"

Liv took a breath and swallowed, then turned to face him. He was blank, but not expressionless. Every conflicting emotion was rolled into one soul crushingly gorgeous man.

"Fallin' too fast for the kind of fella that'll hurt me in the end. The kind of man that can kiss a frown from your face and talk the dress off your back. The kind of man that makes you feel like you are his sun, his reason for life. Until they cheat. Lie. Buy you red roses instead of white tulips because they you confuse you with the girl they've got on the side." She paused, looking for courage. "And she's right..." Olivia bit her lip and wiped away a tear that was too quick to hide. She tried to break Andy's wide-eyed stare. Her voice trapped in throat, and her admission came out a whisper.

"Against my better judgment and fear of being crushed, I'm falling in love with you."

****

It was just the thing he didn't want to hear. She was falling for him, and having her say it first, bold and out loud, while he cowered from the truth filled him with sleazy guilt. How could he tell her now? After she bared her soul and left her heart open for him? His brain fired round after round of condescending criticism, and his heart raced in elation and conflict.

And since God has a fucked-up sense of timing, Andy was already hard for her.

Tears welled in her green eyes. It was torture. There was no simple solution. No stabilizing and cross your fingers until tomorrow. He loved her. He wanted her. And having her would satisfy them both.

Andy rose from the bed and crossed the room in one stride. He heard her suck in a breath, and everything that came next was a welcome and mind-bending blur. He wiped the dampness from her cheek and crushed his mouth over hers. Up until this point every kiss they'd shared he'd forced himself to slow and savor, but there'd be none of that this time. All he could hope for was when the dust settled and the truth came out, she could forgive him.

He kissed her, hard and hungry. In a gasp, Liv retaliated, molding their lips together. Her tongue danced along his, skillfully teasing and tasting with each sinful draw. She wrapped her arms around his neck to bring him closer. His gravity pushed them back, driving her into the wall. Liv came up for air and let the wall support her. Her head fell to the side. Thankful for the dose of flushed skin left open from his baggy sweater, he inhaled, then kissed down her neck and across the curve of her breasts. Taking to heart her promise to let him taste more, he ran his tongue between the deep cleavage. He slid a hand up the side of her shirt, skimming his fingers along curve of her back and up to cup her breast, letting the weight warm his hand. His thumb teased her nipple, and Lord help him—she moaned.

Liv came to life under the work of his tongue and fingertips. His mouth watered, and his cock ached imagining what she'd do as he'd roll his tongue over her slick and pulsing sex. She purred, groaned, called his name. She was the kind of woman that let you know what worked, worked better, and what set her on fire. He could come just listening to her command him where and how to touch her. And he hadn't even seen her naked yet.

She ripped away his white undershirt and climbed onto her toes, pressing the length of her long and perfect body to his. Andy responded in kind and pulled her out of his oversized, shapeless sweater and guided her back to the bed. He took his time. Like a kid on Christmas morning, he wanted to unwrap and imprint her body to memory. He laid her back onto the mattress with a deep, long kiss. She tangled her fingers into his hair and let out a flirty giggle when he sheepishly grabbed her tits like melons at the market. He stood before her, and felt the heat from her lusty gaze as it traveled over his chest and down his stomach. She smirked. Sinful. Greedy. All for him.

He let her enjoyment boost his overinflated ego. "Do you like what you see, Ms. Aberdeen?"

"Maybe."

Andy hovered over her, sliding his hand down the front of her pajama pants. He traced the lace hem to tease the heat between her legs and pressed. She gasped.

"Maybe?" He worked her clit through the satin

and lace of her panties. Liv's warm, honeyed voice sighed with pleasure. "That doesn't sound like a maybe," Andy hissed into her ear. He slid a finger into the wetness and was brilliantly rewarded. A sound so fucking sexy he wanted to make it his ring tone sang from her throat.

A stampede of feet and toddlers whining broke through the thin walls. Andy froze. Liv shot up onto her elbows, a mortified grimace lined her face. He tried to block Lottie's stern voice. It had the potential to be a boner killer. He took his free hand and pressed it to his lips in a silent "Shush". Her cheeks flushed, rosy and radiant. He wanted to throw open the curtains to see her glorious body writhe beneath him in the late afternoon sun, but that would require him to move from that spot. And an alien invasion would have been more likely.

"I think I need to see a bit more," she twanged at a whisper. It went straight to his dick. Already painfully hard, any little thing could tip him over the edge, and hearing that sweet Savannah drawl sure didn't help.

"That can be arranged…"

She pouted. Her bottom lip, red and swollen from his kisses, had the power to unravel him. He wanted those lips around his cock so bad it made his teeth hurt.

If he had one shred of self-control he'd stop. He'd hear the nagging voice of his conscience over the shameless desire pounding through his body. But she was beautiful, kind, and so fucking sexy, any man would lose their mind. And she loved him. There was no going back from that.

He pulled his mind from fucking her mouth by ripping away her leggings and wet panties in a quick, commanding movement. And there she was, naked as the day God brought her into the world, and he couldn't wait to put his mouth on every single inch.

****

Andy stood over Olivia, devouring her with his eyes. Naked in every way, she shivered. Not from the cool air dancing over her nipples. Not from the Prima cotton sliding beneath her skin. Telling Anderson she was falling for him had left her vulnerable. Exposed. He could break her with one word. Except he stood there, grinning like he'd just been given his heart's desire. And a medium rare rib-eye, debating where to cut in.

He sucked in a breath and eased himself down. Face to face, as if to start with a kiss. She raised her chin to meet his lips, but Andy skimmed by with a nibble. A taste. Then moved to her neck, kissing in short, sensuous bursts. Liv squirmed, forcing more contact. He groaned. Low. Rumbly. The sound vibrated up his throat and tingled down her spine. He gripped her waist and grazed his thumb along the swell of her breast. She arched into his touch.

"Be still," he hummed to her throat. His warm breath mixed with the cool surrounding air and sparked in her belly.

Liv closed her eyes. "You started a fire, Andy Cole. You better be ready to stoke the embers."

Andy swirled his tongue around her nipple. She gasped.

"Hmm. Like that?"

Liv rocked her hips upward. "Yes."

Taking his time, Andy quested down her body. He kissed along the outline of her ribs, skimming his fingers along the rivets of bone and sex-scented skin. He found her navel and nipped at the sensitive spot. She giggled and writhed beneath him.

"I see my girl's ticklish." Andy bit at her hip. The quick, cut of his teeth surged to her sex. Agonized, she twisted in his grasp, and her mouth watered. She licked her lips, tasting him on the air.

With a flash of heat, Andy drew her close and engulfed her in a kiss. His tongue slid past her lips and possessed her mouth. Hard. Demanding, the kiss drove her back and into the billowy sheets. Heady and satisfied, Liv purred, rolling her hips at the weight of his body pressed against her pelvis. She tore her hands down his taut back, then around to fumble with his jeans. Desire pounded through her veins and pulsed in her clit. Savoring and anticipation be damned. She wanted more. She needed more.

Andy pulled himself away. Restraint hissed through his teeth. He gazed down, a blend of loving lust curling on his lips. "You have all night to stoke my embers, Liv. But you'll always come first."

He left her no time to react, or say something clever. He grabbed Liv by the knees and yanked her forward. Flat on her back, Andy spread her legs and wedged himself between. He locked his blue eyes to hers and sank into Liv's depths. He kissed an open thigh. Then the other. Liv sucked in a breath as if it had the power to keep her from screaming.

"You will *always* come first," he repeated, running his nose along her cleft. He inhaled, then let out a groan. Hungry. Wanting. His deep, twangy assurance filled her with swoon, but his hooded stare hooked into her heart. It sputtered, trying to process carnal desires with tender affection.

Andy smirked. The perfect blend of sinful and sincere, then dove between her legs.

****

God, she tasted sweet. So sweet he almost couldn't take it. Andy kissed and lapped at Liv's clit, as if her cries of pleasure could absolve his sins. Her sensuous vocals climbed then crested with silence. Liv convulsed around the stroke of his tongue and caress of his fingers. Arching off the mattress, she wove her fingers into his hair and dug her nails into his shoulder. She held him in place, but it wasn't necessary. If he could he'd build a house between her legs, and pay for the real-estate in pussy licks.

He didn't know what he loved about her more, Liv's uninhibited chorus of yesses and purrs or the giggles as she floated back down.

"Sweet baby Jesus," she said, between heaving breaths and staccato laughter.

Andy came up for air, unable to hide a smug, shit-eating grin from his face. He kissed his way up to her hip nipping at the bump of her iliac crest. A tremor shook through her as he slid his fingers from her sex. She flinched, but surged with another round of giggles.

"I'm sorry. I'm just a bit sensitive…"

"Oh, I had no idea." Andy curled up next to her. The cold, silky sheets puckered his skin. The late afternoon sun blazed through skinny beams across Liv's bedroom. She turned into his chest, and nuzzled against his neck. His arms wrapped around her shoulders and back. Natural. Like she'd never leave.

Liv wiggled her toes between his legs searching for warmth. "You can take your pants off now."

"Is that an order?"

She looked up from beneath her lashes and hid a sweet and sexy grin into her pillow. "Don't make a lady say she wants to see her fella's cock. It's indecent."

He stifled the urge to puff up his chest, and rose off her bed. Her eyes widened, burning her gaze along his body. She grinned, then bit her lip.

Liv sat up and put her hands on his. "I think you'd better leave this to a professional."

"Don't y'all just cut people out of their clothes?"

She palmed his erection. Hard, then soft. His breath caught. Slight, rhythmic pressure teased through the denim. "Only when the patient is very, very, bad."

She placed a kiss on his collarbone and tugged the zipper down.

"Careful."

"Always."

She wedged his jeans open, then down his hips. She slid her hands into the waist band of his boxer-briefs and palmed his ass. He hissed and threw a glance at the ceiling, calling for mercy. With a deft swoop, she peeled away the remaining layer. His dick sprang free. It should have been an embarrassment, like a horny teen desperate for third base. She broke her heated gaze and looked down. Call him a shit, but when she pinched her bottom lip between her teeth to hold in a smile, he all but howled.

Desire exploded in his veins. The restraint. The time. All hopes for savoring the moment evaporated into a whirlwind of Olivia-infused lust. He ensnared her waist and down to squeeze her ass. He latched to her lips and kissed. She replied in kind, pulling his tongue in her mouth. She wrapped her long legs around his waist, and he flipped her onto the mattress. The old, wooden frame creaked.

Liv giggled. "I don't think my bed likes what you have planned."

He broke away, gasping for air and cupped a breast in his hand. He teased the tight peak, dying to see her reaction. Her face tightened with want. *So goddamned sexy.*

"I give zero fucks about your bed."

Liv squirmed beneath him and pushed his jeans further past his knees. He kicked them off and knelt before her. She pouted. Sultry. Laced with amusement.

"Good."

He craved to kiss her again, skin on skin, to grind his cock through her wet heat. But he'd never be able to stop. The need for air cleared his head. He fought the magnetic pull of her curves and reached for the nightstand. The condom that fell out of her panties while they slept this morning mocked every selfish move. Flushed with a burst of novice anxiety, his fingers trembled. One lover for half his life and one grief-fueled fuck hardly made him an expert, and her beautiful eyes looked him over with the highest of expectations

After two unsuccessful rips at the foil, Liv grinned. "I've got some trauma shears in my bag."

"Ah, no thanks." Without a doubt the last thing Liv's military grade, industrial scissors cut through were the seam of piss- and blood-covered pants.

She raised herself onto her elbows, then inched upright. Andy dropped his gaze to Liv's tits as they moved through space. "Why don't you let me?" she said with the sweetest Savannah twang.

He eased her back with a kiss. "It's all right. I got it. This is part is my job. Besides, if you put those little hands of yours down there I'm afraid it'll be over sooner than I want."

Liv's sultry smirk reemerged, propping an arm behind her head. Andy pinched the rubber in place then rolled it down. He held in a grimace as the latex strangled his hard-on, then lowered himself over her. Liv reached up to meet him, wrapping a lean calf around his back. She kissed him. Soft, and deceivingly chaste, Liv danced her lips over his and rubbed her clit against his cock. She groaned, arousal flooding between them, drowning his insecurities and doubt.

This wasn't fucking. Or simply sex. He'd fallen for her.

She broke her kiss. "C'mon, cowboy. I'm ready."

That was the kick he needed. He opened a thigh and hoisted her leg around his hip. She smiled. Warm. Tender. Loving affection replaced her lust-filled grin. It was something he never wanted to be without again.

Chapter Eleven

For the average woman, three non-mechanical orgasms in as many hours were pretty amazing statistics. And enough for Olivia to suffer withdrawals the moment Andy left her orbit to order in some late-night Chinese food. Her muscles ached, fingers trembled, but her chest felt hallow and empty. Like something was missing, and if she didn't get a fix she'd likely spiral into the love-struck's version of an alcoholic's DTs.

She never expected to come that third time. Roused from a comatose sleep by a warm, callused hand stroking between her legs, Andy drilled his desire into her backside and nuzzled the curve of her neck. Thoroughly well-fucked and satisfied, she smiled, content to simply roll over and welcome Andy having his wicked way with her. But without so much as a warning the ripping of foil and sheathed latex flushed her hot, as if every drop of blood rushed to her skin and sizzled beneath the surface.

Instant. Intense. Pleasure coiled in Liv's belly. With each roll of Andy's hips, she tightened, then pulled him deeper. Slow and sleepy lovemaking morphed into need. A release, as if she could erase the last twelve months of regret and heartache by a deeper thrust. A seamless, deeper connection.

Blindsided by every sensation as it sang down every nerve, Olivia cried out praising Andy Cole and the Lord above. Split in two from ecstasy, and fear, she knew one thing—it all had to be too good to be true.

Liv slipped into Andy's cotton undershirt, Ziploc-ing his scent under her bathrobe. With her first free minutes alone in God-knows-how-long, she putzed around her room, reorienting her bass-akwards nightshift brain. Night time in Chicago was never dark. The city glowed orange from dusk to dawn, impossible to know the time simply by looking out the window.

She flipped on her flat screen. HGTV hadn't switched to *BeachBody* infomercials, which meant she hadn't sent Andy on an impossible task. China Moon always let her order until the last episode of *Tiny HouseHunters* aired.

A familiar crack echoed through the thin walls. The back stairs creaked from muffled, heavy footsteps. Plastic bags rustled outside her door. Rich, tangy deliciousness hung in the air and danced on her tongue. Excitement fluttered in Liv's chest. Like an addict staring at her next fix, Liv's mouth watered, and it had nothing to do with her thrice-weekly egg-foo-young habit.

She jumped from her desk and ran to open the door, then yanked it open. She fell against the frame taking in his muscular chest, flecked with the perfect dusting of man. "Hi."

Andy beamed, arms full, smile even fuller. "Hi."

He stepped through the doorway. Stark. Cold. Awkwardness breezed over her in his wake. Conversation would come next. The deep stuff. The stuff she always skipped to keep from pulling the past to her present. The stuff sexy-time tingles and infatuation had a way of distracting her from.

He set two plastic sacks down on her hope chest and began emptying the contents onto her comforter. "So, I have to admit I'm a bit jealous of Nguyen."

"Who?"

Andy looked up, a slight curl tugging on his lips. "Your delivery boy. Nguyen. He knew your order when the caller ID came through and tossed in extra crab rangoon because you hate odd numbers."

Liv rolled her eyes. "I really need to stop drunk dialing for my delivery…"

"He did seem pretty heartbroken you didn't answer." Andy motioned to sit on the rug and handed her a paper plate and some chopsticks. "When can I know more about you than Nguyen?"

She sucked on her bottom lip, plump from hours of Anderson's kisses. Lottie flashed in her brain. And so did her secrets. "Charlotte VanSutton, I will skin you alive," she hissed.

Andy laughed, dipping his lettuce wrap in a brown sauce. "Don't blame Charlotte. She just gave me a friendly warning."

Liv's appetite vanished. She poked at her food, praying a distraction would pop into their conversation. Nanny. The twins. Charlotte demanding access to Liv's hidden stash of booze. The best sort of distraction had happened three times already, and the last one damn near killed her. It was time to hike up her big girl britches. Skeletons were just the bones holding a person upright.

Liv's pageant smile defaulted across her face, and she took a deep breath.

"You know," Andy cut in. Liv exhaled hard, thankful her mouth wasn't full of food. "Um. I'll start. There is one thing you really need to know about me. I'm a d—"

"Democrat? Christ on a cracker, I figured that for myself—with all your humanitarian efforts and charities, I knew you had to be somewhat politically purple. I am, too, just don't tell Lottie. I slipped a 'you guys' in once while talking on the phone, and she didn't speak to me for a week."

"Southern people and their pride," he drawled. The sultry twang surged in her belly, flooding her sex with want. She shifted, wishing for panties. A chastity belt. Anything that could have been another protective layer to keep her from jumping onto his cock and riding him six ways to Sunday. And Monday. Then Tuesday.

Amusement twinkled in corner of his eyes. Worry washed away with her quips and his digs at their stereotypical, southern heritage. Simple. Sexy. Every cell started to buzz with desire. God, he really needed to stop turning her on faster than a Savannah Stepford Wife at the Bergdorf's summer clearance.

HGTV progressed to its overnight run of ab roller commercials. She had managed to chat about Logan, his addiction to blonde nursing students, and her Momma. Sure, she skirted much of the scandal and heartbreak, but she'd opened up more to him than anyone, apart from Mrs. Loveitz, since she ran away from Savannah. But she'd get there. They had time.

Liv sat cross-legged, lounging into Andy chest. His bare heat infused with her back. They took turns cracking open fortune cookies and reading the words of wisdom.

"Running from your past, only runs you in circles," he read with a snort. His breath blew across her neck. She wished she could read his face. She didn't have a PhD in men, but it didn't take much to know a fella's huff meant a billion and one different things.

"So how many women do you leave in your wake?" she asked, sugaring the question with her Sweet Peach twang.

Andy cleared his throat, and shifted behind her.

A loud, intrusive knock banged at her door, and before she could groan her favorite curse word, an annoyed Lottie popped through. "Y'all finished? Good. Andy, there's a lightbulb that needs fixin' and the garbage can is full."

"Charlotte VanSutton, did you just barge in my room at 1 AM to get my boyfriend to take out the trash?"

"Yes. And?"

Liv's scalp prickled and she clenched her teeth, rallying out of Andy's lap, but he stopped her with a kiss to her bare shoulder. "Boyfriend, huh? I do love the sound of that." He kissed her again, this time, nipping her earlobe. "How about you be waitin' for me when I get back?" She broke Lottie's indifferent gaze, and purred. Andy's eyes flashed with wicked intent. "Wearing nothing but a very happy smile."

Liv grinned and met his lips. She kissed him soft, quick, scratching her nails through his stubbled jaw. Andy pulled away, unfolding from the floor like an origami of sex. His jeans hung low on his hips, revealing the muscular curve of his ass. If a "six-pack" back was a thing, Andy sure as a hell had it. She tore herself from Andy's marvelous behind and over to Lottie. Charlotte had long perfected the mask of Savannahian snobbery, but there was no hiding her tiny, pursed lip of approval before turning to leave.

Andy followed, then looked over his shoulder. He smoldered swoon from his height. "Got any other projects for me, Lottie? I was told this afternoon I have skilled hands."

Olivia flushed, and uncoiled from her seated position, teasing her robe open to expose a thigh, spreading her legs with a "come-hither" flick of her eyebrow.

Andy threw a glance at the ceiling and cracked a knuckle before shoving his fist into his pocket.

****

Turned on and wet from anticipation, Liv paced in her birthday suit around her bedroom. Maybe Lottie took him to his word and gave him a "honey-do" list a mile long. Her fingers shook, and her clit ached. B.O.B. called to her from her nightstand. Anderson withdrawals could be remedied in three minutes flat, but that's not what she wanted. She wanted more than to get off. She craved the intimacy and affection only Andy could give. A good fuck and the orgasm that went with it were just the ice-cream on her peach cobbler.

Liv wrapped herself in her robe and went on the hunt to find Andy. Fifteen minutes was far too long to make a girl wait for sex. She crept along down the hall, careful to step over noisy floorboards. She'd feel plumb awful if she woke the twins sleeping the floor below in her sexy-time pursuit.

Middle of the night silence echoed through the narrow halls and vast living rooms. Down on the first floor, the guest rooms were all closed, except one. Liv shuffled her bare feet over the hardwood expecting to find Nanny, maybe even Lottie tending to the twins, but a low, croony tenor stopped her in her tracks. Liv peeked around the door. City lights and streetlamps outlined Andy's frame as he stood, rocking in place. A pudgy foot swayed in time as Andy shushed and sang a chorus of "Jesus Loves Me".

Immediate and unstoppable, tears welled behind Liv's eyes. Love and longing. Shame and regret erupted so quick she choked. Andy turned. Liv caught a glimpse of sadness before his face was lost to shadows. She raced on tiptoes to the back stairs to catch her breath and wipe away the rebel tears. She hugged herself and bit her cheek, trying to reel in the sudden burst of pain.

A door clicked shut, followed by Andy's footsteps. In a heartbeat he turned the corner to Liv's back stairs. Bathed in the orange city glow, his carved chest and approachable abs heaved between forced breaths. He licked his lips as if he needed a minute to explain, to find his thoughts. But need surged through Liv's veins, and she threw herself into his arms.

****

Andy caught Liv mid-air, and fell into the wall for support. Heated and hungry, Liv clung to him with a kiss. She sucked the air from his lungs and stroked her tongue past his lips. His switch flipped. The constant dull ache of loss compressed his ribs while calming Lottie's restless little boy. Pain held in by a stitch dehisced, but Liv's warm body seemed to suture him back together.

He came back for breath and kissed her neck, pulling her robe out of the way. Light from the octagon window over his head illuminated Liv's features. Soft and Delicate. Wild and so fucking beautiful. She clawed her fingers down his back and arched into his touch. He opened her robe to tongue between her breasts and cup her ass, pulling her into his erection. Her arousal soaked his fingers, and like Pavlov's dog, his mouth watered.

She rolled her hips over the denim strangling his cock, then reached to fumble with the button. He wanted her hands on his dick so bad, but responsibility flashed red. Time. Place. Condom. Noise.

"Liv, wait, I don't have anything…"

"I'm on the pill. Don't make me beg."

He growled, low, unrestrained. He spun her around to face the wall, slipping his fingers through her slick heat. He exposed her backside and nudged her knees apart. She moaned a sexy as sin yes as his zipper gave way, then silenced her with one deep thrust.

****

Hard. Fast. Andy fucked her like she was the answer to his prayers, but it was Liv who'd called for divine intervention. Grief and longing stabbed at the base of her spine and reached into her fingertips seeing Andy love on Lottie's baby as if it were his own. She needed him. She needed to forget. And she didn't have to ask him twice.

As if conjoined at the soul, Liv came down pulled

back by Andy's deep draws for air. Mind blown, body blown, she waited for the inevitable. The crushing moment Andy withdrew and their connection severed, except he held on and held her against him. He caressed the curve of her hips and swell of her breasts. Kissed the nape of her neck, and along her shoulder, but something was achingly different. He touched her like he had a need only she could fulfil, and he intended to cherish the effects.

When his breathing slowed, he let go. Stiff and awkward, Liv straightened, trying to ignore the immediate emptiness she felt inside. She bit her cheek. A rush of hormones and memories she'd buried deep threatened to make her a looney woman who cried after sex, but he turned her in his arms. She pressed her cheek against his chest, and focused on the "LubDub" sound within his ribs, as if his heart beat only for her.

She trembled from muscle strain and cold. Nothing like having sex upright to remind you to do some squats once in a while. Liv slid her robe back in place, then pulled away.

"Olivia, wait," he whispered.

She looked up to search his face in the shadows. His brows wove together. Worry. Doubt. Maybe even guilt, but all unnecessary. A girl doesn't need their fella to explain themselves after a quickie. Because she'd have to as well.

She managed a smile, and when he didn't return the grin, her stomach fell to her feet. Her breath trapped in her lungs. She was the deer. He was the headlights.

"You need to know something. You're not the only one that fell recklessly in love. I may even have you beat. I think I loved you the moment I found you asleep standing up."

Chapter Twelve

Andy's declaration lifted her from the treacherous waters she drowned in. It was time to move on. Move forward. Loving Andy would do that. And letting him love her back—even more. And as for her secrets and skeletons … what's a few more days?

Her small smile widened. Elated. Damn near ecstatic, but she'd never say it. Now wasn't the time to tempt the juju. Liv wove their fingers together, led Andy up to the narrow stairs, and back to her bedroom. He looked at the immaculate bed, and neatly folded pile of clothes, then cocked her an amused eye.

"When I get antsy, I clean."

He smiled. "Evidently."

She swatted his arm, and strode past, shedding her robe as she walked. Andy coughed, then cleared his throat. "I think you're tryin' to kill me."

Liv turned, a demure pout tightening into a smirk, inching herself onto the mattress. "Tuck me in?"

Something between a growl and groan rumbled from his belly as he sprang for her. She giggled, absorbing his kiss with strokes of her tongue, then slowed. Savoring him. Savoring his lust and affection.

"I love you, Andy Cole. Don't go breaking my heart."

Andy swallowed. His upper arms quaked, holding his body inches from her. She finally hit his max tolerance for sex and sappiness. Her poor fella needed a nap. STAT.

She smiled. Her stomach did a back flip when he returned it out of the corner of his mouth, all lazy and adorable. She fell into her pillows with a yawn big enough to catch flies. "All right, enough of all that. Bedtime."

He laughed and climbed in next to her. Liv knew he was the kind of guy who needed space, but she couldn't help the girlish impulse to spoon into his bare chest. She danced her fingers along his muscles, watching the skin pucker under her touch. His twangy tenor rumbled within his ribs. She tried to listen, but sleep hit her like a wave against the shore.

****

Liv's eyes popped open. Darkness, flecked with neon orange beams, surrounded her. And so did the subdued snores of the man she'd fallen for. Sleep might have hit her like a wave, but insomnia punched back like a hurricane. Without a doubt, she'd been asleep mere minutes. She reached for her cracked iPhone on the nightstand to check the time. Andy's bright blue OtterBox balanced on his wallet. The screen glowed with alerts and messages. Petty girl jealousy and the kind of curiosity that would throw her into the crazy category itched her fingertips.

She jumped from her bed and grabbed only the essentials for cover, then dashed from her room, not stopping until two floors and three hallways separated her from stalker territory. Late night shopping and a glass of Shiraz would keep her distracted. Distracted but with a sizable dent in her savings account.

Safely in the kitchen, she found Charlotte doing the same. Midway through a bottle of red, she had a slew of tabs open on her downstairs desktop ranging from Vera Wang to Wal-Mart. Lottie looked over with one of her disapproving glances.

Liv shrugged into her robe and pulled the sash tight. "Couldn't sleep?"

"Nope. I was rudely woken up by banging on my wall." Liv held her best friend's gaze until it cracked with humor. "Well at least it sounded good."

"Oh, Lot. So. Very. Good. Sorry about the noise, though. Andy was actually up rocking Ashton back to sleep."

Lottie raised her chin, probably debating where on the VEN diagram of boyfriend material that put him. Liv sighed. She wasn't going to win the battle in one night.

"So retail revenge is on the agenda? A Vera maxi-dress and PowerWheel? I like it," Liv said pouring herself a glass from Lottie's bottle, then curled up on the chaise with her favorite cashmere throw.

"Spring'll come sometime … even up here in the North Pole."

Liv lit up. "Does that mean ya'll are stayin?"

Lottie offered a small shrug. "I have no plans to go back. I sent a lawyer to Teddy's office yesterday and that new PA of his said he was in the middle of an 'endothermal tightening' whatever the fuck that is."

"No more boob-jobs and Botox, then?"

"Sadly, no. So I hope those tits of yours stay where they belong. Teddy promised me a new pair after I breastfed those piranhas for a full year." She pursed her lips, sad and disappointed, letting her sassy, southern exterior soften. "She was a patient of his, you know. He claims *she* pursued *him* and he was the innocent victim."

"So Teddy succumbed to the feminine witchcraft of thong panties and a tramp stamp?"

Lottie laughed so hard she choked on a gulp of wine, splattering it all over the living room floor.

"The little twit was there to get a tribal tattoo lasered off her crack!"

Liv and Lottie engaged in the rapid-fire banter of best friends, only slowing to get into the glorious details of how good Andy was in the bedroom, and of course, the back stairs.

"He told me he loved me."

Lottie's face hardened. "Is that all he told you?"

"What else did he need to say? I was shocked when it wasn't 'Deuces, crazy woman, with psycho best friend.'"

"Did you tell him why you moved here?"

She pursed her lips. "The weather obviously. No. We didn't really get into it. He knows about Logan. I think that's enough for now."

"Are you still dumping half your fortune into that trust?"

"My hourly pay hardly constitutes a fortune, Lottie. And my Daddy taught me right. *My* trust will keep me more than comfortable for a long time. The money I make saving lives goes to the right place."

Habit had her turn her gaze to a cherished black and white photo on her mantel piece. Her eyes stung and repressed tears welled in her eyes. Lottie shot from her seat, then sat and cradled her head in her lap.

"No need to be brave, Livy. Let it all out."

****

Of course Liv fell asleep the moment his balls dislodged from his throat long enough to tell her the truth. And of course he knew better than to tell Liv he loved her after sex. If his Dad were alive, he'd smack the back of his head and order him to haul hay-bails until he stopped thinking with his dick.

Three times the words, "doctor" and "divorced" all but fell out of his mouth, but Democrat? Shit, he couldn't even get that right. Sure, his conservative upbringing muddied from red to a pale pink, but to call himself a Democrat was a bit of a stretch.

Andy gazed at Liv's vacant side of the bed. For the last ten years he battled having his days and nights flipped upside down and bass-ackwards, but he never had a problem getting enough rest. Trying to adhere to her sleep—or no sleep—habits might up his chances to get to be near her naked, but it wouldn't result in the six hours he needed to function, save lives, and have the patience he was known for with his residents and med students.

A grey Chicago morning streamed through the curtains of Liv's bedroom. His lovesick heart was disappointed she wasn't there to kiss him good morning, and his cock clearly felt the same. He talked it down, took a quick piss and stared for a long minute at her toothbrush. Were they in a place to share? He licked the fur that stuck to his teeth and tasted stale, musty air in his mouth. He'd kissed the woman up and down. It'd be fine.

He brushed his teeth and thumbed through his phone. He perused the headlines, set up his fantasy football team, and tried not to watch the clock. Fifteen hours had been sucked from Charlotte's deadline, and another huge chunk would be lost to a shift in the Pit. He loved the work, and itched to get his hands dirty, but hated knowing Liv was exactly the kind of coworker he wanted. Quick thinking, smart-mouthed, and kind-hearted. Guilt kept piling up. He was such a selfish shit.

His heavy footsteps creaked against the wood floor. He lightened to a tiptoe, sensing the stillness and quiet of the early morning. His heart went out to Nanny Kemp, and he'd feel like the biggest ass if his clumsy, size thirteens woke the sleeping babies. Downstairs he hoped to find Liv, alone and in a place to talk. Maybe he'd casually mention his profession then make a run for it. He still hadn't figured out his plan when he found Liv, snoring in the lap of her best friend.

"Fair warning … this happens a lot," Charlotte whisper-yelled over the soft, feminine snore he'd begun to love more than the sound of her sighing in pleasure. He smiled, loving her more than he thought possible, until he saw a pile of wadded up tissue on the floor next to Liv's outstretched hand.

"What did you do? You promised me two days!" he sputtered, louder than he meant to. Liv began to stir. She stretched her long body uncurling from the sleeping ball on the chaise.

"Two days for what?" Liv purred, rising to her feet from Lottie's lap. Charlotte shot a dagger from her brown eyes and pursed her lips, apparently choosing to stay silent. Andy found his breath. Fear sucked the oxygen from his lungs. She sauntered over, batting her green doe eyes from beneath red puffy lids. "Two days to buy me something nice?"

"Well now, you've ruined the surprise."

Liv pouted, jutting out her full bottom lip and climbed on her tip toes to give him the good-morning kiss he craved. It made him ache.

"Did someone use my toothbrush?" she twanged, swatting a hand at his chest.

He chuckled. "Guilty."

Liv ran a finger through her copper strands and pressed her hand to her cheeks as if she were suddenly self-conscious and cleared her throat. "Don't mind all this. Just a pair of cackling hens that had too much wine."

Charlotte got up from her spot and gathered the pile of tissues. A stampede of tiny feet could be heard overhead, and Liv broke from his embrace to pick up an ornate, antiqued silver frame that had been lying on the floor just out of arm's reach. She gave it a quick dusting with a corner of her robe and placed it over the fireplace. He hadn't noticed it yesterday sitting front and center. It was Olivia, looking radiant as ever, holding a sleepy baby swaddled in a standard issue hospital blanket.

"So, which one is it? Ashton or Louise?" Andy

asked, swooping in to take a better look at the beautiful photo.

Lottie answered, wearing a forced expression. "That's LouLou. Always Livy's favorite."

Jesus Christ, was the woman ever going to let up and let him prove his love for her best friend?

Liv cleared her throat and wiped at her cheek before turning to face him, wearing the same forced smile as her friend. Red flag.

"Guilty," she said, before returning to his open arms. She face-planted into his chest.

The twins clattered down the hall under the direction of Nanny Kemp. "Whatcha got for the littles to eat this morning, Miss Livy?"

"Eggs and bacon," she answered, rubbing her nose along his sternum.

Charlotte swooped her prized boy in her arms. "I've got it, Nanny. Thank you."

Andy tangled his fingers in Liv's auburn curls and brought her face to his, then sweetly kissed her lips. "As much as I want to stay, I'm afraid I've got to adult today. I'll call you later. Have fun with Lottie and the children."

"Oh, I don't know about that. I won't be doing much but hiding under my covers."

He laughed and held her face to kiss her once more, nibbling at her lip. "Why is that?"

"The rule of threes," she moaned, but not in the sexy way.

Lottie clanged a skillet onto the range and huffed. "Don't get started on that superstitious nonsense."

"It's not nonsense," she grumbled.

"No, it's documented fact," Andy assured her.

Olivia beamed into his cocky half grin. "I knew there was a reason to fall in love with you. I don't want to leave the house unless it's dire. It's Friday the 13th, and a full moon."

Shit. Five bucks someone already put out the free beer sign outside the ambulance bay. "That's only two," he countered with grim optimism.

"Oh, I forgot to mention it's a super moon. It won't happen again this century. I was supposed to work, but someone took pity on me and switched. I worked the last full moon. I'm still recovering."

Andy smiled, sending up a silent thank you to the Lord for the intervention. "I'll take care and be on the lookout for black cats." He bent down to kiss her once more, wary of Lottie's glare. "I love you."

Liv purred, happy and content. His stomach twisted as he pulled away. Putting on his polite, Texas charm he waved and tipped an imaginary hat to Nanny and Charlotte and blew a kiss to Louise. He pointed to address the little boy in her arms. "You're the man of the house there, Ashton. Keep these ladies safe and in line."

Lottie held in a smile. If he'd have blinked, he'd have missed it. Finally, a check in the win column.

Andy stepped outside and was hit with the full force of fall. Grey and listless, the Chicago skyline looked dead. The flicker of hope for a good day extinguished. He crossed his arms over his chest for warmth, pretty sure he'd have to extract his testicles from his abdomen and marched down the steps to the 'L, but was stopped by a wave from a friendly face. Liv's sweet old neighbor Mrs. Loveitz braved the cold to get her daily newspaper.

"Well, howdy, Mrs. Loveitz. Feelin' better I hope?"

Bundled in a full length, black fur and plaid scarf tied around her silver curls, Rose ignited under his warm tone. "Oy, if it isn't the romance hero, Andy Cole."

Olivia's neighbor called him over in a dramatic gesture he couldn't refuse. "Oh, you know when you become an Alter Kroker like me, you basically sit around until you die. All they adjusted some of my medications and sent me packing the next morning."

Andy nodded, taking her morning *Trib,* then escorted her up the steps to her porch. "Sadly, that sounds about right."

She shot him a sideways glance, then waved it off. "My goodness, what a gentleman. I thought this was a lost art. Haven't had a man properly dote on me since my Clyde. So Liv musta said yes to that date. You look well rested and satisfied."

He choked and blushed like a kid caught jerking off by their grandmother. Rose gave him a sly, knowing smile. "Oh, come now. I'm old, not dead."

"Well it's a little cramped in there. Olivia's best friend and children came to visit. And there is only so much rest to be had around kids."

Blaming the kids for his lack of sleep wasn't the biggest fib of the day, but at least he didn't sound like a horny twit.

Mrs. Loveitz perked up. "Lottie's here?"

"She prefers I call that I call her Charlotte."

"Ooo, that's never a good sign."

Andy released Rose's arm at the top of her stairs. "I've been basically threatened with death if I hurt her."

"I wouldn't expect anything less from Charlotte VanSutton. I'll have to drop in and say hello. I haven't seen her since last summer when…" Thick, aged lines around her lips pursed into a frown.

"Why? What happened last summer?" he pressed, fairly certain whatever she said would skirt some truth Liv didn't want him know. Andy glanced at Olivia's building as if it had the power to reveal the secret, but all it did was fill him with guilt and longing.

"Um, Lottie discovered she was pregnant with her twins."

Andy examined Rose's face then turned back to Olivia's front door. A knot tried to form in his stomach. His gut had a way of knowing the universe was about to throw a life at him he wasn't going to be able to save. Some poor soul was going to die because it was time for Anderson Cole to learn a fucking lesson.

The earth seemed to tilt on its axis, and a chill ran up his spine.

"Aww, you poor dear. You'll get used to it. Get yourself a new jacket. A good old Chicago winter is coming."

Chapter Thirteen

Olivia and Charlotte sat immersed in two-thousand thread count sheets on her old four poster bed with a toddler in each lap. Little Louise dozed, full-bellied and slack-jawed onto Liv's chest. Lottie lounged, semi reclined with her prized son nuzzled up to her breast, suckling himself to sleep.

"Do ya think he knows the tap's dry?" Liv asked.

Lottie curled a blonde strand around her finger and smiled. "Don't know. Don't care. It only means he's his Daddy's son."

The babies stirred. "*Shit*," they whisper-yelled in unison and backed out from beneath their respective time-bomb. The antique wood cackled and creaked with their movement. Liv held her breath and looked up to the Lord in a silent plea the children kept snoring. Safe from the tiny binds of LouLou's arms, she watched mesmerized. The sweet girl and precious boy instinctively wove arm in arm. Like those too cute to believe are true twin memes on Facebook, Ashton and Louise clung to each other like their own personal security blanket. An ache knotted in her stomach.

Charlotte wrapped an arm around Liv's shoulders and squeezed, holding her for the full thirty seconds needed to release a dose of oxytocin to nullify the pain she must have felt radiate from her.

"C'mon, Livy. It's never too early for Nanny to make us one of her juleps."

They made a clean getaway and settled at her polished marbled counter while Nanny ground up fresh mint and sugar into the frosty, pewter cups. She had to endure her proud Georgian mumble of discontent when the herb was produced from a plastic bin in the fridge rather than her own personally tended to garden.

Charlotte rambled about Teddy's affair, going on and on about the pricks of their past. "And you never settled, Liv. Leaving Logan after the scandal hit was like a giant 'fuck you' to everything a Savannahian woman is supposed to stand for. And all I ever told Teddy was 'Don't get caught.'"

Nanny placed the cups between the lifelong friends. Pride twinkled in her doughy, black eyes. Liv gripped the neat edges and offered a clink to Lottie. "To all the men in our lives."

They took a dainty sip, mirroring the ladylike habits drilled into their consciousness from Mrs. Lucas's finishing school. The sweet, crispness puckered her skin and danced on her tongue. "I'm sorry you had to go through it, too, Lot. I hate to admit it, but Momma was right. In southern society you're either a Missus or the Mister's Mistress."

Charlotte exhaled a shaky breath. "And my poor babies. You're real lucky you got out without any baggage."

Olivia stiffened, her glass rattling within her fingers. The ache that never went away tore through her, and she shot a glance to her mantel. Tears came next, and she bit into her cheek, hoping to keep them at bay. She'd cried enough last night, and she promised herself she wouldn't grieve every day.

Charlotte slumped, then hung her head. Keenly intuitive, Nanny excused herself to check on the babies. "I'm so sorry, Livy. I wasn't thinking when I said that."

Liv took two beats and found her big girl panties. She wiped her cheeks and took a non-ladylike swig of her julep then plastered her Sweet Peach pageant smile on her face. "I know."

There was a rhythmic knock at the front door. A sudden joy replaced the sadness swirling in her mind.

Even Lottie jumped from her seat as if a burst of happiness came up and bit her in the ass. And it was a race to see who could get to the door first.

A boney elbow jabbed into Liv's ribs. "No fair, you see her every day!" Lottie whined with a sulk to back to the barstool. Liv opened the door with a smirk that screamed victory curled on her mouth.

Mrs. Loveitz waited on the stoop. Her face, lined from a lifetime of joy and sorrow, was pinched tight. The late fall lake rot must be wafting its way west. "Hiya, Rose! C'mon in," Liv twanged and helped her through the entry.

"Hope you don't mind me dropping over."

Olivia gave her a strong hug and kissed her translucent blue cheek. "Heavens no! I hope you're feelin' better," she added with a mindful grab of Rose's hand to feel the radial artery pulse at her wrist.

"Oh, child. I'm fine," Rose assured and strode across the room shrugging out of her liquid, mink fur, and untied her plaid scarf from her curls. Lottie caught in Rose's eye. She grinned, warm and misty, opening her arms to Olivia's honorary sister.

Charlotte leapt from her seat and melted into Rose's grandmotherly embrace while Liv fretted around her kitchen eager to entertain and grabbed her a glass for the tea she kept on hand for her visits.

"It's been too long, Lottie. I heard you were visiting Olivia and that you brought your babies."

"I don't remember tellin' you Lottie was here," Liv said bringing her the drink.

"Oh, you didn't, dear. I ran into that handsome hunk of Texan steak you all but devoured the other day shivering on your front stoop. He told me."

Liv's ears turned pink, but there was no judgment in Rose's smile. She shooed away the tea and motioned to the frost covered pewter cups.

"Bring me a julep. I'm here to gab and gossip."

Liv's heart swelled. It had been over a year since the three of them were in the same room. And it was like a day never passed. The déjà vu was so strong, her belly twinged and ached while she sprawled onto the chaise.

Rose took healthy gulp of her cocktail, smacking her lips with the sweetness. "So tell me, Olivia. Are you aware of how crazy that man is for you?"

****

The gab and cocktail fest lasted a few hours. Rose's perfectly painted face continued to strain, and Liv insisted on taking her home to rest. Lottie and Nanny Kemp decided to hire a driver to take them and the twins to a much raved about Children's Museum on the Northshore. During the lull, Liv was hit with a brilliant way to pass the time. Dressed in nothing but a smile, she shot a series of sexy selfies to distract and tease the "So fucking bored," and "So fucking busy," texts from the "adulting" Andy Cole.

Naughty tingles shot down her spine and between her legs as she hit "send' and climbed into bed take care of the throb surging through her sex. She shut her eyes, and imagined Andy's tongue lapping around her clit and the long, rough thrusts he used when he fucked her on the stairs. But, shit she wanted him. No vibrator on the planet could compare. She almost felt sorry for B.O.B. and offered him a heartfelt breakup soliloquy before taking him out of her nightstand and tossing him into her closet.

Her cell phone chimed. She dashed back to answer. It had to be Andy. God wouldn't be so cruel. But to her disgust and dismay it was work. Fucking work. A mass invite to a mandatory meeting put on by the Chief of Emergency Medicine.

In a heartbeat she went from depraved sex kitten to grumpy cat, but it was silly. She had no reason to be anything but upbeat. Nothing awful had befallen her on the unluckiest of unlucky days. Three orgasms since midnight, a visit from Mrs. Loveitz, a luxury facial with Lottie's fifteen-hundred-dollar placenta cream, and a killer deal on the new Marc Jacobs alligator clutch. She'd be lying if she had anything but glowing things to say about her day so far. She quit her moping and pulled on a pair of old white scrub bottoms reminiscent of her days in Savannah and a County Med ER fleece she had been gifted for ER Nurses Week.

The meeting would be a two-hour blip, easily forgotten. She'd attend the meeting, wave at the poor souls slaving away in the Pit and still have time to primp and prep for a sultry meet up with the man she'd been daydreaming about naked since he marched his fine ass out the door.

Chapter Fourteen

To put it mildly, Andy's day went from bleak to utter shit in six seconds flat. He wasn't ready to blame Liv's rule of threes but there was no way around it, the juju was bad. A three hour wait, ICU holds taking up the rooms needed for patients that kept rolling in and trying to die, and one psychotic old man that kept roaming the department, naked, threatening to "release his hounds," flashing his semi-limp cock to any person willing to look his way.

And then it was gone. The chaotic ebb and flow of the ER emptied the Pit so fast it gave new meaning to the phrase feast or famine.

He turfed the final patient of the hour, and his three residents huddled around the desk drawing straws. Somebody had to do the lumbar puncture on ol' man crazy, cock-flasher, and the fates in their fucked-up glory picked Dr. Martin. CiCi kept her face impassive.

"I'll order some Haldol and Geodon. He'll calm down," Andy advised. Nurse Nora from his first day caught his eye. She grinned, a little too friendly. He tried not to return it when he asked her to medicate the patient.

"Right on it, Dr. Cole," she sang in a sugared voice. Something about it made him cringe, but because he couldn't help himself, his gaze lingered on her ass as she walked by. Not even remotely comparable.

On a downward break of a constant uphill battle, Andy sat back in his rolling chair, and dicked around on his phone. At some point you stop worrying about what looks professional. He could be looking up drug interactions for all anyone knew, but doctors don't spin in their office chair when they find out that Levophed and Meropenem were compatible. Liv had texted twice. Once to say the magic words "I love ya, cowboy," and the other with the more important message that her thighs were still shaking from the best sex of her life. Her own words. It took every ounce of self-control not to high five the confused hallway patient, and strut like a goddamn peacock. He knew he had done his job, but to have to have her admit it so straightforwardly filled him with such obnoxious pride he was pretty sure nothing could fuck up this day.

A call from across the eerily quiet ER pulled his thoughts from Liv's tits. "Hey, Doc?" It was Moe. The short, squat, no-nonsense nurse in charge.

"Yeah?"

"LOL with shortness of breath on bipap coming in in ten." The respite was over.

"All right. Page Respiratory Therapy in case we need to tube her."

Moe nodded and hit the intercom. Dr. Martin emerged from her lumbar puncture with a shit-eating grin plastered on her face.

"Nailed it. Champagne tap," she declared. The other residents followed behind muttering under their breaths. Andy offered a congratulatory high five and reviewed what he expected for the procedural note.

Another tick in the win column, but the upswing couldn't go on forever. Andy shrugged out of his white coat and rolled up his sleeves as Smithson rounded the corner. That was strange. The Chief of ER medicine usually worked banker hours. Seeing him anywhere but the driving range on a Friday afternoon was rare.

"Dr. Cole?"

Andy nodded in acknowledgement and signed a transfer consent Moe shoved under his nose.

"I'm getting resistance from the CEO. He thinks we've got time to get the level four suits flown in from Atlanta."

He didn't see the problem. Getting the level four suits was a huge victory. "We don't?"

"Not if we want to be properly trained. I don't want another Dallas…"

Andy went through the motions in the resuscitation room and gestured for the medic to hand him an intubation box. He snapped together the tongue blade and checked the light. "So you've said. What's the timeline? A few days?"

"If we're lucky."

He grinned. "Well then that's good. I'm feeling like luck will be on our side."

Smithson chuckled. "Heh, I guess I'm not used to such optimism. In any case, I'm calling a mandatory unit wide staff meeting."

Andy froze. "When?"

"This afternoon. I'll need you to head it up. Give the department your firsthand account of what they might be dealing with." Smithson slapped him on the back, grumbling something about being appreciative, but it sailed over his head.

"I don't know what I can say really. I was more of a patient than anything else…" That was the understatement of a lifetime. If being on your deathbed didn't fall into the realm of being a patient nothing did.

"Presenting symptoms, course of treatment, etc."

Andy clenched his jaw, fidgeting with whatever he could get his hands on. "Low grade fever, fatigue. And pray you don't bleed out and die."

"So much for that optimism." Of all the times to be a smart ass. Repressed memories clawed their way into Andy's brain. Blood. So much blood. "The meeting starts at five. Get there when you can," Smithson finished, before heading out of the trauma room.

Andy checked his watch. "That's in two goddamn

hours!"

Smithson shot Andy a hot glance. He glared right back. Andy knew Smithson was doing all that he could to keep his department prepared for a potentially deadly and devastating contagion, but Jesus Christ the other shoe wasn't dropping, it was being hurled towards Earth faster than he could fix.

Moe popped his head around the curtain. "Yeah, looks like they're coding her now. They're coming 'round the ambulance bay."

Andy made sure to mutter his choice curse word and followed the charge nurse to see the commotion. A group of paramedics yelling over one another with one riding along the stretcher performing CPR charged down the hall. There wasn't much to make out except for a plaid, tan and red scarf tied around wooly curls.

Chapter Fifteen

Locking up her front stoop, Liv met the full force of fall. There never seemed to be a gradual downward trend. In Chicago, it went from hot and humid to freeze your nipples off overnight. The cold temps and the prospect of waiting on a windy 'L platform drove her pace down the sidewalk. She rounded the corner at the end of her block and hugged herself, pushing through a frigid blast of air.

The screaming wail of an ambulance hit her with the gust of wind. It took the turn down Liv's street almost on two wheels. Adrenaline shot through her veins. The trauma junkie in her never seemed to be satisfied, and her first instinct was to run back the way she came. But a shiver of rational thought came with the loss of feeling in her cheeks and she loped up the stairs to the oncoming train.

The juju kept shining in her favor. Liv slid right onto the 'L, had her pick of open seats, and was free to read her worn and battered copy of *Twilight* without a conceited eye roll from a girl a decade her junior. The train didn't remain empty for long, but as commuters filled in, everyone smiled and acknowledged each other. Liv had the strange feeling she had fallen asleep and taken the train straight home, but no one wore shorts and NorthFace parkas at the same time riding Belles Ferry or the River St. streetcar.

Several stops down the doors opened, and Torey stepped through. Seeming bored and irritated, she looked over the passengers until she locked eyes with Liv. She beamed at her new friend, and Olivia patted at the open seat next to her. Apparently, unperturbed by the threat of potent cooties, she was dressed chic and lovely, wearing skinny, ankle jeans, an olive-green blazer, and a blush, low-cut shell. She piled her black hair into a high ponytail with a sweepy, eye-catching bang. Liv knew this look. Full-on huntress mode.

"They called you, too?" she asked as her friend settled into the plastic bench. Torey pulled her out her own dog-eared copy of *Fifty Shades* from her purse and arched an eyebrow over the cover.

"Since I'm not a regular staff member, I'm not required to go to Dr. Smithson's dog and pony show. But I'm making an appearance as a liaison from the Woman's and Infant's department. I don't mind really… I'm hoping to run into someone that happens to be a fantastic lay."

Liv flushed. Desire flamed up her neck and over her breasts.

Torey nudged Liv in the shoulder. "Well don't you look well fucked and guilty all of the sudden. I knew you wouldn't be able to hold out that long. But why would any woman want to?"

Silly girl giggles bubbled in Liv's chest. Embarrassed. Amused. Suddenly very aware she'd be judged for a fool.

"Oh my God. That guy has you completely dick-faced, doesn't he?" Torey's eyes widened. She turned in the seat, as if their closeness would prevent any juicy tidbit from floating away unheard.

An ache pulsed between her thighs. Andy flashed in her memory as he worked his tongue over her sex. His always perfect stubble polished her skin raw, leaving a twinge of sinful pain behind. Liv fanned herself with her favorite YA romance diversion and sighed. "It's worse. Heaven help me, Torey, because I am so flippin' in love with him."

"Spill. And I want every dirty and delicious detail."

Liv rolled her eyes. "Girlfriend. Shouldn't I say the same to you? The only reason a woman wears that kind of shirt is to lure in her prey."

"Fine. Leo's a dick. But he wields it like a god. I will never bring him to the 'burbs to meet my parents. And he still cries at the end of *Titanic*. Your turn."

Olivia didn't believe in kissin', tellin', and making everyone part of your private business, but there was something warm and exciting about telling a friend she'd fallen in loon-ely in love. It might have had something to do with the fact Torey wasn't hell bent on making her remember the last time she let herself be swooned to the nines by man who'd proceeded to crush her heart and soul. Whatever the case, it was nice to sit and gab about making love, honest fucking, and all the feels that went with it.

In sync they stood, bracing for their stop. Liv's cell phone buzzed in her pocket. She tore it free, hoping it was Andy. She frowned. It wasn't her Saintly, sex on a stick, but work. She let it go to voicemail. "I can only go as fast as the blue line, people."

****

"Did you get a hold of her?" Andy called from the resuscitation room.

"We tried, doc. Voicemail. She should be on her way in for that meeting Smithson's putting on."

Andy looked over the sterile field to his residents, thankful the blue paper drape covered Rose's face. He almost couldn't stomach intubating her. Her ice blue eyes wouldn't stay shut.

Sweat blurred his vision. Placing the arterial line should be a prize for his favorite student of the day, but in no way would he trust any of them right now.

"Don't stand there and do nothing. Help hang lines. Run your asses down to the pharmacy for drips."

He should have stopped torturing Rose's body twenty minutes ago, but he couldn't. He kept imagining Liv's face. Imagining her shock. Her fury. Imagining the love fade from her eyes when she discovered he was a selfish liar, but above all that, the goddamn doctor that let her friend die.

For all intents and purposes, Rose Loveitz was gone. She did nothing on her own. Her lungs needed the ventilator. Her heart needed the constant current from the transcutaneous pacer, and her major organs needed every pressor he knew of to prevent tissue necrosis. This wasn't saving a life. It was prolonging death. And everyone in the room knew it.

The bright white fluorescents sliced through his temple. If it weren't for the fact he was threading a wire up Rose's femoral artery, he'd throw the cardiac monitor out the window. He didn't need a wailing crisis alarm to know her blood pressure was fifty over dead. When he finished, he tore himself out of his gown and gloves. Like a brat, he kicked a pair of trauma shears that were on the floor and threw his hip into the scrub sink. In the dank recesses of his mind he heard Olivia's warm honeyed voice. Except it wasn't his memory.

"Oh my Lord. I saw her two hours ago. She was fine. What in the hell happened?"

With his back to the room, Andy listened to the hum of morbid conversation. He glanced over his shoulder and rinsed the soap from his arms. She had dropped her bag on the floor and rushed to her side, taking in all the shit he'd subjected Mrs. Loveitz's failing body to. His stomach dropped into his feet. Seeing her so upset ripped his gut wide open.

"What's next? Where's y'all's attending?"

Andy held his breath and tugged off the disposable scrub hat hiding his dark hair, then turned around. "Right here."

****

How many different feelings can a person experience at once? If anyone had ever died from internal conflicting emotions, Liv was pretty sure she'd break into a million pieces and bleed out on the floor.

CiCi Martin, one of Liv's preferred residents, came to put a hand on her shoulder. She was good at reading what patients and families needed in the form of support, but right then, as she gripped Rose's frigid hand, CiCi missed the mark. It took every ounce of self-control not to shrug her off and shoot daggers from her eyes. She needed to save that ammunition for the man she thought she knew standing ten feet away.

"Liv, have you had a chance to meet Dr. Cole?"

How in the world was she supposed to answer that? She held his gaze, hurt welling in her eyes until they brimmed with tears.

"No."

Dr. Martin went through the details of Rose's arrival. The code. What they think happened.

"How long was she down for?" Liv asked.

"Twenty-three minutes," Andy said, finally with the courage to join them around Rose's body. CiCi took it in stride and left the room. Liv smiled at the nurse busying herself with lines and drips. They'd given report to each other a handful of times over the last year, but she could never remember her name. Reading the tension better than CiCi, the sweet, well-seasoned nurse found an excuse to step out for a minute.

"I wanted to tell you—"

She didn't even look up. "We're not talking about this now."

Andy straightened and sucked in a breath. "Does she have family?"

"Me. I'm it."

"Liv, these kinda decisions are—"

"I'm it," she repeated. "Husband's dead. Son died in Desert Storm. Daughter died of breast cancer in '06, and her grandson got caught tryin' to embezzle funds from the Chicago Public Schools. He's serving time down state. I—am—it." Liv turned over Rose's hand and caressed her cool palm with her thumb. It brought her down. The seemingly insignificant action had a way of numbing the hurt. "I'm her medical power of attorney. The paper is in my wallet."

Without a reply, Andy retrieved her bag and called the unit secretaries to make a copy. Liv knew what came next. They usually escorted the family to a private room, call in the chaplain and have a "Come to Jesus" about outcomes and statistics. Except she knew it all. She'd had the same conversation with hundreds of hopeful families. If Rose's heart made it through the night, it'd be a miracle, but her body wouldn't last more than twelve hours before going multi-system organ failure. And even with the post resuscitation cooling measures, being down for more than twenty minutes was enough to destroy neurologic function. Should the impossible happen and her body turned around, she'd never wake up.

Andy's gaze caressed her back and up her neck. It was the first time she wanted to let herself cry. Weep. To sob into the arms of someone she loved. She wanted Andy. She wanted to inhale the skin at his chest, and have him swallow her in his warmth and shush away her tears.

Liv stood at Rose's face and removed the Burberry scarf that covered her coifed perm. It was her gift from last Christmas. An extravagant but much deserved "Thank you" for being a ready friend and companion during the most trying summer of her life. They were kindred spirits born generations apart. She loved Rose and would cherish her friendship forever.

Andy watched, arms folded over his broad chest. The occasional distraction would pop in and out, but he never let himself be pulled away for long. Liv couldn't tell if she loved or loathed his calm presence.

She lowered herself to Rose's ear and whispered the Hebrew hymn she sung every night for two months while Liv ballooned with water weight and protein, praying in her different faith to the same God asking to last one more day.

Mi ha'ish
Hachafetz chayim
Ohev yamim
Lir'ot tov
Netzor leshoncha meira
Us'fatecha midaber mirma
Sur meira
Va'asei tov
Bakesh shalom
Verodfeihu

She followed the psalm with her own silent prayer, selfishly asking for strength knowing Rose's soul was already in good hands. She placed a warm kiss on her cold cheek, and stood to meet Andy's gaze. If he was trying to remain impassive, he was failing miserably. But now wasn't the time figure their shit out.

"It ends now. I'll call her Rabbi. But everything ends now."

****

It's nothing like what the idiots show on TV. From beginning to end it took no more than four minutes. Life support withdrawal rarely happened in the Pit. The crass reality was that the beds were used to save lives. If someone wanted to die peacefully, they went somewhere else to do it. Liv stood next to Andy, hugging herself to prevent reaching for his hand. He'd already offered it twice, and like a petty, resentful twat she ignored it.

The Rabbi and his *Chevra Kadisha* made all the proper preparations. Liv hated feeling glib and unhelpful, but Rose was the first Orthodox Jew she'd ever met and didn't know one thing about how to care for her once her heart stopped beating. She helped remove all the wires and tubes that prolonged the last few hours of her life, and wiped any remaining blood or stomach goo that oozed up the throat during the rounds of CPR. With an all too quick signature, Rose's body was taken away.

Shoulder to shoulder, Liv and Andy watched Rose's body wheeled out on the stretcher. She kept waiting to feel something that wasn't sadness. She adapted her heart early on to not carry the weight of the patients she lost, as otherwise she'd have never lasted her first year in Atlanta before heading home. It was the one thing she could thank Logan for. He'd taught her how to shut that part of her off, yet one by one, tears fell down her cheeks.

Anger prickled behind her sadness. She had every right to cry, but it looked like weakness. Andy didn't know what Rose meant to her. All he'd see was an over emotional girl who couldn't handle real life in the ER. Still she caved.

Lured by his gravity, Liv leaned into him. He sighed and wrapped his arms around her rigid frame, but with the weight of his embrace came the weight of his lies. She shrugged him off and pulled away. She composed herself with a swipe at her damp cheeks.

"No. You don't get to comfort me."

Andy stiffened and blew out a hard breath. The rejection hit him where she hoped it would. He stepped back to rub out the tension in his neck.

"Olivia. Please. You're going to have to let me explain."

She turned on her heel, then reached for her bag. "I don't know when that'll happen, Dr. Cole. Cause right now, they're pagin' you to room three. And I have a mandatory nurses meeting to go to. You have a nice night," she said with her warm twang, and marched out the door.

During the ten-minute walk to the auditorium Liv lost count of the, "I'm sorry's" and "You okay?'s" and the most dreaded, "If you need to talk."

She forced a pleasant expression acknowledging the sentiment, not wanting to fault her coworkers for trying to be supportive. She'd be the first one to offer a coffee or a willing, silent ear, but it was all too soon. The worst part was she couldn't rid her mother's voice from her brain, telling her to put on her big girl panties and smile.

"No one wants to see a sour puss, Olivia," she'd say, and being a dutiful southern daughter, Liv would plaster her pageant smile and stomach the hurt like it was her job to prove her life was nothing but enviable to the rest of Savannah society. But right then, the pain it took to force her cheeks up and lips tight was an eleven out of ten on the pain scale.

Every pair of eyes followed her down the steps. She chose a spot near an exit and sat beside Torey. She allowed a giggle at her friend who vamped up her cherry red lip and cleavage to maximum velocity.

Torey purred and shivered in sin. "I may or may not have a fast pass to sexy time in two hours. Think that's enough time to get a Brazilian? Leo's been a good boy. I think a surprise is in order."

Thankful for the distraction, Liv nodded and

played along. "I've got a great girl in the Ukrainian Village. Danka. She'll clean ya up good."

"Excellent," she hummed and tilted her chin just a bit. "Suck's about your friend, Liv. Go ahead and look upset. No one expects you to smile."

Liv nudged her elbow into petite friend and let her shoulders fall. Her poised posture wilted under the weight of heartbreak and loss. Just like the shrill, nasal disdain in her mother's voice, she couldn't shake the image of Andy standing across the bleached white room, looking like a trauma doc god under the glaring fluorescents. Didn't the Lord have the decency to make him look like a washed out, puny dicked pipsqueak rather than a sexier than hell orgasm wielding wonder in black scrubs?

Why hadn't she questioned the chemistry? Why didn't her gut bubble with alarm when she started to fall way too fast for a guy she knew couldn't exist? The kind of guy she left after her own taste of Savannah's emergency medicine. Why didn't she recoil from her looney, lovestruck behavior that took nine months and over nine hundred miles to fix? Two people did. One was probably halfway through her favorite Shiraz and the other was on her way to a funeral home.

Torey checked her makeup with her cellphone camera. "What do you think 'His Royal Highness,' Dr. Smithson wants to tactically scare us with today? Wasn't this time last year all about that Ebola nonsense? Such a clusterfuck. And for what?"

"Preparedness for an incurable contagion of epidemic proportion?"

"I know you're having a shitty day, so I'm going to let that slide."

To her surprise Liv laughed, truly thankful for Torey and her snarky yet reasonable commentary. She debated going a step further and telling her about Andy. She wasn't ready for the "I told you so," discussion that Lottie would ream into her, but she needed someone to objectively listen to her rip into Anderson and his lie. Basically, she needed someone to agree with whatever came out of her mouth.

The theater lights dimmed and brightened over the speaker's podium. Torey made a quick dash to the front to grab the meeting agenda and notes piled on the ledge.

"You never know when you'll need something to wipe your ass with," she mocked, glancing toward the back. Leo must have caught her eye because she offered a sly, sex kitten smirk and demure wave before sitting back at Liv's side. She mumbled some naughty details that any normal lady would refrain from mentioning, while Liv scanned the meeting outline.

Torey let out a gasp. Olivia didn't need to look over to know why. She felt his heat before he even walked through the door. "Well, that sure as hell isn't Smithson."

Chapter Sixteen

Liv kept her eyes in her lap, forcing even breaths. But remaining calm proved to be impossible. The room erupted with the hum of infatuated, swooning hens. Her first reaction was to turn around and bellow, "Back off bitches. He's mine."

"Well… Mr. Cole is actually *Dr.* Cole," Torey whispered behind her meeting itinerary, her voice dripping with gleeful intrigue. "Did you know this, or is this new information?"

Liv checked her watch. "New. He pronounced my friend dead exactly seventy-eight minutes ago."

Torey blanched. "Damn, Liv. That is all kinds of awful."

Olivia spent the next few minutes explaining the code, what it was like seeing Andy turn around. The shock of his deception was almost harder to reconcile than knowing Rose would never speak to her again.

"I bet he's devastated," Torey said glancing in Andy's direction. "Losing a patient is always hard, but to have *that* one on your conscience…" Torey brought her attention back to Liv. Torey stroked Liv's hair and smiled, a friendly way of saying "Chin up. I gotcha, girl", and clearly a way of changing the topic. "And now you've got the *hottest* doctor in town head over dick for you, I might be a little jealous. You two'll be, like, the ER prom king and queen."

The way Torey looked at her, it was obvious she expected the kind of rapid-fire, deliciously crude girl talk that had made them insta-friends days before. Except Liv couldn't find anything to say. Conflicting emotions aplenty, but nothing that could be made into a sentence.

Torey seemed to read her silence and diagnosed Liv's hang-up in a heartbeat. "Wait. Are you *mad* at him because he didn't tell you he was a physician?"

Olivia shifted in her wooden seat, suddenly very aware of how petty it all seemed on the surface. She picked at her thumbnail until it bled.

"Weren't you the one who lied in the first place? When you guys first met at the library. What did ya say you did?"

"Dog groomer. I know. It's completely hypocritical but—"

"Friend, I'm not judging. Just making sure you see and acknowledge the crazy before I tell you how Andy hasn't taken his eyes off you once since you sat down."

The hum of conversation floating around the large room evaporated into roaring silence. The pressure of Andy's gaze tugged at her heart, and she caved. Of course, he was staring at her. He stared with such strength and longing it was as if he'd wait a lifetime for the smile he hoped was coming. But Lord forgive her for all her faults, a lifetime was probably how long he'd have to wait.

Olivia gathered her bag and jumped from her seat. "I can't sit through this."

"No problem, Liv. I'll take detailed notes."

Andy's gaze might as well have been beams burning into her back as she rushed out of the auditorium. She shoved the door open harder than necessary. The ancient steel frame groaned in protest. If getting up to leave before the whole thing started didn't cause everyone to look at her, the ruckus sure did. She heard Andy's nervous cough and the twang that made her panties wet.

"Good evenin', y'all. I'm Dr. Andy Cole."

The door crashed shut behind her. She made it to an empty service corridor. The one that led to the basement and the morgue. Olivia collapsed against the dingy, concrete wall and slid to the floor, primed to cry. But if she wanted privacy and quiet, she should have known better than to pick a spot yards away from where the bodies that piled up on Friday the thirteenth were taken.

A stretcher that needed some serious WD40 came up from the basement.

"Heya, Liv." It was Javier. The flirty, charge nurse who'd asked her out so many times she'd lost count. The charge nurse that smiled at her like it was his life's mission to see her naked. Tonight was no different. While the attention was hugely flattering, it felt like rubbing hand gel into her hangnail. But she'd seen so much pity in the faces of everyone for the last few hours, it was a welcome distraction.

She unraveled from her less than ladylike squat against the wall. "Hi, Javi. How about you don't go and tattle on me for skippin' out on the mandatory meeting for the year?"

He grinned his half smirk, the one every overinflated male ego in the ER had down to a science. "Only if I get something in return."

Typical. She gritted her teeth and forced her cheeks into a smile. "You want to take me out for a drink?"

Javi grabbed his chest. "Ooo, ouch, Liv. Way to spear me in the heart."

Okay. She could laugh at that.

"It's balls to the wall busy upstairs. Help out for three hours, and I'll take your on-call shift next week."

Liv held in a cringe. Yes, the juju was bad, but it couldn't get worse. "Can you give me disaster pay?"

"The lady drives a hard bargain."

She smiled. This one was genuine. "You should

see me haggle over a pair of shoes."

"Hard ass."

"You'll have no argument from me, sir." She retrieved her bag from the floor and matched Javi's stride, shoving her hands in her pockets. She might have been indulging in a little harmless banter, but she didn't want him to take it much further. "But money talks, Boss."

"Disaster diff? Chump change. I was ready to offer triple time. So I win."

"Just because I'm not one hundred percent altruistic, doesn't mean I'm greedy. Y'all got me for three hours. That's it."

Javier crossed his heart and pointed to the ceiling, solidifying his promise. Since her original sexy time plans had gone to hell in a handbasket, working a princess shift for crazy good money was an acceptable substitute. By then Andy should be done with his shift, and if he did manage to lollygag, she could avoid him, *or* be just visible enough to drive him crazy. She couldn't decide how she intended to play.

****

Of course, she got up and left. What the fuck did he expect? The punishment seemed to fit the crime. Having to smile like a jackass after Olivia shot him full of bullet holes and be forced to relive an experience he'd rather forget, all had the makings for a Heaven-sent ass-whoopin.'

The information he and Smithson decided to cover was pertinent, but unhelpful, and impossible to instill the proper level of alert. After the mess in Texas, every hospital in the US went into scare tactic mode. Preparation and education cost many departments into the millions, his old unit included. Necessary precautions for sure, but beaten to death with an ugly stick so bad the word "contagion" became just as taboo as "quiet". And it had nothing to do with tempting the juju.

None of the equipment or HazMat suits had arrived, so he spent his time discussing how a patient would present. Which was as varied and inconsistent as any viral BS that circulated around every daycare center, old folks' home, and the checkout line at the supermarket. It was a fucking cold—until it wasn't, and by that time you were dead. Smithson had to come down from his ivory tower to handle the important questions. Andy had a grim sense of satisfaction knowing Smithson was just as lousy at addressing the glassy-eyed masses as he was, but at least he could fall back on his homegrown twang and a self-deprecating joke about being a cowboy in the big city. Smithson, known for efficiency, effectiveness, and an extreme lack of funny had a hard time selling the level of awareness needed to keep his staff of over three hundred on the ready.

The auditorium filed out. He stared at Liv's empty seat and her vamped up friend. She had kept her nose glued to the handouts, which probably meant she was hiding her cellphone in her lap. Smithson clapped him on the shoulder, thanking him for his time and muttered some other soliloquy how a person in his position can't be too careful. He probably looked like an ass, but he wasn't in the mood to stroke Smithson's ego and tell him what he was doing was right.

A tall blonde in blue and an even taller brunette medic green came up to introduce themselves. Instantly, Torey's keen, little eyes locked onto him. He clenched his jaw and forced a smile, irritated that he had to put on a show for both. But the only one that mattered was the one that could dig him into a deeper mess then he made for himself.

Yes, he loved the city. No, he hated the weather

and Cubs fan all the way. The brunette was either bold or drew the short straw.

"No. Not married," Andy answered. He knew Torey would be grading the answer and turned his eyes to hers. "But I'm lucky to have found a great girl that I'm very much in love with."

The corner of Torey's lips twitched, and a smile emerged from her judgment. It was a blessing that would work in his favor. ER nurses had excellent bullshit detectors. Torey knew he was telling the truth.

Andy thanked the Lord the conversation didn't go beyond that. Women above the Mason/Dixon had a tendency to be more aggressive than he was used to, and if he wasn't already in love with another woman, there'd be no point denying it, he'd be playing them like an organ in church.

The in-house pager went off at his waist. He should be done with his shift, but he hoped for a reason to stay. If he wasn't going to see Liv tonight, he might as well be at work, and he'd lose his ever lovin' mind cooped up in the suite at the Peninsula.

The page was from CiCi. When was she ever going to feel good on her own two feet? Andy scratched at his chin. He had hoped to get in a quick word with Torey, but she was already playing Leo like an organist on Sunday. It would be a huge violation of the bro code to break up whatever pre-mating ritual the two were engaging in, so he took that as a sign and left.

He compulsively checked his phone for messages or texts on his way back to the Pit, stopping at the door that would open into the chaos to try to call her. He didn't know what he'd say. Except that he was sorry. He also knew the window of regret would be short. Blame being a man. Blame the sin of pride. But he was proud of being a physician. That's who he was at his core, and that didn't mean he should carry the burden of the last guy who'd treated Olivia like garbage. The fact that he was an ER doctor, too, well, that had to be purely coincidental.

He considered it a small victory that the call went to voicemail after six rings. The fact she wasn't blocking his calls was a definite tick in the win column. Hearing her sweet, Savannah twang and imagining the warm smile that usually went with it shot straight to his groin. If his dick and his brain could get on the same page that'd be great. He was about to pour his heart out to her voicemail, but Dr. Martin gestured him in through the glass. It was for the best. No woman wanted to hear a man plead his case over the phone, or worse, cry.

He pushed a button, and the doors opened before him. It had to be in his head, but he felt Olivia's heat the second the he walked through. And as if the staff meeting wasn't punishment enough, his eyes immediately gravitated to Liv working over a stretcher crammed in a corner. Her white scrubs clung to her perky behind that—for the love of God—gave him the slightest glimpse of her lacey, thong panty. His eyes squeezed shut, but it didn't matter. The image would be frozen in his mind forever.

"What's up, CiCi?"

"I paged you as soon as I heard. We got an ambulance call about a forty-something male, SSO, complaining of malaise, and a low-grade temp."

The arrogant ass in him laughed. "If he's Spanish speaking only, how do they know he's complaining of anything?"

CiCi was in Dr. Martin mode, and apparently that meant she didn't laugh at shitty jokes. He straightened and cleared his throat. "Sorry."

"They picked him up from an overrun apartment,

a halfway house for some of the refugees from Central America."

Andy frowned and pinched the bridge of his nose. "And so it begins. Have the secretary call their dispatch and tell them that rig will need to be suspended and those medics contained for three days. I'll assess him outside even before he comes in."

She nodded and made a few notes on a Post-it.

"Want me to tell charge?"

"Nah. I got it." He looked around for that guy he couldn't stand, and sure enough, he was right where you'd think he'd be. Smirking like cock in a henhouse right into Olivia's sexy face.

How wrong would it be to punch him in the throat? Guys like him asked for it with every word that came out of their mouths. It'd be doing the world a service by knocking that dickwad down a peg. He took a calming breath and dug his knuckles into the counter. It didn't help, and neither did staring at the pair like he was waiting for them to do tricks. How could she not feel his eyes on her? How was she not miserable and out of her mind?

He grabbed the first thing in his line of sight and threw a metal clipboard across the counter. It landed with a crash in the lap of the cardiac monitor tech.

"Yeah, thanks, doc. How about you lob it underhanded it next time you wanna have a temper tantrum?"

He should have apologized, but his back was already turned. The doors to the ambulance bay opened, and he marched his sorry ass outside.

It didn't matter that by Texas standards, it was freezing. Anything below fifty might as well be the arctic. The ambulance siren wailed in the distance. Thinking about the patient gave him something to do that wasn't obsess over Olivia and her jerk charge nurse. Work was always the best distraction. The rig backed into the space. The door opened, and out popped a gowned and gloved medic.

"Hey, doc, this is Jorge. He might be a—"

"Yeah, I know, fellas. I'll take him from here. Y'all know this is your last run, right? I'm sure it's nothing. But it's only a seventy-two-hour containment period."

"Yeah, dispatch told us. Three days paid vacation. Already updated my Netflix lineup."

In the event it was a normal 'flu and not the one he was miraculously immune to, Andy pulled out a mask and lazily covered his mouth and nose. He climbed into the ambulance. Pale, listless, the patient struggled to breathe. The nasal cannula forcing oxygen in his nose wasn't cutting it.

"Probably pneumonia," Andy said, taking his stethoscope from around his neck. There was a mumbling of agreement, and he turned his attention to the man lying on the stretcher.

"Hey man. *¿Que pasó?*"

His Spanish was rusty, but still easy for him to understand.

"Been feeling bad since I came on the bus. Really tired. Really cold. I'm not hungry. My Nona called the ambulance when I passed out. And when I woke up. I couldn't see. But I'm better now."

Andy pulled his stethoscope from his ears, falling into the bad habit of listening to the heart and lungs while the patients answered questions. He blinked, trying to process what the patient said. No way he admitted to having a loss of vision after a syncopal episode.

"Did y'all hear him say he passed out and couldn't see?"

The medics looked at each other and shrugged. "Nah, doc. That's the first we've heard of it."

Andy grabbed a penlight from the tool kit next to the stretcher. The monitor started beeping. His oxygen level tanked. Andy flashed the light in his eyes. Jorge winced, then howled in pain.

"*Shit!* Y'all get in that rig and stay there!" The medics shot shifty glances at one another, then laughed.

"Doc, you're not seriously thinkin' it's that blood flu..."

Andy swallow against his dry mouth. He never second-guessed himself. That millisecond delay could cost someone their life, but what if fear had him imagining blood pooling in the tear duct? He slapped on a new glove and gently placed a finger on Jorge's lower lid. He pulled down and flashed the light in his pupil. Jorge bucked in agony. Andy sailed back. He crashed into the rig's wall, shattering the Plexiglas supply cabinet. Something sliced deep into his arm and cut to his flank. His fingers went numb. Shards and supplies rained over them. Jorge began to weep, delirious from pain and fever. Blood oozed from his eyes where tears should be.

Andy jumped out and shoved the two medics in. He braced against the pain in his side. "Y'all have been exposed. Stay in the rig until we get the CDC here to quarantine you." He pulled the stretcher from the grooves that held it in place.

"You're still bringing him in?" one yelled.

The monitor hadn't shut up once. "Yeah. He's dying." He threw a sheet over Jorge's face. It looked awful, but it was the best he could do until he got into the negative-pressure resuscitation room just through the trauma bay doors.

Ignoring the searing in his side and trickle of sticky warmth down his arm, Andy rushed the stretcher through the doors. Jorge writhed in the excruciating pain he knew so well. It would feel like he's on fire from the inside, that his bones would have melted, and the tears he'd cry would be a lava of blood. "I've got you, Jorge. I'll make it better," he lied in miserable Spanish.

Dr. Martin waited in the vestibule and read the urgency on his face. She pulled a pair of gloves from the wall container.

"No!" Andy bellowed. "Just me! Call Smithson. We'll need the respirators and level four HazMat suits."

CiCi stood back. The charge nurse finally took his role seriously and was on the phone, delegating orders around the room. All the glassy eyed masses he had preached to not more than an hour ago watched with horror streaked on their faces. Some took large steps back as if to put further distance between themselves and the deadly air Jorge expelled. Andy careened around the corner and into the trauma room. The light was blinding. Jorge moaned and rubbed his knuckles into his bloody eye sockets. Andy dimmed the lights and grabbed for non-rebreather oxygen mask.

Seamless, chaotic movement erupted outside. Sweat pooled down his back. It was all too real. And too fucking soon. Overhead a loud fan started to churn. At least someone had listened to one word from that godforsaken meeting.

With Jorge settled after a few breaths of one-hundred percent oxygen, Andy grabbed a mask, then headed to the nurses' station to instruct CiCi and the charge nurse until Smithson arrived. Three days. He survived before. He'd do it again and, he hoped, save a man in the process. He scanned every face for Liv's. He exhaled a hard breath, wishing he had seen her once more.

He forced his eyes on the asshat charge nurse.

"No one goes in. Seal it up behind me using the steps I talked about…"

His thought fizzed. Like an answer to an unsaid prayer, Olivia popped into his vision. Unable to focus on anything but her energetic, infectious, smile, Andy paused. She rushed by, pulling her hair away from her face. Her wide eyes locked with his, a trace of an adrenaline infused smirk curled on her lips.

"C'mon, y'all. This guy looks like he's fixin' to die."

If he hadn't been weighed down by an anchor of loving lust, if he hadn't been fixated on her sexy pout and her tits as they bounced through space, if he hadn't succumbed to the biggest flaw of being a man, he would have been able stop her.

Chapter Seventeen

The first thing a nurse does upon entering a patient's room is an across-the-room assessment. It usually starts with the mental tally: is the person talking, crying, texting, sexting, or complaining about the food—because if any of those were a yes, it was a guarantee they were breathing. Every nurse when presented with a new patient preferred the screaming expletive asshole over the obtunded. You can sedate the crazy. The other usually required a hefty dose of life saving. To Liv's worry, this guy fell some scary place in between.

The doors clanged shut so hard the glass rattled in the frame, and Liv flew into autopilot. Noise rumbled outside, but it should've been a stampede. A dozen people should have rushed in behind her. There should have been a battle for elbow room and people calling dibs for procedures. Nurses should have been delegating to the medics, residents giving orders to the nurses, and attendings barking at the residents, but there was nothing. Nothing but the hum of the negative pressure fan and the labored, raspy breaths of a man crying blood.

She tried to ignore the nagging sensation in her stomach. But something was wrong. The kind of wrong that usually meant a trip to the morgue. She took a calming breath and smiled. Fake it 'til you make it pageant training had its perks. Focus on the patient. Anticipate. Intervene. Reassess.

Liv turned up the oxygen and tugged her stethoscope from around her neck. "I don't suppose you speak a lick 'a English…"

Commotion broke outside, startling her attention away from the man on the stretcher. The sliding glass door opened a fraction. "*Olivia*! Don't get close…"

Of course it was Andy. Hearing him say her name

set her body on fire, but her brain was still pissed the fuck off.

"Dr. Cole, do I need to explain to you what a nurse does?" she called back.

A muscular forearm clawed through. Andy let out a frustrated groan, still sexier than hell. Smithson and Javier yelled over his shoulder as he charged through the sliver of open door. For whatever reason, it sounded as if Andy was being bullheaded and defiant.

"For the love of Christ, Liv, what are you doing?"

She hung her stethoscope around her neck. "I'm baking a cake. What does it look like I'm doing?"

He rolled his eyes.

"You don't get to be exasperated. His oxygen saturations were in the effing toilet."

He came up next to her, roughing a hand through his inky hair. "The last thing I am is exasperated…"

He towered over her as she worked. Overwhelming. Suffocating. For a second she couldn't breathe. She wanted more. So much more. But having him so close didn't fix a damn thing. It magnified the stab of deception. Her *own* deceptions. It only served as a reminder for how stupid and hypocritical she was being. Andy hadn't really lied. He was guilty of purposeful omission, a crime she was even more prolific in.

Seamless and silent, they went through the motions, anticipating the other's needs. She still couldn't believe she was the only one in the room, and if she wasn't so damned mad, she'd thank him for helping with the mundane "housekeeping tasks" docs didn't usually bother with. Up until this moment she was sure ER physicians were never taught how to put on a blood pressure cuff.

Liv smiled at his tender, compassionate hand. If possible, hearing him comfort the patient in broken

Spanish made her love him even more. She didn't understand a word, but she felt the empathy surge through his body.

She went through her usual paces, starting an IV and labeling the blood, annoyed and flattered at the attention Andy burned into her backside. She couldn't help herself and popped a hip while writing notes on her handy scrap of paper towel. Andy paused mid-Spanglish sentence. Liv grinned, self-satisfied and petty. She wasn't without flaws, and a tiny part of her relished the notion Andy needed a double take, except in a heartbeat something was different.

Liv turned and let herself be pulled into the concern woven between his eyes. For a moment she forgot why she was angry. She had forgotten the humiliation of foolishly falling for the same lines of crap. If he had just told her the truth from the beginning, she'd chalk it up to having a flipping type. Tall, dark-headed sex gods that happen to save lives for a living.

A wave of nervous energy prickled down her spine. She suppressed it with a few compulsive clicks to her clicky pen before fixing it to her scrub top and dropped the samples into the red Ziploc bag.

"I'm just gonna run these," she said. Explaining the obvious seemed like the only way to fill the growing gap between them. In a heartbeat the air became dense with everything they left unsaid. It was torture. Wanting him. Loving him. And hating him all at the same fucking time.

Her eyes began sting. She blinked away from his gaze. "I'll send in CiCi and that new guy from respiratory. I'm sure you want an arterial blood gas."

Andy stepped toward her and scratched at his chin. "Liv, you can't leave."

She checked her watch. "Yeah, I can. My three

hours are up."

He rubbed the back of his neck and winced. A blotch of deep red tried to seep through his shirt. She had to stop herself rushing over to take a look. He could super glue himself back together.

"If you had just sat through the damned staff meeting you'd—" he started, but of course she wouldn't let him finish.

"Well, you see I really wanted to, but I'd hit my max capacity for bullshit a few hours ago." It was unprofessional and a below the belt dig at his character, but she gave almost zero fucks.

His lips flatlined. Andy went from impassive to pissed off in an instant. The compassion that lightened his blue eyes went black. *Good.* It'd be easier to storm off when he looked like an arrogant, asshat trauma doc rather than the charming and sweet, Anderson Cole she'd fallen in love with. Even if they were one and the same.

Something in his hooded glare shot straight through her heart and down into her belly. She swallowed and sidestepped his dominant pose. He grabbed her arm. Demanding. Electric. Her breath trapped within her throat. "*Neither* of us can leave."

She stopped and looked up. The anger clenched in his jaw relaxed. Love lined his face and flowed through his fingers. "Liv, the patient has Hemorrhagic Fever."

She stared for an awkward second until inadvertent giggles welled in her chest. "Sure he does. And we're just locked in here together for three whole days and see if we die."

He pursed his lips into a frown and broke her gaze by looking through the ceiling.

"Oh my God. Wait. You're not... Are you serious?"

He sighed. "Yes."

Disbelief rippled through her. Nervous energy spiked in her blood, and she shifted from foot to foot. Her heart began to pound. She rambled her fear out loud to keep from throwing up. Andy let the shock sink in for a few seconds before bringing her back to reality.

"And if that ape y'all call a charge nurse has done what I told him to—the sliding door is sealed. You, me, and Jorge over there are contained for seventy-two hours."

Life drained from her face. Her lungs couldn't get enough air. The room with eighteen-foot ceilings and enough space for four stretchers quickly became a coffin. Her fingers began to tingle and cramp. She cupped her hands over her mouth and bent at the waist. Passing out from hyperventilation sure wouldn't help things. Andy placed his hands on her shoulders and traced his callused thumbs in circles into the base of her neck. Comfort infused from his grip. But she jumped away. From him. From Jorge. From the source of toxic air he exhaled.

She needed a minute. Or five. She needed to run herself into tight circles and pace. And bite her fucking nails. All she wanted was to be allowed to freak out like a normal person without an audience.

She turned her back on Andy prepping Jorge for intubation. She heard his Texan drawl infused into a few common medical words. The patronizing proverb that God never gives you more that you can handle popped into her brain. Now would be great time for Him to stop trying to prove the point.

The patient moaned and choked on his gurgling secretions.

She glared at Heaven. "*C'mon…* can't you give a girl second?"

Over her shoulder she heard Andy's warm

chuckle and the screech and hiss of suction. He was certainly handling things like a man unafraid to die.

Olivia straightened and pulled on a fresh pair of big girl panties. But after Rose's death. Andy's surprise. And the awesome knowledge she'd been exposed to a highly infections, deadly contagion with no cure, at this rate she was going to plumb run out.

She sucked in a hard breath, then forced it through tight lips. Her pageant smile reappeared, and so did clarity. Jorge was just a normal patient. Andy was just a normal doctor, even if he was a hotter-than-should-be-legal doctor.

She avoided his gaze as came back to the bedside. Who knew what kind of black hole his baby blues would send her down? Without looking at one another, they went through the effortless, choreographed motions doctors and nurses develop over time. Her first instinct was to smile at their partnership. Caring for patients with Dr. Cole, boyfriend or not, heartbroken or whole, would be a privilege. Jorge was their first patient and, she hoped to God, not their last.

"If you knew what was going on here, why come back? Why put yourself at risk?" She felt his pull, but kept focusing on tasks.

"Do you really need to ask me that?"

She tried to occupy herself by clearing Jorge's airway and fidgeting with his lines, making mental notes of other random things to do for three whole days. Like where she'd pee.

"Why aren't you freaking out?"

Andy glanced at the sealed door and up to the gallery as if he expected an audience. "Remember when I said I'd done some mission work in Central America?"

Torn between a smart assed, woman scorned retort and proper Savannahian civility, she went with the latter and offered a nod. Andy came around the head of the bed, encroached on her space. Deliberate or not it made her ache.

"Last year. Three hundred and eighty-seven days to be exact. I was where Jorge was."

She stopped what she was doing and searched his face. Something made him grimace. "I'd made a half dozen trips to Guatemala over the last few years helping these folks and the orphans left behind. Never so much as a cold, but that time it got me. I was lying in a strange bed, not sure if I was going to close my eyes and never wake up. But I did. I was the first."

The monitor blared to life. Andy swore under his breath. She knew what it meant, what had to happen next. Liv loved her state-of-the-art ER. Every tool and medication she could possibly need were kept at a finger's reach. She even had access to a few units of blood and platelets. The resuscitation room had it all. Except a fucking toilet.

Liv frowned into Jorge's pale, agonized face. "I'll get the meds."

****

Jorge's blood and sputum filled intubation climbed into the "hard-as-fuck" top three, only successful because Olivia's ability to anticipate. For him. And for Jorge.

Taking a minute to appreciate the calm after the crazy, Andy washed his hands in the sink. Liv watched, clicking the hell out of her pen. Blank. Almost stoic, he could see the wheels of thought grinding away as she anticipated where down the rabbit whole Jorge was fixin' to go.

God, she was a good nurse.

They spent the following hour in an awkward silence. Both jumped to Jorge's bedside at the slightest alarm, followed by forced and exponentially uncomfortable doctor and nurse speak. It was enough punishment simply to be locked in a room with a woman you've just seen naked knowing she wants to knee you in the 'nads every six seconds. The unsaid tortured the air.

Finally, the tension broke. A distraction. Smithson appeared in the overhead viewing gallery, as if to make his omnipresence known with an update and chitchat.

The CDC was flying in from Atlanta, and should the patient be stable enough, would be transported to NIH Research Hospital. The medics had been safely quarantined, and because of Andy's quick involvement with their dispatch, their preliminary screens were negative.

Possibly, the best news by far, efforts were in place to use the scrub room as an ante-chamber. He and Liv couldn't leave, but at least they'd get food and supplies that weren't six-month-old saltines. He already thanked the few lucky stars he had left for the ability to pee in a jug and was pretty sure Liv's nurses' bladder would hold indefinitely.

Liv sat at her stool, quite possibly charting her life away on a patient with less a than six percent chance at survival. His stomach turned. Of all the bells and whistles the unit had, he didn't have access to the screen that could tell him the answer to the question both were afraid to ask.

"So, do you think Smithson will be babysitting us all night?"

The question pulled him from his thoughts and shot straight to his groin. Liv didn't look up from her screen, continuing her up-to-the-minute notes while he sat half the room away, doing nothing but doodle in his scratch pad and fixate on Olivia's statistical chances.

She finished clicking at the computer, then stood and stretched. He caught a glimpse of skin along her flank as she pulled the knot that held back her hair and shook out her shimmery curls. It had to be intentional. A means to drive him insane. Mad with want and disappointment.

Andy roughed a hand through his hair and looked into the gallery. The lights above their heads were still on, but it appeared their boss had stepped out for a snooze in the trauma lounge. "Looks like Smithson needed some beauty sleep."

Liv forced a smile and did a once over the intubated and sedate Jorge. With the monitors satisfied by his stabilized vitals, it was sad but true, he'd already become like a piece of furniture. A toxic, time-bomb coffee table. As if she heard the silent pleas for closeness, Liv came to stand a few inches away. Her vanilla and cinnamon scent permeated the air, and Jorge's septic stench became a memory. Her lithe fingers intertwined with his for an agonizing second, then glided them up his forearm to the makeshift Band-Aid CiCi slapped on before he dove into the trauma room. She began her own tender ritual, peeling away the soaked bandage, then cleansing the skin beneath.

Between each swipe of sterile saline, she asked questions with the hushed voice that had a dangerous habit of turning him on. "Was your grand plan just to sleep with me?"

"No. But I would be lying if I didn't admit it was high on my list of priorities."

Her lips curled. "So, we're telling the truth now, are we?"

Liv seemed intent to bust his balls, and he was going to sit there and take the beating like a man. He couldn't help it. He flashed her the smart assed smirk that on more than one occasion turned her cheeks a sexy shade of red and made sure to lay his twang on good and thick. "On my honor as a Texan, Olivia. No more lies. Can you say the same to me?"

She clenched her bottom lip between her teeth and examined the floor. Her conflict ripped a hole in his gut. Nothing she could say would change how he felt about her. She sighed and gave him a tight nod. Something in her silent submission tore away his resolve to be a professional, *and* patient for Liv to give him a green light. He had to kiss her. Like his lungs needed air, he needed the weight and warmth of her lips on his.

Andy wove his fingers into her hair and searched her eyes for protest, any tell that would halt him in his tracks. But need and longing crinkled along her brow. His mouth watered.

"You guys okay down there?" boomed Smithson through the gallery intercom. Anderson shot upright, holding his hands away from Liv's body to prove he wasn't just touching a female coworker in a less than appropriate way.

Liv held her position, casually drawing her attention to Andy's side then turned to address the interruption in the ceiling.

"We're fine, sir. Just tryin' to see what happened here to Dr. Cole." She slid her hands under his shirt, dancing her fingertips along his stomach. His heart started to pound, and as if the whole clusterfuck weren't punishment enough, his dick got hard like a freshman in gym glass.

Liv giggled, warm and amused. "Olfactory, Optic, Oculomotor…"

Andy chuckled and let out a sigh, wishing he could shower her with the love that swelled within his ribs and rub out the ache in his cock by pulling her onto his lap. The sexual teasing had a way of deescalating the situation, and if it weren't for the half dead man, the hum of the ventilator, and the noise from overhead, they could've been anywhere else.

"I'm all right, Allen. Jorge got a good whack at me before I brought him in."

"Good thing you've got Nurse Olivia in there. She'll fix you up," Smithson said between popping chips into his mouth and loud chews. Liv pulled up the rest of his shirt and exposed the damage.

Anderson straightened and held in a wince. He tried for a cavalier smile, but it ended up a grimace.

"Should I be insanely jealous that Smithson gets to call you Olivia?"

"Will it make you buy me something expensive if we get out of here?"

The word "If" made him want to vomit, but if Liv was going to take this in stride, so was he.

He grinned. "Absolutely."

"Then yes. Be very jealous." She turned to glare up at Smithson, who had moved on to slurping down his late-night snack with a swig of Coke and jumbo jug of water. She smiled through gritted teeth.

"We're only starving, with no place to pee except the sink. Think he knows he's being an inconsiderate boss?" she asked, pressing her knees together.

"No, I don't think so."

Liv went through the motions, cleansing the multiple abrasions to his side. He might have been able to talk his hard-on down, but there was no stunting his ego after Liv's eyes went wide with some sort of flustered want. Her hands shook as she sealed the bandage over the wound, jumping off her stool after her fingertips grazed his skin.

He ran a hand over the congealed, rubbery blood

blotting his scrub top and opted for a standard issue blue one from the storage cabinet. Sure, he looked like one of the drunk and disorderlies after they'd pissed themselves, but at least he was clean.

Dozens of eyes fixated on him as he pulled the shirt over his head, but none of them belonged to Liv. The gallery filled with extra bodies using their break time to watch them like monkeys at the zoo. Stupid ER people and their morbid curiosity. He couldn't fault them. He'd do the exact same thing.

"Any idea when we'll get that scrub room up and running, Smithson? I think Olivia would agree. A pizza might be nice."

Idle chatter cackled through the intercom while sly glances bounced between the ladies lining the gallery walls. The few men rolled their eyes. Except one. Javier crossed his arms and glared. It took every ounce of self-control not to sweep Liv in his arm and claim her for Javi's benefit.

They locked eyes. Andy placed a palm against Liv's back and murmured an order for another dose of anti-virals and platelets. He grinned, relishing the win.

"Two hours tops, Anderson. The guys from Atlanta got deferred to St. Louis and should be here by sun up. Flurries came in this evening. You'd think O'Hare had never seen snow before."

He nodded, then turned his attention to Jorge and Liv working over him. He inspected for signs of DIC or hemorrhage. If overwhelming sepsis didn't do you in there always was the pesky little complication of bleeding out. So far there'd only been one episode of hemoptysis and some blood in his urine.

Andy motioned to the phone. Smithson licked his fingers clean and reached for the receiver. For all his streamlined precision, he appeared to be like the rest of them. Pork rinds and diet soda as a means to placate stress.

"How about a little privacy, boss?" he growled, way past the point of southern civility. Smithson went on the defensive about learning procedures and crowd control. It was not what he wanted to hear. "Do I need to remind you that Olivia could be next? And you're treating this like fucking show and tell."

Smithson carried on with valid points about being a teaching hospital and other lines of bullshit that meant nothing until Andy heard the words, "Fine. I'll clear the gallery."

Andy watched Liv through his peripheral vision. The constant ache of attraction rushed to his groin. She rolled her head from side to side, and his mouth watered, remembering the tang of sex on her skin. He wanted to run his tongue along her shoulder. This was hell. He was sure of it.

She grimaced. The pain etched across her face intensified as she cracked a few knuckles and rotated her ankles.

An ache flared. But it wasn't lust. It was fear.

"Allen," he breathed into the phone. He searched the gallery for his eyes. "You need to get me the prelim swabs."

Chapter Eighteen

There's only so much freaking out a girl can take before splitting in two, and Liv was pretty sure she had surpassed her max level of suppressing shit an hour ago. She needed a caffeine drip, PRN shots of her Grandaddy's moonshine, and a few hits of Xanax. Not necessarily in that order. Jorge, on the other hand, needed a central line, pressors, and a rectal tube in exactly that order. Too bad it seemed pretty clear she was closer to being able to mainline coffee than getting Jorge the interventions he needed to stay alive—and to make cleaning up his blood-tinged poop any easier.

Liv dragged her desk right alongside the stretcher. Jorge and all the machines that kept him stable were clustered in the center of the room under the spotlights and heat lamps. He was his own island while she and Andy floated around in a little rowboat of sexual angst and worry.

Her pulse thumped away in her temple. Everything began to ache. Joints. Muscles. Breaking her sexy time dry spell left her sore in places she forgot existed, and it didn't help that Anderson was being all charmingly arrogant, and intensely tender at the same time. If worrying about her own odds at defying death, while trying to save an actively dying man didn't split her down the middle, being tormented by loving lust and her own heartbreaking deceptions sure would.

Andy appeared to be taking the disaster in stride, but that didn't mean he didn't let his apprehension show every now and again.

"Are you sure you feel all right?" he asked. It was the third time he'd asked in the last hour.

She nodded with a rush of red to her cheeks. "My recent workout routine finally caught up with me."

His lips curled in a wry smile, but it didn't relax the tension in his neck.

"And it's not a flipping fever, all right. I've always run a little hot."

Andy rolled his stool across their invisible line of caution and brought her gaze to his. With the gallery deserted, he'd been lax about the way he handled her. And truthfully, she wanted it that way. If she really could die in a few days, she wanted to feel the touch of a man who loved her. Perhaps it was that threat of death that pushed her to accept to Andy's stupid guy decisions, but she sure as hell wasn't ready to admit to it yet.

His blue eyes searched hers. It was as if he knew whatever he'd say would come out wrong or be misconstrued, so he relied on the unsaid to convey his message. His touch was clinical as he gently pulled down her lower lid and flashed a pen light in her eyes. "See nothing to worry about, doc. Not dying yet."

He frowned. "Christ, that's not funny."

"Well … maybe not 'LOL' or anything. He needs a central line. I may be the best stick in town, but this guy's running out of places to hit, and only so many drugs play nice together."

Andy scratched at his chin. "I know, but I don't want to give the guy another place to bleed from."

"Then get it on the first try, silly," she said with a smile. She didn't mean to flirt, but Andy lovingly lapped it up.

"Thank you for that sound piece of nursing advice, Nurse Olivia. But first…" The lights in the scrub room flickered on. The phone rang. Andy jumped from his chair, pulled too close to Olivia to be considered professional, and grabbed the receiver.

Smithson appeared overhead. They had a quick, unpleasant sounding conversation before Andy hung up.

He charged to the sealed door, and Liv followed at a hesitant distance. Andy peeled back layers of trauma tape used to seal them shut. The doors opened a fraction. Sugary sweet marinara, meatballs, and garlic floated through the air. The cheap stuff. But she didn't care. Even on the outskirts of a college town, the only thing open at three AM was Papa John's, and right then, it smelled like steak and lobster swimming in butter and truffle oil.

Andy dove through the crack and retrieved two pizzas and a box of supplies. She'd kiss Smithson if he left her deodorant and a RedBull, but before she got the chance to check, Andy was already in front of her prying open her mouth. And not the way a girl hoped her guy would. He tugged at her chin and popped her cheek to the side, then thrust a sterile swab into the back of her throat.

It was the least sexy thing he'd ever done, and she'd seen him wipe poop from another man's butt crack.

"Sorry," he mumbled double bagging the sample before shoving it through the newly constructed anti-chamber. "I can't think with that looming over our heads."

Liv nodded, touched by his concern, but it chipped away the final brick that dammed up her fear. She turned away from him, her throat tight. God, she wanted to cry. She *needed* a good fucking cry, but nurses didn't. Not at work. Not on the clock. And as sure as the sun would rise tomorrow, Liv expected triple pay.

Andy placed a hand on her shoulder, stopping her retreat. As if he could read her thoughts, he turned her into his chest and held her there. Strong. Protective. And apparently not giving a crap about Smithson's eyes in the ceiling, he brought her face to his and kissed her.

Screw a good ugly cry. A delicate, church-tongued kiss from Dr. Anderson Cole had the effect of two bottles of her favorite red. She pulled away, love drunk and satisfied.

"Shall we dine, cowboy?"

They ate in silence, pressed into the furthest corner of the trauma room. Between chews she stole glances at Jorge then back at Andy, trying not to imagine herself half naked and dying on a stretcher. There had to be a cure. Something they could do besides play catch up to the disease process, but it was a bad idea to travel down the road of "What if?" It meant she'd need to make a call. *The* call. And not the one she owed Lottie or the disaster that would be her mother.

She checked her watch. Eight hours crawled by. Smithson was kind enough to include a cellphone charger. The moment Andy's phone chirped to life, he suggested a *Friends* marathon.

"Netflix and chill, huh?" she teased with a mouth full of greasy pizza.

"I do believe it would qualify as a sixth date," he said, low and swoony, with a smile so genuine her heart fluttered within her ribs. But behind the smile was the fear he couldn't hide. Jorge's monitor wailed. Whatever sorry excuse for a date they were having was over.

They rose to their feet to check on Jorge. No way to sugarcoat it, Jorge looked like shit. Pale. Mottled. Stiff from fever, if it weren't for a weak but steady pulse threading beneath her fingers, she'd be calling the medical examiner's office.

"Seriously, Andy. We're due for another round of PRBC's and platelets. I'm maxed out on all our drips. He needs a—"

"I know." He pinched the bridge of his nose. "All right, let's set up for a central line," he ordered, but Liv was already waist deep in the supply cupboard. "I know you're up there, Smithson. How about you get me a sono machine."

Dressing Andy in his sterile gown gave her a tingle of pride. Like she was sending her soldier into battle. She'd seen dozens, if not a hundred, central lines placed over the seven years she'd been a nurse. Just like IVs and arterial sticks for nurses, some doctors were just better than others. Sometimes it was just a string of shitty luck. Liv didn't know where Andy fell on the spectrum. But if his blind intubation were any indication, Andy'd do the procedure with his eyes closed just for the challenge.

Feeling less than sexy, Liv donned her hat, gloves, and mask before setting up Andy's supplies. Sterile technique, standard precautions, both seemed silly given the circumstances, but it was one more thing to stop her from flying over the cuckoo's nest. Ever since he said the words, "The Blood Flu", the only way to stem anxiety fits and staring at Anderson's ass was to fiddle with her pen, obsessively organize, and disinfect everything the light touched. About as useful as a fish with roller skates, but it kept her busy and made it seem like she had her shit together.

Andy made several injections with an anesthetic through the salad plate sized hole in the sterile drape. Jorge hadn't moved in hours, and his blood pressure was such crap, weaning sedation was a must right after intubation, but they had the good-bad luck that he was so far gone, Jorge didn't need the milk of amnesia IV drip, Porpofol to keep him calm.

Andy eyed the stretcher's position. "Liv, would you—"

Knowing what he needed before he even opened his mouth, she stomped on the pedal and dropped Jorge's head a few degrees. His mask hid the vast majority of his face, but wrinkles sprouted around his baby blues. She made sure he caught the little flirty flick of her eyebrow before turning her gaze downward.

Liv held her breath as Andy made the first and what she hoped would be the only incision in Jorge's neck just above the clavicle. Like a hot knife through butter, the long needle seemed to be swallowed into the hollow of his throat. Smooth. Effortless. Dark venous blood flashed back. She exhaled, and if the roll of Andy's shoulders were any indication, he did, too. It was a victory. One hit meant less risk for bleeding. It would be downhill from here.

But juju be damned, half dead Jorge bucked to life.

****

Blame evolution, but the knee jerk reaction was to flail back and prevent self-harm as Jorge convulsed, wretched and writhed in pain, but Andy held steady clenching his gloved fist around Jorge's shoulder. Blood oozed from the site, but the guidewire was present and accounted for.

Liv let a few of her favorite curse words fly before she flew under the drape. "How can this be happening? His BP is seventy over forty."

Andy knew. It was all part of the disease. The fucked up, bass-akwards disease that violently took a person's life. The tighter his fingers held the line steady the more Jorge flailed. It was no use barking orders at Liv and how to handle the crazy. She was doing the best she could, and he'd be a lying, cocky prick if he thought for a second he could do any better.

She dropped to her knees before his feet and grabbed Jorge's arm. Andy tried not to focus on how twenty-four hours before she was in the same exact position doing something very different. The ventilator screeched in revolt, and Jorge was seconds shy of coughing up his intubation tube. That was a good boner killer.

Liv whipped out a slipknot wrist restraint in six seconds flat. She tugged her mask down, gasping for breath. "I usually don't show off that skill until the tenth date."

A man shouldn't grin during the seconds that split life and death. But that's what he did. He loved her. Wanted her. And Christ forgive him, while Liv busied herself with trying to keep Jorge safe, calm, and alive, he used all of his energy to beg the Lord to skip Jorge and save Olivia.

The constant alarm drew an audience. Smithson was either delirious with sleep deprivation, or he was being an ass. "You guys think he needs a little sedation?"

"No. None at all. He's handling it *fine*," Andy said. Sweat prickled along his forehead and dripped down his back. Jorge's blood saturated the thin, paper gown and stuck between his gloved fingers. Bright white lights conflicted with his brain's need for sleep, and the goggles he wore began to mist. He was a fucking mess, but Liv was as sexy as ever tucking a stray strand of copper back into her scrub cap. She beamed with trite, southern civility into the gawkers in the gallery while she rummaged through drawers and cabinets.

"Must be nice to micromanage from up there, Dr. Smithson. Would you like to change places? 'Cause, I'm awful tired."

The gallery went silent. Smithson muttered something that resembled an apology as Jorge weakened. Blood tinged tears trickled down his cheeks. Seeing Jorge's pain ripped him in shreds.

Liv stood at the bedside drawing the medication from the vial, the needless cap wedged between her teeth.

"Five of Versed?"

"Whatever he needs," Andy advised. Liv patted an unopened vial taped over her heart, expecting him to say just that.

She dove under the drape, while he threaded the central line catheter down the guide wire. Liv tried to talk Jorge down. Singing sweet lies in her warm, honeyed twang about how they'd get him feeling better, how they'd help him rest, and how he was in good hands with him as his doctor.

Liv reemerged as he placed the last stitch securing the central line into Jorge's jugular. Exhaustion replaced her radiant sexiness. Exhaustion that had nothing to do with insomnia. Straight up mental and physical burn out.

A smear of bright red doused her cheek. Fear prickled Andy's scalp. He ripped himself out of the gown and gloves, then crossed the room to make sure she was okay.

"Don't worry about me. I'm fine. He's bleeding from his gums."

"Shit. If he goes into DIC, Liv, he's gone."

She nodded and rubbed her temples.

He wiped her cheek with the hem of his throwaway scrub shirt, and like an old habit, she braced her hands on his hips and rested her forehead against his chest.

"Baby. Take a nap."

She crinkled her nose.

"Are you too modern and self-sufficient for a man to call you 'Baby'?"

"No. I loved that. It's the nap part."

Andy tilted her chin to lock their eyes. Her green eyes brightened to emeralds under the fluorescents. It had to be her strong-willed, southern woman pride.

"Jesus Christ, Liv, no one would think less of you if you needed to take a thirty-minute nap. Don't go telling people, but I do know how to hang blood and write down vital signs."

Her smile made his heart ache and cock twitch, but the sexy grin dissolved in a gulp of air.

He searched her eyes. "What's the matter?"

She squeezed them shut as if it was his gaze that caused her such pain. The thought alone gutted him from stem to stern.

"Look at me." He had no intention of forcing her, and his heart just about stopped when she finally did. "Tell me what's wrong."

"No. It's fine. I'm being stupid is all…" she muttered, shaking her head. If he let her, she'd walk away. Dismiss her feelings or fears and shelve it for another day. Except she might not have that luxury. Why was she so hell bent on not opening up? He might not have been honest about *what* he was, but he sure as hell was honest about *who* he was.

He frowned. What had broken her so badly she felt he wouldn't want to bear her burdens? He didn't care about their medical director, and the hordes of nosey people in the gallery, or that she smelled more of Jorge's bloody sweat than her usual vanilla and cinnamon. Andy held her heart to heart and wove his fingers into her hair. "Let me be here for you."

She rubbed her face into his shirt, as if she intended to burrow under the flesh and bone, then turned her gaze to Jorge. Grey. Listless. Crying tears of blood. "Andy, I'm afraid that if I close my eyes … I'll never wake up."

****

Through some genetic weakness, Andy convinced her to sleep. Power naps used to be her thing.

In nursing school, she had it down to a science. While she did her time in Hot-Lanta's busiest trauma center working twelve day stretches because she was addicted to the adrenaline and prestige, tricking the brain to survive on forty-minute cycles of sleep was essential for survival.

She curled into an upright ball, wedged between a cold, chrome storage cabinet and the spare ventilator. Not as bad as falling asleep waiting for the 'L, but close. Andy sat at her feet, knees tucked under his chin, back to the wall as if his presence could keep the bad juju at arm's length. Except she knew better. Shit happened in threes, and it took more than a call to Heaven and a sex on a stick ED physician to keep it away.

Liv snored herself awake, blinking in the bright light. A trickle of drool hung on her lower lip. She should've been mortified, but Andy already had a first class look at her less than sexy sleep habits. He stood at the other side of the room talking in a hushed voice into the telephone. Her pupils rebelled in exhaustion, squinting him in focus. He rubbed the back of his neck, then hugged his arm over his chest. She didn't expect him to be an emotionless robot, but panic tweaked in her belly. She needed to smack some chewing gum or click the hell out of her clicky pen, STAT, except both were victims of Jorge's recent tantrum.

Andy turned around, his worry transformed. Joy. Elation. But above all relief. He hung up the phone and crossed the room in three long strides.

"Negative, baby. The screens are negative. A few more hours and we'll have confirmation." He pulled her from the floor with enough strength her shoulders popped. His arms coiled around her waist and spreading the width of her back and up her ribs. He sealed his lips to hers. Hard. Demanding. Unrelenting in his quest to kiss life into her. A kiss that sent tingles up her spine and goosebumps down her arms. So wrong. So right. And so inappropriate if she didn't have the excuse she might die in a few days.

He stepped back and read the flush on her cheeks. She shot a demure glance at poor half-dead Jorge, then their boss in the ceiling. A sheepish, apologetic grin curled on his lips for manhandling her with little care of time or place.

"Oh yeah, everyone knows and have been taking bets to as to when we'd have sex in the supply closet."

Her blush deepened and crawled down her chest. Nothing was more embarrassing than being outed as a couple because they had less control than a pair of hormonal teenagers. Still, she floated in the way he looked at her. His gaze hit her right in the heart and right between her legs. "Think we'll fit?"

Andy took a palm full of her behind and squeezed.

"Down, boy," she whispered to the sudden build of desire pressed into her pelvis.

Andy's lips hardened. Of course. Something bad had to follow the good. "So, the CDC is stuck in Joliet. The flurries turned into a mid-October blizzard, and I-355 is under two feet of snow. Needless to say, Jorge is stuck with us for a while longer."

Liv turned her eyes to Smithson and the fresh-as-a-daisy day shift charge nurse. Maybe she'd cave and put on the paper panties Smithson gifted from the Mom and Baby floor. "My triple time just doubled," she grumbled knowing her demands would be laughed at, but when she took her Nightingale pledge and signed on the dotted line of her contract, she never imagined this kind of situation would be part of the deal.

Money and sick people as job security should

never be a nurse's motivation. Even on the hardest days Liv loved her job, but the money she made saving lives didn't pay for her preference for Louboutin's, alligator clutches, and newest innovation in skincare. The money had purpose. It helped ensure a future for a person she'd never see again.

"You know, Liv, when I texted you a plan to enact sexy time revenge, this wasn't the direction I thought you'd go," yawned a girlie voice watching the Olivia and Andy show. Torey's little black head popped through the standing room only gallery lurkers. She either found a chair to stand on, or was sitting on the shoulders of her new steady, Leo.

Liv unwound herself from Andy's grip, did a quick once over of Jorge for good measure, and signaled for Torey to grab the phone. Torey pushed through the group of dayshift-ers Liv didn't know wearing an elite grin.

"I knew there was a reason to talk to you on the train last week. You're famous. So am I by association."

Behind her, Andy thumbed through Jorge's serial, i-Stat lab results, then tweaked the ventilator settings. Her heart threatened to burst when he dabbed blood away from Jorge's face, and grabbed a new gown from the linen cart.

Torey gasped. "Well I'll be goddammed? Is he going to change his sheets?"

Olivia straightened with pride. "He sure is. Will you go ahead and tell all those wet-pantied vultures in there, he's mine?"

Torey giggled and glared at the swooning women cramped in the twenty by ten space.

"No time for the usual witty pleasantries, I'm afraid. I'm really glad to see you."

"Of course you are, I'm awesome."

Liv laughed and looked up into the gallery. "Do you work tonight?"

Torey shook her head and stroked Leo's bicep.

"Well if you can spare Leo his own sexy time. I need you to do me a huge favor."

She put on her serious face. "Do ya need me to cut someone? Blondie behind me looks pretty pissed."

"Harder than that, friend. I need you head over to my house to go on a panty run for me."

"Vixen," she purred. "How hot on the hot scale?"

Liv shifted from foot to foot. A thong seemed like such a good idea when she imagined Andy peeling it off with his teeth. "Make it a matching set of sevens."

Torey nodded in approval at her practicality, and mumbled something to a hidden person behind her. She turned back around, mid eyeroll. "Sometimes I wonder how I lasted here for five years. Give me an hour."

That fixed one hurdle. She'd feel like a new woman after a fresh pair of britches. She usually kept a spare set of everything in her locker, but she blew through those her last shift during "banana bag" discount night.

"And as if I haven't asked too much as it is, I need you to run to that liquor store on Clarke and buy a friend of mine a case of Jack Daniels."

Chapter Nineteen

Liv knew Torey was a rare gem in the friendship world, but her willingness to drop everything and be her panty go-for, *and* the means to liquor up Lottie before Liv called in an hour tipped her into the saintly category. Andy and Dr. Smithson spent the morning on a conference call with the suits from Atlanta still stuck in BFE, Illinois.

Her silly girl mind wandered, doodling Mrs. Cole on a scrap piece of paper. She needed to come clean. It was time. It was time to see if he really was the kind of man he swore up and down to be after discovering her closet was half full of skeletons. The black kind of secrets a woman would rather carry to her grave than tarnish the image she was supposed to uphold. The secrets and shame that make a girl run away from home and her family to a frigid, blue state with the hope no one, especially her Momma, would want to come find her.

By the grace of God, a new clicky pen materialized in the second box of goodies left in the ante-chamber, along with black tar coffee, a dozen Krispy Kremes, and a gallon jug of water. She'd had her fill of squatting over the hopper in the dirty utility closet and had resolved to turn into a raisin before having another sip of liquid.

She compulsively clicked her pen, waiting for the fifteenth lab draw to complete. The little gun spit out Jorge's results, which lo and behold were worse than an hour before. She crinkled her nose and turned to Andy with his feet propped up at her makeshift nurse's desk. She sure did love him, but the temptation to kick the back leg of the chair itched her feet.

"You know, I've been thinking…"

"That's no good. I don't like my girl to have a brain," Andy interjected, more hillbilly than handsome.

Liv laughed and stuck up her middle finger. "Jorge's blood type is AB. Why don't we try a transfusion from you? Isn't that what fixed the missionary physician that survived Ebola last fall? I think he even paid it forward with the nurses in Dallas."

"It didn't work for the patient—he still died. I don't think the transfusion fixed him, Liv. That was statistics and good luck."

She shrugged. "Then what are we doing in here, Anderson?"

He rubbed his temples and gave her an appeasing smile. "You're right. We'll try. But I have to warn you, I'm terrified of needles."

She leaned into his space and ran a finger over the rope of a vein that run up his forearm. "That's good. I've got a fourteen gauge with your name on it."

A loud bang shook the glass in the gallery above them. The door must have crashed open, then slammed shut. The noise broke their moment and Andy's balance. He fell backward like a kid falling asleep in detention.

"Olivia-Grace MacArthur Aberdeen. You have six seconds to tell me what the hell is going on down there."

Charlotte VanSutton clinked her stilettos up the tile stairs in a blaze of Savahannian glory. Her chocolate locks flowed with a fresh blow out rivaling Duchess Kate, and her dewy complexion could only come from Jean Luc at the Four Seasons. "I swear to God, Livy, you had better have a damn good reason you didn't call the moment you got locked in there with Doc McFibberPants."

Andy rose from his seat. Liv knew he wasn't in the mood to be hounded, nor patient and polite. He'd already given her the CliffsNote synopsis of Lottie's threat and the subsequent promise to cut off his balls if he kept lying.

"Glad to see you've been busy, Lot," Olivia said, gesturing to her fifteen-hundred-dollar makeover.

The proud line of her lips softened, and she shrugged out of her trench. "I needed to put a dent in Teddy's AMX Black. Are you all right?"

She wished there wasn't ten feet and two inches of glass between them. If there was one thing her stuck-up, childhood BFF was good for, it was a hug. "The preliminary tests are negative. Other than a case of bad breath, and panty rot I think I'll survive."

"You don't have bad breath," Andy jumped in.

Liv looked over with a wink.

"Mind your business, Dr. Cole," Charlotte snipped. "Is there some way we can have a proper hen hack without everyone and their brother listening?"

Liv motioned to the receiver. Lottie reciprocated on the other end. "So, I guess this is what'll be like if one of us ends up in prison. You don't have to worry about the panty rot. I brought you some new underpinnings," she said and held up a plastic Jewel bag. Liv cringed seeing her fine, Parisian lingerie in a grocery sack. "Speakin' a which, you owe that sweet friend of yours, a new pair… She came knocking on the door at six in the morning, and I went looking for your Granddaddy's gun."

"I really wish you hadn't come all the way down here. I *am* fine." She felt Andy's eyes caress her back. "It should only be one more day, and the fellas from the CDC will come and take over."

Lottie nodded, subdued, like the fire she flew in with suddenly fizzled. Liv saw right through her best friend's brash exterior, knowing it was to cover the huge lump of fear in her throat.

"How's my LouLou?"

"Kickin' ass and takin' names. As usual." A hard pause cleaved their easy banter. A glare cut in to the glass hiding Lottie's face. "I'm sorry about Rose."

Olivia straightened, then hung her head. Suppressed grief welled in her eyes. As if he could sense her pain, Andy came over and placed a comforting hand along her back.

"I talked to Smithson. We should get started, Liv." He darted a glace to Lottie that was more arrogant asshat than arrogant charmer before walking away.

A low rumble came through the receiver. Liv's tears melted away with a laugh. "Don't you go growling at my boyfriend, Mrs. VanSutton."

She huffed. "So, have you told your boyfriend why we hate men like him?"

"I think you might be overgeneralizing men in the profession, Charlotte dear."

Liv almost heard Lottie's eyes roll and looked over her shoulder. Andy stood at Jorge's feet, arms folded over his chest. Intense thought weighed on his features. She wished she could rub out the tension in his neck.

Once again, the door banged open. Smithson appeared in the gallery, stealing some of Lottie's space. In a bizarre but predictable beat, Lottie flashed the late middle-aged physician her trademark Miss Georgia Sweet Peach smile and batted her eyelashes. Charlotte VanSutton sure had a soft spot for silver foxes.

"Sorry to interrupt, ladies," Smithson said through the main intercom. Andy turned around. "But it seems visitors are arriving for everyone. Anderson … your um … your wife is here."

Liv's mouth popped as if to scream and spun on

her heel. She stared his deception in the face. He didn't deny, cower, or have the decency to drop onto his knees and grovel.

Her fingers clenched and she bit her cheek to prevent from flying into the less than professional category.

Charlotte on the other hand had no reason to hold back. Her cackle could be heard in hell. "Over generalizing my ass."

****

In medicine when your patient is fixin' to die, there stood a fairly decent chance whatever you do will help in *some* way. A Band-Aid over a bullet whole will at least try to stem the bleeding. This was one of those rare moments Andy wished God would grant him a "do-over," because with every attempt to put out a fire, it didn't just blow up in his face, it swallowed him whole and sprouted five more.

Liv's green eyes pierced Andy's skin with the precision of a scalpel. He didn't even have time to look shocked or confused. Or figure out how to plead his case. He just stood there wearing the same glib, mortified expression that appears when your mom finds your stash of porn.

"Well, Jesus Christ. Of course, you're married."

He rushed to her side. She folded in on herself and stared at the floor. He shot contempt at the gallery. It wasn't Smithson's fault, but someone had to absorb his anger, and if he so much as looked at Charlotte and her purse-lipped judgment he'd lose his mind. And there was still the fucking task of saving a dying man.

"I'm not married. I'm divorced." Bile burned the back of his throat. He hadn't said it before, and for some reason, it made him feel like a shit rather than a man free from the clutches of a cold, vindictive wife.

Liv took a deep breath and marched to the supply cabinet, intent to use her job as a means to avoid talking to him. He wanted to touch her. He wanted to give her some space. He wanted to put his fist through the goddamned wall. She took an arm full of supplies and motioned with her chin for him to sit.

He did as she instructed and rested an outstretched forearm on a rolling table. Overhead, Smithson cleared his throat before ruining another moment. "Anderson, your *ex*-wife—seems pretty insistent on coming up. Something about being your emergency contact—"

"Allen," he boomed, looking into the gallery. "I don't care what line of bull you need to sell. Get Greta out of here."

"If your ex flew up here on her broomstick, I'll show her my pitchfork. I'll handle it," Charlotte said with a sweet smile that made the grown man next to her blush. "Shall I fetch a shovel, Dr. Cole?"

Andy snorted, not wanting to give Lottie the satisfaction of making him laugh. Liv kept working, stiff backed and silent. She waved at her friend with a gloved hand.

"Andy, you find a way to fix this, and remember, Livy, I'll need a play by play."

Lottie's high heels clicked down the stairs. He imagined the waiting room erupting in flames when Charlotte faced off with Greta. Liv wrapped a tourniquet around his arm. The slip-knotted rubber snapped and pinched his skin. After a few pounds of his heart, his arm began to throb, then turn a ruddy blue. A punishment he'd have to take. But when her hand gripped the larger than necessary IV catheter, a panicked sweat dotted his lip.

"And when was I going to be privy to this

important piece of information?" she asked, swiping an alcohol pad over his numb and pulsing arm.

"Liv, I never lied about being married. I didn't want to bring it up."

She met his gaze, a huge "What the fuck, asshole?" plastered across her face.

Her hands started to shake. Her thin, nimble fingers couldn't seem to open the package holding her very sharp, very large IV. He reached over to help, but he should've known the offer would be less than welcome.

"I don't need your help," she said with fraying patience. She slammed her fist on the counter. "Of course, it never came up. You were too busy trying to sleep with me."

That was the line. He'd take the beating when it was deserved, but that kind of dig was so far out of bounds it was in a different time zone. He flicked the tourniquet loose and rallied off the rolling stool. She could be mad. She was within her right. But he wasn't the kind of creep that would fuck her first and throw her away the next morning. Besides.

"That's a heck of an accusation coming from you, Olivia. I know very well you've got some pretty big secrets you don't want to share. Do I question you character for not tellin' 'em to me? *Would* I make you feel like less of a good person for your *choice* to tell me or not?"

Liv brought her eyes to his. Bright. Bold. And unrelentingly broken. He cupped her cheek. He wanted his words to come out right. He wanted to take away every tiny piece of doubt or pain his cowardice caused, but he wasn't built that way. Doctors are clinical. Analytical. Too fucking practical for their own good.

Purple shadows dug into her ivory and cream skin beneath her emerald eyes encased in red. If a tear fell down her cheek, he'd take the IV and jab it in his own arm.

She bit her lip. "All right, Andy. No more lies."

Chapter Twenty

Liv squeezed the roller clamp draining dark red blood from Andy's arm. He sat semi-reclined while she collected what they hoped would be a lifesaving blood transfusion. She carefully measured the blood as it drained from his arm, and clamped the sample. The last thing anyone needed was for Andy to be in hypovolemic shock on the floor.

For the last half hour, Andy talked. She listened. And tried not to let the sting of deception slice into her heart. He gave her a weak smile. "On a scale of zero to ten, how much do hate me?"

Liv frowned, more at herself then Andy's half-truths. "I don't hate you. It's just... Being a doctor. Being *married*—"

"I'm not marr—"

"*Divorced*," she bit out. "Doctor. Divorced. Both very important details you could have told me."

He rolled his eyes to the ceiling, and shook his head. "Said the pot to the kettle."

Liv flinched, looking away. Snark bubbled inside, but she deserved that line.

Andy heaved himself upright, any remaining color draining from his face. It didn't take spot on nursing intuition to know he couldn't tolerate much more. She pressed her fingers into his wrist. His pulse threaded beneath her fingertips. "All right. That's got to be enough. Dr. Cole. You need more iron in your diet."

His eyes flickered to life. "I'm famished," he whispered in a way that hit her right in her sweet spot. She leaned into his space, strategically placing the curve of her cleavage right in front of his nose while she grabbed for a bandage. Charlotte and Torey had some explaining to do. What was supposed to be a sensible, subtle sexy number seven turned into a nine-point-five sheer, demi-balconette. Lingerie meant to be seen, lusted after, reserved for special occasions, not layered between her two-day old scrubs and an Old Navy tank top. Occasions where boob sweat was the result of rigorous, marathon lovemaking, not repositioning an almost dead body. Andy grazed a free hand to discreetly flirt with her breast.

"Easy there, cowboy. I'm still mad at you," she lied. How could she? She was just as guilty. Liv peeled a tiny corner of the IV tape away from his skin. "Fast or slow?"

A sound so hot her toes curled, rumbled from his throat. "Can a man have both?"

Liv bit her lip, loving the way he squirmed, then yanked the tape from his skin taking with it a three-inch strip of arm hair and probably the first layer of his epidermis.

He jolted backward, clutching his arm to his chest. "Jesus Christ, Liv."

Not being mad, didn't mean off the hook. A wheezy laugh broke Liv's smug silence.

"Oh Andy, ya think that's bad..." Torey chimed in during what must have been a game of revolving spectators. "You need a trip to visit Ms. Danka. She'll clean ya up good."

Liv pouted in play pity while she secured self-adhering pink wrap to his arm. She kissed his scowl. Andy's frustration flipped into a smile, and he swung his legs over the side.

"I wouldn't do that—"

His feet touched the floor, and his legs wobbled. Liv threw her arms out to catch him, but her two hundred pounds of beefcake collapsed them in a heap. She landed in a less than ladylike position, with Andy sprawled beneath her.

"You all right?" she asked feeling around the back of his head. Something made him grunt the air from his lungs when they hit the ground.

He cleared his throat and shifted. Hot. Hard. And completely ill-timed he drove his arousal into her pelvis. "I think you need to check it out. It's achin' pretty bad."

Liv stifled a satisfied grin with a swivel of her hips before pushing off the ground. "That'll require a doctor's order."

He groaned with what must be a serious case of blue balls and tried to follow. This time she forced him to stay put.

"Let me at least check your BP before you get up." She turned, ignoring his proud, twangy muttering as she walked away, then set up the transfusion. Liv released the roller clamp and glanced at Heaven, hoping the miracle intervention would turn Jorge around.

"Liv, I didn't tell you about Greta because I wasn't ready to—" Andy said, trying to dig out of the Greta-sized hole he made.

She waved him off. "Somethin' ain't right…"

Andy propped himself into the opposite corner. "What's wrong?"

Liv looked over Jorge for a long beat, then reviewed his vitals. "He's cold. And his heart rate's up to one-thirty."

"It's gotta be all the pressors."

Liv raised a skeptical eyebrow, and grabbed the manual blood pressure cuff from her supply cart. She sat at Andy's side, trying not fixate on the monitor over Jorge's bed. Knowing she stank, Liv kept a too proud distance. The next thing in Smithson's care-package had better be some Lady Speedstick, but Andy drew her close and scratched his full, two-day beard into her armpit. Liv smiled. She wasn't the only addict needing a fix.

She shoved her stethoscope in her ears and squeezed air into the cuff. "Eighty-eight over sixty-two. I'll get you some OJ and graham crackers."

****

Call him a cliché, but while he hated to see her go, he loved to watch her leave. The loss of his lifesaving pint, had sapped his strength and froze him inside out. Being too weak to stand, let alone help Liv move and care for Jorge, assaulted his fucking ego, but he would've pussed out hours ago if he knew Liv would strip to her skin tight, sweat dampened tank top after cranking up the heat lamps.

Andy stared, jealous and embarrassingly turned on by the attention she gave half-dead Jorge. Punishment for being an ass, but a punishment he'd gladly accept.

She wiped at the sheen dotting her forehead and glanced at the empty gallery. As if the lack of an audience gave her permission be tired, she rolled her neck and stretched.

He motioned for her to sit, hoping she wasn't harboring some subconscious resentment. "Come sit down, baby."

Her lips pursed into a grim line.

"He's not goin' anywhere."

Lazily, Andy opened his arms to her, and she smiled. Finally, a tick in the win column.

Mid-squat Jorge's monitor wailed. Except there was nothing. No movement or outward sign of crisis. Tasting her scent on the air, he half hoped she'd ignore it, but she shot up, halting his pursuit after her with a look he knew better than to tempt.

"His O2 sats are sixty, his heart rate is just climbing…" she muttered aloud for her processing and his benefit.

Before he could tell her to troubleshoot the ventilator, Liv was already going through the motions in her calm, controlled, and sexy as hell manner, but the alarms didn't quit. Andy heaved himself onto a chair to get a better look. The effort required was an embarrassment.

"God, he looks like shit…"

"Thanks for that astute assessment, Dr. Cole," she said, wiping another layer of sweat from her brow.

The revolving door of gallery gawkers heard the commotion. People with nothing to do but lurk stampeded up the stairs. Liv appeared to ignore it and took a cleansing breath. She tore her stethoscope from her neck, then pressed it to Jorge's chest. He could make the argument he was staring at Jorge, but there was no denying it. He was staring at her, the curve of her hips, the plump perfection of her breasts spilling like sin out the top of her lacey underthings. But he was really staring because she was amazing. She just also happened to be the sexiest woman he'd ever seen.

He glanced at the gallery hoping to see Smithson, but found Javier enjoying an eyeful. That was the kick in the ass he needed. Andy forced himself upright and over to Jorge's bedside, making sure the ape saw his hand slide up the small of Liv's back before hitting the silence button.

Liv pulled her stethoscope from her ears and pinched the bridge of her nose. "His heart and lung sounds are more diminished than an hour ago."

He took a moment to listen for himself while Olivia rushed away. Immediately, he knew something was wrong. Jorge's heart sounds weren't diminished, they were virtually non-existent, as if the heart was swimming through stew. He flicked the dying man's ribs, hoping for a hollow resonance to vibrate in his chest. Except the sound was dense. Full.

"Shit. Smithson!" he called. "This guy's chest is full of blood."

Anticipating his needs, Olivia brought over the ultrasound machine, the only piece of life-saving technology he had. Smithson emerged through the rumbling anxious spectators. "Dammit. Think the central line caused the hemothorax?"

His knee jerk reaction was to shout at the top of his lungs, but seeing Liv so calm and in control reined him in.

"Does it even matter now?" he hissed swiping the wand over Jorge's thoracic cavity. Liv pulled a sample of blood from the central line, hit silence and suctioned copious, frothy red sputum from the tube down Jorge's throat. Smithson backed away, trying to get an ETA from the CDC.

In a synchronized beat, Jorge stabilized, satisfying the monitors and machines. Andy took a moment to breathe. Think. Anticipate. And drove the transducer deep into Jorge's chest, but the grey blob never materialized on screen.

His vision blurred, darkening into a tunnel. The room began to spin. He gripped the stretcher like it had the power to ground him to the Earth.

Fast and furious, Liv clicked her pen. The sound drilled through his temple. "It couldn't be a bad insert. His bleedin' times are the best they've been since we got caught in this whole mess."

Andy couldn't find words. He couldn't find air. He couldn't find steady ground beneath his feet. Black spots melted into his eyes, and the bleached light from above started to buzz and hiss.

He fell back. The collapse took forever, but he

wasn't falling. Liv eased him into a chair.

She dosed him with ice cold water laced with salt. He opened his eyes, squinting against the light. Liv welled with tears, then blinked them back.

"Oh, thank God," she sighed, resting her forehead against his. She trembled, and not from the classic crash of adrenaline "I need you, Andy Cole. Don't go scarin' me like that."

Andy gasped for air. "He needs a chest tube."

Liv pinched her eyes shut, and rubbed the heels of her palms into the sockets like she couldn't stand to see what was before her. Like she finally understood trying to save Jorge was like trying to disprove Newton's third law—everything they did they'd be hit with an equal opposite reaction.

"You're right. If he's not bleeding from the stick, it's something else. Let's drain his chest. Then auto-transfuse what's left."

She fell to her knees. Smithson buzzed overhead with a useless update. The CDC team and their resources were still over two hours away. They might as well have been on the goddamn moon. He placed a weak, damp palm to her cheek as a tear ran down her face.

She looked over at Jorge's waxy, grey body. "It's no use."

He forced her eyes back on him and smiled. Genuine. Confident. And full of love for the exhausted woman kneeling before him. "Then what are we doing here, Olivia?"

She sucked in a breath like she was ready to challenge his use of her own logic. But he pressed on.

"We can do this. You and me. We're gonna get through it. And so will he," Andy said. It was a lie. But it was a flawless lie. He didn't expect Jorge to last through the night.

Turning his mind off to the noise, the chaos, and the pounding of blood in his ears, he pulled Liv in for a kiss. He needed it. She needed it. And apparently everyone in the gallery did, too, because there was an eruption of immature cheers and catcalling.

"Now I'm dizzy for a whole 'nother reason," he twanged.

He'd never forget the grin that split Olivia's face. She stood, his eyes following the length of her body as she did. "Will that be a STAT thoracostomy tray, Dr. Cole?"

"Mm, I love it when you talk dirty to me."

****

Setting up the chest tube tray, filling the chambers with sterile saline, attaching the suction canister, and making sure everything was clamped and ready to go took little time. The closet control freak in her liked doing the technical stuff on her own, but when it came to the cleanup, she missed the village it took to save lives. The overfull linen baskets and garbage trickled out of the dirty utility closet and into the trauma room.

Sexier than hell, Andy prepped at the sink. Taut and defined, his muscles slid beneath his thin white shirt as he meticulously scrubbed between each finger. Hit with a surge of swoon, she dropped a bottle of rubbing alcohol. Then a sponge. Apparently, Liv's suspicious case of the dropsies was enough for Javi to contribute his two cents.

"Need me come down there and show you how it's done, Liv?" Javi asked, arms folded over his chest. Through the glare against the gallery window, she couldn't make out his expression. Teasing or not, it wasn't the time nor place.

She smiled and clung to her Savannahian civility,

feeling patience flee her body.

Andy came to her side, drying his forearms with a paper towel, feeling no such obligation.

"I don't know how that'd be possible, Javier. I'm pretty sure that head of yours wouldn't fit through the doors. Olivia won't call you out on being a prick, but I sure will."

The gallery went silent at the pissing match laid out before them. The gaggle of women lining the walls all but fell over at the sexy showing of testosterone, herself included. But lives had to be saved.

Liv silenced the monitor for what felt like the millionth time that morning and tied a surgical mask around her face.

"You fellas finished? Last I checked, chest tubes don't insert themselves."

Andy followed. Javi's stare singed her backside until the unit called him away.

"I don't need you to fight my battles, Dr. Cole," she said, squirting bottles of iodine onto Jorge's chest and the sponges she dropped on Andy's sterile field.

He slapped on his latex gloves, then wiped Jorge's chest clean. Using his free hand, he felt for landmarks. Liv stood at his side, armed and ready with an open ten blade for him to retrieve.

In one fluid movement, he pulled the scalpel and sliced through Jorge's sixth and seventh intercostal space. "I know you don't," he said, plugging his left first finger into Jorge's chest. With his right, he worked the hemostats into the wound and spread open the meat between the ribs.

Liv held her breath. A hot flash of adrenaline started at her scalp and pounded into her toes. Blood gushed from Jorge's chest. Liv dropped a tube that rivaled a garden hose into his open palm, and he shoved it into the hole in Jorge's thoracic cavity.

"But what kinda man would I be if I didn't want to be your hero, Olivia?" he finished without looking in her direction. Unprompted, she met the end of the tube with the drainage hose and unclamped the system. Dark red blood flowed like oil from his chest into the collection canister. The whole thing took less than a minute, and she finally allowed herself to breathe.

She cleaned up while Andy sutured the chest tube in place. Almost immediately Jorge's vitals began to improve. But the juju reared its head. Jorge dropped into shock.

"Good thing we saved our victory dance for later..." Olivia said, prepping the autotransfuser, a trauma nurse toy only seen on old ER reruns. New-grad nerves prickled her skin, but most trauma nurses worked a lifetime and never used the archaic piece of technology that gave Jorge back the blood he lost *and* any remnants Andy sacrificed. Just under four-hundred milliliters of blood came out then right back in—anymore meant a trip to the operating room—but that was the textbook solution. There was no black and white in this clusterfuck of grey.

She stood at Jorge's feet and rubbed her temples. The amount of effort to save one person. A person who should have died hours ago. A life she fought to save at the potential cost of her own. Would she want such efforts made? Futile and agonizing. What an appealing mix. Andy came and stood behind her. He slid his hands over her hips and kissed the back of her neck.

"Christ, Liv you're on fire." He pulled away mumbling under his breath, then called for Smithson before switching off the heat lamps. His brows pulled tight, he seemed to assess her from across the room. He saw her as a patient, and it pissed her off.

Liv rolled her eyes as he approached with a thermometer.

"Keep that up, and I'll take it the other way."

"Mm," she purred. "That had better be a promise, Dr. Cole."

Air hissed through his teeth, and he checked his watch. His baby blues dilated.

She ignored her fatigue, and an overwhelming case of the "unsexies", feeling her boob sweat pool in her eight-hundred-dollar bra, and glanced at the supply cabinet. Two people could fit—or contort—if need be.

Andy laughed and popped open her mouth with his thumb, gently placing the thermometer under her tongue. "Oh, Olivia. What I want to do to you will require a helluva lot more room."

Chapter Twenty-One

Her eyes watered. Fever. Hands down. The optimism she usually relied on couldn't be faked as he wiped an icy washcloth along her neck and face. Andy insisted on a second swab and had Smithson run it to the lab himself. "It's a waste of everyone's time, Andy. By the time it comes back, I'll be just like our pal over there."

His lips flat-lined. "Don't talk like that."

Lottie appeared overhead for a quick "come to Jesus" with Andy about his witch of an ex-wife; apparently, even *she* couldn't corral her crazy. And for Charlotte VanSutton to admit another woman bested her was a huge blow to her ego.

"I tell you, Anderson Cole, I don't care if she makes the best pecan pie this side of the Mississippi, there isn't one redeeming quality about her, but if she knows what's good for her, she should leave y'all alone."

Andy grinned, but said nothing as if to pretend he wasn't listening in on their hen hack. Charlotte went on with all the little details Liv had too much pride to ask. Hair? Boxed. Tan? Fake. Wardrobe? Neiman's Bargain Basement. Sure, it was bitchy and lacked class, but Lottie was just doing her job as Liv's best friend to boost her up.

Liv decided against telling Lottie about the fever. What good would it do? Besides, she got to see a very pleased Lottie charm the widower pants off Smithson. She all but purred when he invited her to the cafeteria for a coffee.

Liv and Andy feasted on stale turkey sandwiches and pudding from the ER's free lunch stash. The unsaid wedged a hole between them. If it came down to talking about her statistical chances of dying in less than forty-eight hours, or discussing Andy's ex-wife, the ex-wife seemed like an easier pill to swallow.

"So, when did things between you and Greta start to go bad?"

Staring blankly at their conjoined fingers, Andy's eyes turned glassy. He didn't respond, so she gave them a squeeze. To her horror, he winced.

"Things didn't go bad for us, Olivia. We had a—"

A shrill, nasally twang cut in from overhead. "Is this the part where you tell your new girlfriend how you blame me for the death of our son?"

Greta Grey—*Cole*—came into view, and Andy went cold in her grip. If only he'd given Lottie the go-ahead to use a shovel. "Are you gonna tell her about how you let our tragedy break up our marriage? How you quit on me, Anderson?"

Liv turned. Agony, repressed but raw, raked across Andy's face. The kind of pain that still sucked the air from her lungs when having to tell a person their child died. He swallowed as if he needed to force down resentment. Death of a son. Unfathomable. Incomparable. She'd never be able to tell him now.

Andy began to quake. She called his name, warm and low, the same way he'd never been able to refuse. She wanted him to look at her. Not Greta. Not the memories that still tore him apart.

She tried again, putting a hand on his face to force his gaze. But he wouldn't give in, as if he intended to bear Greta's punishment, and deny himself the comfort only Liv could give.

"Are you going to tell her how as a husband *you* failed *me*?"

Liv shot to her feet. "That's enough outta you, ma'am."

"I think you mean *Mrs.* Cole," she drawled, purposely elongating her married name is if it bore power over her.

"Oh, bless your heart," Liv retaliated in the trademark condescending tone learned from her Momma. "According to Anderson, not for the last ten weeks and five days. I know what you're tryin' to do here—"

"Only making sure he doesn't come across as St. Andy to the empty-headed masses who fall for sweet words, charm, and the backhanded sin of pride."

Chagrin prickled down her spine. Behind her, Andy rose to his feet. His heat infused with her back, and the embarrassment fizzled. She laced her fingers with his. "No man is perfect, Greta. No woman can stake that claim, either."

Greta shifted her gaze and ran a rattled hand through her big hair then crossed her arms, but it wasn't in defiance.

Andy stepped out of Liv's warmth and walked closer to the gallery. "Thank you for hurryin' up here. I wasn't thinking when I put you down as my emergency contact. After twelve years that'll be a hard habit to break."

Liv turned away to give him and Greta the privacy they deserved but wouldn't get, but he reached for her.

"This is Olivia. And she knows firsthand how right you are about the kinda man I am. And for some odd reason I haven't run her off yet."

"Well, we are locked in the same room for another twenty hours," Liv quipped to the tile floor.

Greta scoffed. "So, she's funny, too?"

Andy laughed through his nose. "Maybe not LOL funny. But yes," he said, gallantly defending her lame joke.

She swatted his arm. During a silent beat, the tone turned. Addressing the elephant in the room seemed like a good idea. Liv found Greta's grim gaze through the glass.

"I'm sorry about your son."

Andy squeezed her fingers, but in that instant, it burned. She let him go fearing what her eyes would reveal, and went over to check on Jorge. She went through her hourly assessment, but it was mindless routine. She could have been assessing a stuffed jack-a-lope for the amount of attention she gave him. Liv tried to shut out Andy and Greta's conversation, wishing that for the sake of her sanity they'd pick up the phone rather than use the intercom.

Andy sighed. "I've never blamed you for what happened to Jackson."

"Of course you do. Why else would you come back up here? To punish me."

"Distance. I came back to Chicago for distance. Maybe if you left that godforsaken town you'd find some closure, yourself."

Liv tossed a curious glance to the gallery. It wasn't eavesdropping. They were having the conversation out loud for God and all Creation.

"It's home, Andy. It's where our boy is buried," Greta countered, riddled with pain and guilt. A knot twisted in Liv's gut. Her eyes began to sting. She bit into her cheek to keep her tears from falling and stuck her nose in Jorge's chart.

A sound, even more damaged and damning, erupted from Andy's chest. "No, it's the place where you relish in the pity and prayers of others. Where I'm the ludicrous, absentee father who wasn't there to save his son from drowning during bath time because I was too busy playing hero halfway around the world."

The gallery door swung open, and a nervous chuckle came from the ground floor. Genteel banter floated in. Lottie's twang, layered on so sweet it was likely to send Smithson into diabetic coma, but the flirt fest did an abrupt 'about-face".

"Mrs. C—, Greta," stuttered Smithson, as they came up the tile stairs. After that, it was safe to say, the train from crazy town entered the station. Lottie charged past Smithson, her chocolate tresses billowing around her face. Angelic, except for the look that spouted horns curled on her red painted lips.

"Oh, you poor thing. You must not be very bright, because when I said, 'Andy's doin' just fine,' What I really meant was 'He doesn't want deal with your brand of crazy', which, Greta, dear, is why he sent me."

Greta stared daggers from the gallery, as if she expected Andy to interfere on her behalf. Liv found some dignity when he ignored Greta and came to her side. She caught a glimpse of Greta's defeat, but just as guilty of the "backhanded sin of pride," Greta straightened her shoulders and walked off with one last dig at Charlotte, this time directing it at Smithson. "Jesus Christ, Allen. From Mellie to … this? She must be rolling over her in grave."

Greta stormed out, leaving an awkward lull in her wake. True to her character, Lottie broke the tension the only way she knew how. "Well that seemed highly unnecessary. Does hospital coffee translate into something I don't know up here in all of this liberal codswallop?"

Andy slid a hand around Liv's waist and held her to his side. She anticipated it, and was already trying to pull out of his grip. She wanted his touch, but couldn't look him in the eye. She needed a diversion. "Lottie, you need to stop sayin' whatever pops into that head of yours."

Lottie scoffed. If Liv had to take bets on which would be more likely, she'd bet on a snowman's chance in hell before Charlotte VanSutton selectively chose her words.

Liv kept Andy at a distance using Jorge as a barrier between them. "So, you had a son?" she asked, feather light, as if the weight of the revelation would crush them.

"Jackson. He … last year. July. I was on the damned mission trip. God saved me. But took my little boy."

She'd endured the same month of devastation. An irony no one should share. Her heart broke. For him. And for her.

Andy squeezed his eyes shut and pinched the bridge of his nose as if it held the power to suppress grief from leaking unto every cell in his body. Liv knew the feeling. The sucker punch to the stomach. The unrelenting guilt, sadness, and self-loathing.

Hard wired to say the least helpful words to a grieving person, Liv shook the urge to say "I'm sorry", but she didn't want to stand there like she had the expectation he "man up" and compose himself. Liv reached an open hand over Jorge's body. Relief relaxed in his shoulders when he laced their fingers together.

"She's right though, Liv. I couldn't talk about Greta because *I* failed her. She needed me. To be strong. She needed me to be a better man, and I couldn't. Greta held our little boy in her arms as he died, and I couldn't even find it in myself to try and save her. Or save us."

There, she had it. No more lies. Olivia saw Andy for what he was, *who* he was, and it only made her love him more. Andy didn't deny his skeletons. He was trying to evade the man the skeletons seemed to create. A feeling she knew too well.

Andy cleared his throat and kissed their conjoined hands before letting her go to swipe at his cheeks. "So now that you know I'm a lying, selfish coward I suspect you wish I had just been an axe murderer?"

Liv couldn't stifle her ironic smirk given the seriousness of the question. Humor was the easy way to defuse tension. It's the only way to survive life in the ER. "Enough arrogance and charm to be one of the most prolific serial killers," she mused, reciting her best friend's insight.

Lottie and Smithson had kept a quiet vigilance over the room, but after hearing a line of her own snarky banter quoted, she must have felt the need to take credit. "Everybody wants to be me..." she sighed with such drama it rivaled Ms. O'Hara. "Y'all okay? This will be the only time I admit this, but I'm sorry. I had no idea your ex-wife would be so bold as to challenge my wrath—"

"It's more than all right," Andy cut in with adoration in his eyes. "Looks like Liv and I need that kinda motivation to lay all our cards on the table."

Apparently still not over the tingles of new love, Liv's heart fluttered, but being guilty of the same sins meant nothing, not when he was trying to live with the death of a child and she with the guilt of giving hers up.

"That's good. It was about time you told him about Georgia," Lottie said.

Olivia shot a laser glance at the gallery. Best friend telepathy didn't seem to have the greatest effect through tempered glass. Tears welled in her eyes. Lottie paled then cupped a hand over her mouth.

Andy flashed her the lazy half grin brimmed with swoon. "What about Georgia?"

After years of having to conceal her thoughts and

feelings, Liv immediately fell back on her pageant persona and gave him the smile he had yet to look away from.

"Oh, you know, just how it's the best state in the Confederacy."

Chapter Twenty-Two

Two hours. That was it. Two more hours until Jorge could be passed off to someone else. In the ER, it's treat 'em and street 'em. Not sit at the bedside and watch them try not to die. It should have been a victory Jorge clung on this long, but he couldn't shake the fear if somehow Jorge pulled through, what it meant for Olivia. *His* Olivia.

He didn't deserve her. He didn't deserve her kindness. Her understanding. He didn't deserve the way he looked in her eyes. Back home he drowned in false sympathy and gossip. In a town of two thousand everyone knew everyone's business and made it *their* business.

His marriage had been over for months, but the final straw came from Greta's "well intended" friend stopping by with her third batch of chili. All the prayer circles, grief groups, and donations made in the name of Jackson Cole to the *United Mission Center* had long since stopped, but his little boy's death was a wound that wouldn't heal. Greta's friend and dozens just like her, picked at the fledging scab until his pain was as raw as the day he watched Jackson's tiny coffin be lowered into the red Texas clay.

"Maybe that was God's way of sayin' you should be spending more time 'round here, Andy."

To this day it set him on fire. The entitled sense of judgment spewing from their fake empathetic faces. For fuck's sake, he judged himself enough. He didn't need it, didn't *deserve* it, from relative strangers. He slammed the door in her face, got on a plane and threw himself back into the dying masses who only knew him as the doctor that didn't die.

"Whatcha thinkin' about, cowboy?" Olivia asked looking up from her notes.

Shit. What *wasn't* he thinking about?

He grinned and tapped her clicky pen against his temple, hoping to formulate a sentence that wasn't, "I want to fuck you so badly I can taste it."

His pause drew a smirk, as if she could read his ill-timed guy brain. She straightened and threw her hair off her shoulders, painstakingly similar to the seductive control she wielded riding his cock. "I'll have you know, my fever's gone, but I'm still feeling a bit … hot."

She pulled her copper waves into a messy bun, welding it together with a pen she had clipped to her tank then fanned herself with a stack of papers from her makeshift desk.

His whole body went hard. "It's an awful irony to be immune to the Blood Flu only to die from blue balls."

Her sultry stare turned giddy, a welcome relief. Another second of her green eyes devouring him with want and he'd bend her over the table, Jorge and viewers in the gallery be damned.

"Well, don't you know all the right things to say to a girl to make her feel special?"

The little machine running lab tests spit out the latest bit of good-news. Liv's giddiness turned into downright exhilaration. She jumped from her seat thrusting her fist in the air, but Andy went deaf to her words, fixated on the way her breasts bounced and the sliver of skin at her waist.

"C'mon, cowboy, this is great news! Dr. Smithson!" she called crossing the room. She brought the little slip of paper for Andy to review. Adding insult to injury, she stood before him dancing her tits in front of his face.

"I swear, woman, you're tryin' to kill me." Andy

rose and took the slip of paper to read himself. "I'll be damned..." Shock wasn't the word. "Allen. You up there?"

Smithson huffed up the stairs. "What's going on?"

"It's his bleeding times. Lactate, everything. It's all ... better." Was it wrong he didn't want to whoop and holler? He needed Liv's second set of test results. Maybe then he could slap himself on the back at a good save.

"But why the bleeding in his chest?" Smithson interjected with his personal blend of subdued caution.

Andy shrugged. "No idea."

"But his output's been minimal. After the auto-transfusion, it's been pretty much dry," Liv added, poring through her scribbles. "If his blood gas is good, think we could extubate? He's got to have some worried family that can stop by?"

"Eh. Not yet I'm afraid. The whole compound is under mandatory quarantine. It won't be over until later tomorrow."

Olivia frowned and nibbled on her lip in a way that made his heart burst. She was such a better person than he'd ever be. She had every right to be asking when *she* was getting out of there—what about *her,* and never once had that come out of her mouth.

"No one else has come up with symptoms?" Andy asked.

Smithson bowed his head. "They found an elderly woman that died in her sleep. Took her real quick. And there was a scare with an infant, but turned out to be straight up flu type B. If source one is improving—do you think the guys from Atlanta would be better allocated to the refugee compound?"

That was an intense call. He wasn't sure he should be the one who made it. He looked at Olivia. Her fire should be out. Her drive and the ability to give a crap should have lapsed when she learned she was risking her life for a stranger. Liv wasn't a soldier. She was a nurse, and dying for someone wasn't part of the Florence Nightingale pledge.

"What do you think, Liv?"

She smacked her gum and flashed him the smile that went straight to his groin. "We got this. I don't want them to steal my thunder."

He laughed and came to her side. "That's such an ER nurse thing to say."

She shrugged and allowed him a quick pat on the behind before returning to Jorge's needs. Which apparently this hour was a sponge down and to shampoo his hair. Andy scratched at the back of his head. It wasn't the first time he found himself jealous of the near dead man.

"There ya have it. Send them to the compound. Liv and I can manage here for now." He motioned to the phone. He knew it looked seedy and suspicious, but he didn't want to talk about Olivia like she wasn't there.

"How much longer?" He pressed after picking up the receiver.

Smithson narrowed his eyes and took a hesitant breath. "You're not her doc—"

"Cut the crap, Allen."

"Second swab is positive. I'm having them run it again."

****

Anyone good at their job in the medical field had to have a game face, the default "RBF" worn when presented with the sad or gruesome. An unreadable, resting bitch face came in handy more often than a pair of hemostats.

Andy hung up the phone and turned back,

wearing manufactured ambivalence. Blame the spot on bullshit detector every ER nurse is born with, but not six seconds before he had been imagining her in every state of naked, with her mouth around his cock and now he glanced in her direction with the kind of apathy you give the quadriplegic before grabbing his limp penis to place a foley. Except, Andy wasn't hiding pity. It was fear.

Her stomach dropped to her feet. She couldn't breathe. In the game of Russian roulette, it was her turn to pull the trigger. "Let me guess… You got some great news to tell me."

Andy rolled his eyes. Sarcasm probably wasn't the best defense mechanism. What did he expect? She wasn't the kind of woman to fall to her knees and weep. But if death was truly knocking on her door, someone had better bring her a bottle of the 2009 Balthazar and a hit of weed. Guzzling expensive wine and trying pot were easy ticks off her bucket list.

"We don't know anything yet," Andy said, grabbing his penlight from her desk. He cupped his calloused palm over her cheek. She turned into it like a needy kitten and closed her eyes. "Let me look."

She complied with her pageant smile, this time opting for a quick prayer that the signs weren't there, that she wasn't going to be spending the last hours of her life in agony with Andy feeling obligated to stay behind and watch.

He flashed the light in her eyes. She braced herself for a jolt to sear into her brain, but there was nothing. Andy tugged the delicate skin below her eye even more.

"You make me wrinkle, Dr. Cole, you're payin' for the Botox."

He let out a reflexive laugh and flashed the light a second time, repeating it over her other eye. A nervous smile crept on his face.

"Looks good."

Liv pushed aside her selfish worry and put on her big girl panties.

"So what do you think? Was it the anti-virals, the Fresh Frozen Plasma? Your magic blood?"

He pinched the bridge of his nose and plopped down on her rolling stool. He swiveled his hips back and forth in a way that caught her britches on fire. "Luck?"

"Hogwash. You were the lucky one."

He shrugged.

"'Bout time you learned to pick your battles," she teased.

Andy rose from his stool and planted a kiss on her lips before stealing her stethoscope. Every cell in her body sizzled. Sex on a stick took a minute to listen to Jorge's chest. He smiled as if to accept the finality of good news, except he exploded. He charged away from her as if to keep Liv out of the line of his outburst. He choked her stethoscope between his hands until his fingers blanched white. Her beloved purple Litmann was about to be a casualty of Dr. Cole's temper.

"This was the wrong call. I should have never brought him in here." Andy glared over at Jorge as if he suddenly resented him looking so pink and plumped up with blood products.

Liv shook her head. There was no way he meant that.

"The department didn't have everything it needed, and I brought him in anyway. After Rose. You. That fucking meeting. I needed something to fix. But if I had just waited a damn minute maybe you wouldn't be in here risking your life…"

Liv went to Jorge's side and grabbed his hand. "He is someone's son. Father. Husband. He's alive because you cared enough to try and save him."

He launched himself at her. Hard and possessive, he grabbed her arm and drew back. He inhaled her malty, sweetness and almost caved. The urge to kiss her and forget the whole thing was so strong it burned like fire in his veins. "None of that matters, Liv. None of it matters if *you* don't walk out of here with me. Every time I see you wince, stretch, or wipe a drop of sweat from your chest I want to slit my wrists for bringing him in here."

She gasped, feeling his guilt pull in his words. "I don't blame you."

"It's not about blame," he said, his face twisting as if his analytical, trauma doc brain tried to beat out the primitive male portion that had a habit of fucking everything up. "I accept this is my fault. All of it. That if I hadn't been thinking with my dick that first day maybe … I love you. And if you died because of my fucking need to be the hero, I'd never be able to forgive myself. It's how I lost Jackson—and Jesus Christ you'd think I'd have learned the damned lesson."

She placed her fingers on his cheek. Her nails roughed through the coarse, unkempt beard, and she smiled. Liv filled with the kind of sappy bliss only seen in *Lifetime* movies "So you love me, huh?"

Andy's face, once contorted with worry, split into joy. "Yeah. Yeah, I do."

There wasn't time for a kiss to solidify their moment.

In an unwelcomed beat Smithson appeared overhead. "Everything all right down there, Anderson?"

Andy stared into Liv's eyes. His gaze hardened. Determined as if he would accept nothing but her survival.

"I need three rounds of antivirals prepared."

****

Liv perched on her rolling desk chair holding in a wince. And a few screams of her favorite cuss word as Andy dug around the crook of her arm for an elusive vein. Still, she could only take so much.

"You're really bad at this," she teased. Second poke or not, she wanted to bat his hand away and do it herself.

Andy frowned and flicked the light switch. Bad time for a little joke to lighten the tension. The dank trauma room buzzed to life under the fluorescents. In order to keep some semblance of normalcy, they had cycled the lights to mimic day and night hours. The gallery overhead was abandoned, except for one lonely housekeeper who apparently needed a nap.

"I told you to drink more," Andy grumbled finally hitting a flash of dark red.

"Says the guy that doesn't have to pee in a sink."

That drew a smile. She kissed him, and it disappeared just as quick.

"Can I get an ETA for when you intend to stop punishing yourself?" she asked.

With more tenderness than she probably deserved, Andy taped the edges of the IV then looked her in the eye. "When I know you'll walk out of here the same way you walked in."

She threw a glance at Jorge.

"It's you I care about. You are the only person that matters in here."

She opened her mouth to protest, but he released the roller clamp on the IV bag and walked away. They had to make it through the night. That was it. Jorge had five hours left of his active contagion period, and if she hadn't developed symptoms of the violent, viral assault on her immune system resulting in a bloody, painful death by then, well she'd better not say.

Andy pored over Jorge's chart, assessed his ventilator settings. He grinned, getting close to Jorge's face to speak in warm, encouraging tones. Her heart swelled, tears prickling behind her tired eyes. She leaned back to rest her head. The small bag of fluids rippled down the plastic tube and drained into her arm. Primed to pray, Liv closed her eyes. She needed a dose of strength. Courage. Something she and Andy could hold on to and get them through the night with Jorge alive and well on the other side.

Her arm went numb. Ice crystalized in her veins, then turned to fire. Pain seared through her shoulder, across her chest and into her neck. It started to close. Swell. Her tongue felt huge and floppy in her mouth. She forced a sound from her throat. Nothing. No noise meant no breath and her lungs screamed for air.

Panic fluttered in her heart. Black spots darted before her eyes.

Anaphylaxis.

She clawed at the insatiable itch in the back of her throat. She groped, blind for the clamp to stop the drip. She climbed to her knees and pulled in a wheezy, tight breath willing Andy to turn around.

****

Andy hovered over Jorge's stretcher, playing an epic game of "If this, Then that," in his mind. Jorge blinked. A clear, pristine tear pooled, then fell down his cheek. It was relief. Andy knew the feeling. He'd been there. Felt it. Lived it.

Andy explained the process of removing his breathing tube the best way he could, given the limits of his medical Spanglish, thankful his time in Guatemala fell over two consecutive birthdays.

"Get ready to blow out the candles, buddy," he said, in less than fluent Spanish and turned over his shoulder. Liv's infusion should have been done. He'd been so caught in his own thoughts, he didn't question the lack of sexy, southern banter. When she wasn't there eyeing him with wicked intent he was glad to assume she allowed herself a nap, but he couldn't help but feel like a plane without wings. It wasn't that as a doctor he needed a nurse. It was simply, as a man, he needed Olivia.

Fumbling around the supply cart, he found a syringe and sucked the air out of the bubble holding the ET tube in place then counted for his and Jorge's benefit. "On tres. Uno. Dos. Tres."

Jorge forced an exhale, the tube out with it. He coughed, taking in his first non-mechanical breath in almost three days. A smile split Andy's face. He grabbed at his chest for his stethoscope, forgetting he'd been using Olivia's as a nice excuse to peer down her shirt whenever he wanted to listen to Jorge's lungs.

Andy scanned Jorge's vitals. Satisfied for the moment, he assured him he'd be right back and went over the hidden corner of the room he and Liv deemed their "boudoir". She must have crashed hard, her feet extended out in a less than ladylike way.

He shoved her little desk with a hip. "Sorry to wake you, baby… Oh. God."

Chapter Twenty-Three

"Livy!" he called, diving down to gather her in his arms. Limp, cold. Blue. Covered in blood. His brain fired a mile a millisecond. First survey. Pulse? Yes. Breathing. No. "Smithson? Smithson!" Andy bellowed into the middle of the night silence. He looked up, hoping to see the sleeping housekeeper, but the gallery was empty.

He forced two breaths into her purple mouth, examining the rise and fall of her chest. No movement. Blotchy red, streaks tracked up her arm. Blood oozed from the tiny puncture in its crook. The IV dangled at her side.

"Shit. Allergy."

He scooped her off the floor, eyeing Jorge in the process. He wanted to shove him off the stretcher, but had to be satisfied with placing Liv's long and lean body on the polished chrome counter. Her arm fell over the edge, blood dripped on the floor. He bellowed for Smithson. Anybody.

He threw Jorge's oxygen mask over her face, but it'd be useless if he didn't reverse the anaphylactic shock. He needed Epinephrine. Benadryl. And a working IV site. He rushed to the locked medication cabinet and began poking at the touch screen. It squawked in protest.

For fuck's sake. Why wouldn't a physician have access to the machine dispensing the medication they ordered? Rage bubbled from his chest. He kicked the block of metal. Every curse word under the sun burst out his mouth, and the first solid object he could get his hands on became a tool to pry it apart.

Behind him Jorge dozed, peaceful, and blissfully unaware of his doctor's panic-riddled temper tantrum. To his right, Liv lay motionless, teetering on the brink of consciousness. This wasn't hell. This was hell's redheaded, middle stepchild.

He pummeled the machine, calling on every invisible force for help. The gallery doors banged open, feet pounded up the stairs. It wasn't Smithson. It was the ape, Javier. Salt in the fucking wound.

"You gonna pay for that, Doc?"

"I need your login and password!" Andy commanded with another whack at the machine. It wasn't going to work; it wasn't a damned piñata. But he couldn't stand there and do nothing, plus it felt good to beat the shit out of it.

"No way. Have Liv get in there for you."

"Are you as blind as you are a dipshit?" He motioned to Liv lying a few feet away, unconscious with her blood dripping to the floor. In defense of the ape, it was hard to see something directly below his feet.

"Shit. What happened? Um," he rubbed his forehead as if he needed to conjure up a long-buried memory. He probably typed the password so often, it didn't require thought. "Login's my last name. Palermo. Password. Titties twenty-three."

Andy threw the med pole aside and let the words sink in as he punched the buttons on the Pyxis keyboard. There wasn't time to laugh, but he absolutely shot a cockeyed glance at the gallery as the drawer popped open.

Javier stiffened, indignant. "What's wrong with a tribute to boobs and 'His Airness'?"

"Nothing but halfway to middle age with the password of a giant douche," Andy answered fishing the medications from the draw. "Tell Smithson Epi and antihistamines shouldn't be locked up."

Meds in hand, he ran back to Olivia. Ruddy and

pale, this time she opened her eyes when he called her name. Strangled wheezes screeched from her throat. But she was conscious. A win.

"Why did you have to pull out your IV, woman?"

Liv's purple lips flipped as she struggled to breathe. He drew up the anaphylactic cocktail into large syringe, flicking the air from the tip.

"I need to main line this, baby. Okay?"

"You main line that Epinephrine, you'll throw her into arrhythmia, doc!" Javi shouted through the glass.

Andy clenched his teeth and slapped at her arm, hoping a vein would magically appear. "I can fix SVT and some vomiting… I can't crich her by myself."

Her eyes fluttered then rolled back into her skull. Andy grumbled a string of profanity. A new swarm piled in to gawk at his train-wreck. Smithson, irritable and unapologetic, climbed the steps.

"What's going on down there?"

Much to Andy's surprise the ape explained the obvious, and Andy focused on finding a place to get Liv the medications as fast as possible. Frantic, her heart raced within her ribs. Andy held her upright in his arms. Her head fell to the side, exposing the delicate line of her collarbone and neck. There was his answer. While the rest of her venous system clamped down from hypoxia, her jugular vein distended from increased pulmonary pressures. He cringed. Injecting a one-inch needle into her neck turned his stomach. But it was Liv's only option.

He kissed her icy lips as if they were the cure to an unsteady hand, then swiped antiseptic over the bulging, rope running from her jaw to disappear beneath her clavicle. The needle pierced the skin. Liv twitched. Blood flashed into the syringe, and he slammed the plunger with his thumb.

Ten seconds. Epinephrine took ten seconds to circulate. He held a sponge to her neck and gathered her in his arms to sit on the floor. Instantly she began to quake. Her pulse bounded through her extremities. Her dusky, pallid complexation flushed pink. The mask blowing pure oxygen in her face began to mist from short, rapid breaths. Her eyes opened.

"Liv? Ya with me, baby?"

"Cold. I'm cold."

Shit. Vasoconstriction. Tremors. And her thin, white tank, half sopping from the toxic, anti-virals froze Liv to the bone.

He sat her against the battered Pyxis and retrieved the last warm blanket. With little care to his audience, he peeled her out of her wet clothes, then did the same. He engulfed her with his warmth, then sealed them in the toasty bath blanket.

He hummed in her ear. The hiss from the non-rebreather mask scrambled his thoughts. Definitely, a good thing. She might have been sixty seconds from dead, but that didn't stop his dick from noticing her hard, rosy nipples straining through another sexy as sin, lacy black bra.

His fingers trailed up and down her side, rippling over the faint outline of her ribs and lean stomach. The tremors weakened. Her breaths came easier. And because she was as stubborn as she was beautiful, she pulled the mask off her face before her lungs would have been ready.

"Apparently, I'm allergic to anti-virals." Liv looked him in the eye. It took every ounce of self-control not to cry like a little kid learning their first lesson about the family pet who went to live on MeMaw's farm.

Adrenaline evaporated. He wove his fingers into her hair and pulled her into a fierce kiss. Hard.

Demanding he held her against him, and he didn't let go until his head began to spin. "Please don't do that to me again."

The pressure to man up burned into his scalp. He cleared his throat and pulled away.

She grinned, tired, lazy. "I'll try." Her warm honeyed twang and plump red lips shot straight to his cock.

He grimaced, pushing down the ache of unresolved want. "Wear the damned oxygen, Olivia."

"Whatever you say, Dr. Cole."

****

Crammed next to Jorge's stretcher and the battered medication Pyxis, Liv tried not to roll her eyes. She had no idea how long Andy intended to treat her like a patient. It started sweet, but quickly ventured into the irritating category. He was a hoverer, and while the tingles of new love and attraction craved closeness, her knee jerk reaction was to tell him to back the fuck up. But that was a stupid fight to pick. He loved her, and she loved him, so she wore the pulse oximeter on her finger, and the nasal cannula in her nose even though her saturations had been ninety-eight or better for the last hour.

"I'm fine. I promise," she assured with a smile. The one that made him blush and bite his lip, but his gaze wavered.

"You were dead. In my arms. Cold. Not breathing—"

She grabbed his hand and laced them together. "And you saved me."

Andy ground his molars together and scratched at his chin. Anderson Cole was a worried mess, but he was sexier than hell doing it.

Liv finally got some breathing room when Andy

spoke to the suits from Atlanta. No other deaths. No other patients with symptoms. A definite tick in the good juju column. This had to be it. Their up-swing. Rose. Exposure. Anaphylaxis. Not dead. Upswing.

"When are we going to pull his chest-tube?" she asked to Andy's sexier than hell back. Ass. His whole tense backside.

He turned around raising an amused eyebrow. "Always so eager to get the procedure. *We're* not pulling anything."

She groaned, annoyed he knew her so well, then glanced at Jorge, rubbing his sternum. "Sorry, buddy, I tried."

Wired and jittery, Liv removed her oxygen and went on the hunt for rations. Andy frowned from across the room. She answered his unsaid protest with a just as passive shrug. Unless, he intended to keep her tied down, or otherwise … occupied, he needed to ease up.

Something had to get her back on pointe. Epi and Benadryl may have saved her life, but the medications fogged her brain. If Smithson learned his lesson, the answer to every night-shifters prayers would be there in the form of a sixteen ounce can of toxic energy. She dug through the box and found beloved lime-ick Monster.

Liv popped the tab. Her mouth watered. The first sip burst on her tongue. Her surroundings sharpened. More enticing than Andy's sexy chest peeking through his white t-shirt, she moaned. "Oh, you know just how to touch a girl…"

Liv kissed the black and green tall-boy. Andy's eyes widened, but a voice overhead yanked away his attention. The tartness began to fade. She smacked her tongue. Rust and salt lingered on her lips. Clear and potent, blood seeped into her mouth.

"Since Mr. Vasquez's prognosis is far improved,

we feel a statement from the both of you would speak volumes. Nothing big. Local news and government officials. It would mean a lot to—"

"No way, Allen. Not until we know for sure Olivia is going to be all right."

Liv rolled her eyes and went back to Jorge. Being talked about like she wasn't there always got stuck in her craw. She dropped into a deep squat to check out the chest tube drainage canister.

"That's what we wanted to tell you, Dr. Cole. All of Ms. Aberdeen's repeat screens are now resulting negative," interjected an unfamiliar, matter-of-fact voice.

The reply caught her off guard. She her lost her balance and fell flat onto her ass with no way to pass it off as sexy or intentional.

Andy shuffled his feet and looked down. Relief. Elation. He'd probably fist bump the air if there hadn't been an audience to judge his manliness. His grin was infectious. She returned it, but shot a curious glance to Smithson in the gallery. Composed. Dignified, but completely lacked the same sentiment.

She lumbered off her hiney with Andy's steady hand wavering a bit beneath her weight. Gravity really wanted her ass on the floor.

"How can y'all know for sure? It's only been three hours since we sent the swabs and blood work."

"We ran the screens ourselves with the rest of the quarantined population. Our testing capabilities are quicker and are far superior in their accuracy."

An involuntary smile crept on her face, but she kept her eyes on Smithson. Blank. Impassive. The emotionless mask people in the business of saving lives learn to wear.

Andy wrapped his arms around her waist and buried his scruff into her neck. "All right, I'll do whatever y'all want. So long as Liv's okay. I'll sing fucking show tunes. I don't care." He held her so tight, she was sure her head would pop like a ripe, axillary abscess.

Dots danced before her eyes. "Easy, cowboy."

He squeezed harder. "No."

She grabbed a syringe filled with ice cold saline and squirted it up his back. He jumped away, then retaliated with a smack at her behind, eying her with delicious, sinful intent. "Dangerous game to play when we'll be outta here in a few hours."

She wanted to revel in it. Lap it up. Bat her lashes and flash him a dip of cleavage. But her nagging nurse's suspicion kept her eyes focused on the gallery. The fellas in the cheap suits all but slapped each other on the back as Smithson shook his head, a faint frown tugging at his cheeks.

Andy couldn't stop smiling while she couldn't ignore a metallic taste gumming up her mouth.

****

Liv fidgeted with her watch and clicked her pen in rhythm to the new Taylor Swift, giving zero fucks about blatant rule breaking. Her nursing manager had yet to stop by, and if the wicked witch of the west suddenly appeared and had a problem with jimmy-rigging the ancient desktop speakers to play annoying pop music, well, Liv had a middle finger waiting with her manager's name on it.

They had an hour left. One hour until she'd step outside and inhale commuter exhaust and Lake rot. It should curl her stomach. But she'd give anything to rid the embedded stink of her sweat and Jorge's blood, and clear her lungs with Chicago's city air. She couldn't wait to melt into her shower, eat a juicy Johnny's Beef with extra peppers, and sleep like a tit-faced baby. She wanted to believe the blood oozing in her mouth meant nothing.

Liv stood over Jorge, hoping to read his mind. He was going to rub himself bald right below his left nipple. She reached for his hand. "Hey, buddy. You need to stop that."

Jorge locked eyes on hers, wide, like he stared into an impending doom. She smiled, but Jorge's fear didn't lift. She went so far as to flirt a little, telling him ladies preferred a symmetrically hairy chest, but he didn't break.

Liv looked up and found Andy staring at her boobs from across the stretcher. Caught, he grinned, sheepish and unapologetic, as if to say, "So what? They're mine." The little thought sizzled inside, but Jorge fought her grip, this time to scratch so hard he broke the skin.

"Andy, something's wrong..."

He sat up, mirroring her movements. "I'm really tired of you sayin' that."

She shrugged. No arguing the truth.

He rose to his feet with a pensive, all-encompassing glance, sifting through possibility after possibility. Filing the "what-if's" from the "if this, then that". Her cheeks flushed. Want and warmth pumped through her body just by watching the man think.

"Jorge. *¿Que pasó?*"

Andy took the better part of a minute trying to get Jorge to verbalize anything he could comprehend. Liv fell into her routine and putzed with the monitor. "His pressures are up. Maybe we jumped the gun on extubating."

He frowned and said nothing.

Liv inspected the large, dressing covering the hole in his ribs and the opaque, silicone tube draining his chest. A thick, glob of red seemed to plug up the tube.

What was the first rule of nursing school? Always wash your hands and don't milk the chest tube?

"Dr. Cole, I think the tube needs to be stripped."

Apparently in arrogant trauma doc mode, Andy replied with a half-assed nod and continued to inventory and anticipate. She took it as a verbal order, and grabbed her hemostats and some four-by-four gauze pads. Lubing up the cotton, she coated her trusty fix-all nursing pliers and slid it up the tube. It stretched, thinning out the red glob, but it didn't break apart.

"Something sure as hell ain't right. It's a clot."

He shook his head and looked down his nose. "That's not possible."

She shot a warning glance right back into the baby blues that made her knees weak. "Do you always condescendingly contradict your nurses in front of patients, or is this some overstep of familiarity on your part because you've seen me naked?"

He clenched his jaw, all foxy and pissed off. She crossed a line, but called him on his crap. Either way he should know better than to use that kind of asshat tone with her. But of course, clotting didn't seem possible. The entire disease process ruined the body's ability to clot. Thus the whole unpleasant complication of exsanguination.

Jorge started to writhe, rolling from side to side as if whichever way he rested set his skin on fire. Anxiety bubbled in her gut. The good kind. The good kind of stress that jump starts your instincts. Immediately, she fired through tasks, checking her lines for patency, grabbing lab tubes, and warming up the ventilator should Jorge need to be put back down.

Javier materialized in the gallery. Contorted in some form of spite or jealousy, he crossed his arms. "Looks like a party down there."

In the best mood of her life, Liv couldn't come up with a clever line to put him in his place, but apparently, she wasn't who he wanted to have a chat with.

"Hey, Doc," he called.

Andy cracked a knuckle and looked up. She half expected the glass to burst from the torpedoes of testosterone, but Javier broke their gaze.

"Don't do the interview."

Chapter Twenty-Four

Conflict ripped through Andy's spine. His shoulders slumped. High on the good news Liv would be all right he'd have agreed to anything. He knew why Smithson and the medical board would want to put on a show. As much as it sucked giant donkey balls, a hospital was a business. A Joint Commission, insurance company and government-controlled business.

He tried to read into Javi's flat lined expression through the distance. "I gave my word."

"Whatever, man, don't listen to me. Do what you want."

The monitor wailed, and Jorge groaned with pain. It didn't make sense. It was supposed to be over. Jesus Christ, it had to be over.

Olivia called him back. "What's next?"

Javi's judgment needled him in the back, while Liv's wide eyes looked to him for strength and direction. He clenched a fist and beat the counter before turning to the chaos.

Jorge cried and clawed at his sternum. "*Pecho. Mi pecho.*"

Synapsis fired. Dots connected. He shoved aside his exhaustion, and grasped for the end of his fraying rope. "Let's re-intubate, and I'll take a look with the ultra-sound machine."

Wind syphoned through the anti-chamber. A huge, bright white figure with a yellow hood and hoses up the back appeared. The HazMat suits should have triggered relief. It should have been a light at the end of the clusterfucked tunnel. He searched for Smithson through the layers of protective plastic and tempered glass, but when the medical director turned around, he seemed to look anywhere but his gaze. A crew of cameras and reporters were just beyond the door. Something pinched in his gut.

He stole a glance at Olivia and up into the gallery. Javier wasn't wearing his usual smug indignation. He clasped a hand over his mouth as if to hold back vomit. Their eyes connected. Slow and deliberate, Javier shook his head.

Andy took the cue and turned his back on Smithson. He might have agreed to become the hospital poster boy, but now wasn't the time. For all of his brilliance, it seemed like Smithson couldn't read the room for shit.

"Allen, don't even bother coming in here. Something's wrong. Jorge's fixin' to crump."

Liv approached with the bedside sono-machine and medications. He had her run enzymes, bleeding times, and chemistries. But if a fat, glob of blood clotted in the chest tube, the risk of a pulmonary embolus seemed ripe for the picking. If the juju was ever going to start turning around, now would be a good fucking time.

She beamed a confident smile. It had to be fake. There was no way in hell she believed in him or anything they were doing that much.

A small group of reporters, cameras, men he recognized as members of the board clamored for a spot close behind the glass. *Fools.* If they had any respect for the virus that floated behind the fragile layer, they'd run the other way.

"In case those HazMat suits have made y'all deaf and blind, now's not a good time."

He pressed the probe into Jorge's chest, closing his mind to the distractions and noise surrounding him. At first pass, he saw nothing but the familiar, mechanical swoosh of blood pounding through Jorge's heart. But it couldn't be right. A grown man didn't howl in pain like that for the hell of it.

He stared at the black and white image until an anxious sweat dotted his forehead and his eyes crossed. Looking for a clot in the vast vasculature of the lungs was harder than finding a diamond in a sea of sand.

His thoughts jumbled. Olivia. Jackson. Greta. Jorge. His pupils took in information, but his brain couldn't process a damned thing. His hair fell in his eyes. He brushed it away with his forearm and squinted Jorge back into focus.

Liv permeated his air as she bent before him to check the chest tube and lines. He breathed her in, and like an addict getting his fix, he settled. Regrouped. He'd become an embarrassment without her.

Another swipe and press into Jorge's ribs then down. Liv watched. Concern weighed on her features, but hope gleamed in her eyes. He stared. Intense. Unyielding. Love swelled in his chest so tight it choked him. He coughed up composure and glanced back at the ultrasound screen.

And there it was. Clear as day. "It's an aortic dissection," Andy said, wiping at his brow. "Smithson! We need the OR now."

****

Liv looked over the patient she'd begun to know better than herself. "I knew something was wrong. How did I miss it?"

Smithson shuffled in the antechamber. The bright white plastic suit and yellow hood muffled most of reply. "He's got one hour left."

"Look at him. He doesn't have thirty seconds."

Monitors wailed, every wire attached to a machine beeped and screamed warning of Jorge's imminent demise. Jorge's chest tube had been dry for a day, and now cherry red, arterial blood began to seep from his fraying aorta.

Liv prepped for a mass transfusion. Six plastic bags of dark red hung over her head. With her beloved Sharpie, she marked each to correspond with an IV line and port on the rapid infuser. In her career, she'd seen three aortic dissections. Most patients died before ever getting through the door. The few that did, all died within minutes. But she hadn't come this far to have Jorge die because they couldn't get him to surgery.

Stubborn, furious tears burned behind her eyelids. She bit them back and glared at the gallery. The CDC had done nothing except make promises they had no intentions to keep. But Olivia was hell bent on keeping hers.

Andy swiped the transducer over Jorge's middle. It didn't take an MD behind her name to see the giant, bulging artery running through center of the body. The solution was instant.

"Open him up," she sputtered.

He shook his head, not a refusal but confusion.

"What?" he asked.

"You could open him up. Open him up and clamp off the dissection. They'll have to get him to the OR then."

He sucked in a hard breath and grimaced. "I can't make that kind of call. First do no harm, remember?"

"You can!" she insisted and rushed to his side. "You already did—the moment you brought him in here."

"And look where it got us—you."

She wove her fingers into the hem of his shirt and forced herself in his eye line. It was the first time he'd ever resisted their lure. The chaos of the room began to fade. Jorge's pale, pallid, lifelessness seemed to blend into the background. It was just her and him.

"We can fix this."

He looked down. In the hours they had spent locked in the room they'd gone belly up and bass-ackwards. His panty dropping, trauma doc swagger had dwindled into self-criticism and doubt. Wide eyed and lost, he squinted her into focus. In a heartbeat he changed. Hardened. His blue eyes deepened. Andy grabbed onto the hope she looked to him with. Somewhere, she flipped the switch.

He nodded. Short. Simple. And she shot into action.

In a breath, Jorge was put back down. Andy didn't bother with his broken Spanglish. There wasn't time, and he was so fucking tired of lying to him. Seamless, they worked hip to hip to prep then slice. He eyed Smithson through the glass. Three minutes was all he needed. A hard cut from bottom of the ribs down to the belly button so he could pull apart organs and dig around for his bulging central artery.

It was a blatant overstep. Jorge needed surgery, not an ER attending desperate for a save, but the statistics and juju were not on his side.

Liv draped him in a gown and covered Jorge's face and crotch with sterile towels. Smithson's eyes widened, taking in Olivia and her movements. They connected just as she opened and presented Andy with the blunt end of a ten-blade. Smithson's sputters of protest were sucked up by the ventilation system.

The scalpel was hot between his fingers. "I suggest you get surgery down here. STAT."

Chapter Twenty-Five

It was wronger than wrong, but Liv wanted a camera. Like a skydiver documenting an epic drop, the urge to snap a selfie as she suctioned pints of blood from Jorge's chest coursed through her veins. Even with a lifetime of lifesaving left, she was pretty sure very little would top this, and she'd seen a guy chopped in half by the Metra train. Across the stretcher, fine lines of excitement poked out the edge of Andy's mask as he dug around Jorge's thoracic cavity, and the gallery overflowed with the rest of the adrenaline junkie freaks who thrived on life in the ER.

Andy called for a clamp. Liv slapped it into his open palm. Behind her, the sealed door ripped open. Smithson burst inside. Billowy, plastic suits squeaked along the tile.

"What in the hell are you doing, Anderson?"

"Saving his life, for the fourth goddamn time."

Smithson eyed the field. Jorge's insides were pried apart. Directly in the center quivered Jorge's aorta, a threadbare firehose pulsing with the frantic rate of his heart. Andy worked the clamp tight in his fist. The bulging artery shrank then stilled.

"The three of you have an hour left under quarantine! This *could* have waited."

"Nothing you can do about it, now. He needs bypass and a graft. Clock's ticking."

"And really, Dr. Smithson, Jorge's done his time. Technically Dr. Cole and I are the only ones still under quarantine," Liv added without looking up from her task. Refilling Jorge's tank with donor, packed red blood cells was a never-ending battle, and the reason mass transfusion protocols required two nurses. It looked like

Andy got the easier end of the deal, and he just finished filleting the man open.

Liv caught Andy in a split-second glance. Love and respect brimmed in his eyes. She flushed turning to lovesick mush when he tore off his gloves and ripped away the surgical mask. Happy pride grinning from ear to ear.

The suits from the CDC filed into the scrub room used as the antechamber, all sans high level Personal Protective Equipment, having a silent conversation of discreet looks and shrugs.

Something was off. Javi, Moe, and two other day shift charges nurse stood by the newly opened entrance. She spotted her elusive ER Nursing Director in scrubs two decades out of date. Her gut twisted. Maybe she was just tired of being observed, and scrutinized.

She turned her back on the audience and pulled a sterile drape over Jorge's face and wide-open middle.

Andy cleared his throat. "It's Monday, right? Who's on for cardio-thoracic? If y'all can't get your shit together, I might as well unclamp and let him bleed out on the floor."

There had been an eerie absence of noise after Andy secured the dissecting artery, but in a hot beat, everything and anything that had an alarm went off.

"Allen! Surgery. *Now!*"

Liv threw him a pair of new gloves and dove back into Jorge's belly. God, she loved to watch him work, but there wasn't time to sit and fawn over her trauma doc boyfriend. She looked through the ceiling to the Lord on the other side. They needed a miracle—and lots of fucking hands. Smithson pulled off the negative pressure hood and tore his body free of the plastic suit. Dozens of bodies filed in elbowing for room. It's what should have happened three days ago. It made zero sense.

A beefy scrub tech shoved her out of the way and assumed control of the sterile field. Javi rifled through her fourth round of packed red blood cells.

Liv let out an inadvertent, possessive growl. "Get your grubby hands off my rapid infuser."

"Now isn't the time to be territorial. You're going on three days of no sleep and sloshing around with epinephrine and Benadryl in your system."

She frowned.

Javier flashed a quick glance at Anderson over his shoulder. "Look, I'm not trying to be a dick. I care, you know?"

Olivia nodded, and ripped off her bloody gloves, snapping them into a pile of garbage on the floor. Her first instinct was to look for Andy, but he was lost in the sea of black scrubs and surgical gowns. She hid from the chaos under the blue paper sheet near Jorge's face.

"C'mon, buddy. Hold out just a while longer. Can you do that for me? Give us a few more minutes before you give up."

She stroked his cheek then ran her fingers through Jorge's thick, chocolate hair and pressed her forehead to his. ER nurses didn't get close to their patients—it's a survival technique. The mantra was, "Treat 'em and street 'em," not just to make room for more patients, but to keep boundaries. Distance. Anything to keep from shouldering the pain of constant loss. Any nurse that wanted to last more than six months needed to figure that out before taking boards, or they should really consider a job waitressing—it was essentially the same thing with far less blood and people trying to die.

The scab from Rose's death started to dehisce. She wasn't strong enough to have two people she cared about die when all she could do was sit back and watch.

A voice boomed through the trauma room's ambient noise. "We've lost a pulse."

She pawed at his neck. "No! Don't you dare!" Liv commanded to his blank face, then threw her weight onto his sternum. Hard and fast, she beat hope through Jorge's body. Hard and fast, she prayed for God to grant a miracle.

Seconds passed like an eternity until a body joined her under the drape. Hands gripped her arm.

She shoved her shoulder into the mass pulling her away. "Get the hell away from me!"

Liv kept her rhythm and glanced back. Andy staggered a few steps, then straightened. He should have been mad, but failure lined his face. Defeat. And it was unacceptable.

Anger fueled her fire, until tears burned in her eyes.

Andy approached her, palms raised, then dwarfed his hands over hers. "We've done our part, baby. It's over. He's gone."

There she had it. Jorge was going to die. Not from the incurable contagion everyone feared. Not from sepsis or infection. Somehow, he defied the odds, but couldn't beat unlucky genetics and the rule of threes.

Bile seeped up her throat. "After everything we've done… This can't be it."

Strength left her body, and the compressions of Jorge's heart followed. She collapsed onto her knees with Andy right behind. He eased her down, and held her tight, weaving his hands into her hair. The room stilled. Jorge's hand fell to the side, like he knew she needed it. Liv laced her fingers with his, and through the silence came a beep. And another. And another.

"Oh, sweet Jesus," she cried. Andy picked her off his lap, and she dove for his neck. A pulse. Strong.

Undeniable.

The relief seared like fire in her veins and sucked the air from her lungs. She couldn't find words, but found Andy over her shoulder. She nodded.

The flat line of Andy's mouth pressed into a smile. "He's not dead yet, y'all. Move him!"

Together they hurried in stride, flowing with the current of bodies toward the door. Liv refused to let go of Jorge's hand. Letting go might fuck with the juju.

Andy's heat fused with her back. He threw out orders and directions as they made their way to the exit, leading the team with the kind confidence that made her swoon. They reached the door. Her lungs burned. Hungry for the fresh air of freedom, but a strong, tattooed arm yanked her back.

Javier shadowed by a stern, zero fucks given Dr. Martin stopped her tracks. "That's as far as you go. Liv. You guys need a decon and debriefing."

****

She wasn't high on the save. It didn't feel like all the other lives Liv intervened on God's behalf. It was like He did her a favor. He granted her a tried and true miracle, the kind you get once a lifetime. Perhaps it was a touch early to cash in that chip ... but right then, as she watched Jorge be wheeled up and out of the Pit, under the microscopic eye of everyone she worked with, she was glad the Lord answered her prayer.

The reward for saving a life while being stuck in a room for three days, having to pee in a sink, eat stale crackers, all under the glowing prospect of death was a freezing cold shower and scrub down with steel wool. Liv wanted to scream at the injustice. Call out the thankless, coarse treatment, but she'd go through the motions if it meant she was that much closer to her two-thousand thread count, high-calorie comfort food, and naked cuddle time with her trauma doc boyfriend. And maybe a vacation.

In the decontamination showers, Javi dangled a washcloth in Liv's face wearing a dickish smirk. Liv blushed. Tired. Smelly and feeling all around unsexy didn't mean dead.

"You're outta your goddamn mind," Andy hissed, apparently past the point of giving a shit.

"Don't get your lasso in a knot, Doc. I'm just messing around. CiCi is here for Liv."

Olivia's mouth watered. The combination of testosterone and clenched, chiseled jaw perfection would set a better blaze than a lit match and lighter fluid.

"Javier, you're going to get your ass beat if you're not careful."

He shrugged too casually to be trusted and flashed a quick glance to Dr. Martin. The silent second screamed with unsaid feeling. God, they were so busted.

Liv grinned, taking her towel from CiCi. She staggered into the sterile, three by three aluminum shower. To her right, Andy did the same. His gaze, tender but wanting, washed over her as she pulled the plastic curtain along a rusty rod. A head taller than the decontamination cubicle, Andy peered over the wall.

She contorted out of her top and tossed it into a red biohazard bag. Air hissed through his teeth. Sure she stank and was sweatier than a Democrat at an NRA rally, but it didn't seem to bother Andy one bit. Timing be damned. Decontamination babysitters be damned. It turned her on.

"Like what you see, cowboy?" she tempted, resisting the urge to look up. There was no telling what she'd succumb to if he drilled his baby blues into her, but his pull went way past magnetic. Every cell in her body cried out for him. Like an addict, she caved.

He devoured her with his eyes, then grinned. It hit her like a morphine rush. Want. Relief. Together they'd saved a life, a life the rule of threes pegged for death. And she was safe. Bad juju hung over her head like a black cloud ready to pour, but Andy was always there holding the umbrella. He loved her. No doubt about it.

"Think I need to see a bit mo—" He cut mid-word as freezing water flooded over their heads.

"Scrub clock starts now," a voice barked over the deluge.

That was un-fucking-necessary. Furious, she hugged herself for cover. "Forget Dr. Cole, you're going to answer to me."

She ripped open the curtain expecting to see Javi's smart assed look of innocence, but it was CiCi. Timid, quiet, and with her hand on the door that would leave Liv and Andy in absolute privacy for the first time in forever. Except, decons were done with an audience. Always.

Dr. Martin smiled, pointing to the clock, then scurried through the heavy door seconds before it slammed shut.

Andy threw aside the curtain and reached Liv in one step. There wasn't time for a clever quip, or seductive smile. He wrapped his arms around her waist and pulled her from the frigid downpour. In a heartbeat, his mouth was on hers, sliding his tongue past her lips. Hot and unrelenting, he claimed her with a kiss.

His weight pushed them from the water and to the other wall. Liv groped at his wet shirt, running her hands over his chest. Andy groaned, breaking contact with her lips to pull his shirt over his head. He dove between her breasts, then peeled her bra strap down her shoulder, and popped a nipple free from the black, lace cup. His thumb teased the tight peak while the other caressed circles into the small of her back.

She sighed. Her clit pulsed with want. She drew him in, wanting the weight of his erection against her belly. She loved tall men, but at six-three she couldn't rub her swollen sex over his cock. He must have read her dirty mind. Andy gripped her ass, then lifted her off her feet. She wrapped her legs around his middle. The connection was instant.

She gasped, feeling his urgency and mirrored it. He set her on a linen cart. She ran her tongue along all her favorite parts that weren't waist down. His neck, his collarbone, all the delicious places that haunted her memory as he tore away the remaining shreds of delicate lace holding her breasts in the air.

The throb between her legs grew. She pawed at the knot of his scrubs. He grabbed for her hands and groaned, exhaling his frustration. Restraint.

"It's been days, Liv. I don't have anything—"

"I don't care. I want you." She held him tight with her legs and crushed her body to his. Liv took charge of his kiss. Their movements. "*I* need you."

Andy wove his fingers into her hair and brought her gaze to his. He ran a thumb over her lips, taking in the purple rings painted beneath her eyes, and the flush in her cheeks. "Jesus, Olivia. I love you."

Her heart burst. *Everything* burst. She beamed, lovestruck and looney. "I love you, too, Dr. Cole," she twanged, "but we have a lifetime to whisper sweet nothings. Right now we have three minutes to—"

He didn't let her finish. He sealed his mouth over hers sliding his hands down the back of her scrubs to palm her ass. She giggled into his mouth when he squeezed and lifted her just enough to peel her pants down her thighs. Liv didn't bother with the knot that slung his scrubs dangerously low on his waist. If there were time she'd pause and admire the happy trail and tight V that led the way to his cock as it sprang free.

He kneed her legs spread and brought a hand to the hot spot between her thighs. His thumb pulsed over her clit, and he dipped a finger into her wetness. She rolled her hips over his working fingers and purred. Sinful pressure built behind her navel.

She moaned, and her head fell back, driving her pelvis down. She tightened, drawing his fingers deeper. Faster. A flick of his thumb and she'd come for days, but Andy removed his hand. He brought his fingers to his mouth and sucked and savored. "If there isn't time to eat your pussy, this will have to do."

It was a line right out of her smut of the month book, but sweet baby Jesus, it hit the spot. He gripped her waist and yanked her closer to the edge. Already wide, he lifted her leg to deepen his angle. Her head fell to the side. Andy kissed the hollow of her throat and between her breasts, then filled her with one thrust.

Her breath caught in her throat. Hard. Rhythmic, he slammed into her again. And again. The build was instant, picking up where his fingers left off. He pulled her to him so her breasts bounced in time, rubbing her clit as he worked. She tried to swallow her moan, but a man should be rewarded when they did something right. So fucking right.

One moan opened the flood gates. Andy cupped a hand over her mouth to catch the pleasure, but didn't slow down. Every sound that purred from her throat spurred him faster between her legs.

Pleasure grew, swelling deep within her belly, rolling up her spine and out her mouth. She choked on ragged breaths, calling to God. Jesus. And of course, Andy Cole.

"Like that, baby?"

She writhed beneath him, working her body to match his movements. He dipped her back. New angle. New sensation. The kind of good that deserved a scream of yesses, but holding onto a sliver of consciousness, she bit her lip and whispered, "More."

Andy obeyed. He slammed into her once again, palming a callused hand around her breast. Rough. Demanding. His want over her pleasure. It must have pushed him past control. He gripped her sides, arching her toward his chest and kissed her. Gentle. Tender. A simple lover's kiss, and a stark disparity to the lust he fucked into her.

The waves of her orgasm surged the second their lips touched. "Come for me, Olivia."

He removed his hand as if it was the barrier to her ecstasy. Her muffled cries amplified.

Andy growled, brought his lips to her throat as if to taste the vibrations. "That sound. So sexy. It'll be the death of me…"

She let out a giggle, but it was stifled by another thrust. And another. The tidal wave of her orgasm crested. She hit the plateau and floated at the apex until she crashed into climax with Andy following right behind.

****

He couldn't move. Not on his life. Andy knew they were seconds away from embarrassing discovery, but he couldn't fucking move. He rested his forehead against Liv's while she came down. Her chest heaved as she caught her breath. Unintentional. And sexy as hell.

"Glad we got that out of the way," he crooned, adjusting upright.

Olivia smiled. The one that made everything go all catawampus and patted at the battered, rolling sex cart. "The perfect height. I think this deserves a special spot in my boudoir."

He kissed her nose and offered her a hand. "Anything my lady wishes."

She hopped down and wavered when her feet hit the floor. Liv reached out with both hands, one for balance, and the other to root to Andy.

He crouched to her height. Immediately inventorying for any signs of syncope. Liv pressed her knuckles into her temple and winced. His heart, still on sex rebound, froze in his chest.

"Everything all right?"

Her full lips pressed into a pout. "Please don't look at me like I'm a patient. I'm just suffering from a little post-coital wooziness."

He stood a little straighter, resisting the urge to puff up his chest and glanced at the towering digital clock with the countdown stopped, flashing "O-O-thirty.'

Caressing her hip, Andy guided Olivia back under the spray and lathered up a washcloth. "May I?"

Her green eyes flickered to life. "Please do, cowboy."

He laughed and started massaging her neck with suds. "Would you believe I've never ridden a horse in my life?"

She grinned and submerged her face under the warmer water. "Seriously?"

"Texan's honor."

"We'll have to remedy that, Dr. Cole. Say on the beach in Cabo?"

He kissed her wet, puckered lips. "You're speaking my language."

A hollow whack echoed the metal door. They sprang apart, like a pair of necking kids caught by Bible-thumping adults.

"Time's up. You guys had better be decent,"

hollered the asshat through a crack in the frame.

Andy rolled his eyes. "Just a sec," he called back and swooped Liv in his arms. He pressed their hearts together then kissed her lips. Equal parts hard and soft, it was one he wanted to savor.

There was another bang. She squirmed in his embrace, but he held tight and slid his tongue into her willing mouth. Blessed with a better resolve, Liv pushed him off.

"Well, I do declare, Anderson Cole, you want to take advantage of me."

His cock twitched. That O'Hara act was a first-class ticket to boner town. "Yes, ma'am," he crooned, letting his drawl linger.

She giggled and shoved him out, then into his own shower stall. "Shoo!"

The door swung open. He caught a glimpse of CiCi, and if the mortified gasp he heard as he pulled the curtain were any indication, she caught a glimpse of his lily-white behind.

On the other side of the wall, Olivia hummed to herself. The same subdued lullaby from the other day. His brain and dick responded like a horny virgin while the rest of him filled to the brim with sap. Unmanly sap. But he wouldn't have had it any other way. Loving the woman was more natural than breathing, and trying to deny it would be as impossible as breathing without air.

He contorted under the water and rinsed away the briny, medical soap imagining what came next. From the second he saw Rose coding on his table, the moment he stupidly let Liv march in the trauma room, the fever and the well-timed visit from his ex-wife, he couldn't help but fixate on the rule of threes. What a crock of shit. When it came to him and Liv, it was more like whatever could go wrong, will. And not to tempt the juju now that it swung in their favor. Hearing her sweet, Savannah twang mindlessly banter with CiCi, he allowed himself the luxury of picturing their future.

"I know you said Cabo, baby, but after all this I'm thinking Maui. I have a friend down in Austin that has a place on the water who owes me a favor."

Andy rubbed the suds from his eyes expecting to hear her warm, honeyed voice sass out a reply.

He waited a beat, resisting the urge to pop his head over the short person's shower stall. But she said nothing. His insides twisted.

"Liv?" he called, panic surging in his chest.

CiCi chimed in. "Liv, I stole you a real towel."

A muffled splat replied. The shoddy metal divider swayed. Soap singed in his eyes. He squeezed them shut and backed away, pawing water from his face.

Silence held in the air. The hard downpour suspended in space. Hours of blackness passed with just one blink. In his life, time never slowed to savor the good. Time slowed to imprint the bad.

He forced his eyes open. Olivia's outstretched hand lay at his feet.

Chapter Twenty-Six

It had to be a joke. A subconscious mind trick with a serious dose of déjà vu. Any second now Liv would slither her lithe, sexy body under the divider and rise onto her knees and wrap her lips around his cock.

Half tempted to nudge her hand with his bare foot, Andy willed his fantasy true, but on the other side of the curtain, CiCi let out a gasp. The deluge pooling around his feet turned pink.

He threw himself out of the shower. CiCi was already on her hands and knees, covering Liv's paleness with a blood tinged towel. She pressed her fingers onto Liv's carotid artery. Their eyes connected. Time stopped.

CiCi pinched her lips together, but relaxed her shoulders.

"She just passed out. Maybe the water was too hot, and she got lightheaded," she said, using her rational Dr. Martin tone. With a dart of her eyes, CiCi's face flushed.

"Doc. Do you mind not free balling in front of my girl?" Javi called from over his shoulder.

A pair of scrubs hit Andy in the chest. He wasn't in the mind to be embarrassed, nor apologize for thinking Javi'd been a girlfriend steeling douchebag for the last week. But he did toss him a glance of thanks. It went unappreciated. Javier stood with his back facing the shower calling for assistance on his walkie.

Andy contorted his wet legs into the scrubs pants, fixated on Liv cradled in CiCi's lap. She palpated the tangled mess of auburn curls for injury. His gut twisted. She wasn't opening her eyes.

Andy dove to the floor and scooped her up. "I got it." She folded in his arms. Even in acute anaphylaxis she had more fight.

He inventoried her cool, pale skin, the sallow, purple swirl under her eyes and cupped her cheek like she was made of blown glass. His first instinct was to shake her out of the cruel trick she must have been playing.

The hum of Javier and CiCi's discussion sharpened. He tried to block out their judgment. If he looked as destroyed and desperate as he felt then, he more than deserved a minute to compose himself.

He cleared his throat and found a final shred of dignity. "Livy, you with me, baby?"

She stirred. The shred threatened to evaporate.

Liv whimpered, then winced. "Javier, you had better not be callin' a rapid response."

Andy rolled his eyes. "Good Lord, woman you're trying to kill me. Are you all right? You're shaking. When was the last time you ate?"

He started to ramble. Finally, the critical thinking process kicked in. He grabbed another towel from the sexcapades linen cart, and worked the harsh cotton over her arms and chest trying to sop up the wetness.

CiCi and Javier kept their faces toward the door. His insides set to boil. "Palermo," he said so low it rivaled a growl. The attack on his last name got his attention. "I want a STAT blood sugar and a wheelchair. Dr. Martin, find Smithson. I'm taking her home."

Javier's face sparked. Andy knew it wasn't defiance, but that was how his body reacted. He went rigid. The weight of Liv in his arms tethered him down, and he calmed himself with a quick inhale of her dewy skin.

"Don't be a jerk to the nurses, Dr. Cole," she warned in her Savannah twang. The sweet upturn of her lips sucked all his manliness dry. Tears squeezed behind his eyes, and he laughed. Javier and CiCi started bickering in the kind of forced whispers perfected by closeted lovers. Andy felt a pang of sympathy and turned his attention back to Olivia.

Andy swallowed her in his arms and helped her upright. She pinched her lip between her teeth as if to hold back a scream.

"Baby, what hurts?"

She shook her head. He knew the next thing she'd try to say was "I'm fine".

"Don't lie to me."

The metal door swung open. Smithson marched in with the suits from the CDC. Liv wrenched her eyes shut and turned her face into his chest. He couldn't tell if she was hiding from the light, or from the sudden audience. Andy threw himself over Liv's body covered by nothing more than a wet towel.

"Christ, Allen. Give us a minute. It was just a syncopal episode. Probably a little low blood sugar. I don't remember the last time she ate."

Olivia continued to squirm. A rusty, metallic tang broke through the blend of bleach and antiseptic. The smell of clotted blood collected on his tongue and warmth oozed down his side. The three-inch gash down his flank from the ambulance tussle must have ripped open. Too occupied, he felt nothing. His hands floated over her head and neck, trying to provide comfort and palpate for injury while he read the silent glances and forced expressions.

Exhaustion seemed to wilt Smithson's shoulders as he approached. His green surgical scrubs were dotted a deep red. His gaze darted around the decontamination stall and eventually down at Olivia wrapped in his arms. The evasion of eye contact felt intentional. Andy looked back to Javier with CiCi pulled protectively into his side.

And that's when he saw it. Pity.

"No! She's not sick!" he cried, making the connection before his body had a chance to respond. "She needs rest and to get the hell out of here."

He rallied off the floor, holding Liv tight against the frantic pounding in his chest. A stretcher crashed through the metal divider. The tiny room swarmed with bodies.

"No!" he bellowed. His voice sounded foreign bouncing off the polished steel walls. Smithson put a hand on his shoulder and the other on Olivia's cheek. Andy drew back as if Smithson were the poison making Liv limp and listless. "I swear to God, Allen. Don't touch her."

Smithson froze, then offered up his palms in surrender. Andy hoisted Liv's dead weight close and shifted from foot to foot. The walls closed in, and like a raging lunatic he paced in place expecting the sea of people to part before him.

As if she felt him unravel, Liv murmured a reminder to play nice. Even in the midst of pain and what should have been naked embarrassment, she had better control over herself. He inhaled the air along her temple and settled. Never in his life had he needed someone the way he needed Olivia. He fell too hard. Too fast. And if something happened. There'd be no coming back.

"Sorry," he said, directing it at Smithson, but for everyone's benefit. The apology was sincere, but it didn't derail his intent and when they weren't given room to leave, his patience fizzled. "I'm going to take her home. Now."

He crossed the tiny space with a large step, then stopped. Liv's warm honeyed voice came out strangled, stopping him in his tracks.

"Andy," she breathed.

He knew the tone, knew the words that came next.

"Something's wrong."

Chapter Twenty-Seven

The trauma room wasn't big enough. White wash walls with miles of cable and wire enclosed on him like a vise. The scent of blood—*her* blood—replaced her vanilla and cinnamon.

He dove among the chaos, wanting to be everywhere and nowhere at the same goddamn time. He elbowed for space to work over Liv's limp, pallid body. It was torture. Seeing her, her pain, knowing there was nothing he could do.

"You told me—to my face—that she was safe!" Andy cried out, tearing his hands through his hair. Smithson ignored his accusation, already treating him like a belligerent boyfriend raging in the background.

Liv retched. Her gaunt shoulders arched off the stretcher. A gush of bright red erupted from her mouth. He grabbed for suction. Another body and pair of hands rammed into his side. The long plastic tube slammed against the back of her throat. She choked.

"Give me some goddamn space!" he screamed. Desperation stormed through his body. The room went still. Liv opened her eyes and licked her blood-caked lips. Andy swooped in to get near, but Javier held him back.

He fought against the ape's arms. "What the fuck are you doing?"

Javi threw his weight into Andy's chest. Andy shot contempt right back. "In here. You're not her doctor. Understand?"

Andy paused, struck with the reality he couldn't be both. Liv slurred his name. He jerked out of his way, but Javier grabbed him. "I can't imagine what you're going through, but she needs you, and you sure as shit need her, so get it together. You're three seconds away from me throwing your ass into the waiting room. You hear me, *Anderson*?"

The emphasis pulled him back. He swallowed and looked over at Olivia. CiCi and Torey stood over her and pointed in his direction. She stretched out her hand. She reached for him like she knew he needed a tether. Javier released his hold. Andy crossed the room with one stride. He wove his fingers into hers, knotting his free hand into her hair. Her pale lips turned up with the contact. A half dozen people poked, prodded, assessed, and intervened. Javier was right. He wasn't her doctor. This was what he was meant to do.

"How are you feelin', baby?" he asked.

Her eyebrows knit together. Confusion. Worry. Pain. He couldn't tell which. "Dr. Martin … Torey…" she slurred, sucking air between each word. "They said…"

Andy looked over his shoulder for CiCi. Smithson. Anyone that could tell him what the hell was happening. "It's okay. You're going to be fine."

She rolled her eyes. "You can't lie for shit, Andy Cole."

"So said the dog groomer."

Liv giggled, but the effort drew a gagging cough. More frothy, pink sputum trickled out her mouth. Pulmonary Hemorrhage. Esophageal tear. Disseminated intervascular coagulation. He snapped his jaw tight to keep from running his mouth. But HIPPA be damned, someone had better start talking soon.

Javier, CiCi, and Smithson stood shoulder to shoulder with an older woman with cropped grey hair and faded, ill-fitting scrubs. He recognized her immediately as Nurse Granger. Head nurse during his residency and now County Med's chief nursing officer and ER nursing director. The nurse yin to Smithson's medical director yang. They stared him down like he was a terminal threat.

A respiratory therapist handed Smithson Liv's latest labs. He turned to stone, and CiCi bit her lip. In the opposite corner of the room there was movement, but Javi held his gaze as if he had the power to funnel his reaction. A screech and squeal pierced the air, and the ventilator chirped to life.

****

It was impossible to focus. To listen. The noise made it unbearable. Swoosh. Hum. Hiss. Swoosh. Hum. Hiss. It was as if she heard her own heart forcing the blood through her brain. Shrill, nasally voices seared through her dura. The only break came from Andy. His rolling, Texas tenor was like a swipe of lidocaine over an aching wound.

"The exposure was just strong enough to attack the vasculature. That's why she's not quarantined," explained one of the men from the CDC. It must have been for Andy's benefit. In his core, he was a doctor, and as much as she hated it, she was a puzzle he'd want to solve. "We could try a transfusion. From you." he continued, "Mr. Vasquez—"

"Jesus Christ. Don't you think I've already thought of that? We're incompatible," he spit like their rival blood types was a reflection on their relationship. She squeezed his fingers. The effort to call his name was too much.

Someone fixed a mask over her face. She tried to gulp down the forced oxygen, but her breath was trapped in sludge. Above her, a flare of light struck the polished sliver of a tongue blade as it snapped together. The earthy, medicinal tang of iodine cut through the smell of rust. Foreign hands wiped the cold antiseptic along her right chest and up her neck. A breathing tube and central line came next. Jorge flashed before her eyes. Then Rose. Their bodies, listless and bleeding from the attempts to save their life. Her eyes began to sting, pink tears clouding her vision.

Andy appeared overhead, and the pinch of a needle below her collarbone disappeared. She smiled and pawed at the mask, trying to make her tongue work in her mouth. He shook his head, but grinned.

"Don't go taking that off. And be still. They're trying to get a line in you, baby."

She persisted. "Lottie. You need to get Lottie here. Before…"

He pressed the mask back over her mouth. "I'll get her here. I promise." He turned over his shoulder to address another person with a front row seat to her doom. Her stomach dropped seeing Torey's expressionless face as she disappeared out the door.

Cardiac and oxygen monitors wailed a crisis duet. Seconds flew by, spiraling faster into her own demise. Time was running out, and all of her unfinished business lurked in her foggy, hypoxic mind. Everything she ignored. Everything she shoved down, blackening her soul. Her Momma. Logan. Her damning sin of pride. The whole reason she never went back. The unbreakable tie to the city she'd never call home.

Her biggest regret imprinted on her consciousness. She squeezed her eyes tight, wanting to eliminate the image, but it forced her tears.

"It's all right, baby. They'll be done soon," he murmured over the swooshing, hiss in her brain then ranted about pain medication. She shook her head and pulled at her mask once more.

Andy leaned closer. She inhaled his malty air, and her pain eased. She opened her eyes, hoping his love was the last thing she would see.

Javier stepped in with a red vial clutched between his fingers. Time was up. "Oxygen Sat's are seventy, Liv. We need to do this."

Andy's composed smile faltered, but he nodded in Javi's direction. There wouldn't be time for Lottie to arrive. The bright light and chaos of the room began to dim.

"No heroics," she sputtered, desperate for her final wishes to be heard. The room went silent. The half dozen bodies seemed to freeze in midair. People in the business of saving lives expect everything done, except when it came to themselves. "A week on the vent. No trach."

Andy gripped her hand and caressed her cheek. She turned into the callused warmth. "C'mon, baby. Don't talk like that."

She looked away and searched for Smithson. Her eyes found his. "No compressions."

"Olivia. No. You can't mean—"

She silenced him with her bloodstained gaze. "Promise me. No CPR."

Andy's brows knit together and brought her hand to his cheek. He ran his nose over the thin skin along her wrist. Goosebumps puckered along her arm, and she scratched his unkempt beard.

Andy answered with a solemn nod. The room scrambled back to life. Smithson barked orders in his dominant prose. "Seven-o ET tube. Andy do you want to step out?"

"I'm fine," he said and kissed her lips. "I love you, Livy. I'm gonna be right here."

With strength she didn't know was left, she smiled. "I love you, too. Tell Lottie when she..." she paused to suck in air. A weight crushed against her sternum that had nothing to do with the fact she couldn't breathe. "Tell Lottie. It all goes to her. Everything goes to Georgia."

****

In the ten years he'd been a doctor, he'd preformed countless intubations. Young. Old. Some lived, more died. That was the reality. He'd see more people die than he'd ever come close to saving. And it sure as sure as hell tarnished the pride from telling people you save lives for a living. When a save happened, it was exhilarating. For a brief moment, all the other losses fade and a man can breathe free from the guilt that comes with being human.

"Anderson," Smithson said, interrupting his moment of selfish loathing. His crinkled brow mirrored his slept in, worked in surgical scrubs. "We've got her stabilized. We're going to move Olivia to a private room."

Andy's scalp prickled. Anger simmered down his spine. He rose from his chair, and glowered at the senior physician and the gallery full of gawkers. "Now you give a damn about her privacy?"

"You know this wasn't a black and white situation."

"I was ready to be your fucking poster boy, Allen. All praise, County Med for handling the next contagion with no loss of life or spread of infection. And you lied. To me. To *her*," he bit out, scratching at his jaw.

Smithson shook his head. Insistent. "No. It wasn't a lie. Olivia's secondary screens were—and still are—negative. But what did happen, or what we can only assume happened, was that her immune system fought the virus and inactivated the strain, but the exposure was still strong enough to attack the vasculature."

Andy turned his back. He didn't care what

Smithson had to say. None of it mattered. Liv had a five percent chance— and because of her fucking request— even less. How could she expect that of him? How could she ask him to sit back and not do everything in his earthly power to save her?

Clinky heels echoed at a manic pace down the hall. They grew into a run. Charlotte appeared in the doorway, windswept and breathless. She paled, her brown eyes widening. "Oh my, Livy…"

Smithson stepped toward her, but Andy held him back. Explaining everything to Lottie was his responsibility. He'd failed at everything else, but at least he could do right by Olivia's best friend.

Lottie straightened and smoothed her hair. She gave Smithson a small, forced smile as he passed.

"Can I bring you a coffee, Lottie?" he asked.

"Thank you. That'd be very kind."

Dr. Smithson left, pausing at the door. "We'll be moving her in a few minutes."

Andy hoped for beat of composure, but Lottie dove right in. "What the in the hell happened, Anderson? I thought she was fine."

His insides turned to fire. It wasn't an accusation, but it sure as shit felt like one and apparently his face said as much.

"I'm not blaming you," she continued, dropping her bag to the floor. Used to the expectations of chivalry, she turned her back just enough to show she expected him to remove her coat.

His life and happiness balanced on the head of needle, but he couldn't help but smile. Lottie went to Liv's side and stroked her face. She scrunched her nose and ran a slender finger along the stiff hospital gown. "Don't worry, Livy. I'll get you out of this eyesore."

She turned back with the sort of openness that

meant she was ready. Ready for him to be upfront and honest. In a few short minutes he vomited a play by play that lead up to the last twenty-four hours, starting with Liv's insistent and amazing role in Jorge's recovery. It was important to start with Jorge, since focusing on his miraculous outcome was the only thing that gave the fucking situation meaning.

Lottie didn't smile. Behind the expressionless face he'd come to think only people in medicine knew how to wear, he saw the quick processes of thought. "And her chances."

His mouth opened to answer, but he couldn't move air to speak. "We don't have everyth—"

"Don't mollycoddle me, Andy. What are the chances my Livy wakes up?"

"Five percent."

Lottie's defiant flare flickered. She cracked, sucking in a tight breath, but in a beat Charlotte VanSutton returned. She pursed her lips and cleared her throat.

"I have some calls to make. Did she say anything … anything for me?"

Javier arrived with a few medics. They gathered her belongings and prepped her for transport. Portable monitors bleeped on, and they worked around Andy and Charlotte as if they were imaginary figures in the room.

Andy rubbed his temples. He'll never forget the last hour of his life, but conjuring up the memories tore his heart out.

"Yeah. Um. Something about Georgia. It all goes to Georgia. Why? For all her southern belle pride, she made it sound like she hated where she came from."

Lottie bit her lip and glanced down. She took Liv's hand, eyeing Javier and his transport medics with suspicion. They must have felt the ire of her judgment.

Javi backed away like she was the medusa and stepped out of the room.

"Savannah is where she's from. Georgia is her daughter."

Chapter Twenty-Eight

"You'll make it, Bubbela," said a comforting, familiar voice. Rose Loveitz paved her way through Liv's consciousness, her brain fighting the sedation and opioid haze. Dreamlike memories clawed forward. "Two days left. Now. Come. Sit. I didn't schlep all this over here for *my* health. Matza balls have magic powers."

"I bet that was the line Logan used to lure in nursing student number five," Lottie snarled, swallowing her ginger ale.

Liv lumbered, puffy and five years past due, to her chaise. She hugged her belly for support, and Lottie hurried over to help her sit. It wouldn't have been the first time she missed the chair, landing flat on her ass. A twinge rolled beneath her ribs. A foot. The baby girl, days from being born, didn't like the change in position. Liv pressed her palm into the tiny extremity. Tears welled in her eyes.

"You'd think a person would get tired of being kicked around," she quipped, but she couldn't bring herself to smile. There was no point in pretending her heart wasn't breaking.

"They're a really sweet family, Olivia," Rose assured her. "Agreeing to all your terms. I bet they'd even let you pick where she goes to college."

Behind them Charlotte huffed, pushing the tray with steaming broth and a fat, doughy ball before her swollen belly. Liv frowned and bit her lip.

Rose nudged her arm, intuitively pushing her to take a bite. "I understand why you haven't told that schlump of a man about the baby. Are you sure you can't tell your Mother?"

Liv swirled a spoon through the steam and

stretched her hand over the width of her stomach, then looked down.

Lottie clasped her hand over Olivia's and fired a laundry list of curse words directed at Liv's mother. "That witch'll be lucky if Livy ever speaks to her again."

The fog of Olivia's mind began to thicken. Another dose of Versed pushed through her veins. The memory smudged, then faded. Blackness enveloped her consciousness, but the final words her Momma ever spoke rang clear.

"Call off that engagement, Olivia-Grace, and you had better get rid of more than the three carats on your left hand by this time next week."

****

Andy paced the short distance between the window and door. Liv's new room had the privacy she deserved, but the monitors and machines keeping Liv alive, sucked up every inch of space. Trapped within her coffin, warm, bright sunshine streamed through mocking his hell.

"Her own mother?" he asked, disgust biting into his words. Charlotte spent the better part of an hour explaining what Liv had been too proud and broken to admit. Her decision to move to Chicago wasn't a decision at all, but a way to save the child left behind by an asshole that couldn't keep his dick in his pants.

"Savannah society loves a scandal. Except when it hits close to home. Calling off an engagement is a seven on the hot gossip scale, a cheating fiancé was a nine, and an out-of-wedlock pregnancy for the former Miss Savannah would have been a ten. So, she ran all the way to this metropolitan travesty so she could put her sweet baby up for adoption and go back home, but you can see how far she made it."

Andy stared, transfixed, by the mechanical rise

and fall of Olivia's chest. Her creamy skin turned translucent, almost blue from blood loss.

"So that's what she couldn't tell me? About her decision to save an innocent life?"

Lottie came to his side and grabbed for his hand. "No. That she couldn't overcome her own pride to keep her. If Livy's biggest regret is giving up her baby girl, her biggest fear is that deep down, she's still her Momma's daughter. Always more concerned about what other people think."

The ventilator bleeped, the smell of rust bit through the air. Frothy, pink sputum crept up the tube. Andy clenched his fingers to keep from being anything but Liv's boyfriend, but the seconds crawled by. Olivia's oxygen levels dipped then plummeted. Lottie paled, and stepped back.

Liv retched around the tube, pink tears seeping down her sallow cheeks. "She needs more sedation. I'm here, baby. I'm here," he soothed, pulling off the bloody secretions she drowned in. She stilled, the screeching alarms satisfied for a moment. He took a shaky breath, Liv's honeyed twang chiding his behavior toward the nurses still played in his ears, but something inside burst. The dam of restraint gave way, and rage erupted from his chest.

He stormed into the nurses' station, blazing ire into every pair of eyes he met. "What the hell is going on out here? Does she have to fucking die to get someone's attention?"

A waifish charge nurse tried to corral and placate his outburst. She recited a bunch of canned crap ingrained from years of "What to do if someone loses their shit," training. None of it registered. And the forced, condescending tone she used to talk him down threw fuel into his fire.

He reached the central block of computers, and threw aside chart after chart looking for Liv's. Families of patients hovering near death poked their feeble heads from behind glass doors.

"I want a nurse outside her room at all times. You got me? And someone page Dr. Smithson."

"Anderson," called Lottie from Liv's doorway. She opened a hand to him. An offering. A show of support and understanding. But it wasn't what he needed. He needed to rage. To scream. To purge himself of the anger and uselessness he was trapped in. His insides churned. Memories played in his mind. His parents. His boy. His Olivia.

His frantic gaze found Charlotte's brown eyes. Calm and reassuring, they brought him back. His fire extinguished, but in swept sadness. Tears he knew couldn't be held back burned in his eye sockets. "I ahh…" he started, but his voice cracked. He cleared his throat and pointed to the emergency exit. "I need a minute."

****

Ask any physician to name the best place in the hospital that isn't the sleep room and they'll say the roof. Clarity. Peace. Or an easy way out was always available on the roof. Andy charged up the stairs taking two at a time, as if Olivia's ghost chased at his heels. His thighs burned. His lungs screamed for air. He'd never felt more than thirty-five years, but the effort needed to barrel up fifteen flights to the helipad was a far cry from the man he was a decade ago. Outrunning the horrors from his first pediatric code. Shelbie Meyers. Age three. Blunt chest and abdominal trauma. Blown orbital. Sexual assault. The three hours he spent trying to save her life easily shaved three years off his.

He shoved the rusty door open with his hip and

fell into the sunshine. The first breath of fresh air sucked life into his lungs, then exhaled his rage. Right at Heaven.

With no one but God and the pigeons to judge he ranted like a lunatic, firing curse words into the sky until his tears and anger ran dry. No matter the cause, yelling expletives at the top of your lungs always seemed to be the remedy that wasn't Thorazine or Haldol. But he deserved it. Every "goddamn, Jesus fucking Christ," every kick at the dusty ground was some form of back pay for times he couldn't detach from the tragedies he had to shoulder as a physician and as a man.

Dizzy from sunlight and gulping down air, he sat with his knees to his chest. The sun traveled, slow and lazy overhead. The pager at his waist buzzed. He squinted to read the text. Smithson. It could have been Liv. Or his walking papers. Right then. It didn't matter.

The door crunched open. He startled, with the noise and break of solitude. The foot that came through he knew as well as the back of his hand. Greta.

"I knew I'd find you up here," she said. To Andy's surprise her voice wasn't nails on a chalkboard, but something familiar. Comforting.

She sat at his side and handed him a cardboard coffee cup. His lips turned into an involuntary smile. Charred black caffeine wasn't the smell that hit his nose.

"It's your favorite."

Andy breathed in the buttery, malt of whiskey and swirled the cup in his hands. He took a swallow and shut his eyes to enjoy the sting and burn as the liquid coated his throat. "Thank you."

Greta shrugged. "Is she going to live?"

Andy sighed through his nose. "No chitchat? You're just going to dive in?"

Greta held his dejected gaze. She knew his crap

this way to Sunday. Avoidance was his middle name.

His shoulders fell. "I dunno."

"What does your gut say?"

"That I'm being punished for something."

Greta dropped her hands at her sides. "Don't be so melodramatic."

"Thanks for your six seconds of compassion, Greta."

"Everyone dies, Andy. It's not your job to save—"

"Except it *is* my job," he bit out, balling his hands to a fist. He shot to his feet, leaving Greta to follow. He spun around to rid himself of her judgment, then took another gulp of whiskey draining the cup with one swallow.

"No. Your job is to help the sick. Take away pain. You're not God."

He clenched his jaw shut to keep from running his mouth. It wasn't the first time she called him on his hero/God complex. She'd never understand. He was trained to save people. It was his skill. His art. Some people paint, play music, wrote fucking books. He cut people open, stopped the bleeding, and put them back together again. And it sure as shit sucked seeing his efforts not end in a life saved.

His pager buzzed again. He ignored it. Greta looped her pinky with his. The same way she did when they were seniors in their Baptist high school, leaving room for the Holy Ghost. It brought him back. He loved her once, and in some small way, still did.

She cleared her throat. "One thing's for sure. You'll never forgive yourself if you're not there this time."

"To what? Watch her die?" A helicopter churned in the sky, floating toward the landing pad.

Greta stepped into his vision. Pain raked over her features. She watched the efforts. Witnessed the turmoil and crisis doctors and nurses faced every day as they fought fate. "Yes."

Andy winced. A sucker punch of honesty lodged itself into his windpipe, and he couldn't breathe. Greta was never one for sugarcoating. But just as like always, Greta softened. "To be there and say good-bye."

Andy met her eyes. Golden brown, warm. The first thing he fell in love with. Empathy pulled her lips tight and eventually into a smile. Something between them fused together. Healed. Scarred.

Wind funneled around them, and Greta's auburn hair blew around her sun-kissed shoulders. She pointed to the incoming hot unload. "That's my cue, Anderson. I'm heading home. You know my number." She took a step to leave, but something pulled her back. "Maybe she'll turn around. You did."

He smiled at the woman he'd loved for half his life. "Thank you."

She disappeared through the rusty door. An ancient elevator door slid open, and out popped Javier, Dr. Martin, and two medics. "What's coming?"

"Fifteen-footfall from scaffold. Bilateral long bone fractures, probable pelvis," Javier rattled off, pulling gloves from his pocket.

"Need a hand?"

Javi tossed him a pair. "Yep."

Chapter Twenty-Nine

The golden hour of trauma resuscitation was a junkie's best fix. Mechanical. Seamless. Silencing a young man's cries of pain by aligning a jagged femur with slow, monstrous traction and stabilizing a boggy pelvis cleared his head. Almost made him forget.

As a man, he needed permission and privacy to rage. To allow himself to feel. That's what he found on the roof, a way to funnel his rage into relieving another person's suffering. A cathartic release of the powerlessness that came from Liv being at the mercy of fate.

Andy rubbed out the tension in his neck and shoulders as the rest of the trauma team rushed the kid to surgery. Hoisting a broken limb and pulling against spastic muscles were a trauma doc's version of dead lifts.

He followed at a distance. He didn't want to be involved with the "What if" conversation. He didn't want to be the one spouting off statistics and probabilities that the boy will come out alive and whole. CiCi took the reins with the tearful family. She had a direct, but compassionate way. A skill no classroom or attending could teach. Empathy was something a person was born with. Dr. Martin was born to be a doctor, and if he heard one more privileged, brown nose dickwad call her a token in a white man's world they'd be working every scrotum and rectal abscess for three months.

Andy wedged himself into the elevator behind the stretcher, family, and the rest of the trauma team wishing he'd melt into the steel encasement. Curious gazes, snide grimaces, and pitiful glances bounced from person to person, finally casting their judgment on him like rattlers ready to strike.

He ground his molars together and fixed his eyes on the doors, willing them to open. Andy's pager buzzed at his waist. Then chimed. Then buzzed again. Javier and CiCi's gaze drilled into his sternum.

The old intercom buzzed through metal elevator. "Dr. Cole, to the ICU STAT. Dr. Cole, to the ICU STAT."

His heart stopped. Strangled within his ribs. Crammed in the corner, Andy pushed through the bodies and equipment, all but screaming for people to get out of his way. He locked onto Javi for a panicked beat before jabbing at the button to stop on the next floor.

Dr. Martin adjusted a wire hanging from her patient's bed and tried to smile. "It's not a code blue. Maybe she woke up."

He scrubbed at his face, unable to grasp onto the hope in her voice. The door opened, and he fell through the crack, apologizing over his shoulder to the family for the disruption. He charged down the hall at a run, his sneakers betraying any chance at keeping quiet. A team of people huddled at the mouth of Olivia's room, with an emphatic and fiery Lottie at the center.

"Thank you, Jesus. Andy. Allen. No one here will tell me a damned thing."

Dr. Smithson crossed his arms as Andy slowed to a winded stop. He peered into Olivia's room, then bent at the knees. It wasn't the sprint that trapped the air in his lungs. But Olivia. Blood seeped from beneath her frail frame, pooling into dark blotches onto the floor. Two nurses primed a half dozen bags of dark red to infuse through hoses tunneled into Liv's arms and chest, while another manually squeezed a bag of yellow plasma.

The medical director spouted numbers and statistics. None registered. Charlotte tapped the toe of her pointy shoes and grabbed for him. He straightened, his eyes starting to sting.

"Anderson?" Dr. Smithson prompted.

Apparently, he missed the bullet.

"What?"

"The bleeding…" Smithson repeated, uncrossing his arms. He flashed a look at Charlotte wringing her fingers into a knot. "We know where she's bleeding."

All the other bodies filed out, leaving one. A woman. Navy. Obstetrics.

"Olivia's beta HCG is five-point-five."

****

His lips went numb. His hands shot to his face. Andy took a step toward Olivia's all but lifeless body. Shame swirled in his gut. His selfishness was going to kill her. How many times had he said the fucking condescending sentence, "It only takes one time, to get a woman pregnant?"

And for Liv, it had to have been the time he fucked her on the back stairs. Intense. Unplanned. And unprotected.

"On the pill. Don't make me beg," she panted, into his neck. In a primal beat, he'd turned her into the wall and nudged her legs apart. Get her off and pull out. Get her off and pull out, he told himself, but a sound he knew would be the death of him coiled around his cock, obliterating his control. And sure enough his lack of restraint left a timebomb in her belly.

Lottie gasped. Shock? Horror? Mad-as-hell? She gaped at Olivia's lifelessness. "Livy's pregnant?"

Andy's mouth opened to sputter a defense, but words never materialized.

Smithson cleared his throat. "In the smallest sense of the word."

The medical director's grey eyes locked with Andy's for a heartbeat. It was a placating, shit explanation. A woman was never just a little bit pregnant, and now the tiny cluster of cells proliferating into his child had started to skip itself down one of Liv's Fallopian tubes looking for a cushy place to land. And she was bleeding. Bad. The kind of bad that stopped a beating heart in less than an hour. The crucial hour he'd spent playing hero when he should have been at Liv's side.

Andy pushed past Lottie and approached Liv's bed. Suddenly, the Earth turned on its axis. Gravity no longer rooted him to the surface. Liv tethered him down, and he was sure to drift away without her.

Charlotte cupped a hand over her mouth. Her slender fingers nervously worked over her diamond rings. Her lips moved as if chanting in prayer, but knowing Lottie, she was probably way past God and dabbling in some womanhood voodoo.

The adrenaline spark had been a distraction; now reality shocked into his gut. He kissed her sallow cheek and inhaled her air. His insides ached.

"How many units?" Andy asked the room.

A salt and peppered nurse flipped the transfusion switch. "These make fifteen."

Andy raked his hands through his hair. Charlotte reached for him, but like a fucking coward, he couldn't look her in the face. He kept himself fixed on Olivia and the mess he created. Seeing the woman he loved on the brink of death had to be punishment enough.

"Smithson?" he called over his shoulder. He needed an update. A plan. One where watching Liv die wasn't on the agenda.

Smithson held up a finger, caught in a hurried and hushed discussion with the high-risk-obstetrics attending, a specialty he'd never have been able to stomach. Frazzled, uncontrolled curls framed a whisper pale face hardened with the task of saving a dying woman or… He couldn't finish the thought.

Andy released Lottie's clammy grip and went to the pair standing in the ICU doorway, with Lottie's delicate heels clinking behind. Smithson and the OB's conversation stopped. Both eyed him like a nosey, ingrate family member. "I swear to God if either of you two mention fucking HIPPA—"

The obstetrician shook her head. "Hello, Dr. Cole. I'm Maggie Ford. Dr. Smithson paged me as a consult."

He swallowed and roughed a hand over his chin. "What d—"

"We need evacuate the pregnancy. And pray it doesn't come to a hyst—"

Andy threw his hands up. The only protest he could manage.

It had to come to this. The only thing an ER doc needed to know about the uterus was that it bled like a stuck pig. And it was all his fault. If he were to protest, they'd call him selfish, a stupid Christian conservative that couldn't distance his beliefs from medicine, but it was Liv who'd fled her life in Savannah to protect a child that wasn't planned.

He knew what Liv's choice would be, but *her* life was the one that mattered.

A young, fresh faced girl helped change the sheets. The peach night dress Lottie brought fell away. Liv's porcelain skin was cracked. Mottled. Blotches of purple bruises matching the size of his hand developed at both hips and breasts. Bright red pinpoints dotted the skin around her eyes and neck. The same petechiae scarred his chest and back.

He couldn't find his voice. To agree. To say the words would terminate his child and God forbid ruin

Liv's chances of ever carrying another baby.

"Anderson," Smithson encouraged. Seconds clicked into minutes they wouldn't get back.

"I can't … I can't make that decision. For her."

Stone-faced, Lottie stepped up. "Well you don't have to. Liv's only next of kin is her wretched mother. But I'm her power of attorney. And I say do whatever she needs."

Dr. Ford nodded. Her mechanical switch flipped. "I'll have my team up here in ten," she said pulling her hair into a knot. Dr. Ford marched away, her clogs dragging along the floor. He wished his switch would flip. To see Liv in black and white, to be able turn off his heart and his brain on.

Smithson grabbed his arm, and offered an empathetic glance before side stepping out of the room. Charlotte dug through her handbag and pulled out her cellphone. Immediately, she punched at the screen.

He followed her through the crammed room, unconsciously staring at Liv's skeletal belly covered by crisp sheets, specked with blood. "You know that's not what Olivia would want, Charlotte. Not after what she went through."

"Livy didn't make me her POA to make decisions the way *she'd* make them. The day she signed those godforsaken papers she signed away a lifetime of happiness. Giving up Georgia was the wrong choice. I know it. She knows it. And I'll be damned if I let her do it again."

Lottie glared at Liv, but it quickly softened into something more than pain.

"God, what I wouldn't give for a cigar and Jack Daniels," she grumbled, ditching her wealthy pretenses.

Andy perched himself on Liv's bed. He inventoried her features and took her cold hand in his.

Her pulse fluttered, as if her heart were flying away.

Lottie paced in a circle, talking on her cellphone. "She's dying, Eleanor, but if you think you've got time to time to stop by Louis Vuitton on Michigan Ave, then by all means. I don't think Livy'll miss you," she bit out before hitting "end". "The nerve of that woman. Momma in nothing but DNA. The only reason I called her up here was so that Livy would have a reason to wake up and tell her the titty lift Teddy gave her came out uneven."

A rush of nurses and scrub technicians filed in. An anesthesiologist assumed his spot at the head of Liv's bed. Andy moved to a stool and laced his fingers with hers, ignoring the "gas man's" downcast judgment.

"Yes, he's allowed to stay," Dr. Ford announced as if she heard the running thoughts of everyone in the room. "But, Mrs. VanSutton, you may—"

Lottie threw up a hand. She looked to Heaven with a pleading expression as she strode to the door. Andy caught her eye turning the corner. Despair.

A scrub tech offered her a sterile towel to dry her outstretched arms while another held open her drape. Olivia's heart rate began to climb. Andy pressed his fingers into her wrist as if he had the power to slow it down, and held his breath.

"I want q-ten-minute Hemoglobins," the OB ordered. "Have the blood bank on stand by for mass transfusion protocol. Every unit type specific comes to this room."

A large box on wheels with a half dozen canisters and hoses attached to the side rolled in after her. At once he recognized the vacuum, the rudimentary means to yank out Liv's bleeding uterus and the microscopic cluster of cells driving her to exsanguinate.

His heart stopped. Dr. Ford must have read the horror on his face.

"I won't know the extent of the hemorrhage until I'm there, but I'll save whatever I can," she added in the purposely even voice doctors used to prevent unrealistic outcomes. Reality was easier to stomach when people stopped pretending miracles existed.

Andy squeezed his eyes shut, waiting for the scrub tech to pin up the drape. He had no desire to watch. At last the blue curtain was secured, and the vacuum churned on.

"A word please, Alex," Dr. Ford announced. All around the room, heads bowed and hands clasped together. Irritation prickled up his neck and down his arms. They were wasting time. Liv's pulse threaded beneath his fingers. If they needed to pray, they should do it on their own time. The anesthesiologist spoke from behind his mask. Deep and solemn, prepared words he must have said hundreds of times. People in business of saving lives had their thing. Their superstitions. Their means to ward off the juju. He never bothered with such nonsense. Calling on God's hand to aid them in His plan was usually the kind of thing that made his eyes roll, but something in the prayer hit him square in the chest.

Hope.

****

Consciousness has a funny way of fucking with you. There's no asleep. No awake. No way to decipher fact from fiction, except, through the fog Olivia smelled Lottie's Chanel, felt Andy's callused fingers, and saw her precious Georgia. Memories materialized. Senses heightened, but there was no way to know if medications clogged up Liv's brain or the natural course of dying that pushed her buried memories forward.

Hazy July sun filtered through pale green curtains. A cheery glow cast over the bland post-partum suite. The clock hanging over the bed ticked too fast to be real. An hour was all she needed. Or so she lied to herself. With each tiny breath that passed through her daughter, she recited the promise of only one more minute.

A rose and cream little girl with a full head of strawberry blonde peach fuzz snuggled tight into Liv's breast, as if she intended to burrow back inside, and with a monstrous bite the baby latched. Fast and furious. Lazy and slow, her baby began to nurse. Liv was in awe.

"Do they really come out and just ... know what to do?" she asked her constant bedside companion. Unlike Charlotte and her preening requirements, Mrs. Loveitz never left Liv's side. Through her thirty-hour labor, six superhuman pushes, an episiotomy, and her first trip to the bathroom, Rose was there. Young hip to arthritic hip.

Rose stroked the sleepy infant's pudgy cheek, encouraging another burst of short sucks and a deep swallow. "Babies are smart."

"Well, let's hope Georgia has Logan's IQ and Liv's everything else," Lottie interjected from the doorway. Her best friend whirled in like she owned the place, setting down a bag of toiletries and breast pump supplies. "I know it's the best way to get all that ... boob juice flowing, but are you sure you want to—"

"I just wanted know what it felt like. What *she* felt like ... and when she's done. I'll be done." Liv glanced at the bedside table and the small stack of papers smudged with fresh ink and tears. Lottie nodded. Rose stroked her messy curls and brought her lips to Georgia's ear. She whispered the Hebrew Psalm that had been Liv's only source of comfort for the last six months.

The baby fell asleep in Liv's arms. And it was time. Her golden hour was up. Her eyes burned, but she had no tears left. Lottie pulled out her cell phone, and Liv shook her head, a sob caught in her throat.

"No, Lot. I said I didn't want pictures."

Charlotte's brown eyes drew together. "Trust me on this, Livy. You'll want just one. And so will she—one day."

Liv pulled her night dress around her shoulders, and Rose swaddled Georgia in the nursery blanket. Charlotte crinkled her nose. "Don't worry, baby girl, Auntie will get you out of that eyesore. All right, Livy, smile like it doesn't hurt."

Muscle memory complied, and Olivia put on her Sweet Peach pageant tooth filled grin. The camera flashed, and pain resumed on her face.

"Why don't you meet them, dear? The social worker said her new parents would love to meet you," Rose asked bringing over the clear, plastic bassinet. The healthy baby version of a stretcher.

"They're not her parents," Lottie grumbled.

"They are her parents. I know you think I'm making a bad decision—"

"Yes. I do think it's a bad decision, Olivia. You did this so you could come home. But now I know for sure you'll never be able to come back. While your life and blood lives in this godforsaken city, you will never go back to Savannah. So what's the point?"

Liv opened her mouth, lips numb and heart breaking.

"And I swear to God, if you say your Momma I will cut your hair while you sleep."

Liv exhaled and shook her head. Lottie wouldn't understand. "I'm giving her a family—that's something she'd never get from me."

Charlotte unfolded her arms and wiped at her cheek. "Oh Dior, why isn't your waterproof mascara worth the forty dollars I spend?" She kissed the bundled baby's cheek and the top of Liv's head before turning to leave. "I love you. Finish up here and hurry to the house. You should see the new counters and antique brass fixtures. *So chic, et tre`s belle. Vieux monde perfection francais magnifique.*"

Charlotte VanSutton understood the decisions Olivia-Grace MacArthur Aberdeen had to make. It was the way they'd been raised, like the understanding beauty comes with pain. No one likes a bikini wax, or plucking their eyebrows, but a woman did it anyway. And smiled through the whole goddamn thing.

Rose muttered a Yiddish phrase Liv should've known and took the sleeping baby from her arms. Lottie paused, but didn't turn around. She had always been the strong one, and apparently that meant hiding her tears while staring at the door. "Don't worry, Livy. This won't be the last time you hold a baby in your arms."

Chapter Thirty

The buzzing hum of a vacuum would haunt Andy for the rest of his life. Dr. Ford was done in under an hour. Five more units of blood infused and half the supply of donor platelets. Hospital staff lined up for hours to donate to the "Blood Flu Campaign" which morphed into the biggest PR stunt medicine had ever seen with Olivia at the center. But he didn't have the energy to care.

The last sterile drape was removed. Andy finally had the courage to glance over the lower half of Liv's body. If she survived, she'd never forgive him. But at least she'd be alive.

Dr. Ford explained the outcome to Lottie, killing off a piece of his soul with each word. "The bleeding was significant. She'll have some scarring, but I managed to save her uterus and stem the active hemorrhage."

Charlotte's eyes fell, like she had been holding out for a miracle. Or perhaps it simply hit her; Liv had lost another baby. Still, she smiled with a sort of graciousness he didn't have the ability to fake.

The room darkened with early evening. He didn't bother with a light. It would only magnify Liv's lack of healthy color. Her pulse raced beneath his fingers. The monitors bleeped in and out of crisis. A heart rate of one-thirty and a blood pressure under one hundred were sure signs of secondary shock. Nurses and medics filtered in and out, melting into the background. They'd stopped offering conversation hours ago, and he didn't even notice when they came and went.

The only interactions he allowed were with Smithson and Charlotte. Nanny Kemp had brought the children for what she called "Snack and Snuggle time", and was somewhere in the lobby. Smithson made hourly rounds between Liv and Jorge. He was extubated and already speaking with family, and Andy felt a need to check in. And truth be told he'd never spoken to a person after slicing them open and clamping off their aorta. If ER docs had a bucket list, that'd be close to the top. But that meant leaving Liv's side, and he simply couldn't.

Liv's heartrate began to stabilize. Her color began to improve. But it wasn't enough. Blood still seeped from every hole they put in her body. The "Oh Shit Knot of Worry" sank in his gut and doubled in size. Disseminated intervascular coagulation would be the final, irreversible, nail in her coffin. He clenched his fist around the red fucking bracelet with the letters DNR.

Chaos and noise drifted into Liv's room. A loud, accelerating beep alarmed from a bedside monitor. He looked up. Liv's heart ticked away at a steady seventy-two. Weak. But not hers. Flashes of blue, green and black descended upon the next open door. Overhead the intercom boomed. "Code Blue."

Andy sucked in a breath. "Sonofabitch."

****

"Time of death, 20:49," Smithson announced. Immediate and anticlimactic, the room stilled. No trick plays, no fancy procedures, no more cut and runs. Jorge Vasquez died in minutes, the exact way fate demanded the first time he went ahead and fucked with the juju. Everything in medicine came with a cost, a side effect. Reversing the blood flu and a hack job repair of a central artery meant one thing. Clots. Lots of them. And Jorge threw a pulmonary embolus faster than you could say, "Tag, you're it."

Andy held Jorge's wife close while she sobbed in Spanish and bits of broken English. Twelve hours ago, he had his fingers inches from his heart, and now he was dead. It was all for fucking nothing.

He was supposed to comfort her, to have the right thing to say. Everyone in the damned room looked at him with the expectation he'd have the magic words to get her to stop crying, but the well he went to for compassion and empathy was dry. He unraveled himself from Isobel's devastated grip and went back to Liv's room next door.

A small group of ICU nurses and technicians convened around a computer, their backs to the crowd. "She'll be number three," one murmured. "We need to knock on some wood fast, you guys... I have a gut feeling Southern Belle won't last until midnight."

Andy stopped. A wall of dread halted his tracks, and his heart right along with it. He stared like it had the power to change destiny, but the knife of reality stabbed between his ribs, then turned a quarter dial.

The elevator dinged, and the doors rattled open. Lottie's clinky heels announced her arrival. "What's going on, Andy?"

The superstitious trio stiffened and caught his gaze. He scratched at his chin and swallowed a flare of resentment. "Nothing."

Lottie wove her arm into his, leaning into him as they walked. "Her Momma's landed," she drawled with disdain.

Andy checked his watch. "Is she on her way?"

"Damned if I know. She's supposed to be, but if I know Eleanor Aberdeen-Maxfield, she's using this time to snoop around her dying daughter's house."

Lottie released Andy's arm and went to Liv's bedside and pecked her cheek. They stood there in silence. He hoped it came across as pensive. Vigilant. But really it was because he was at a loss. And terrified. If Liv was going to turn around, it'd be now. The internal cause of her bleeding stopped. He raked his hands through his hair and rubbed his temples.

"Livy swears I'm the strong one. But I tell you, Anderson. Seeing my best friend like this. I'm not so sure." She reached into her purse and pulled out a Thermos. "This is the closest thing to a flask Miss Goodie-two-shoes has in her possession." Lottie took a deep swallow and looked up. "She has to make it. Do everything you can. I don't care what she said. Do it for me. For yourself. For that little girl she loves more than life."

A frumpy woman with night-shifter bags welded beneath her eyes appeared at the door. "Mrs. VanSutton?" she called.

Lottie cleared her throat and turned on her expensive heels, a forced expression on her face. "Yes, my dear."

"Security called from downstairs. A woman claiming to be Ms. Aberdeen's mother is at the desk."

"Thank you, Tisha." She turned back and shook her hair over her shoulders and pulled a tube of lipstick from her purse. For a brisk few seconds, Lottie primped in the dingy ICU mirror. "Show time. How do I look?"

"Beautiful," Andy answered, automatic, except he meant it.

Charlotte, lifted her chin as if to say "I know" and grabbed for her bag.

It occurred to him that if Liv and her mother were estranged as she led him to believe, she was in for a surprise. "Does she know about me?"

A conniving smirk curled on Lottie's red painted lips. "In a manner of speaking."

She clinked out, swaying her hips as she walked. It was a power move. A mind trick. Something Lottie needed to do to blow away the cobwebs of fear. Andy sat on the doctor's stool and rolled to Liv's bedside. He took her hand and pressed it to his cheek.

He'd never understood why family spoke to their unconscious loved ones. More superstitious nonsense spouted by chaplains and social workers. Something that got in the way of him doing his job because there's always that scene in their favorite TV shows. That stupid godforsaken scene where they pour their heart out to the person they love seconds away from dying—and because they finally come clean and say the magic words their loved one wakes up, like it was the power of their words that dragged them back from the pearly gates of Heaven or seven circles of hell. But it was bullshit. All of it. And yet, words bubbled in his chest.

"Come back to me, baby. Please. I'm not one for begging. And I'm sure the good Lord is tempting you to stay, but please. Come back to me. To Lottie. She loves you. *I* love you. This is where I'm supposed to promise you, God, the Devil, whoever, that I'll be a better man. The kind of man you deserve … but I can't promise you that. I promise I will honor you. Cherish you. Worship you. And if you let me. Give you a happily ever after."

The rhythmic, mechanical rise and fall of her chest lulled him to sleep. He fought the urge to shut his eyes. "Please, baby. Come back to me."

Andy bored his gaze into Liv's pallid face, holding onto the hope for the kinds of miracles only seen on television. The Devil in the back of his mind cackled when she didn't stir. Twitch. Make a move to prove she heard his plea. He closed his eyes and ground his molars together. Like an old habit pressed his fingers into the quick, thready pulse beneath the delicate skin at her wrist.

Liv's heart fluttered then slowed, then fluttered once again. The soft, ding of arrhythmia chimed overhead. Off, then on. And off again. His eyes popped open. Liv's full lips quivered around the plastic tube reaching into her lungs. Her left thumb jerked in his grip.

He sucked in a breath. "Liv?" he called out in a whisper. Saying it too loud might fuck with the juju. Her eyelids fluttered, and her slender fingers gave a slight squeeze.

Andy jumped from his seat. "Olivia! Oh, dear God. I'm here. Don't be scared. I'm here, okay?" he reassured. He grabbed for a call button, but the arrhythmia alarm went off once again. He looked her over, expecting some outward cause for alarm. A misplaced EKG lead. Interference. But nothing. Her heart rate climbed to a flutter, then paused beneath his fingers. He looked up, just to see the monitor wail in crisis. Ventricular Tachycardia.

"No. No. *No!*" Andy cried into the air. His other hand flew to the open hollow of her throat and pushed the button for a STAT blood pressure. At the base of her neck he felt a faint, feverish pulse. In a breath, it slowed and strengthened. He let out a sigh.

"Jesus Christ, Livy, don't do that to me…"

Liv's grip on Andy's hand tightened, while the other pawed at the sheets. She arched and bucked her shoulders, breathing over the ventilator's demands. Andy held her down. "Baby, give them a few seconds."

He turned toward the door, expecting a rush of bodies. There was no way a run of V-tach went unnoticed in the ICU. Liv continued to fight her sedation and the panic felt forced to breathe through a straw.

He shushed in her ear, trying to find a delicate balance of pressure and resistance to keep her calm, but prevent her from hurting herself. Any extra movement could have violent consequences. Seconds flew by, and Liv's strength gave way. Her body sank into the mattress.

A wave of relief rolled his shoulders, but anger boiled inside staring around an empty room.

The crisis alarm wailed overhead. He looked up. Liv's heart rate climbed. He read the green line of electrical activity shooting through her strained heart. Erratic. Disorganized. A wavy, wide-complex wiggle where a synchronized, symmetrical normal sinus should be. Torsades. Rare. Lethal.

"She needs mag," he bellowed to no one. "Someone call pharmacy. She needs Magnesium Sulfate. Two-thousand milligram bolus."

He should run to the nurses' station. Call pharmacy himself, but he couldn't move. He hovered in her space and pressed his fingers into her throat. Nothing. Andy clawed at her neck.

Her pinky-pale lips darkened. Ruddy. Blue. Dead.

Chapter Thirty-One

No pulse. No blood pressure. No circulating oxygen. Liv's heart quivered within her ribs. The mass transfusions replaced her blood volume but depleted her body of electrolytes, the precious spark that set the heart's tempo. First instinct was to swat at the Code Blue button fixed to the wall. If the first rule of Med school was don't date the nurses, second was know how to call a code. But Liv had made her wishes known. No heroics.

A swell of noise rolled in from the hall. The thirty second crisis alarm was enough to catch the attention of the ICU staff. But they didn't hurry. They knew nothing was to be done. Rushing to a DNR was as helpful as giving the morbidly obese diabetic sugar free Jell-O.

Andy raked his hands through his hair, then cupped his mouth as if to contain a scream. Liv was there. Awake. Her life balanced on the head of pin, and he could fix it. Save her. How could she ask him to sit back and watch her die?

Fuck that.

Andy cranked up her ventilator and knotted his fist between her breasts and pounded life into her stalled heart. One by one, her ribs cracked then gave way. He looked down. Liv's rigid frame absorbed the blows. Like a cruel punishment, her doe, green eyes opened to slits as if to eye him in judgment.

"I'm sorry, baby. You can give me hell later, okay?"

"Dr. Cole!" shrieked a voice from the doorway. A wide eyed first year intern that still saw the medical world in black and white back peddled into a crowd of seasoned nurses and residents. "She's a DNR. She's wearing a bracelet."

If his world wasn't about to cave in, he'd laugh. "I know what she said, y'all. But she's waking up. It's magnesium deficiency from all the transfusions. DNR doesn't mean 'Do Not Treat'." Bodies filled in. Annoyingly tentative, they shot each other shifty glances. "If you're not here to help, you can fucking go."

At last a face he recognized came through. Torey caught his eye and wheeled over the crash cart. First thing she did was pull out the defibrillator pads to instant gasps and protests.

"Oh please. You guys know it's the right thing to do. Quit being such pansies. Or do I need to call the Pit for some nurses with balls."

On cue, Javier and CiCi ran through the door, elbowing the ICU team out of the way. "Trosades? Liv'll be pissed she missed it," Javi said.

"She'd be a two-gram bolus, right?" Dr. Martin clarified, rummaging through the crash cart. She retrieved a small bag of normal saline while Javier pulled out the bright blue vial and popped the plastic top.

"What's your girl weigh, Doc? Buck twenty-five?"

Andy shrugged. He never stopped to think about how little she weighed all the times he gripped her by the ass and wrapped her legs around his waist. Javier's guess was as good as any.

At Liv's side, Torey flipped on the defibrillator. Andy looked to Heaven, hoping it wouldn't come to that. His neck and shoulders screamed in pain. His muscles rebelled. He'd been coding her for two full minutes. A respiratory therapist in wrinkled teal unraveled from the stoic group of bystanders and moved to the head of Liv's bed. Another nurse followed. There was a tap at Andy's shoulder, a willing, able body to take over the mess he started. He backed away, and an older nurse with a long grey braid counted aloud for the RT to keep time.

Andy's arms folded over his chest to keep from shaking and stared at Olivia. Serenity amongst absolute chaos. CiCi handed Torey the syringe with the lifesaving electrolyte.

Someone scoffed. "I'm finding Smithson." He didn't need to turn around to know who it belonged to. Some self-righteous nursing supervisor or second year resident who thought they knew better.

"Don't bother. I'm right here," he announced. Everyone turned to watch his entrance. The sea of hospital staff parted. Smithson marched forward, a stone-faced Lottie right behind. On her heel waltzed Liv's mirrored twin. A carbon copy of peaches, cream, and copper curls. Her face, pinched in boredom went slack. She stopped, needing to grab the doorframe.

The ICU resident stepped up. Like a proverbial tattletale, the young twit with brand new creases in his white coat opened his mouth. Andy glared at him. A doctor in everything except experience.

Smithson stopped the resident with a hand, not even offering a look of acknowledgement and went to Andy's side, pacing the length of Liv's bed. Torey hovered with her thumb on the plunger, ready to slam the magnesium into Liv's system. He wished she'd just do it, but everyone had limits when it came to blatant rule breaking.

The need to plead his case fired through Andy's body, but if he was going to be on trial at least it was for trying to save Olivia's life. "Sir, she's had inconsistent runs of V-tach, but closer—"

"It's all right, Anderson. We'll keep going," he said, offering a nod directed at Torey. Immediately she squeezed the plunger, then released the roller clamp. The nurse compressing Liv's heart focused on the task. All of the hushed criticism, and skeptical one liners went silent, as if the eerie quiet somehow moved the medicine faster through her body.

Every set of eyes drew in on Liv while Andy folded his arms and stared at the ceiling. Lottie joined his side. She pried her dainty hand into the crook of Andy's elbow. He looked down, her lips blanched white.

Smithson cleared his throat. "Let's stop compressions and see what we got. And have some Sodium Bicarb ready."

The nurse pulled her hands away, and for a split second he imagined Liv sit up and look around the room like it'd all been a joke. But she was as still as death. All traces of consciousness had disappeared. It hadn't worked. The red, squiggled line on the cardiac monitor blazed in his face.

Furious, Andy pulled himself from Lottie's grip and crossed the room in one stride. Razor sharp, Liv came into focus, and so did what he had to do. He might not have been Liv's doctor, but she was his responsibility. The responsibility you willingly shoulder when you love someone.

Andy pointed to the nurse with her conjoined hands hovering over Liv's breastbone and over to Torey. "Resume compressions. I want that Amp of BiCarb in now. CiCi, get pharmacy on the phone. I want a mag and epi drip. Javier charge the defib to three-hundred. And anyone that isn't family or part of the code team is out." He reached the head of Olivia's bed and turned around. Gawkers still lined the walls. "Now," he commanded.

They scurried, some muttering, most looking over their shoulders to see Dr. Cole in action, in control, and how Smithson intended to let it play.

Andy checked his watch. "I want thirty seconds of compressions to circulate the meds, and then we shock." His stomach twitched saying the word. He ignored it and scanned the room for stragglers, or anyone with the balls to challenge him, stopping on Lottie. Her gaze fixated on the torture his selfishness subjected Liv's body to. Cracked rib after cracked rib, Lottie hid her terror behind a white knuckled fist.

Smithson spoke to her at a whisper. She gave him a tight shake of her chin. A refusal.

The defibrillator signaled ready. The aged, seasoned nurse stepped back while the RT forced one final breath into Liv's lungs. "All clear," he announced.

Javier stood at the crash cart, primed to press "shock". They locked eyes.

"Now."

Chapter Thirty-Two

Time slowed. Stretched. Adrenaline coursed through Andy's body, heightening his senses, but imprinted the horror in his mind forever. During the three seconds Liv's body hung in the air, muscles spastic, face twisted from over two-hundred jules of electricity, he had an eon of time to imagine the life he wanted with her.

She landed on the mattress, arms and feet spread. The monitor wailed before he could read Liv's heart rhythm.

Anguish sliced into his gut. "Again."

Javier jumped to Liv's bedside and relieved the nurse doing compressions. She wiped her brow, her lips in pulled anger, as if she bore the burden of Liv's persistent lethal arrhythmia. Precise and strong, Javi beat life through Liv's body while the defibrillator reset.

The twenty by twenty room tightened around him. The small windows lining the walls were just big enough for a soul to pass through. Torey motioned for his attention at the crash cart. "I have epinephrine and amiodarone drawn and ready," she said, waving both medications flagged with tape.

He took an unsteady breath and rubbed his temples. It wasn't supposed to be like this. Just a means of fixing what was wrong, but he was thankful Torey was able to keep a level head and anticipate Liv's needs. He nodded and gave the order for Epinephrine. Near the door, CiCi repeated the dose and time administered. The flicker of hope that fluttered in his chest sank with each passing second.

A young pharmacist with heavy, black glasses dodged elbows and well-intended grabs from nurses who didn't expect him to get close. Like lab, pharmacy had a bad rap, and consequently, they were severely underutilized.

"Thanks for comin' up here so quick," Andy said. The pharmacist attached the drip to an intravenous pump and punched through the settings.

"Oh, I came before anyone called. Laboratory couldn't get a hold of anyone in the ICU, so they called me to get a drip started. I figured they'd need a STAT infusion with a Mag level less than one. I ran when I heard you guys called a code blue."

Andy straightened. "ICU staff too busy gossipin' about the 'southern belle fixin' to die' rather than answer the damn phone…"

The defibrillator signaled ready.

"Not gossiping, Dr. Cole. I do believe we were all-hands-on deck with Mr. Vasquez," said the seasoned nurse that had just spent the better part of five minutes making sure Liv's heart kept beating. She looked over her shoulder with a steely, zero fucks given gaze. "Everyone clear."

Click.

Electricity scored through Liv's heart. Her delicate frame arched upright and suspended in air. During the seconds that spanned a lifetime he calculated odds and outcomes. Statistics driven into his brain by medical school and residency, verified by years of experience. Sour, bitter bile seeped up his throat. This was it. His final chance.

****

It should be dark. Peaceful. Darkness headed by a glowing, white light. Such bullshit. Liv saw Heaven. Like a passenger on an overcrowded bus, she hung out the window as she rode past St. Peter at the pearly gates. If she didn't know better she'd assume the Kingdom's keeper was nose deep in Candy Crush and accidentally let her bus drive by because there's no question a bus filled with two dozen babies, a handful of kindergarten teachers, five nuns, and one ER nurse, even if she liked to cuss a little, was destined for hell.

The incandescent glow luring her to Heaven condensed into a florescent brown that burned through her eyelids. Bleeps and high-pitched screeching bled through the chorus of angels. Rust and salt rested on her tongue where wine had been. Her ribs cracked to a steady, unmistakable one hundred beats per minute. The BeeGee's popped into Liv's semi-conscious brain. The most apt time to sing "Stayin' Alive" would be when someone's trying to save your life.

With each compression, consciousness returned. And with each bit of consciousness brought pain. Everywhere. The kind of pain that made the ten out of ten look like a bee sting. But it also brought voices. Through the rhythmic blows to her sternum she latched her awakening mind to the voices as if they held the power to lasso her back.

First came Lottie. Muffled, like listening through layers of salt-water and sand, Lottie's sweet, Savannah twang locked in Liv's ribs. The frantic, quiver of her heart slowed then sputtered as Liv clung to the smell of Chanel no. 5 and the sisterly love in Lottie's voice.

Then came Andy. Her Andy. The Andy she loved and lusted for after one smile and swoony caress of her name. Her proud, selfless man who put his calling to save lives above his own happiness. His Texan tenor boomed over the beeps, dings, hisses, and hums. His voice sparked in her core. Warmth rolled out, thawing death from her fingers. The malty tang of his sweat and familiar, callused grip sensed over her body. He was close. Just like before when she teetered between Earthly life and life eternal. Tempted by the promises of one and the guarantees of the other. But unlike before when she foolishly believed she was at the mercy of fate, Liv dug in her heels against the lurking darkness.

Click.

****

"Twenty minutes with no spontaneous recirculation," CiCi announced, precise and matter of fact, as if it were a simple training exercise and not the end all, be all of Andy's existence. Javier hunched over Liv's body, bone white and deceivingly determined in his attempt circulate the last round of cardiac life support medications, but everyone saw it was all he could do to keep from crumbling.

Liv's electrolytes had stabilized. She should be fixed. But somewhere she was still irrevocably broken. The heat from every pair of eyes burned through his scrubs. They waited on him. People in the business of saving lives knew what came next. But that meant he'd have to say it was over. To say with finality, he'd never speak to the woman he loved again. To admit he failed her, that medicine failed her.

Andy paced in a tiny line. A calm hand touched his shoulder, pulling him to a stop. Lottie, graceful and with more affection than he deserved, smiled.

"It's time, Andy. You did everything you could. We need to let her go," she whispered. "Livy's probably already got herself a prime penthouse across the street from Mother Teresa and Florence Nightingale. She won't blame you. So, let her go."

"But she was right there. Awake. I thought I could…"

"I know," Lottie said with an empathetic shrug.

He turned back to Liv with Javier tirelessly working over her. She was gone.

He opened his mouth, and cleared his throat

clogged with despair. "Al—"

"No. Not yet. Please, y'all," pleaded a frail, Savannah drawl. "Don't stop. She's my baby girl. Try one more time." Olivia's mother finally spoke.

In the chaos and attention to detail, he'd forgotten Eleanor had arrived. She stood alone, like an afterthought, next to the wall with extra gloves and supplies. Elegance carried in her shoulders, but regret weighed on her features. The poised passive-aggressiveness he envisioned for Olivia's mother was nowhere to be found.

Andy stared at Liv's spitting image for a long beat. He pitied the hope glowing from her emerald eyes. If there was anything the last week of his life imprinted on his mind, hope was useless. A waste. Hope was for fools with no concept of reality, and for the last week he was that goddamned fool.

He nodded. Ingrained empathy tugged on his broken heart.

Lottie hurried to her side and gave her a supportive arm to lean on. If she harbored any resentment toward Olivia's less than perfect mother, it didn't show.

Two steps ahead, Torey charged the defibrillator, but Dr. Martin jumped in with uncharacteristic excitement. "A study," she exclaimed, pinching the bridge of her nose. CiCi sputtered through her thoughts, then regurgitated a buried factoid she must have read. "Yeah. Um, there was a study by Fort Worth, Texas EMS, actually... Double sequence defibrillation for refractory v-fib."

"It was a finding. Not a study," Andy said recalling the article. "Just a bunch of medics searching for a Hail Mary for persistent fibrillation."

"Yep. Five out of five to be exact."

Andy glanced back to Charlotte and Eleanor, both wide-eyed and hopeful, latching on to CiCi's burst of enthusiasm. "Please, Dr. Cole," Olivia's mother whispered.

He rubbed his temples and tried not to look at Liv's body. Before he could give the okay, Smithson was already scrolling through his iPhone for the study. He gave his own orders, calling for a second defibrillator.

The black cloud overhead cracked. Something in his chest lifted. The room came alive with movement and urgency. The hope he brushed off was contagious. Everyone seemed to grab on. Call him a fool, but so did he.

Andy rifled through the crash cart for another pair of defib pads, while more nurses and medics worked at the head of the bed. Javier stopped compressions and yanked her upright to expose her back. Andy slapped an electrode in place, then eased her down and breathed her in. She might have been seconds away from dead, but she still smelled of vanilla and cinnamon. He ached. In every form of the word.

Andy nestled the last defib pad carefully between her breasts. He kissed her cheek as if to apologize for the seven-hundred and twenty joules of electricity, moments from striking through her body. The second defibrillator signaled ready.

"I love you," Andy said pulling away. He locked eyes with Smithson, his fingers set to shock.

Chapter Thirty-Three

It wasn't like in the movies. The whole out of body experience was a millisecond blip of time compared to the agonizing days the people Liv loved had endured. Guilt swelled as she came to. The same tweak of shame after a luscious vacation knowing your coworkers had been up to their ass in full moon craziness, while you overindulged in liquor and sunshine.

Andy held her fingers to his bearded cheek. The coarse, silky hairs instantly registered in Liv's brain. Strength returned with her senses, and she scratched her nails along his jaw. She opened her eyes against a sterile brightness. Familiar but far out, her surroundings smudged together so she could focus all her energy on Andy. Her Andy. Her Andy that refused to give up.

He shot up with her touch. Worry. Exhaustion. The weight of his own guilt creased his face and swirled beneath his blue eyes.

"Hi…" he whispered, as if saying it too loud would shatter the world around him.

Liv swallowed. Her mouth and throat were raw. "You look like hell, cowboy."

"Well, that's where I've been."

Andy rose to his feet and looked her over. He smiled. The kind of smile that would take a lifetime to forget. The kind that would make her heart skip a beat, if it weren't under the control of an antiarrhythmic. She flushed, both nervous and embarrassed by the attention. She struggled to bring a hand to cover her face.

"Don't do that," he said weaving his fingers into hers. "I haven't seen you anything but pale for days…"

She dropped her eyes to her lap. The need to apologize itched the top of her mouth, but she stopped herself by diluting the tension. She grinned. Weakly. "So how many people saw my boobs?"

Andy groaned. "Jesus, Olivia. I thought I lost you." He eased himself on to her hospital bed. The air mattress hissed beneath their combined weight, and he pulled her into his arms. Liv pressed her ear to his chest. She breathed in his clean woodsy sent and shut her eyes to focus on the lub-dub of his heart that beat only for her.

Liv prickled with delight, but Andy stiffened and sat up. Guilt seeped from every pore. But why? She was the twit that had asked him to deny the very essence of who he was by demanding no heroics. It'd be a mistake she'd live with forever. One that nearly cost the man she loved his livelihood and happiness. The wheels of thought seemed to grind within his skull.

She grabbed his hand and squeezed. "I'm not mad. I know what you did. What you had to do." She rubbed her aching sternum. A ten out of ten and worth every stinking second.

He clenched his molars in the way that made her swoon and looked away.

"Anderson," she said, calling him back. She intended to wait as long as he needed to meet her eyes, a stifling ten Mississippis. And when he did, there was no holding in the waterworks. "I was wrong to ask that of you. Of everybody."

Pain stabbed through her broken ribs. She bit her cheek to keep from wincing. Andy shook his head, opening his mouth as if to flipping argue.

Liv raised her hand to hold him off. "For all the time we spend trying to save lives ... we seem to only remember the tragedy. The pain. Suffering. But you ... you fought for a miracle. I am alive because you refused to give up."

Andy stood and crossed his arms. Cold air rushed

between them, hitting her square in the heart.

"I couldn't live with myself if I had … but, Liv I need to tell you—"

Manners be damned, she rolled her eyes. "Will you stop? Please. I'm trying to thank you for saving my life. For believing what we do isn't just 'black and *right*'."

Andy looked up and searched her face. He studied her with hope brimming in his eyes.

"For giving me my chance at a happily ever after…"

His cheeks twitched. Like to allow a real smile would tempt the juju.

Her over-medicated heart pounded within her ribs waiting for his lopsided, half-grin. A sure sign he believed her, that the whole clusterfuck was over and they could bury their guilt in the flower bed.

A quick knock on door broke their moment. She had hundreds of people to see and thank, but nothing was more important than absolving Andy of whatever sins weighed on his conscience. The door swooshed open, and she cursed her hoarse throat for the inability to call out in her sugared twang to give them a damn minute.

Subdued and stone faced, Smithson charged through the doorway but stopped. His silver gaze connected with Liv, and his face split into a smile.

"Hey, Olivia! Welcome back," Smithson exclaimed, dodging around her crammed ICU suite. He slowed under Andy's downcast gaze. "I'm sorry, you guys. If I'm interrupting someth—"

"Not really, sir. Just making sure Dr. Cole knows a good save when it comes up and bites him in the ass," she sang in her sweetest Savannah Sweet Peach voice.

At last Andy grinned, and this time, her heart fluttered. The monitor above fixed above her head chimed red.

"Well now *you're* trying to kill me..." she said, hopelessly fanning her face.

The silly retort seemed to shoot right into his heart. He laughed. Full. Genuine. And dived back to the bed and claimed her with a kiss. Hard and soft, tender and strong, Andy slipped his tongue past her lips. He gripped his calloused hands over her cheek and traced his thumb over her jaw. She shuddered. It turned into a desperate gasp for air.

"I love you," Andy sputtered between hungry pecks at her lips. The dam that held back her tears cracked with joy. Salty drops of happiness streamed down her cheeks. He kissed her face as if her tears were the elixir of eternal life. "I promised a happily ever after. You will have it."

Liv giggled. Sappy, giddy girl euphoria rippled through her with his declaration. "I love you, too, cowboy," she mumbled between his kisses and wrapped her arms around his waist. His ripped, tight, sexier than hell waist. Her fingers danced along the sliver of skin, and her breath caught in her throat. Primitive. Uncontrolled. Desire spiked in her blood.

"Ahem." Smithson coughed, fortunately halting her ill-timed lust for the man she loved. Andy pulled away, a sly, knowing smirk plastered on his face. He settled at her side holding her hands in his lap.

The rest of Liv's room came into focus. Like Andy had flipped a switch. He saved her life, and now her soul.

The grin on her senior physician's face stiffened. "You'll have to take it easy for a while, Olivia."

"This," she said innocently gesturing between herself and Andy. "Wasn't my fault."

Andy laughed, his eyes washing over her with

tenderness. Never in her life had she felt more cherished. He broke their gaze and looked back at Smithson. Her two favorite physicians shared a silent conversation. The air went cold.

"Where's my Lottie?" Liv asked to break the ice.

Smithson straightened and removed Liv's chart from the end of her bed, tucking it under his arm. "Probably getting the cafeteria to serve fried okra," he replied, affection warming his face. He reached into a pocket of his starched, white coat and pulled out his cellphone, but it wasn't needed.

"Oh, I broke that horse last week," Lottie crooned from the doorway. "A real southern woman can't go a day without." Charlotte breezed past Dr. Smithson with a sweet grab at his arm. He smiled with the not so subtle contact.

Lottie hurried through the room, dodging machines and supply carts in her path. Andy jumped from Liv's side and joined Smithson at the foot of her bed. He knew the level of crazy that was about the paint the puke green ICU walls.

With each stride of her Louboutin flats her expression changed. Her crinkled brow relaxed, and by the time she came to squish Liv's shoulders in a hug and kiss her cheek, she smiled. But as she stood, the smile pinched back into anger.

Lottie swatted at Liv's arm. "Do you have any idea what you put *him* through?"

"I'm sorry, Lot—"

"Don't apologize to *me. I* was fine."

Olivia held her best friend's gaze, letting the fire extinguish before she tried to reply. In a beat she softened, then nestled against her on the rickety hospital bed. "Jesus, Livy. I'm so glad you're all right."

Andy made a noncommittal noise, then went over

to kiss Charlotte's cheek. He grumbled an exhausted greeting and headed for the door. She wished he'd stay. Take away her independent woman card, but she'd be fine if he never left her side.

Lottie smiled, shockingly genuine, then pressed on like it never happened. "But so help me God, you owe me five-hundred dollars for every wrinkle or grey hair that sprouted over the last week."

Charlotte rambled in her warm, Savannah twang about her babies and a few tidbits of gossip as if Liv had been on a vacation rather than the threshold of Heaven. Her Momma came into view behind Lottie's billowy chocolate locks tethered to Andy's forearm. A shadow clung to her Momma's porcelain features. Timid. Out of place. And frail. Eleanor was all but swallowed by her Chanel herringbone jacket and quaffed copper curls a shade too light. A far cry from the domineering woman she'd battled since birth. A cataclysmic crash of remorse and regret hung between them.

The second their jeweled eyes met, the earth shifted, and she knew. Cancer.

Liv's gut twisted. "Hi, Momma."

Lottie took her cue and rose from Liv's side. Eleanor approached, her eyes cast down as if to wait for approval. Liv reached for her, palms up and open.

"Oh baby-girl," she cried, taking Liv's hands in hers.

Charlotte raised her chin and squinted down her nose, but all it took was one glance. She'd see the forgiveness and longing in Liv's eyes and backed away. Lottie offered her a small smile and left her room on the arm of Dr. Smithson. Andy stood with his hands on his hips in front of the rectangle row of prison windows, his gaze calling for an order to stay or go.

"Can you bring my Momma some sweet tea,

Andy?"

He nodded, and took his cue.

Liv surveyed her Momma for a short time, trying to calculate how long it had been. Anger and sorrow made the last year and a half pass like cold molasses. But now wasn't the time to dwell. Someone had to be the better person, even if that meant shouldering a lifetime of resentment.

Eleanor quickly pulled her hands from Liv's, apparently still following her unspoken thirty-second rule of maternal contact, and retrieved a frilly, embroidered handkerchief from her handbag to dab at her eyes. "I don't even know where to begin. Or how…"

"You could start with, 'I'm sorry, Olivia'." So much for being the better person.

Eleanor straightened. "I'm sorry, Olivia. Lord knows I've wanted to say that to you the moment you left."

Liv tried to sit up. For some stupid reason, lying there made her feel weak, and she wanted to be damn sure her Momma wasn't motivated by pity. Her ribs crunched together as she moved upright, reaching for the button to do it for her. She tried to hold it in, but she grimaced anyway.

"Oh, don't be a martyr, Olivia," she said, stiff and annoyed, and pressed the button for her. She simmered as the bed crawled upright. Finally, eye to eye Liv saw her Momma's true nature. Hidden behind Chanel pressed powder and years of ingrained expectations, Eleanor Louise Aberdeen-Maxfield was just a simple southern woman, Savannah stone on the outside, Georgia peach at her center.

"You've done very well up here on your own. Your Daddy'd be very proud of you."

Liv smiled. "*Only* Daddy?"

Eleanor pressed her lips together. That was as close as to a smile as she'd ever get. A wrinkle was never worth the expression of a lady's feelings. "Bless his heart, poor Logan is being accused of prescription fraud. He and that jezebel were apparently selling off prescription pads or some other nonsense. Awful scandal," she said raising an eyebrow. "I like your Anderson. He's quite the charming fella, even if he *is* a Texan."

Liv laughed. "Well at least he's not a Yankee, Momma."

"Your Daddy'd roll over in his grave." A small chuckle was swallowed by a cough. Eleanor's shoulders fell, and she gripped the bedside table for balance.

Liv frowned and, propriety be damned, grabbed her mother's hand. "How much time, Momma?"

She sighed and squeezed back. "No time will ever be enough."

****

"Anderson, wait," Charlotte called from the end of the hall. She motioned for him to hold the elevator. She and Smithson held back in a discussion. A discussion he couldn't bring himself to be a part of the moment his Medical Director uttered "D and C", and Lottie replied with "Not yet".

The damage done by dishonesty disguised as an act of kindness was enough make him vomit the truth the instant Olivia woke up.

Andy shuffled out of the way of patients, stretchers, and other staff coming off the elevator. Lottie's heels and trademark, Savannahian sass, livened up the chatter as she approached. He held in a grin. No matter the woman's faults, there was no way around the fact she'd become a hospital favorite.

"I know you want me to tell her—"

313

"She needs to know, Charlotte. I can't lie to her again."

"*You* had no part in the decision. The truth isn't something you need to bear. Give me three days. As long as I gave you."

Andy snorted. "And remember how great it all turned out?"

Lottie straightened and arched her brow. "Livy and I are more than best friends. We're sisters of our own choosing. I carry a little more weight than being a 'supreme lay with abs to die for'."

Andy smiled despite himself. "Did she really say that?"

Lottie rolled her eyes. "God. Like, five times in three hours. But what I'm trying to get your guy brain to understand is … Liv and I can survive it. She loves you, but it's that fragile kind of love that if you look at it sideways it'll crack into billions of pieces. For Livy and me, sure the truth'll sting, but nothing our friendship can't overcome."

Andy crossed his arms and nodded at the floor. After all the promises he made to God, and to Liv, the idea he'd be keeping the lost pregnancy a secret tortured his soul. Maybe it was the Devil after all who heard his plea.

****

Flipping the juju the bird, Liv was moved to a regular medical room. Smaller in size, but without all the life-saving machinery, the room seemed to be double the ICU suite. More prison style windows, late 80s décor and a bathroom sink never shut off, it was hardly glamorous, but it was one step away from the lavish comforts of home.

Stories about the fate-defying southern belle, ER nurse and her hunky trauma doc were the hospital hot gossip. Quite a feat considering an affluent Mayoral candidate was admitted to psych for his addiction to hookers and porn. Blame her silly, pageant girl narcissism, but that was the sorta talk Liv reveled in.

She couldn't remember the last time she and her Momma spoke heart to heart. Truth be told, it had probably never happened, but as it was when death and dying hung in the air, people managed to let go of the pretentious rules of life and simply tried to live.

"I named her Georgia," Liv said with Charlotte by her side. Keenly aware of Andy's gaze, she avoided any trigger that would pull her his way. She could handle her Momma's judgment. But not from the man she loved.

The shame that usually went with the mention of her daughter's name never materialized. Instead, a tiny bubble of pride floated overhead. "Seven pounds, seven ounces, and a full head of the MacArthur family red peach fuzz."

Charlotte gave Olivia her cellphone. She beamed at the image, Georgia's memory fresh on the surface, then handed it to Eleanor. Liv braced herself for a stab of disappointment. If there was one thing she learned as Miss Savannah '05 and graduating summa cum laude from Vanderbilt, nothing stung more than one of her Momma's stoic reactions. The best she could hope for was a pursed-lip, nod of approval—except she smiled. Gushed. All but fell out of her chair with exalted joy.

"Oh, my darling, she is just beautiful. Cheeks for days as they say!"

Liv gaped at her mother. Shocked wasn't the word. Habitually suspicious of any emotion that wasn't disdain, she kept waiting for a snide, cruel smirk or a classic Eleanor Aberdeen-Maxfield's backhanded compliment. "Truly, dear," she continued, wiping at her cheek. "So very, lovely. I dare say even prettier than you, and you won every county in the state!"

Liv didn't know how to respond to this side of her mother, and apparently her resting bitch face said as much.

"By golly, Olivia, would you stop looking at me like you expect me to sprout horns?"

"Horns? No," Lottie chimed.

"You're more of a pointy hat sorta woman, wouldn't you say?"

Eleanor laughed, and Liv reached for Lottie's hand, then squeezed.

"That best friend telepathy is getting kinda scary, don't y'all think?" Andy surmised. Liv finally allowed herself to look his way. He gave her the smile that filled her to the brim with swoon. A deep flush blossomed across her chest and up her neck. "But your Momma's right, there, Livy. She sure is beautiful."

Regret formed a lump in the back of her throat. She swallowed it down, but it hit her gut and swelled to a softball. "She's loved. Cherished. And wants for nothing by a family that prayed for a miracle. And my Georgia was a miracle."

Eleanor dabbed her handkerchief along her cheek and smiled. "A beautiful blessin' in disguise."

The tone turned. The air in her lungs turned solid, and she couldn't breathe. "Can we have a minute, y'all?" she murmured looking at Andy then over to Charlotte.

"'Course, baby," Andy said swooping in with a kiss. He offered an arm to Lottie, who needed more encouragement. She threw shoulders back swayed her hips as she power strode to the door.

"I'll be back in the time it takes to have a pretend cigarette. That's about the only redeeming thing about this city."

Liv caught Andy's eye as he left. He winked.

Cool. Casual. And sexy as sin. Damn, she was a lucky woman.

Turning back to her mother, Liv fixed her eyes on the dusty, fake greenery in the corner. "I heard you, Momma. I heard you ask for one more try. Lottie. Andy. Everyone. They were ready to let me go. But you..."

Liv smoothed the hem of her floral bathrobe needing a beat of composure, but tears fell anyway. True on boohoo-ing and not tears for dramatic effect were Momma's kryptonite. She wiped them away before they had the chance to make a sloppy mess of the mascara Lottie insisted on when she moved from the ICU. "Sorry. I don't mean to blub—"

"Oh, baby girl..." Eleanor whispered, heaving herself from the chair to nestle next to her daughter. She wrapped her bony arms around Liv's shoulders and embraced her in a way Liv hadn't experienced since falling off her dapple pony at the Georgia State Fair over twenty years ago. Spindly fingers held her against the skin and bones of Eleanor's ribcage. "Go on and cry. Let me comfort you the way I should have the day your Daddy died and Logan broke your heart. And if there is one lesson out of all this, we never know how much time we're going have."

The sad, but true words seemed to hold them closer, until Eleanor shifted, then sat up with a huff. A string of rare curse words hissed under her breath.

"Momma," Liv chided, having never heard full on sailor mode vulgarity escape her mother's mouth. That was how her love for the f-bomb was born. Southern-born ladies just didn't cuss for God and all of Creation to hear.

"It's this goddamn wig," she said, pulling off the auburn mass of curls and tossing it at their feet. Liv caught their reflection in the small mirror hanging over a sorry excuse for a writing desk. Eleanor's porcelain white skull glowed in the brown fluorescents. Her stomach dropped to her feet. "I have a lot to make up for. And it begins now. With this. God wouldn't give me cancer, and take you before I had the chance to make it right."

Eleanor gripped her daughter's chin and forced Liv's gaze. Green eyes locked onto hers and softened, inventorying Liv's face as if to commit it to memory. "I love you, Olivia-Grace. I'm so very proud of the woman you became in spite of the horrible example I set for you. And I'm so very sorry for the pain, sadness, and the scars my failure as a mother I know have caused. And it is my intent to tell you that every day until it is my last."

A new well of tears sprang in Liv's eyes. They fell without restraint, and she shut her eyes, breathing in her Momma's soft soap and perfume. With each passing second, her insides started to ache so much she couldn't breathe, but she pulled away and plastered her fake it 'til you make it smile across her face. Her mother returned it.

Eleanor cleared her throat and wiped at her cheek. "So, I know you and Lottie prefer Vera, but really, Olivia, Monique Lhuillier is so much more elegant."

Liv giggled and flipped her debutante switch. "And Lawd forbid a woman look anything less."

"Remember that awful Badgley Mischka confection your step-cousin bought off the rack? Did nothing for her figure. All hips," she said, with a dainty shake of her chin.

Liv clung to her Momma with a sigh. "And no tits."

****

The buzzword floating through County Med's halls was "miraculous". An expected six-week recovery compounded into less than twenty-four hours. Liv's ingrained ER nurse trepidation simmered on low, but it was easy to ignore. She'd been granted a miracle. And it would be a bitch slap in the Lord's face not to revel in His blessings.

Liv sat in bed, squinting herself into focus in the tiny bedside mirror. She examined the bright red suture line at the base of her neck cringing at the bright pink suture line. Every nurse, doctor, telemetry technician, and housekeeper stopped by to give nosey but good-natured well wishes, but she should have taken the offer from Dr. Rubin in plastics. The dialysis catheter and central line stiches were sure to scar.

Vanity clawed at her nerves. She fiddled with some blush and mascara anxiously waiting on Lottie with fresh clothes and for Andy to come around with the car. That's *if* Smithson's fancy car survived the escort. Charlotte learned to tolerate the 'L, but her Momma would eat glass before she would subject herself to such. She hoped Charlotte kept herself together, if not for Liv's sake, then for the silver fox she was sweet on.

A knock came at the door. Liv pulled the hem of her robe to cover her neck, then fluffed her hair. "C'mon in," she chimed.

In the game of revolving visitors she sort of worked with, obstetrics had the next turn. Dr. Maggie Ford strode through with a stack of papers folded under her arm, rubbing hand sanitizer though her fingers. Liv smiled, genuine and pleased. Kind hearted and quick witted, Dr. Ford always laughed at Liv's not so funny jokes. She was a blast to work with when on call for the Pit.

"Nice to see you sitting up. You gave us all quite a scare over the last week."

She shrugged, guilt tugging a little on her spine. "What can I say, us Southern Belles just love to be the center of attention."

Dr. Ford pressed her lips together.

Liv kept waiting for a smart-assed, Manhattanite retort, but the silence dragged. She pushed through the awkwardness with her pageant smile. "Well, seems I'll be discharged this afternoon. Just waiting on my best friend and my knight in sexy black scrubs to blow this popsicle stand."

Again. No response from the OB attending that had on numerous occasions played heated rounds of "Fuck, Marry, Kill" between patients crashing through the door.

Nerves spiked in her blood. Her fingers tingled, then trembled into fists. Dr. Ford wasn't there to shoot-the-shit.

"Olivia, we need to discuss your follow-up."

****

Andy crossed his arms and glanced around County Med's dingy, outdated lobby. The eighties brass everything gave off a dirty bronze glow. A far cry from the sleek, state of the art ER and ICU he'd spent the last agonizing week encased in. Charlotte jabbered in his ear. Liv's mother, her asshat soon-to-be ex-husband, and redemption were the bullet points for her rant as they waited for the elevator to Liv's floor.

A wide-eyed nursing resident in scarlet scrubs caught his eye. Bright red for red-alert, Liv would have mused. A new grad giddy from gossip. Andy meant to smile, but his reflection revealed a grimace. Hospital celebrity status came with gawkers, headaches, and bold assholes trying for chitchat while he took a piss. All crosses he'd willingly bear, because today he got to take Olivia home.

The doors opened. Lottie grabbed his arm and pulled him through, parting the sea of staff and visitors like a shark in a minnow pond. As if she owned the place. And it had nothing to do with the fact the ER Medical Director was wrapped around her little finger.

Andy dropped her heavy leather bag on the elevator floor, then quickly slugged it to his other shoulder. He didn't know what Tory Burch was, but he was fairly certain it didn't come from Wal-Mart.

As if she could read his mind, Lottie squeezed his elbow. "For the last time, Anderson, I know what I'm doing. Just let me get Livy home. The truth and what comes from it won't fall on your shoulders."

"Christ, Lot. It *should* come from me. Last I check you weren't the one who—"

"Fucked her on the back stairs. Didn't pull out. Didn't stop her from going into Jorge's room. Saved Liv's life when she told you not to? What else am I missing?" Charlotte rattled off with a tick at her fingers.

Andy held her gaze. Hard. Until his throat closed and eyes watered. The elevator dinged. Andy choked on his composure as the doors slid open. An elderly man wearing a green volunteer's vest shuffled in pushing a popcorn machine. He gave Andy a cordial nod. Andy replied in kind, hoping the man shared his hatred of small talk. But hope was lost when the volunteer caught sight of Charlotte.

"Why, hello, Ms. Lottie. Do you have your littles with you today? I've got a fresh batch cooking."

Lottie batted her eyelashes and beamed right back. "Hello to you, too, Dr. Gus. No chillens today. How's your hip?"

The old man rubbed at his side. "Better, today. Sunshine always helps."

"You sure it's not *moon*shine?" Lottie challenged. The pair bantered back and forth until the elevator dinged at the next floor.

Andy took a closer look at the volunteer's badge. Dr. Gus Greenburg, County Med ER Medical Director from 1980-2010. Charlotte VanSutton sure had a type, charming the pants off two consecutive executives. He couldn't help but smile at Lottie. At her strength. Her devotion. Her uncanny ability to put people in their place with one glance. Last week, he was sure she'd be the impossible best friend he'd never be able to satisfy. But all it took was proof of his love for Liv and she'd become his biggest source for empathy and understanding. Especially, since he didn't deserve it. He owed her so much.

She waited for the doors to shut them in privacy before diving back into their conversation. "I know you are hurting. I know you blame yourself, and that in some heartbreaking way, telling Livy the truth would be your … penance … to whoever answered your prayers, but I promise. This is the best way. You've seen firsthand the kind of decisions she makes when she thinks people will judge her. I love Olivia, but you are *in* love with her. The difference between seeing the forest for the trees and a brick wall."

Lottie's logic swam in his brain. He looked over with a lopsided grin. She shrugged. "Hell. I'm tired. What I'm trying to say is. The juju—or whatever that nonsense Livy says—just wouldn't be in your favor."

Chapter Thirty-Four

Olivia gaped at the OB as she approached her bedside, only breaking when Dr. Ford pulled the rolling stool to sit. A million different emotions pummeled her mind. Even a sliver of tainted joy. Dr. Ford's specialty delivered miracles. "My what?"

"Your follow-up."

Olivia's heart swelled with each beat. She rubbed at her sternum, biting back the smallest of smiles. Her chest always ached, but this time it wasn't the burn of Andy's lifesaving compressions. "I don't know what you're talking about. Cardiac and kidney. I haven't heard anything about needing to see OB. Why…"

Dr. Ford placed a stack of papers next to Olivia's open hand. One sheet connected with her fingertip and cut like a blade. "Liv, you won't be needing an *obstetric* follow-up."

The blade became an axe, hacking away at her happily ever after.

"What are you … what…" she stammered, failing, refusing to make the connections. The ache between her breasts vanished. Emptiness ballooned in her belly. The clock on the wall seemed to tick louder with each passing second spiraling into a panic.

As if she sensed Liv's instinct to flee, Dr. Ford grabbed her arm and held tight. "You were bleeding."

"Hello, Captain Obvious. I was sick with the Blood Flu!"

"You weren't sick," she said, pulling back to lock her hazel eyes on Liv's. "But you were *bleeding* from what would have been an intrauterine pregnancy."

Time stopped. The words bounced around her brain, then rooted in her chest. Shame. Regret.

Devastation coiled through her heart's four chambers strangling her central organ.

"No," she demanded. "I'm careful. I'd never let that happen aga—"

Dr. Ford cut her off. "Low-dose BCP, irregular sleep habits, and a two-day course of antibiotics for tuberculosis precautions right before you met Andy…"

And there it was. Just like before. All her fucking fault. Liv squeezed her eyes shut. Seeing is believing. And she refused.

"I'm sorry, but it was a pregnancy your body could not sustain…"

Vomit rose in Liv's throat. She wanted to beg, and scream, plead for her to stop. The hole left by Georgia never healed, bandaged daily by duct tape and denial.

"The preliminary implantation bleeding quickly became—" Dr. Ford paused, forcing Liv to open her eyes and return her gaze. The instant their eyes met, a knife gouged into her chest.

"Catastrophic."

Liv gasped. Choked. An infinity of "no" cemented in her trachea, and she couldn't breathe. Through the cracked door, Lottie's voice floated into her room. Andy's swoony tenor parleyed with Charlotte's Savannah twang. Love and heartbreak ripped through her broken insides.

Dr. Ford cleared her throat. "A decision had to be made…"

****

When the elevator doors dinged open and Olivia's room came into view it took every ounce of self-control—and the mega-ton bag of girl crap to keep Andy from running down the hall and into Liv's arms. Lottie filled his head with the kind of hope that made a man the stupid kind of giddy. The stupid kind of giddy that made a man forget his happiness balanced on the head of a pin, that with one breath could all be over.

Charlotte gave him reassuring smile, immediately recognizing the pretend pageant face Liv relied on all too often. A part of him deflated. Fucking hope.

"Livy dear, you'd be proud of me. Twenty minutes with your Momma and we didn't erupt in flames. It must be something in the water up here…" she said as she strode through the door, then skidding to a stop. Andy dominoed right behind.

"Geeze, Lot. Brake lights," he muttered, dropping Liv's bag into a rickety desk chair. Andy waited for Liv and Lottie's banter to fill the room, but silence suspended time. Andy froze.

Dr. Maggie Ford sat at Liv's bedside. Immediate and intense, loss clawed at his throat. He swallowed it back, unable to move. His heart wasn't ready to see the high-risk OB, and no amount of time would make him ready to see her hovering in Olivia's orbit. She squared her shoulders, blocking Liv from view. The one person he needed to see. The only person who mattered.

Dr. Ford rose, and Liv's lovely face came into view. He hoped for anger. Hatred. Something other than sadness. Fires he could extinguish. A gash he could suture. Defeat was dead on arrival.

Liv clutched Dr. Ford's procedural notes so tight her hands shook. Tears fell.

The self-loathing and regret rooting Andy in place evaporated. With two long strides, he was there.

Andy pulled the paper the from her hands, crumpling the words "dilate and curettage" and "abortion", in bold print in one palm, reaching for her tear-stained cheek with the other. He braced for the inevitable moment she'd push him away, but she grabbed his hands and held him there. Liv turned into the pressure and warmth as if he were the cure to her broken heart.

His mouth opened to apologize. Grovel. Make good on his promise for a happily ever after, but Olivia started first. A stuttering ramble of sorry after sorry.

"It was my fault. All my fault. I put you ... I couldn't..."

Andy kissed her cheek, forehead, and pulled her against his chest. He felt Lottie's gaze dissect Liv's reaction.

"Jesus Christ, Liv. You have no reason to be sorry. *I* should've...."

Liv sat up and pulled away. She looked into his eyes, and his stomach did a back flip. Not from the usual, but from the intense, openness rimming her green eyes. "I asked the impossible from you. I will never blame you for the choice *you* made—to fight for my life. It was the right thing to do. And I love you, so much more for it."

An anchor lifted from Andy's chest. Relief replaced the weight of uncertainty. He smiled. Beamed. But it went unwitnessed. Liv turned to Lottie several steps away.

A small knowing smirk curled along Lottie's lip. The one said, "See, I knew Liv'd understand". Charlotte's smirk grew into the grin that meant she was about to sass out a quip about always being right, but Olivia's gaze went frigid.

"But *you*," Liv hissed. "Of all the people in this world, I would have thought at least *you*, Charlotte Geneva Fields-VanSutton, would know I would have *never* let anyone kill my baby. I would have rather died. *You* know that."

Charlotte paled. Fear flickered across her face, and she bit back a frown. After a beat, Lottie straightened accepting Liv's lash of words with honor and without complaint. "I'm so—"

"For fuck's sake, Lot," Liv sobbed in a tone he knew so well. The same breathless pleading he used to ask God why he saved him instead of his little boy.

Olivia heaved herself from her hospital bed and stood to meet Charlotte's height. For the first time, he saw Lottie bend, breaking Liv's irate gaze to stare at the floor. Not even when Liv's life hung in the balance did Charlotte show a sliver of weakness. "After all I went through with Georgia. How could *you* do that to me?"

Charlotte blinked rapidly, sucker-punched by Liv's absolute and unforgiving pain.

Comprehension seemed to tear through her spine, and she crumbled. Lottie was wrong. Olivia would never forgive her, but they'd both made decisions to save Olivia's life. He wouldn't let their lifetime of friendship be lost over the choice he didn't have the balls to make.

Andy shot to his feet. "It wasn't Charlotte's decision," he bellowed, bearing Charlotte's sins.

Olivia turned. Locked him into focus. Hard. Critical. Her bullshit detector alight across her face.

Andy crossed his arms. "It was mine. I knew she was your POA and that she'd never agree to terminate. So, I lied to Charlotte. I won't even apologize for it. I had to do everything."

Liv's lips flat-lined. She took a step, and her robe fell open. Two red, angry incisions tracked up her throat and across her chest. The visual reminder of Liv so close to death could have killed him right there.

"Including the murder of our child ... killing our *chance*..." she swallowed, like the truth burned a hole in her throat.

A knife of longing plunged into his back. This lie would be the death of him. "Yes."

Liv crossed the room with mechanical steps. The

warmth he loved turned to fire. A fire of hate. Hate he foolishly believed he could fix, except not one shred of emotion betrayed Olivia's reply.

"You lying, arrogant bastard. You are a doctor. Not God. I never want to see you again."

Chapter Thirty-Five

Whoever came up with the bullshit line, "Hindsight is twenty-twenty" must have been a man, and Liv desperately wanted to ninja kick him in the nut sack. Outwardly healed, but forever scarred, Liv returned home haunted by the fantasy of a happily ever after and the man she loved.

Telling Anderson she never wanted to see him again should have broken the curse. Ghost-busted any lingering love, lust, or silly-girl feels keeping her from finding peace or closure. She had it with Logan. His flagrant affairs broke her heart, killing a tiny piece of her soul and self-esteem, but telling the cheating asshole he'd never see her again severed whatever connection they had. She had been able to move away, have his child, and give her precious miracle to another family, yet never had any desire to hear his voice or feel his hands touch her face.

For a week, Olivia refused to leave her bed, claiming weakness, exhaustion, burnout, but it was a lie. Andy's scent was embedded in the Egyptian cotton, and she needed the smell of sandalwood and sweat like an asthmatic needing air.

The need was pure survival, and she hated him for it.

Goal for day ten of the return-to-work mandatory counseling was to take a bath. Except, day ten came and went.

"Will you actually turn the water on at some point?" Lottie asked, looking down at Liv curled in her clawfoot tub with her bedspread snuggled tight around her. She inhaled a dose of Andy. Maybe this would be it. Be enough.

Relief rippled through her heart, but it didn't keep. It never did. Like an addict, she always needed more.

Liv couldn't bring herself to answer. Charlotte turned, grumbling under her breath. Their best friend telepathy had been on different wavelengths since she'd been home. A new form of longing knotted her stomach. And it hurt almost as much as the void left by Andy and his broken promises.

Little LouLou peered around the doorframe. Lottie swooped in her arms and hummed in her ear. Children had been banned from Liv's top floor. Not under her request, but her Momma's. Eleanor's type-A rigidness spilled into every facet of Olivia's household during her stay. To Liv's surprise, Lottie allowed Eleanor to run the roost, but the greatest surprise came from Liv's genuine appreciation of her Momma's effort.

Olivia's honorary niece waved her pudgy little fingers from over Charlotte's shoulders and gurgled out a "Bye-Bye", surely, Nanny's latest feat.

Anger and sadness. Longing. Loss. Every shitty emotion one could feel festered where her womb should be. Nothing that healed, nothing that lessened with time.

Every day after Georgia, Olivia lived in denial. Every day she bargained with herself and the Lord … one more paycheck, one more good deed, one more life saved, and she could finally let go. Except, the quest for peace after heartache was like a snake eating its own tail. A never-ending cycle that eventually consumes you whole.

Liv laid her head against the cool, pristine tile and cried. The emergency room had been her salvation. Her only saving grace, how could she go back now? If the four walls of her bedroom smelled of the man she loved, the four walls which contained them for that fateful week would reek of torment.

A knock came at her door. Daylight turned to black. She'd cried away more than half the day. A slight improvement. The knock came again, followed by a frail call of her name. Liv's heart lifted a fraction. "C'mon in, Momma."

Eleanor crept through the door. Even with the medicinal pot and Nanny's Savannah fried everything, her Momma's already thin frame had become down right skeletal. Stress. The MacArthur women never wore it well.

Olivia pulled herself into a sitting position with her knees tucked beneath her chin. With nothing to do but count minutes and cry, Liv could only figure she was there to talk about something that would be the lemon juice in her bleeding hangnail.

Eleanor perched herself on a velveteen bath stool. "Well, baby girl. It's about time I head back home."

Forget the lemon juice. Her Momma going back to Savannah was more of a wasp sting washed with peroxide. Liv frowned and bit her lip. For the last week, Eleanor showered her with the kind of mother's love reserved for Hallmark Cards and Lifetime movies. With the Grand Canyon sized distance between her and Lottie, she wasn't ready for it to be over. The years lost to resentment and bruised pride they'd never get back.

Liv threw a heated glance to the ceiling. The Lord had become proficient at showing her the best of something and stealing it away. "I can't thank you enough for comin' up here. You've made this ... almost..."

"Bearable?" Eleanor finished with a grim smile. Liv snort-laughed, then quickly fell into sobs. She rose on her knees as if to beg, wringing her fingers between her Andy-scented sheets.

"Momma. Must you go? I know I've been a plumb awful host, but I'm feeling better. I can take care of you. Make sure Dr. Parsons gets your meds and treatments all square up here."

Eleanor pulled away, a flicker of the "Old Momma" flashing across her face. The same woman who preached the gospel that Savannah women never cried.

Olivia retreated, burying her hurt by looking at the floor.

"Baby girl. Look at me."

Liv found a shred of dignity deep in her bones and looked up.

"Wretched cold, or not. There is nowhere in this world I would rather be than with you. But I'm—" Eleanor paused to wipe at her cheek.

"These last few days. Being here, being your Momma, just watching you sleep has been the only medicine my cancer has needed." Eleanor, reached up and removed her wig, coiffing the curls in her lap. "Besides, I fired that old quack Parsons. I won't be gone long. Just a few things I need to take care of. Your Aunt Millie is chomping for gossip. I need to snuff her out before she gets the chance to stoke her popularity with your … our family business."

Liv nodded, torn between appreciative and annoyed. How much of it was to protect her place in Savannah Society?

"Besides. You have Charlotte."

"We're not exactly…"

"Is there an ending to that sentence?"

Liv shook her head, locked onto the look her Momma was known for. Stern. Full of judgment and disdain, but in a beat she softened, reaching over to caress Liv's cheek.

Liv breathed in the soft, powdery smell of her

Momma's perfume and flashed back fifteen years to the one and only time love and tenderness transcended from words to a mother's touch, to the night she watched her Daddy drop dead at the Sunday pulpit, to the night she vowed to do everything she could to save someone from the pain she felt, to the night the Lord revealed her calling.

"Go to him. If you think your heart is breaking, baby girl. Just imagine what Andy's going through."

She flinched at the mention of his name. A thumbtack into the sole of her soul.

"He's hurting, and you need to own that."

The ebb and flow of grief fueled from sadness into a rage. "Oh, the same way you 'own' the expectation I get an abortion if I didn't marry a cheating bastard with a good family name?"

Eleanor stiffened, as if to ignore Liv's outburst the way a mother ignores her toddler's temper tantrum in the toy aisle. She stood, rigid pride straining between her shoulders as she adjusted her auburn wig back in place.

"Thank you, darling daughter, for proving a point."

"Oh, am I to be blessed with an Eleanor Aberdeen-Maxfield life lesson?"

"Not my life lesson. Your Daddy's. Matthew 6:14 'For if you forgive men when they sin against you, your Heavenly Father will also forgive you.' For all of your white knight nonsense, you never seemed to learn how to forgive. Yourself. Or anyone else."

"Forgive?" Liv almost screeched, throwing the Andy-tainted bedsheets aside as if they burned her. "Mother. He—"

"Saved your life, Olivia. I thought your time away from me, from home, would have changed you. Given you some perspective, but then again … how much do people really ever change? Through your eyes a person is either a victim…" Eleanor paused, the usual dramatic second where her words commanded a locked pair of eyes. "Or a villain. And if I knew you still would need a villain to blame, I'd have fallen on that blade. It sure would have saved Charlotte, Anderson, and yourself a whole lot of heartache."

****

Andy spent the better part of a week waiting for his lies to kill him. That would be the most humane thing the Lord could have done. He waited in the bitter cold by the lake, on the 'L around the loop and watched for hours as happy fucking people took upside down selfies in the stupid Bean. But as the hours turned to days, and the days sprawled to a week, it was clear God wouldn't be granting His mercy.

Leaving Liv's side as she burned with hatred rivaled the memory of her hovering near death, or the crunch of her ribs as he compressed her heart. Almost as bad as the hiss and hum of Dr. Ford ending one life to save another. And now another city he called home was haunted by the ghosts of lives and loves lost.

There wasn't a pair of bootstraps big enough to pull him out of the living hell that was life without Liv. The only solution was a distraction. And the only distraction a doctor needed was work. As much as his insides ached for Olivia, his fingers itched to slice, and suture.

Andy stared down the double glass doors to the County Med Ambulance bay immune to the wail of sirens, city noise, and bitter cold. His one mercy came in the form of shitty weather. Rain. Flurries. Freezing fog, a perfect shit-storm of Chicago gloom perfectly echoed his mood, but today God decided to fuck with him.

Sunshine. Fucking sunshine. Liv was everywhere

in it. In every flick of gold and red, pink and peach, Liv appeared, slicing into his heart.

The glass doors flashed open. Liv came alive in a cheery refracted sunbeam. He took it like a knife to the jugular, recovering with pressure and a wince, just in time for the goddamn doors to slide shut. Nightfall couldn't come soon enough.

A tall mass of muscle in royal blue trotted between glass enclosed vestibule. Javier smudged into focus, arms crossed, hopping up and down. The universal dance for warmth reserved for the walk-in morgue and occasional dip into the wintery outdoors.

"You coming in, Doc?"

Andy grit his teeth and shook his head. If it were only that simple.

Javier rubbed his arms and joined him outside turning his face into the sun. Too many shifts in a row, a person loses all sense of day versus night, and Javi drank up the sunshine like an Old Style in the bleachers at Wrigley Field in July.

Jealousy prickled up his spine. Jealous of Javi's freedom and ability to bottle his feelings better than he ever did.

"Have they made you see the shrink, yet?" he asked, shivering in place.

"I've been hard to find, but no. No shrink."

Javi nodded. Two weeks of sleepless nights and restless days weaved between dark eyebrows. Silence filled between them faster than he could shovel out with a forced smile and a wave good-bye.

"So ... have you talked—I"

"Ah. No. Listen. I just wanted to let Smithson know I'm taking a leave." Andy shoved his fists into his jacket pockets and turned from the shadows into the sun. The brightness blinded his way out. He squeezed his eyes shut waiting for his vision to return. When Liv finally faded from behind his eyes, he found Javier's gaze. "I … umm. I never got a chance to thank you. For everything. Tell CiCi she's amazing. And to not let those asshats get the best of her."

"Andy. Wait. C'mon, man," Javier said, stumbling over his words and a concrete curb. "Give me ten minutes. We can get a coffee."

Andy laughed, wanting nothing more than to throw the Lord a giant middle finger.

"All right. No coffee. Mas Tequila."

"Did CiCi put you up to this?"

"So what if she did?" Javier scrubbed at his beard and crossed his arms against the cold.

Andy waited. He owed Javier so much. He didn't deserve his compassion and patient ear. The wounds left by Liv and his lies were too fresh. Too deep. The only thing that could save him now was a distraction, and he had to get there as fast as he could.

"I really appreciate the offer, but I can't. I can't be here," Andy said waving at the brick and glass façade to charge back into the hellish sun.

"Where are you going then?"

A wave of heat and humidity washed over his cheeks and down his chest. A memory. The only place he'd ever been granted peace after heartache. "To save lives."

Chapter Thirty-Six

Olivia wrapped herself in a down parka. An air-temp of thirty and into the teens with lakefront wind gusts might not have gotten the natives in a tizzy, but wasn't about to give Lottie a reason to march her ass back upstairs and under her covers.

Happiness hung in the air like a noose ready to grab hold and slowly suffocate the air from her lungs. Guilt and the sort of boredom that could drive a woman mad was just as deadly as the blood flu. Her room was a coffin. And she had to get out.

With Eleanor a week deep into her life back in Savannah society, she had to find her way back to something. Even if it meant tempting the wrath of a particularly ornery best friend.

Lottie'd become a tyrant presiding over her "recovery". Liv, Lottie, Eleanor, and Dr. Hugs-a-lot hospital therapist knew the word was as fickle as a Georgia winter, but something had to be done. And to Liv that meant finding a way to get back to work. Maybe not the Pit. Maybe not with "people", but somewhere where she could feel useful. Needed. And not broken.

Using a reserved supply of inner O'Hara charm on her male physicians and the luxury of lying over the phone, she coerced the cardiologist and kidney doctors she didn't need a follow-up appointment. Swore up and down she was "all healed", knowing full well "all better" would never be an option.

Any woman would see through her bullshit. Which was why she had to brave the cold and Lottie's pensive glare to battle Dr. Ford.

"You know I don't approve of this. It's too soon, Liv. You don't have to work."

"Yes, I do. Maybe not 'work' work … but I just can't sit here anymore. Work was the only way I could move on after Georgia."

"Spoiler alert. You never moved on after Georgia."

Liv sighed and zipped her jacket up to her nose. "I know…"

Her thoughts and words drifted, then fizzled. The hole in her chest quickly filled with sadness.

Lottie's eyes pulled together in her "are-you-fucking-kidding me" face. Over the last month whenever she let herself wallow in front of Charlotte, she always seemed to lose her patience. Liv couldn't put into words how shitty that made her feel, and Lottie never seemed to want to explain why she was being a shitty best friend. After a lackluster Halloween and a botched Thanksgiving their telepathy went from different wavelengths to non-existent. They were like the couple staying together for the sake of their kids.

"Wear your hat," Charlotte grumbled before turning into a cluster of little people noise. Nanny and the children toddled into the kitchen. Her pseudo niece and nephew had been the one bright spot during her six weeks of dark.

Liv smiled, sure Lottie felt the ice melt between them. "No way. It's two blocks. It took five tries to get this topknot to look like I didn't try that hard," she mused, expecting Lottie to share in the smile, but the one beat could have been one billion. Liv swallowed a lump of loneliness before it swelled into something she wouldn't be able to fake. "Ahh, right. The hat."

Liv grabbed the slouchy cap and pulled in over her ears. LouLou wrapped her roll-y arms around her thigh, and Liv bent down for a quick kiss. When she stood, woozy black dots flashed across tunneled vision, and Liv wavered. Nausea rolled in her stomach. The room rolled with it. She squeezed her eyes shut, praying the moment of dizziness didn't become a full on "fallin'-out".

Lottie reached for her. Love and understanding transfused from her grip, but when she opened her eyes, Lottie's fuzzy expression read resentment laced with disappointment. "Be careful please? Someone won't always be around to save your thankless, skinny ass."

****

Charlotte's words sank in her stomach. Guilt rooted so deep she couldn't move. And the moment she sat down in the cheery and plush armchair in Dr. Ford's waiting room she knew it was a mistake. Bright colors, happy, pregnant women, beaming but bleary-faced new fathers holding squishy, fresh infants surrounded her on all sides. Small children crawling over round, protruding bellies ready to drop a baby with one hard sneeze had to be punishment for something. Maybe this was it. Her penance. If she could endure the smell of talcum powder and overflowing oxytocin, then she'd be free from the bonds of love and loss.

Liv shifted in her seat avoiding every pair of eyes. Except one. Lovely onyx eyes almost sought her out. Alone. Terrified. Screaming in silent pain. The kind of pain that flipped her ingrained nursing switch.

Liv crossed the room, darting around strollers, car-seats and diaper bags with polite nods and "excuse me"s and sat next to the woman.

"Hi. Mind if I sit here?"

The woman pressed her lips into a tight grimace that probably was a close to a smile as she could get.

"Thanks, lots of poopy butts over there. I'm Liv."

"Bree. Think Dr. Ford's running a little late?"

"Rumor mill as of two hours ago, she had back to

back scary STAT deliveries. Uterine accrete, I think."

Bree's grimace turned into a layman's look of WTF.

"I'm an ER nurse. I get nosey."

Bree tried to laugh, but it seemed to bring on a stab of pain. She flinched bracing into her left hip bone. "Speaking of nosey. When did your pain start?"

The first thing Bree tried to do was wave off the pain, as if it were nothing, but it was probably more of a polite attempt to tell Liv to mind her own business. "I'm fine. I'll just wait for Dr. Ford," she said with a dismissive shrug.

"Ahh. No. I've seen 'fine'. You, ma'am, are not fine." Liv's voice rose from a quiet whisper to one of authority.

"Yesterday. Woke me up from a sound sleep."

Liv leaned closer, trying to assume some resemblance of privacy to the bored and curious glances. "And your last period?"

Bree huffed. "Few and infrequent. I have an IUD. Husband just left back overseas. I don't pay attention."

Panic crept up Liv's neck and prickled her scalp. "Can I take your pulse?" she asked in a tone Bree wouldn't interpret as an option.

She offered her hand. Liv pressed her fingers to the underside of her wrist. Her heart fluttered, barely palpable. A thin sheen of clammy sweat broke out at her hairline. Left lower abdominal pain. Clear signs of shock.

Liv jumped to her feet. The masses around her watched.

"I'm going to get one of her nurses to come out here."

Bree nodded, faintly, as if the will to argue took too much effort. Liv charged to the small nurses' desk. The ladies gave her the smile she knew too well, the "oh you again" smirk of annoyance. It took every ounce of self-control not to give it back. Only meaner. Better. More effective.

"You have a patient out here in pretty severe, left lower quadrant pain. She's tachycardic and diaphoretic. I think she's got a ripe ectopic."

The three women stared as if she were speaking a different language, but with the mention buzzed word "ectopic", an older nurse came from an exam room. Her short grey hair and etched face said she was the well-seasoned, no-nonsense woman Liv needed to speak to.

Liv crossed an invisible line. "Ma'am. You have a patient of Dr. Ford's out here that at least needs a set of vitals and a quick look with the ultrasound. She probably needs a trip to the ER."

"Miss. You can't come back here," interjected a talking head Liv ignored.

The older nurse put her file down and examined Liv's face. Was it a flicker of recognition or just the passing nurse's judgement assessing the level of crazy?

"And you are?"

"I'm Olivia Aberdeen. I'm an ER nurse at County Med waiting for my own follow-up with Dr. Ford. But this lady can't wait."

Apparently only her name was needed to grease the wheels. The trio of talking heads stopped their guffs and eye rolling long enough to listen to Nurse Barbara call the shots. Barbara followed Liv with a wheelchair and with more strength she would have guessed heaved Bree into a semi sitting position.

Liv grabbed her hand. "Okay, hon. Things are going to start happening really fast."

Bree mumbled what sounded like an understanding. People around them spread the like Moses and the Red Sea, and out popped a sonographer from his dark cubby in the back.

Liv rattled off the bullet to the ultrasound technician while Barbara told the staff to send for an ambulance and call to Dr. Ford's private line. Liv helped remove Bree's Chicago layers. All flipping four of them. After the third fleece she hissed her favorite cuss word, seriously missing her trauma sheers.

The sono machine turned on, a low hum echoed in the eight by twelve closet. It slowed the moment. Slowed her thoughts. The quarantine clawed forward. Jorge. Blood. But most of all. Andy.

Bree was eased back to recline in the seat. She immediately let out a howl. The sonographer leapt away. "I didn't touch her!"

"No. It's my shoulder. Something hurts in my shoulder," Bree sobbed.

Liv and Barbara locked eyes, coming to the same, instant conclusion.

"She's already bleeding out."

****

Bree wavered in and out of consciousness for the paramedics. Liv kept an even head. Even hand. Fear and memories kept themselves behind the veil of her mind, relying on life-saving autopilot to keep from losing control.

Until the dam broke. Her heart and lungs could have vaporized for as much effort it took to breathe. Her hands could have turned to stumps for as little she could make them do. Self-pity and despair clouded any attempt to be useful, and she had to step away. Like a nervous new grad who couldn't dissociate herself from the stress of saving lives.

Barbara and the medics finished packaging Bree for transport. Liv circulated in the background pacing in a tight line. How can something she loved cause her such pain? Debilitating. Disabling. Pain.

She caught Bree's gaze as she slid into the ambulance, chaos swirling around her. A scared, pleading expression tugged at Liv's heart and reeled her in like a fish on a hook. But this time, Liv approached as a kindred soul. Not someone hell-bent on changing fate.

Barbara offered Liv a hand as she climbed into the squealing ambulance. "I can only imagine how impossible it was to wake up and have so much taken from you. Maggie lights a candle every time she has to end one life to save another. She lit two for you that day. One for what she took from you…"

A medic nudged her elbow and gave her the ready-to-go face. She nodded, but held up a finger asking for a fifteen second pause.

"And the other?"

"So that you could forgive those who had to make the choice."

Barbara stepped back, and the doors slammed shut. Liv pressed her knuckles into her temple as if it could imprint Barbara's words into her brain. The ambulance sped forward, jarring Liv's inertia into the seat-bench. The medics worked as if she weren't there, and Liv grabbed Bree's hand. "Can I call someone for you?"

Bree's oxygen masked fogged with a haggard breath. "No. Not until it's over. I don't want him distracted."

Liv nodded, once again feeling their souls connect through similar tragedy. She sat back, the word forgiveness jostling in her brain with every quick turn and sudden stop. She reached for her cellphone and slid her thumb across the glass. Her finger hovered over Andy's name just like the last three hundred times since he broke her heart and she his, but this time it didn't hover over "delete".

Something flourished in her chest. Warm. Whole. The same soothing heat Andy radiated while she wavered between life and death. She didn't need to find a way to forgive. Forgiveness found her.

But she had one call to make first. And sure enough, it was answered on one ring.

"County Med ER, this is the Charge Nurse, Javier the Extraordinaire."

"Heya, Javi. It's Liv."

Silence met her as a reply, like the mere mention of her name cracked his flirty, full of shit Mr. Machismo act he was known for. Liv imagined his cocky grin fade from his face, and the perpetual knife of guilt stabbed between her breasts. The same place Andy, Javier, and so many other people fought to save her life.

"Hey," he said disbelief dragging out the word. "You know, Liv, if you missed me, you have my number. You didn't need to call the bat line."

Liv frowned, closing her eyes to the chaos of the ambulance. Snark and sarcasm were an ER nurse's best defense mechanism.

"You're right. But I'm bringing you a patient. Thirty-year-old female. Ruptured ectopic, with a large hemoperitoneum, with referred pain to her shoulder. Shocky. Tachycardic. You'll need to pull Dr. Ford from antepartum. She's not answering her nurses' call."

Javier laughed. And just like that she was forgiven. "Jesus, Liv. Left you alone for six weeks and look at all the trouble you cause."

Chapter Thirty-Seven

Dr. Ford, Javier, and a team from L&D met Liv and Bree in the ambulance bay ready to unload. Like a silly girl who's read too many romance novels slathered in fantasy and cheese, Liv hoped Andy would be there, too. Tall, brooding, dressed in his sexy-as-sin in black scrubs, with a too tired to care twelve o'clock shadow meant to hide, but really revealed the equal hell he'd been struggling through. But he wasn't. This was reality, and Liv knew it was her turn to work for her knight in shining armor and the happily ever after.

The elevator doors slid shut. Liv threw a prayer up to Heaven, and Dr. Ford threw a thankful, empathetic glance over her shoulder. The kind of look that said, "Yep. It hurts. Always does." It also meant she was in the clear. The next time she'd see Maggie Ford, she'd be Olivia Aberdeen, awesome ER nurse, and Dr. Ford would be the same feisty and foul-mouthed OB/Gyn Liv loved to save lives with. The hurt would still be there, but nothing that kept a person from living.

She turned to Javier. His brave, cocky grin wavered, and then he crossed his arms as if to stop himself from doing something unmanly.

Liv saved him the embarrassment, and pulled him into a side hug reserved for two quasi-flirty friends in very serious relationships. "Thank you. For being an ass, and not listening to me."

"Well, you can always count on me to never listen when a chick is talking."

Liv's friendly embrace turned into the junk-punch you give your big brother.

"So, um … is he here?" she asked, looking at the floor. When he didn't quip out a reply, she met his gaze.

Javi's mischievous, dark eyes warmed in something like comfort. Maybe it was the worry that telling her the truth would wipe the smile off her face.

Javier shook his head. "Dr. Cole hasn't been here. Not since—"

"So, the rumor *is* true?" cut in a familiar, matter-of-fact voice.

Liv jumped and grabbed at her chest. She hadn't recouped from the excitement and adrenaline of helping Bree. Any other startles and she was likely to end up with her ass on the floor. She turned and found the ER medical director breezing down the physicians' hall. She deflated, absently expecting Andy to be striding right behind. "Nurse Olivia Aberdeen is gracing County Med with her presence? So, I take it you're ready to come back?"

"Ah, Not quite yet, Dr. Smithson. Just keeping the ER in business."

Javi and Smithson shared in a quick chuckle. "Lottie warned me you might try and make an appearance. She swears this place is your magnetic north."

Liv rolled her eyes, but there was no arguing that truth. Javi's charge nurse pager buzzed at this waist. He grabbed it with a flash of excitement.

"Duty calls, Liv. I gotta run, good to see you. Just call the cell next time. See ya, Doc," he said with a minor salute to his superior and loped off to the Pit.

Liv traced the ground with her Converse, and avoided Smithson's eyes. "Have you heard from Anderson? Javi said he hasn't been at work."

"Ah. No. I haven't. He took a leave."

Liv frowned, but she should have expected that much. He'd been in Chicago all of three fucking minutes before being dragged into her suckfest of tragedy and fate. He had no ties to the city; it probably hurt just to breathe the air.

She'd been to the gates of Heaven and came right back to be with him. Texas wasn't that far.

"So I take it, he went home?" she asked fiddling with the zipper of her now too hot parka. Unladylike beads of sweat pooled between her breasts, and suddenly she didn't want to hear the answer.

"I guess you could say that," Smithson admitted. Liv looked up and tried to read his face. He rubbed at his brow, wincing, as if it hurt just to think. She braced against the steel elevator doors and sucked in a steadying breath. The smell of hospital antiseptic always settled her nerves.

"He went back to Guatemala. I've tried calling, texting. He won't even answer an email. I don't know how to get a hold of him."

Liv went slack. Her poised, pageant-girl posture wilted under the weight of disappointment and guilt. She knew her words had cut him to the core, and Andy wasn't the kind of man to rub a little dirt in the wounds she caused and carry on, but she never expected him to run so far. So far from her. But she'd make it right. God. Please let her make it right.

She swallowed a bitter pill of self-resolve and raised her chin. Defiance in the face of despair.

"I know how. Give me Greta Cole's phone number."

****

Liv sat at her writing desk, knees bouncing, freshly painted French tips clicking against the laptop keyboard. Greta Cole wasn't the most difficult person to get a hold of, but she seemed hell bent on putting Olivia through the paces.

Two emails. Four days of stunted, unhelpful text

messaging and finally she'd been granted a "face-to-face" phone call.

"I don't know why you're bothering with her at all, Livy. She's remarkably unlikeable," Charlotte said while combing through LouLou's baby blonde locks. The ice between them seemed thaw after Liv declared she wanted to find Andy and apologize. Still, she tiptoed around the change. Thinner ice meant it was easier to fall through the crack and drown.

"Getting to Andy through Greta feels like the right thing to do."

"Olivia-Grace MacArthur Aberdeen, I believe you have lost all privileges to what you feel is right."

Liv held in a sigh. Just like her Momma, and any southern lady worth her weight in sweet tea and sass, Lottie could layer on the patronizing wisdom better than MAC lipstick. Her finger hovered over the call button. She closed her eyes and prayed for a dose of patience and clicked "dial".

Greta Cole answered on the first ring, greeting her exactly the way Liv expected. Tight lipped. Severe. Like she knew she had her and Andy's happiness by the throat and could squeeze the life right out of it.

"You made him run back to that mess faster than I ever could. For all that precious, southern belle BS, it appears you can break a man just as soon as batting your eyelashes at them."

Liv tossed a glance at Charlotte, who didn't look up from preening her toddler's hair. But that didn't stop a satisfied smirk from appearing on her face.

"I umm. I suppose I deserved that."

Lottie grunted. "That's for damn sure."

"I don't know how much he told you, but if anyone can help me get to him. I know you can…" Liv picked at her thumbnail. "Please, Greta. I need to apologize."

"Oh princess, I know every sad detail. What makes you think he would want to hear your apology?" Before Liv could surmise any kind of reply, Greta pressed on. "If you knew anything by now, Andy's world is black and white. He can't see the forest for the trees."

Behind her Charlotte let huff that was a ten out of ten on the over-dramatic scale. "Everyone just wants to be me…"

Olivia squinted her into "What in the Sam Hill focus", and by the looks of it, Texan women were just as acquainted with silent cast of judgment. But to her credit Greta added her own unladylike eyeroll.

"I told Anderson the exact same thing about you, Livy. In the elevator the day you were going to be discharged. I knew you'd be all high and mighty and never see any perspective that wasn't your own sense of what is morally right. But I never thought…"

Something pulled Lottie into a pause.

"Thought what?" Olivia prompted.

Lottie popped Louise off her lap and shook her head. The century-old settee creaked beneath the shift in weight, and like a twit Liv held her breath. Somehow the sound of great-granny's prized parlor loveseat felt like the final crack in the ice giving way.

"Livy, one day I hope you realize that sitting up there on that moral high horse of yours makes your ass look fat."

Charlotte marched her baby girl out of Liv's room in a way that felt permanent.

"Lottie, wait, how can—"

She was met with silence and a slammed door as a reply. Greta, on the other hand, was already on the offensive.

Liv spun in her seat, and Greta spewed her

venom. "If you only knew how much your friend went to battle for you. And Andy. I've never seen anyone be so ungrateful."

Reflexively, anger prickled up Olivia's neck until her cheeks blazed. She didn't need to be scolded by someone like Greta, even if the argument rang true. Olivia straightened, keeping her mind on the task at hand. "I know how my actions could be perceived that way. Retrospect goggles are always 20/20. I'm sure even you would agree to that."

Greta arched an over-Botoxed eyebrow. Liv read her silence feeling more like a "frenemy" than a foe.

"I don't presume to think God would grant me *another* do-over. But I have to at least try."

"I hear that. And I respect ya all the more for it. After Jackson, I was far too gone in my own grief and rage. I couldn't forgive myself, let alone Anderson. I carry that regret to this day, but I think you owe Andy more than an apology. You owe him the truth. And not in the convoluted, scandalous reveal kind of way. Andy is a simple man. He's a damn good doctor, and you asked him to break with the most fundamental part of that job."

Greta sat back like a TV crime detective hammering down his last bit of evidence. Liv appreciated the technology that allowed for video chats, but right then, it gave Greta a power over her that would have been neutralized by sharing the same oxygen.

Liv cracked a knuckle and balled her nerves into her fists. "It was never about going against the 'Do Not Resuscitate'," she said through gritted teeth. An ache flushed within her ribs, but it was nothing compared to the pain stabbing in her belly. "It was the fact he made the—"

"Good Lord, you need to climb off that high horse before you break that pretty, little neck. The *choice* you blame Anderson for was never his to begin with. He fought with Allen and your friend for what he believed *you'd* want. Didn't matter that the doctor side of his brain knew better."

The distinct clamor of shattered glass traveled up the air vents, and Greta went silent as if the noise perfectly emphasized her point. The sharpened edges to Lottie's twang suggested either a fight with Teddy, or another wine-induced argument with herself. Both were as volatile as a hangry toddler refusing a nap.

Liv's jaw fell open, and Greta's words snapped into place with the kind of weight that could knock the wind right out of the lungs.

"Charlotte would have set me on fire if I had spoken out of turn against you, and you were going drop kick her out of your life even worse than the way you did your mother. And when Andy saw what you were going to throw away at the cost of what you believe to be right and wrong... Like a lovesick, white knight, Andy jumped on that grenade."

Every state of shock sputtered though her consciousness. Someone had just pulled the curtain to reveal the Great and Powerful Oz to be nothing more than a charlatan, and Liv was at the mercy of feeling like a blind fool.

Embarrassment seared up her spine until tears sprang in her eyes. Lottie made another loud declaration, this time leaving no question as to the end target to her temper tantrum.

"Eleanor, I know I promised I'd stick it out. But I can't. She's... Oh, dammit all to hell, I know. I know she needs me."

Liv stole a glance at Greta. Her smugness softened into a look she hadn't seen before. "I know you want to fix things with Andy, but that there is something that needs tendin' to first."

Something between a laugh and a sob caught in Liv's throat. "Christ on a cracker, these will be some expensive as fuck apologies."

****

Lottie lounged in Liv's clawfoot tub sipping a Diet Coke with fresh lime, each twin snuggled into her side. Nanny Kemp retrieved the pair of dead weight toddlers to put them down for the night. They exchanged some mental shorthand, and Lottie looked on with such fond appreciation, Liv's heart swelled in her chest. It was plain their relationship had surged past one of the traditional southern Nanny and her stuck-up employer, but to one of mutual affection and a solidifying love for the children. Their friendship had been something Lottie relied on during the months Liv had had her head on backwards.

Olivia offered up a dainty, perfume bottle flask from her vanity. Charlotte chased her sip of Diet Coke with a healthy swig of the good whiskey Liv never liked to share.

"I will say this, hightailing it to squalorville to is about as basic as a pair of Uggs on a 60-degree day."

Liv laughed and held out two feather weight peasant dresses. Lottie pointed to the cream and mint embroidered frock, and Liv rolled it into her carry-on knapsack.

"I was hoping it came across as grand and romantic, but we're all entitled to our wrong opinion."

Flipping Liv the bird, Lottie stuck out her tongue. A smile as wide as the Mississippi split Liv's face. The potency of a heartbroken and absent best friend was more apparent right after the littlest things. Three hours of boohooing and tear-slopped "I'm sorry"s had only scratched the surface.

"But I just got ya back, Livy. Can we even trust what that pterodactyl told you? I refuse to believe the only solution is for you to fly twenty thousand miles and putting yourself in harm's way."

Liv stashed a few pairs of socks, and a hopeful cache of sultry underpinnings into the top bag and zipped it shut. The task of paring down her Guatemala-or-Bust skin care routine would require at least an hour and half bottle of Rose.

"I believe Andy would dive so deep into work he doesn't come up for air unless dragged by his hair. Besides. I'm not above begging. But I'm a lot more … *persuasive* in person. If you know what I mean."

"So Andy has a coma-inducing blow job in his future. Make sure he signs a waiver."

"Lot, use this time to go home, eat some chicken and dumplin's, square things away with Teddy—"

Lottie's cellphone chimed. "Oh I know you're right. You don't need to rub my nose in it," she whined and hoisted herself from the tub. She preened her carnalized chocolate tresses before swiping at the screen.

If Liv's smile was as wide as the Mississippi, Lottie's was the Grand Canyon. "What has you looking like you snagged the last Goyard Satchel of the season at a zillion percent off?"

Lottie blushed but brushed it off with a shrug. "Nothing. Just being silly."

Olivia grinned. "Uh huh. Carlotte VanSutton, have you ensnared yourself a silver fox for a boyfriend?"

Chapter Thirty-Eight

Andy grabbed the hem of his shirt and wiped sweat from his eyes. He wouldn't call moving a half dozen cots and crushing boxes "backbreaking", but the heat and humidity were enough to make a man sweat just thinking about the work he had to do.

He dusted, swept, and primed fifty or so fluid boluses for the clinic. A day's worth of work done before sunrise.

The work had become mindless. Routine. Just what he needed. Until a fresh round of the blood flu ripped through his village. Six days. Sixteen deaths. The total could have doubled, but the moment his feet touched the soil, Andy implemented new triage and quarantine parameters that seemed to stem much of the contagion.

The rural community nestled between acres of rainforest and the foothills of the Sierra Madre Mountains had seen hundreds die over the last year, many that could have been prevented with simple education and preparation. Now, the small, religious town which relied heavily on prayer to heal the sick had a small dose of modern medicine. And if there was one lesson he learned in Chicago, a good doctor needed both.

By midday, his modest medical clinic usually saw over twenty patients. Most were work-related finger injuries with a few serious, adrenaline pumping amputations and flesh de-glovings. The afternoons somehow became reserved for peds. Routine check-ups, life-saving vaccines, dental care, and hauling clean drinking water for families with no able-bodied men became the norm. Until word spread about the American doctor who survived the blood flu who appeared to be back for good.

Worried mothers and fathers traveled hundreds of miles, bypassing big-city hospitals with long waits and dismissive staff for the personalized time and attention Dr. Andy was known for. Days were long. Draining. But he found peace. Exhausting, ever-loving, peace.

Andy swooped a listless little boy into his arms and laid him on a cot. Solei, a local woman with a knack for finding a good vein, rivaling even Liv's abilities, wrapped a tourniquet around the child's bone thin upper arm.

They'd met during his exposure the year before. She was one of the few people who treated the bleeding masses, himself included, who never got sick. Solei seemed untouchable, and during his medical mission after the death of his son, she was the only one who never asked questions. And he was grateful she kept with the tradition.

Andy did his best to explain his suspicions in Spanish. Six weeks and he still couldn't sputter and comprehend fast enough. Half the time he ended up confusing his nouns, telling a woman her testicle was inflamed or a man that his breasts will lactate. Solei became the universal, shitstorm translator.

Andy felt over the boy's head, neck and belly assessing for outward injury, then pressed his fingers into the notch at his elbow. The child's pulse threaded beneath the surface with no fever.

He fired questions at the frantic parents with Solei pulling double duty, drawing blood and directing the answers.

"When did he start acting sick?"

A spitfire of Spanish bounced back and forth.

"About two weeks. Weight loss, always thirsty," Solei interpreted from the mother's lung-full reply.

Falling into an old habit, he rattled his thoughts aloud as if CiCi or another resident were there to process and put the pieces together. Solei grinned over her freckled shoulder. He almost smiled back.

"I sure wish you could talk to me, little guy."

The boy opened his eyes. "I can. You did not ask," rasped a tiny voice.

Andy laughed and looked to Heaven. Solei did the same. The parents collapsed into each other as their son showed his first signs of responsiveness.

"My name is Oliver." The boy sucked in and blew out air as if he were breathing through wet sand. "And I'm not little. I am five," the boy said in proud, precise English.

A twinge knotted in Andy's side. He had to be named Oliver. Across the cot, the mother welled with maternal pride.

Through short, shallow gasps, Oliver spoke to his mother in the only sort of Spanish he knew. Slow.

Oliver's breath hit him square in the face. Sweet. Too sweet. He opened his mouth and exhaled nail-polish remover.

"Solei, bring me the glucometer, please."

Their eyes met, and Solei gave him a tiny smile so full of affection it made his stomach hurt. He couldn't return it. Not now. Not ever. But he appreciated her work-ethic and seemingly endless supply of understanding. The last thing he wanted to do was hurt her.

Her slender fingers met the back of his hand as she handed him the blood sugar meter. Warm. Kind. But nothing more than the contact of another body.

With the intensity of the moment passed, Andy conversed with Oliver's parents. After a few swipes at his finger and a tiny little stick, all was revealed. "Your blood sugar is six fifty." The boy wrenched his face tight, as if to prove his bravery, but the moment his mother wrapped him in her arms, he squished against her chest.

Andy released the roller clamp on his fluids, and administered a shot of insulin into his skinny thigh. He took his time to explain the need for a transfer. He might have been known for miracles, but Oliver had better chances at the pediatric hospital, even if that meant the long trek to Guatemala City.

The family chatted with Solei and a few other families waiting their turn to be treated. Community and a true appreciation of the word "emergency" prevented any animosity from those he screened as stable.

He stepped out into the evening air, and the wooden door snapped shut. He may never get used to humidity, but he sure could get use to the quiet. Nature's quiet. Bugs. Birds. The far-off call of the wild. Just enough background noise to keep from getting lost in his thoughts. Any good distraction was the result of a constant lack of reminders.

He stretched, arm overhead, hoping it would ease the ache twisting in his side. The sun set in the expanse, painting the sky in gold and red. Always fucking red. Olivia lived in the sunshine, but she called to him from the red. Deep. Primal. The one stitch he could never sever.

His eyes played tricks on his heart. Liv came alive in the distance. Her copper curls bending rays of light carved a halo around her head. He pinched the bridge of his nose, then took a breath. Vanilla and cinnamon. He stiffened, the blow too much and not enough. Liv's rosy image floated closer. So close it couldn't be real.

"Hey, cowboy. Think you could use another set

of hands?"

****

Liv held her breath. Maybe she hadn't said the words at all. She'd practiced the line hundreds of times over thousands of miles. For the last twenty, sweat-soaked hours she was the crazy lady who talked to herself. To God. To Andy. Hoping whatever fell out of her mouth the first time she saw him would be the right thing.

There was no way she said it. Because he was too gorgeous to have her brain focus on anything but his tan. And muscles. Caramelized, beefcake muscles, drizzled with sexy veins running up his arms. And how the weeks of pain she caused deepened his beautiful blue eyes.

Except he ran to her. Liv dropped her Wal-Mart chic backpack to the ground and found her stride. With three long beats she was there, then leapt into his open arms. He held her tight. Impossibly tight, but still not close enough.

"Are you really here?" Andy said burying his nose in her hair. "I've just seen you so many times—"

"It's me. I'm here. And I'm sorry. So sorry," she sputtered before she remembered the big, eloquent speech worthy of all the heartache her stupidity and selfishness caused.

Andy inhaled, and Liv felt him freeze in her arms. He pulled away, slightly, like a lung full of her smell was a stab in his ribs. She braced for the inevitable moment he'd let go and for reality to fill the space between.

Terminal disappointment pulsed through her body. She forced a Sweet Peach, self-deprecating *grin*ace. "I'm usually better with surprises … and apologies for that matter."

Andy flashed a smile. Probably a reflex. Just like the too short to be fair embrace. It was something innate he now associated with pain. Liv fought the urge to recoil, to retreat into humiliation and heartache.

Liv took a full step back and smoothed her hair, wishing Andy'd say something.

Anything.

After an agonizing ten heartbeats Andy sucked in a breath, and Liv jumped in. Mindless small talk was the easiest preventative medicine for a Type A, spoiled pageant princess who never learned to handle rejection with any sort of grace or dignity.

"My golly, what a set up y'all have down here. And these trees?" Liv rambled nonsense, darting her gaze around Andy's medical compound. Dread burrowed into her stomach. With each poorly constructed sentence and limply superficial comment about the humidity the scales tipped closer and closer into the psychotic category.

And while she made sure to bring her favorite hyaluronic acid serum and enough happy pills to last a month, she was thirty seconds away from needing a hefty hit from a B50-2.

Andy seemed to squint her into focus, but she didn't dare grant herself permission to read his face. Another decade of awkward wedged its way between them while she prayed for some sort of divine intervention. But it was a useless request. She'd cashed in that chip ages ago.

"Jesus, Andy. Say something before I'm so far gone even fifty of Benadryl, two of Ativan and a Haldol chaser won't calm me d—"

Andy reached for her waist, then silenced with a kiss. A toe-curling, heartbreaking kiss. His tongue slid along her lips, soft, delicate, as if to taste for authenticity. As if the Devil tempted him too many times before, then plunged into her mouth.

Her head spun. Her weakened heart pounded in

an irregular SOS. A warning. Six seconds until her brain blacked out, but Andy pulled away. Oxygen refilled her lungs in sweet relief while the rest of her ached with unresolved need.

Andy set her toes to the ground. His eyes brightened, and he skimmed her cheek with his fingertips. Liv turned into the affection like a cat craving more. And at last he smiled. Lazy. Adorable. Full of swoon. She needed a dose of her heart medicine, but she needed Andy more. She didn't care if it killed her, she'd never be able to stop looking at his face.

"Sorry 'bout all that, but I wasn't even sure you were real 'til ya mumbled something about swamp-ass and LaPerla panty rot."

Liv went limp in his arms with laughter. Chortle after chortle, Liv laughed until she sobbed, shoulders heaving. Unladylike snot threatened to add to her full-on hysterics and running mascara. She sucked in some slow, deep breaths and tried to keep from hyperventilating, suddenly more acutely aware of her not so private surroundings.

Andy pulled her in so they were heart to heart, and it only made her want to cry more. She'd broken *him,* and there he was comforting *her.* He kissed her hair and shushed along her temple in a way that made her feel cherished.

But that didn't mean forgiven.

"Anderson Cole, can you ever forgive me? I know it was you who really fought for what I would have wanted. Even though I was wrong. I know how it must have killed you to go through all of that. And then for me to say such horrible things…" Grief clogged her throat so tight she choked on her words. His fingers brushed along the contours of her neck, her collarbone, then dipped into the sweat dotting her chest. "I was pridefully shortsighted, selfish, and it's nothing I can take back."

Andy signed and dusted kisses into her hairline. "If I say all is forgiven will you buy me something real nice when we get out of here?"

"On my honor as a redhead," Liv crooned, nuzzling her nose into his sternum.

"Oh, I don't know about that. I've known too many redheads."

Olivia breathed in the tang of hard labor and the raw outdoors. Her mouth watered, and it took every ounce of self-control not to lick the sheen right off the exposed skin at his chest.

"Mmm. Touché. I'll come up with something better after I've been thoroughly checked for ticks."

Andy grabbed for her bag, and heaved it over a shoulder, pulling Liv into the other. "Good God, woman, what do you have in here?"

"Little of this. Little of that. A girl never knows what to pack when she has to hunt down the man she loves in the middle of the jungle."

Andy laughed, warming her already flushed skin. "It's not the jungle. And we're not as remote as one would guess. I even have WiFi. But you still have to pee in a sink."

"Good thing I'm well acquainted with that skill."

Andy paused, steps away from a large wooden cottage. A cobblestone path led to an even larger basic structure, like two double-wide trailers stuck together. One window box A/C raged on full blast. A line of people pressed themselves to the surrounding windows, soaking in the forced air and the reunion playing out before them. Liv chuckled at the irony.

"I'm so glad you're here, Livy. I love you, so much. Too much, if that's fucking possible. I found a way to survive after Jackson. But without you ... I ... I know you need children, maybe we can—"

Liv placed her hand over his heart. Strong, regular. A perfect constant. "I love you. We have the rest of our lives to talk and make plans. I'm not going anywhere, and right now, by the looks of it you've got a room full of patients," she said, stepping away to twist her frizzy mane into a knot at the base of her neck. "Where do you need me, Dr. Cole?"

Liv's gaze traveled along the sickly people until she locked eyes with a dark, swirling beauty. Exotic. Lovely. And jealous.

Andy placed a hand along the small of her back, leading her to the double, double-wide with a line out the door. "I have the perfect welcome gift. A very large fella who hasn't pooped in twelve days. He needs a soap suds enema. STAT."

She stopped, reveling in the smile crinkling Andy's brow and the joy glossing his eyes.

"I love it when you talk dirty to me."

****

"I hope you like Chef Boyardee," Andy said, humor hanging on his drawl. They'd cleared out the clinic an hour ahead of schedule. He and Olivia had fallen right back into a perfect rhythm. They moved the meat, with only the occasional translational hiccup with Solei left to connect the dots.

A slight frost iced over Solei's usually warm exterior after Liv introduced herself. Andy was probably making a mountain out of a molehill, but there was no denying the shift in their dynamic the moment Liv crossed the threshold.

Olivia leaned forward and uncrossed her legs. Her sweat dampened tank clung to her in all the right places. "You know I'm a lady with a rather unladylike appetite," she said with the same humor sweetening the sultry edges to her Savannah twang.

Andy kissed the top of her head and joined her at the dinette with bowls full of steaming, fresh veggies and broth. Hunks of heavy sourdough bread basted with roasted garlic and melted butter floated over top. "I know the place ain't much to look at, but the kind folks around here make sure I'm well fed."

Already warned off of the tripled heat from the poblano and jalapeno peppers, Olivia took a careful sip of the soup. "Nah. It's charming and cute to boot. I only wish I hadn't offended your help."

Andy offered her a tight, appeasing smile. "Like I said earlier, baby, I think you came as a shock. And all y'all nurses are the same. Don't want anyone to come 'round and steal your thunder."

"Oh, I know. It just gives me an icky feeling. I'm not usually disliked,"

Andy reached across the table and grabbed for the Cholula. Liv looked him over with a "whatever, buddy, your funeral" sort of smugness and rested her spoon against the bowl. He felt her green gaze dissecting his movements, and nerves tightened around his chest. Liv rose from her seat and came to sit astride his lap. Face to face.

Andy rocked the chair back and made room. She peeled out of her ribbed white tank-top and searched his eyes. Lust and longing glowed in the gold flecks of her irises and something inside broke, and he bit back a wave of sap.

Liv cupped both cheeks and placed a delicate kiss on his lips. "I'm so sorry, Anderson. I didn't trust in your goodness. I couldn't tell you my secrets because I was so ashamed of myself. And was too afraid of what you'd think. About Georgia. About how I let my pride stand in the way of being that precious girl's mother. And when I learned about Jackson, and all the pain you went through, I feared your judgment."

Teetering between horny and heartache, Andy was afraid to breathe. Liv needed to bare part of her soul. But she was also in nothing more than a sheer, lacy underthing and a pair of ass-hugging denim shorts that left nothing to the imagination where he was a hard breeze away from thrusting her up against the kitchen counter and diving between her breasts. The restraint required to keep from grazing his thumb over her tight nipple was almost as bad as the day he had stop himself from keeping her heart beating.

Liv added insult to injury by roughing her nails down the front of his shirt and grabbing it by the hem. She pulled it over his head with expert finesse, dropping it to the ground like an afterthought. Her tits held up and together were a teasing finger length away. The sweetness of sex seemed to hug every curve of Liv's body.

"I love you, baby. Simple as that. You're a good and genuine person. Skeletons do nothin' but hold a person up."

Liv seemed to bite back a sob, and it sucker-punched the air out of his lungs. He'd go a lifetime proving what he said to be true. She laced their fingers together, seeming to marvel at how they fit. It was sweet as fuck, but not enough. Every cell burned with need.

"Good Lord, Olivia, I have to touch you," he forced out at a whisper. Like saying it too loud would somehow pop the real to life fantasy of a happily ever after. "Please."

She grinned, the special one that made everything go belly up and bass-akwards. "As you wish, cowboy. As you wish."

The End

www.elliskaye.com

EVERNIGHT PUBLISHING ®

www.evernightpublishing.com